Courtesy of the author

A portrait of the writer as a young man

About the Author

LAWRENCE BLOCK is a *New York Times* bestselling author and one of the most widely recognized names in the crime fiction genre. He has been named a Grand Master by the Mystery Writers of America and is a four-time winner of the prestigious Edgar and Shamus Awards, as well as a recipient of prizes in France, Germany, and Japan. He received the Diamond Dagger from the British Crime Writers' Association, only the third American (after Sara Paretsky and Ed McBain) to be given this award. He is a prolific author, having written more than fifty books and numerous short stories, and is a devoted New Yorker who spends much of his time traveling. Readers can visit his Web site at www.lawrenceblock.com.

ONE NIGHT STANDS
AND LOST
WEEKENDS

ONE NIGHT STANDS AND LOST WEEKENDS

LAWRENCE BLOCK

HARPER

NEW YORK • LONDON • TORONTO • SYDNEY

HARPER

The stories in this book were published as *One Night Stands* in 1999 by Crippen & Landru Publishers, and the novellas in this book were published as *The Lost Cases of Ed London* in 2001, also by Crippen & Landru Publishers.

Pages 367–368 constitute an extension of this copyright page.

FIRST HARPER PAPERBACK PUBLISHED 2008.

Library of Congress Cataloging-in-Publication Data:

Block, Lawrence.
  One night stands ; and, Lost weekends / Lawrence Block.
    p. cm
  "The stories were originally published as One Night Stands in 1999 and the novellas as The Lost Cases of Ed London in 2001 by Crippen & Landru Publishers"—T.p. verso.
  ISBN 978-0-06-158214-1
    1. Detective and Mystery Stories, American. I. Block, Lawrence. Lost Cases of Ed London. II. Title. III. Title: One night stands and lost weekends. IV. Title: Lost cases of Ed London.

PS3552.L63O64 2008
813'.54—dc22   2008003500

08 09 10 11 12 OV/RRD 10 9 8 7 6 5 4 3 2 1

To the gormless young man
who wrote these stories
and the hapless editors who bought them

CONTENTS

The Lost Cases of Ed London

INTRODUCTION

IN 1999 THE SMALL PRESS PUBLISHER Crippen & Landru brought out a limited hardcover edition of twenty-five previously uncollected early stories of mine. I called the book *One Night Stands,* as most of the stories were written in a single session.

The Lost Cases of Ed London followed two years later, consisting of three novelettes narrated by a private detective whose name you can very likely infer.

I was by no means convinced that any of these stories needed to return to print, and yet I didn't want to deprive collectors and specialists of access to them. So I chose to limit their availability to these hardcover collector's editions, and not to allow them to be reprinted in paperback form.

Here you have the contents of both volumes, assembled together in a handsome but reasonably priced trade paperback edition. How come? What happened that led me to change my mind?

More important, I think, is what didn't happen. No one who bought either book wrote to the publisher to demand his money back or to me to savage me for foisting such crap upon the reading public. Now this doesn't necessarily mean that anybody *liked* the stories; for all I know, collectors bought them and admired them and placed them with pride upon their shelves, never bothering to read the damned things. While I might have worried that reissuing them would damage whatever remains of my reputation, well, it didn't.

And here's something that did happen: Sometime in the mid-nineties I got an e-mail from my friend Evan Hunter. He'd been approached by Charles Ardai of Hard Case Crime about the possibility of HCC's reissue of a group of stories Evan had written and published some forty years earlier. They featured a Bowery derelict named Matt Cordell, a former cop who pulls himself together sufficiently to handle a case and then falls apart again. Evan wasn't sure he wanted to see those stories back in print, and he wondered what my experience had been with the publisher and with reissuing early work.

I was able to vouch for Ardai and Hard Case Crime, and I was also able to put in a word for Matt Cordell. I remembered those stories well—I'd read all of them when they appeared—and I assured Evan that neither he nor they had anything to apologize for. "And for what it's worth," I said, "here's how I make this sort of decision. When I'm faced with two courses of action, I try to pick the one that brings money into the house."

Why should I sit in judgment of my early work? Why should I limit its readership to collectors with full wallets? Why not opt instead for the choice that will bring in a few dollars?

ONCE I'D COME AROUND to that way of thinking, I didn't need to do a lot of heavy lifting. My publishers and I agreed that both books should be combined into a single volume, or if you prefer, a double volume—English is a curious language, isn't it? And was there a title that might serve for such a book?

I still liked *One Night Stands* as a title, but it didn't really fit the Ed London novelettes. They'd taken longer to write—a few days, certainly. I couldn't remember whether I'd written them on the weekend or during the week—I could barely recall having written them at all, to tell you the truth—but as soon as the new title came to mind I liked it, and so did the good people at HarperCollins.

We also decided that the original introductions should stay, and so you'll find them here, one immediately after this one, the other preceding the novelettes.

THERE'S ONE OTHER THING I should talk about here, and that's a story that was included in *One Night Stands* as a separate pamphlet. It's tucked into the main body of this new edition, but it isn't mentioned in the original introduction, and I probably ought to remedy that.

The story was my only real attempt at science fiction, a genre I rather liked and certainly respected, but not one to which my talents and imagination seemed to lend themselves. My agent liked the story and sent it everywhere, and it always came back, until it landed at *Science Fiction Stories,* that market of last resort edited by Robert A. W. Lowndes. (They paid half a cent a word, but my agency insisted they get a minimum of ten dollars for a story. They took their one buck commission, and I netted nine dollars. Funny what you remember.)

Laurence Janifer, a friend of mine who liked the story far more than it could possibly have deserved, brought it to the attention of Judith Merril, known as the "little mother of science fiction," who chose it for her very prestigious best-of-the-year collection. Go figure.

The planet on which the story takes place is called Althea in a nod to the Richard Lovelace poem "To Althea from Prison," which begins, "Stone walls do not a prison make." I accordingly called the story "Make a Prison," although that's not a very good title, is it? If I had wanted a good title, all I had to do was move on to the poem's second line: "Nor iron bars a cage." Now *that's* a title. And, since I get to decide these things, that's the title it's going to have from now on, starting right here in this volume: "Nor Iron Bars a Cage." The rest of the story's not much, Larry Janifer and Judy Merril notwithstanding, but that's a damn nice title.

Lawrence Block
New York
2008

ONE NIGHT STANDS

Introduction
IF MEMORY SERVES . . .

IN 1956, FROM THE BEGINNING OF AUGUST through the end of October, I lived in Greenwich Village and worked in the mail room at Pines Publications. I was a student at Antioch College, in Yellow Springs, Ohio, which sounds like a hell of a commute, but that's not how it worked. At Antioch students spent two terms a year studying on campus and two terms working at jobs the school arranged for them, presumably designed to give them hands-on experience in their intended vocational area. Like a majority of students, I had spent my entire freshman year on campus. Now, at the onset of my second year, I was ready to begin my first co-op job. I knew I wanted to be a writer, so I went through the school's list and picked a job at a publishing house.

Pines published a paperback line, Popular Library, a batch of comic books, and a couple dozen magazines, including some of the last remaining pulps in existence. (*Ranch Romances*, I recall, was one of them. It was what the title would lead you to believe.) I worked five days a week from nine to five, shunting interoffice mail from one desk to another, and doing whatever else they told me to do. My weekly salary was forty bucks, and every Friday I got a pay envelope with $34 in it.

I lived in the Village, at 54 Barrow Street, where I shared a one-bedroom apartment with two other Antioch co-ops. My share of the monthly rent was $30, so I guess it fit the traditional guideline of a week's pay. I know I never had any money, but I never missed any meals, either, and God knows it was an exciting place to be and an exciting time to be there. (I was eighteen, and on my own, so I suppose any place would have been exciting, but at the time I thought the Village was the best place in the world. Now, all these years later, I haven't changed my mind about that.)

I didn't do much writing during those months. I'd realized three years earlier that writing was what I wanted to do, and every now and then I actually wrote something. Poems, mostly, and story fragments. I sent things to magazines and they sent them back. At Antioch, I taped the rejection slips on the wall over my desk, like the heads of animals I'd slain. Sort of.

One weekend afternoon, I sat down at the kitchen table on Barrow Street and wrote "You Can't Lose." It was pretty much the way it appears here, but it didn't end. It just sort of trailed off. I showed it to a couple of friends. I probably showed it to a girlfriend, in the hope that it would get me laid, and it probably didn't work. Then I forgot about it, and at the end of October I went back to campus.

Where at some point I remembered the story and dug it out and sent it to a magazine called *Manhunt*. All I knew about *Manhunt* was that most of the stories in Evan Hunter's collection *The Jungle Kids* had first appeared in its pages. I'd admired those stories, and it struck me that a magazine that would publish them might like my story. So I sent it off, and it stayed there for a while, and then back it came.

With a note enclosed from the editor. He liked it, but pointed out that it didn't have an ending, and that it rather needed one. If I could come up with a twist ending, a snappier ending, he'd like to see it again. So I found a newsstand that carried *Manhunt*, bought a copy, read it, and wrote a new ending, one which at least proved

I'd read O. Henry's "The Man at the Top." (My narrator ends with the triumphant boast that his ill-gotten gains are due to increase dramatically, because he's just invested the whole thing in some gold mine stock. Or something.)

I sent this off, and it came back with another note, saying the new ending was predictable and didn't really work, but thanks for trying. And that was that.

Then several months later the school year was coming to a close, and I was due to head off to Cape Cod and find a co-op job on my own. One night near the end of term I couldn't sleep, and I lay there thinking, and thought of the right way to finish the story. I went home to Buffalo to visit my folks, drove out to Cape Cod, and wrote a new ending for the story. The acceptance process was slow—*Manhunt* had what we've since learned to call a cash-flow problem—but, long story short, they bought it. Paid a hundred bucks for it.

My first sale.

I LEFT THE CAPE after a month or so and wound up back in New York, where I got a job as an editor at a literary agency, reading scripts and writing letters to wannabe writers, telling them how talented they were and how this particular story didn't work, but by all means send us another story and another reading fee.

I lived in a residential hotel on West 103rd Street, where my $65-a-month rent was again a fourth of my salary. And, nights and weekends, I wrote stories, which the agency I worked for submitted to various magazines. Most of the stories were crime fiction. I hadn't yet decided I was going to be a crime fiction writer—I don't know that that's a decision I ever made—but in the meantime I read extensively in the field. There was a shop on Eighth Avenue off Times Square where they sold back copies of *Manhunt* and other digest-sized magazines (*Trapped, Guilty, Off-Beat, Keyhole, Murder,* and so on) at two for a quarter. I bought every one of these I could find, and I read them cover to cover. Some I liked and some I didn't, but somewhere along the way I must have internalized the sense of what made a story, and I wrote some of my own.

They sold, most of them, sooner or later. Sometimes to *Manhunt*, but more often to its imitators. *Trapped* and *Guilty* paid a cent and a half per word, so they were the first choice after *Manhunt* passed. Then came Pontiac Publications, at a penny a word. (Their magazines had titles like *Sure Fire* and *Twisted* and *Off-Beat*, and every story title had an exclamation mark at the end. I longed to call a story "One Dull Night" so that they could call it "One Dull Night!")

After I'd been a month or so at the literary agency, it was clear to me I was learning more than I'd ever learn in college, and that I'd be crazy to stop now. So I dropped out and stayed right where I was. In the spring, I decided I'd learned as much as I was going to at the job, and that a student draft deferment was, after all, better than a poke in the eye with a sharp bayonet. I went back to Antioch.

By the time I got there, I was writing books. "Sex novels" was what we called them, though they'd now get labeled "soft-core porn." I wrote one to order the summer before I returned to Antioch, and the publisher wanted more. So that's what I did instead of classwork. And I also went on writing crime stories. At the end of that academic year, in the summer of 1959, I dropped out again, and this time it took. I started writing a book a month for one sex novel publisher, and other books for other publishers, and from that point the crime short stories were few and far between.

WHEN DOUG GREENE AND I discussed bringing out a collection of these early stories, he brought up the subject of an introduction. "You can read through the stories," he said, "and write some sort of preface."

"One or the other," I said. "You decide which."

I have a lot of trouble looking at my early work. I rarely like the way it's written, and I especially dislike the glimpse it gives me of the unutterably callow youth who produced it. I like that kid and wish him well, but read what he wrote? The hell with that.

You know what? I'm *afraid* to read them. I'm scared I'll decide not to publish them after all, and it's too late for that.

So an uncharacteristic attack of honesty compels me to advise you that I am in the curious position of introducing you to a couple of dozen short stories that I myself haven't read in forty years.

Someone else suggested that some of the stories might require revision, because attitudes expressed in them are out-of-date and politically incorrect. No way, I told him. First of all, one of the few interesting things about them is that they're of their time. I'd much rather burn them than update them. And screw political rectitude, anyway. You want to go through *Huckleberry Finn* and change the name of Huck's companion to African-American Jim? Be my fucking guest, but leave me out of it.

A FEW THINGS YOU MIGHT WANT TO KNOW:

1. A few of these stories, as indicated in the bibliographical notes at the back, were published under pen names. This only happened when I wound up with more than one story in the same issue of a magazine. W. W. Scott, who edited *Trapped* and *Guilty*, would make up a pen name when this occurred, generally by working a variation on the author's usual byline. Thus "B. L. Lawrence." The guy at Pontiac asked what pen name to use in similar circumstances, and I provided the name "Sheldon Lord." Were there other pen names? Maybe, because there have been editors in the business who had house names that they used at such times. Maybe they used them on stories of mine. I don't think this ever happened, but at this point I'd have no way of knowing. And no reason whatever to care . . .

2. There's a story in here called "Look Death in the Eye" that deserves comment. It may strike some readers as curiously familiar. I wrote it way back when, while I was working for the literary agent, and it sold to Pontiac, and I lost all track of it. Didn't have a copy, didn't know where to find one.

And I found myself thinking about the story. What I really liked about it was the last line, and that, really, was all I remembered. So I re-created the story from memory, right up to the last line, which I recalled word for imperishable word. I hammered it out and sent it off to a fellow named Bruce Fitzgerald, who was editing a magazine called *For Women Only*. (It was a beefcake magazine, as it happens, composed of outtake photos from *Blueboy*, a gay magazine. The stories and articles interspersed among the nude male pix in *For Women Only* were ostensibly slanted to female readers, of which I doubt the magazine had more than twenty nationwide. The idea was that, by being purportedly for women, it could get on newsstands closed to gay publications, where its true audience would, uh, sniff it out. Its name notwithstanding, it was really for *men* only. Publishing is a wonderful business.)

Bruce liked the story, but felt it was a little too graphic for his female readers, even though we all knew they didn't exist. Could he use it without the last line?

Without the last line, of course, there's no story. And the only reason I wrote the story a second time was so that I could reuse the last line. So I displayed artistic integrity I never knew I had and withdrew the story. I don't know what difference I thought it would make, since nobody read anything in that magazine anyway, but for once I just couldn't stop myself from doing the right thing. *Gallery* wound up taking it, last line and all. It was published as "Hot Eyes, Cold Eyes," and was later included in my second collection, *Like a Lamb to Slaughter*.

3. The title deserves explanation. Most of these stories were written in a single sitting. I would get an idea and sit down at the typewriter and hammer it out. You can hold a short-story idea entirely in the mind, especially the sort of brief and uncomplicated story that most of these are. A weekday evening or a weekend afternoon was generally time enough to see one of these stories through to the end.

It still often is. I still write stories rapidly, and sometimes complete one in a single setting. The major difference, it seems to me, is that the gestation period has gotten a lot longer. I'll nowadays let a story idea percolate or ferment or stew for days or weeks or months. Back then I tended to strike as soon as the iron was hot, or, occasionally, before it had really warmed up.

I'VE HAD THREE COLLECTIONS of short stories published, plus a small-press collection of the Ehrengraf stories and *Hit Man*, an episodic novel comprising the Keller stories. *One Night Stands* consists of stories deliberately omitted from these collections (or ones I'd lost track of, but if I'd had them handy I'd still have left them out).

What have we got here, then? A box labeled "pieces of string too small to save"? If they weren't worth collecting, why have I collected them?

I've been guided by the same principle (or, some might argue, the same lack thereof) that has led me to republish some early crime novels that I'd be hard put to read without cringing. The fact that I can't read them with pleasure doesn't mean someone else couldn't, or shouldn't. I've decided it's not my job to judge my early work. Let other people make what they will of it.

Then, too, I'm not unmindful of the interests of collectors and readers with a special interest in an author—in this instance, myself. I don't collect books, but I have other collecting interests, and I understand the mind set. Of course a collector would want a writer's early work, to read or simply to have and to hold, and why should I deprive him of the opportunity? And why shouldn't some scholar with a thesis to write have access to that early work?

At the same time, I don't think these stories are much good, or representative of my mature work. For God's sake, when I wrote these my typewriter still had training wheels on it. So I've decided *One Night Stands* should have limited distribution, going not to general readers but to collectors and specialists. Thus it's being published only in a limited collector edition, and not, as is generally the case with Crippen & Landru publications, in trade paperback as well.

Enough! This introduction has passed the 2500-word mark, which makes it longer than many of the stories it's introducing. It's taken most of the morning to write it, too. May you, Dear Reader, like the tomcat who had the affair with the skunk, enjoy these stories as much as you can stand.

Lawrence Block
Greenwich Village
1999

THE BAD NIGHT

THE SHORTER OF THE TWO BOYS had wiry black hair and a twisted smile. He also had a knife, and the tip of the blade was pressed against Dan's faded gabardine jacket. "Why'd you have to get in the way?" he asked, softly. "Every bull from here to Memphis is after us, and Pops here has to . . ."

"Shut up." The older boy was taller, with blond hair that tumbled over his forehead. He, too, had a knife.

"Why? He ain't going to tell anybody . . ."

"Shut up, Benny." He turned to Dan, smiling. "We need money, maybe some food. We better make it over to your shack."

"No shack," Dan said. He gestured toward an opening in the wall of rock that edged the valley. "I live in the cave over there."

Benny started to laugh, and the blade of his knife pierced Dan's skin and drew blood. "A cave!" he exploded. "Dig, Zeke—he's a hermit!"

Zeke didn't laugh. "C'mon," he said. "To the cave."

They walked slowly across the field toward the mouth of the

cave. Dan felt the sweat forming on his forehead, felt the old fa-miliar sensation that he hadn't felt since Korea. He was afraid, as afraid as he'd ever been in his life.

"Faster," Benny said, and again Dan felt the knife prick skin. It didn't make sense. He'd lived through a world war and a police ac-tion, and now two kids from Memphis were going to kill him. Two kids who called him "Pops."

The veins stood out on his temples, and he could feel the sweat running down his face to the stubble of beard on his chin. "Why did he get in the way?" the kid had asked. Hell, he didn't mean to get in anyone's way. Just wanted to go off by himself, fool around with a little prospecting, and relax for a while.

They were almost at the entrance of the cave. Now they would take his money, eat his food, and put a switchblade knife between his ribs. He was finished, unless he managed to get to his gun in time. There was a shiny black .45 waiting on his shelf, if only he could get to it before Benny got to him with the knife.

"Here it is," he said. He stepped inside the cave, the two boys right behind him. It was a large cave, wide and roomy and branch-ing out much wider in the rear. On one side was his mattress, on the other his trunk and four orange-crate shelves.

"Let's go," said Zeke. "Bring out the dough and some food. We ain't got all night."

"Yeah," Benny echoed. "We gotta roll, man. Make it fast or I stick you, dig?" He prodded Dan with a knife for emphasis.

"Wait a minute." Dan's eyes darted desperately to the crates and lighted on the kerosene lantern. "Let me light the lamp over there. It's getting kind of dark in here."

Benny looked at Zeke, who shrugged. "Okay," he said. "But don't try anything." Dan walked across to the side of the cave, and Benny followed with the knife.

Fumbling in his pocket for a match, Dan glanced down to the middle shelf of the crate where the gun nestled cozily amidst a packet of letters and a pair of socks. If only he could get it, and if only it were loaded. Was it loaded? He couldn't remember.

"Hurry it up," Zeke said. It was now or never, Dan thought. He lifted the pack of matches from his pocket, tensed his body, and fell forward.

At the same time he lashed out viciously with his foot and heard a dull grunt of pain as he connected solidly with Benny's belly. His right hand snaked out for the gun and closed around it, his fingers caressing the smooth metal of the butt. All in one motion he took it and whirled around, his finger tight against the trigger. The boys scampered for the rear of the cave. Then, before he could get a shot off, his right ankle buckled and he fell to the floor. For a moment everything went black as the pain shot up and down his leg. He gritted his teeth until the floor stopped spinning.

Dan glanced around the cave, and the two boys seemed to have disappeared. He tried to stand, but the stab of pain in his ankle told him it was useless. The ankle was broken.

He could hear Zeke, cursing dully from the back of the cave. They hadn't left, then. He had them trapped.

After a time the cursing stopped. "Hey, Pops!" Zeke called. "That was pretty sharp, you know?"

Dan didn't answer.

"Sharp," the boy repeated. "You faked us good, but what'll it get you? You can't move, Pops."

Dan started. He scrutinized the rear walls of the cave but could see nothing.

"Peek-a-boo," Zeke called. "I can see you real good, Pops. There's a cool little crack in the rock, you know? I can see you clear as anything. You still got your gun, but you can't go anywhere."

"Neither can you," Dan answered, in spite of himself. "You can't come out without getting shot. You two little bastards can stay there until I get some help."

The boy's laugh rang hollowly in the cave. "Help? You expecting company, Pops? Bet there's a whole mess of people in a real rush to come here. This cave's a big attraction, huh?"

Dan ran a hand over his forehead. The boy was right—the world didn't exactly beat a path to his door. Daley would drop by in the morning with the mail, but he couldn't figure on anyone showing before then. It was a stalemate; he couldn't get the boys, and they couldn't get him.

"I can wait," he called. "My friend comes up at eleven every morning, and we can just sit it out until then. Have a nice wait, kids. Enjoy yourselves. When the cops get hold of you it won't be much fun."

This time they both laughed—high, shrill laughs that chilled Dan to the bone. The laughter echoed and bounced between the walls, and Dan felt his blood come to a boil. "Laugh!" he yelled, savagely. "Laugh your heads off, you little bastards!"

"Pops," called a voice—Benny's, this time. "The laugh's on you, Pops. Know what time it is?"

"It's nine o'clock, Pops. Nine at night. It's fourteen hours 'til your friend comes. Think you can stay awake for fourteen hours? That's a long time, you know."

Dan drew in a breath sharply. Suddenly, he felt very tired. Very tired and hopelessly old.

"He's right," Zeke said. "There's two of us, Pops, and we still got our blades. You might get real sleepy tonight. Just have to sit there all night with your eyes wide open, while one of us sleeps and the other one watches you. After a while your eyes'll close up and that'll be the end. You'll be too sleepy to feel the knife."

The boy went on, but Dan didn't listen to the rest. He let out his breath slowly and stared at the gun in his hand, wondering idly whether or not it was loaded.

He knew what happened when a man had to force himself to stay awake. He'd seen a sentry who fell asleep at his post six miles north of Inchon. He'd looked like a man asleep, until Dan had noticed the slit that ran across his throat from ear to ear. He probably never knew what was happening, never felt the knife slice his life away.

Could he stay awake? He didn't know. He glanced at his watch, noting that the boy had been right—it was just a few minutes past nine. He'd been on his feet all day since 8:30 in the morning, and it had been a rough day, with plenty of walking and climbing. He felt tired already, and he had fourteen more hours to go. His ankle throbbed dully but steadily, a slow and persistent ache. He knew it was draining him of the energy he would need to remain awake through the night.

"You may not have to wait until you fall asleep," Zeke called. "It's getting real dark, man. You won't be able to see too good. We can sneak up, like."

Dan looked around for the lantern and was relieved to find it at his side, where it had fallen in the scuffle. He set it upright and made ready to light it, then realized how little kerosene he had in it. Probably not enough to last the night. He'd save it until he couldn't see without it.

"Okay," said Zeke. "So you got the lamp. You'll still fall asleep."

The minutes crawled by and the shadows grew longer. Dan sat very still on the floor of the cave. The boys talked among themselves, and occasionally he caught snatches of their conversation. They'd started in Memphis, headed west, pulled a series of small holdups, and one of them—Benny, he guessed—had knifed the proprietor of a delicatessen. The man had died.

Killers. A couple of punk kids, but they had killed already and they would kill again. Zeke, he thought, would kill if he had to, but Benny was a different sort. Benny would kill whenever he got the chance.

Dan had met that kind before. There was a guy in his platoon, a tall, lean boy from the hills. And one day the platoon had taken seven young Chinese as prisoners. And the tall, lean boy from the hills had stepped up to each of the POWs in turn, and placed his pistol to the back of each head, quickly and methodically blowing out the brains of each of them. The Americans were too dumbfounded to stop him. Dan had been violently sick, and the memory still churned inside him.

He shook himself suddenly and took several deep breaths in rapid succession. He had almost fallen asleep that time. His eyes remained open, but his arms and legs were completely relaxed. He had heard about that—falling asleep bit by bit, until your mind wandered into dream-channels that seemed vividly real. He moved his arms around to speed the circulation and touched his injured ankle gingerly. It was sore to the touch and swelling rapidly.

There was a laugh from the rear of the cave. "Almost," said Zeke. "You're an old man, Pops. Pretty soon you'll be dropping the gun. Why don't you just give it up?"

Damn you, thought Dan. He looked at his watch—10:20. It was dark now inside the cave, too dark for him to make out the outline of the rear wall. He'd have to chance running out of kerosene.

He struck a match and lit the lantern, warming his hands over it. It felt good. He hefted the gun in his hand. Was there a bullet left? The gun was full three days ago, but he had shot at some squirrels since then. How many times had he fired it? Five? Six? He couldn't remember.

Nor was it possible to tell by the weight. He could judge between a full gun and an empty one, but one bullet either way didn't make that much of a difference.

He noticed himself blinking more and more frequently, as his eyes struggled to shut against his will. He forced himself to look first at the lantern, then off into the darkened area of the cave. *Just so it isn't steady*, he thought. *Vary it, mix it up, just so you don't get accustomed to one position.* He moved his arms from time to time, shifted his weight, and changed the position of his legs as much as the broken ankle would permit.

The boys spoke less, then stopped talking altogether. It was almost midnight when he heard Zeke's voice, soft but clear in the near-silence of the night.

"Pops," the boy said, "Benny's sleeping. Isn't that nice?"

He didn't answer. There was no point in wasting energy; he needed every drop of it just to keep awake.

"I said he's asleep," the boy repeated. "Just closed his eyes and floated right off. Sleeping like a baby."

Stop it, Dan thought fiercely. *Don't talk about it, you bastard. Don't even mention the word.*

But Zeke knew what he was doing. "Sleeping. Wouldn't you like to take a little nap right now, Pops? Be real easy, you know? Just close your eyes, lean back . . ."

No. His hand tightened on the butt of the gun, squeezing hard. He started to sweat again, and then a cold chill came over him.

"Relax," the voice cooed. "You're real tired. You want to catch a little sleep. Close your eyes. Go ahead—close them."

Dan's eyelids dropped by themselves at the command, and he had to struggle to lift them again. He was being hypnotized, crudely but efficiently.

"Damn you!" he roared. *"God damn you!"* The boy chuckled. Zeke's chuckle grew into a laugh, and Dan could feel his pulse racing. He shouldn't have blown up. He had to relax, had to take things slowly and easily.

Zeke began again, slowly and methodically urging him to sleep, but Dan forced his mind to ignore the suggestions. It wasn't easy.

His body was beginning to rebel as he alternately sweated and shivered. His ankle ached with a vengeance until he wanted to put a bullet through it. But for all he knew the gun was empty. He didn't dare break it open to check. Zeke was watching him constantly, commenting on every move he made. If the gun *was* empty . . .

He began glancing at his watch with increasing frequency. It seemed as though time was standing still for him, as though he and the two devils were suspended in a stalemate for eternity. But the weight of his eyelids and the nagging aches of his body assured him that this was not the case. He grew weaker and more tired with each passing second.

A few minutes past one, his grip relaxed and the gun nearly dropped from his hand. He swore and the boy laughed.

Is it loaded? Dammit, is it loaded? And then, suddenly, *what the hell difference does it make?*

He realized that it made no difference at all. Whether the gun was empty or full, they *thought* it was full. And because they thought he held a loaded gun, they were waiting for him to fall asleep. As long as . . .

"Pops," the voice interrupted him, "Zeke's gonna have a little nap. Ain't he lucky?"

Shut up.

"You'll be sleeping soon, Pops. Then I'll have a chance to cut you good. Dig?" Benny had none of the hypnotic effect of Zeke, but his words dug at Dan's brain and broke his train of thought.

Dan clenched his hands into fists and bit his lip so hard that he tasted blood in his mouth. If they *thought* he was awake, and that the gun was loaded, they wouldn't approach him. The real thing didn't matter. It was what they thought.

"I don't think I'll give it to you quick, Pops. I'll just take that gun away and do a nice slow job. Think you'll like that? I'm good with a blade. Real good."

Now how could he sleep, yet make them think he was awake? They could watch him clearly, watch the eyes shut and the gun fall. His fingers would relax, so slowly that he wouldn't ever feel it, and the gun would slip, gently to the floor. How could he fake it?

"Think you're tough, Pops? You won't be so tough. I'll cut you up *so* slow. You'll bawl, you know? A big guy like you, you'll bawl like a baby."

Of course, he could put out the lantern. Then they couldn't see whether or not he slept. He reached for the lantern, then hesitated. It wouldn't work.

Without the lantern, he wouldn't be able to see them either. They could sneak up, just as Zeke had suggested. And he knew that he would never be able to stay awake in the darkness. He'd fall asleep within minutes.

"Go to sleep, Pops. Go to sleep, you rotten bastard."

Dan blinked rapidly and sucked in a large mouthful of air. Time was passing, and it was on their side. But . . . and suddenly he had it! As soon as he fell asleep, they would know it. And he would fall asleep before help came. But if they *thought* he was asleep. Just like the gun, the truth of the picture didn't matter.

For the next five minutes he sat very still, scarcely moving at all. Then, slowly and carefully, he let his eyelids drop shut. He breathed deeply and rhythmically. He relaxed.

Benny's taunts had ceased, and he could hear the boy's quiet breathing at the rear of the cave. Slowly, bit by bit, he let his fingers relax and his fist open, until the gun dropped from his grip and bounced gently upon the earth.

Minutes passed. Then he heard movement at the rear of the cave, followed by the clean, metallic *click* of the switchblade knife. They would be coming soon. He kept his eyes closed and his breathing regular.

A hushed whisper, followed by more movement and another click, informed him that Zeke was also awake. He waited, tense as a drum. His left arm began to itch insistently, but he didn't even consider scratching it. He let it itch and bit harder on his lip until the blood came.

There was more movement. He was able to sense, even with his eyes closed, that they stood in plain sight of him now. He could see them clearly in his mind—Zeke cautious, expressionless; Benny anxious, his eyes gleaming.

Here they come. You can even hear them breathing. They're getting closer, and you only get one chance. Get ready . . .

Now!

In one movement he snapped open his eyes and grabbed for the gun. They were barely ten feet away, rooted in their tracks as he came to life before their eyes. He raised the gun, hooked his finger around the trigger, and leveled it at Zeke's chest.

"Drop 'em," he said. "Drop the knives."

Benny gaped like a fish. His hand trembled and the knife fell to the earth.

"Now you," Dan ordered. "Drop it!"

There was no smile on Zeke's face now. The deadpan expression was gone, too, and fear mingled with surprise replaced it. He dropped the knife.

"Now kick them across the floor." They did as he said.

He let out a breath, finally. "Okay," he said. "Now, you both lie down on your bellies, facing me. Zeke, you start crawling over here. Benny, you better stay right where you are."

Zeke inched his way forward. When he was within reach, Dan chopped him viciously across the head with the barrel of the gun. "Go to sleep," he said. "Pleasant dreams, fella."

He lifted the gun and pointed it at Benny. "Now you," he snapped. "Get over here."

"No! Please!"

"Maybe you want a bullet instead, Benny? This is a big gun, you know? Makes a big hole."

Benny didn't say anything.

"Get over here!"

The first swipe of the gun barrel knocked Benny unconscious. Dan hit him again, anyway.

He worked quickly. He tore their clothing into strips and bound their ankles and wrists securely. They'd be unable to get loose for a good long while. Long before then Daley would arrive with the mail, and that would be that.

Dan settled back, turned out the lamp, and went to sleep.

THE BADGER GAME

BARON FOLLOWED THE BELLHOP from the elevator to the room. The bellhop opened the door for him and followed him inside, depositing the single brown leather suitcase on the floor. His hand was ready at once to accept the crisp dollar bill Baron handed to him.

"Will there be anything else, sir?" The boy's eyes indicated that "anything else" took in a wide range of possible services.

Baron considered. A woman might be pleasant, but there would be plenty of time for that later. Besides, he liked to take what he wanted without paying for it.

He dismissed the bellhop with a curt shake of his head and turned away from him. When the door closed behind the boy he kicked off his shoes and stretched out full-length upon the bed.

Richard Baron did not look like a criminal. His clothes were expensive without being flashy—his shoes were black Italian loafers that had cost him thirty dollars a pair and the gray flannel suit cut in the latest continental style had set him back a little over two hundred. His shirts were all white-on-white and had been made to his measurements.

The average Joe would have pegged him for a successful young businessman from the West Coast. Somebody with a little more on the ball might have made him for a hustler in the Organization—not a muscle boy, but somebody with an angle.

Baron was a con man.

It was, he reflected, a good life. For the moment he had nothing to do but relax, and it wasn't hard to relax with a full wallet and $15,000 in his suitcase, fifteen grand in tens and twenties that he could spend whenever he got around to it. The oil man in Dallas hadn't stopped payment on his check and wouldn't even think of it.

The oil man now thought he was the owner of several hundred acres in Canada loaded with uranium. As it happened, the oil man now owned a few hundred totally worthless stock certificates. By the time he found out he had been taken, he wouldn't even remember what Baron looked like.

The oil man had put up a little over $75,000. Baron's end of the deal was twenty grand, and it would take awhile to spend it. Not as long as it might take most people, because Baron liked to live somewhat better than most people did. The better restaurants, the better nightclubs, and the better women all helped lift his life to a higher plane. He drank nothing but Jack Daniels and ate nothing but blood-rare steak.

Actually, expensive living was essential in his occupation. It seems as though marks would only permit themselves to be swindled by men who appeared to be rich. A threadbare pinstripe might do for a sneak thief, but a confidence man had to come on strong if he wanted to score.

Now he could bide his time. Tulsa wasn't exactly the place he would choose for a vacation, but the telegram from Lou Farmer had indicated that Lou had a mark hanging fire in Denver that might be ripe any day. A trip to Miami or New York was out until the mark fell one way or the other.

Baron hauled himself up from the bed and stripped for a shower. He was thirty-five but in better physical shape than when he'd

been twenty and working the short con in railway stations, grifting hard for ten bucks here and twenty bucks there.

He'd come a long way in fifteen years. A grifter's money went
quickly, but Baron had a growing bank account in New York and a
healthy stack of dough in the stock market. Not in the kind of wild
moose pasture that he sold to the marks, but a solid mutual fund
that grew steadily and paid a nice dividend. A few more heavy
scores and he'd be able to lay off for the rest of his life.

He toweled himself dry after the shower and shaved with
a straight razor, applying a few drops of aftershave lotion and a
few more of an expensive cologne that he liked. He dressed again,
changing to a pair of charcoal slacks and a light brown cashmere
sport jacket.

He locked the suitcase and left it in the closet, not really worried
that the lock would be broken. It didn't matter if it was; the money
was snug in the case's false bottom.

It was too early for dinner and he walked leisurely through
downtown Tulsa. It was amazing, he thought to himself, the way
the average guy never noticed what was happening. He spotted
a cannon mob grifting the other side of the street, working their
way through the pockets of passing shoppers. Baron picked out the
hook easily and watched him work, dipping easily into a mark's
back pocket and passing the wallet to one of the other members of
the mob in a second. Smooth.

Just for the hell of it he crossed the street at the end of the block
and doubled back the other way. The cannons were moving toward him and he let one of the prat men bump him gently while
he pretended to study the display in a shoe store. Only because he
was concentrating was he able to feel the wire's hand dip into his
pocket, reaching for his wallet.

Baron said: "Nix."

He half-whispered the word so that nobody but the wire would
hear it. But the wire got the message. Instantly the hand was with-
drawn and the wallet remained where it was.

Baron smiled to himself and moved on. Again the prat man
jostled him, this time mumbling "sorry" under his breath. Baron's

smile widened. The thief was indicating he was sorry he had made
Baron for a mark.

It was always a source of pleasure to him the way a thief could
communicate to another thief without a mark ever catching on. He
and Farmer and the others in his outfit could talk over the head of
a mark forever. And just the one word, "nix," had put the cannon
mob wise to who he was.

Baron glanced at his watch. It was 6:30 now and he was hungry.
He walked to the curb and caught a cab.

"Take me to the best steakhouse in town," he told the driver.

At the restaurant he had a double shot of Jack Daniels on the
rocks and a rare sirloin an inch and a half thick. He finished off
with a pony of drambuie, inhaling the rich vapor of the cordial and
enjoying the warm feeling as it trailed down his throat to his stomach. He paid the check and tipped the waiter generously.

He bought a paper at a corner newsstand and glanced at the
entertainment page. There were only a few nightclubs in Tulsa and
none of them seemed particularly appealing. How would he spend
the evening?

A woman would be pleasant. He considered taking the bellhop up
on his offer but gave up the idea. Later, perhaps, but not tonight.

Instead he caught a cab back to his hotel and wandered into the
bar. He'd just have a few drinks and then catch a full night's sleep.
If there was a woman to be picked up he would pick her up, and if
there wasn't he wouldn't be too disappointed.

At the bar he took the furthest stool from the door and ordered
a shot of Jack Daniels with a water chaser. He tossed off the shot
and was lifting the glass of water to his lips when he spotted the
blonde.

He saw her before she saw him. She was tall, just a few inches
shorter than he was. And her hair was long and golden. The plain
black cocktail dress emphasized her high, full breasts and her long,
tapered legs.

Her face was good, too, except for a slightly hard look about it.
Looks, he decided. Plenty of looks, but not a hell of a lot of class.

Automatically he wondered what angle she was working. She

didn't come on like a hustler, but it was a cinch she was pushing her looks in one way or another. He sipped the chaser and waited for her to make her play.

He didn't have long to wait. Her eyes surveyed the room rapidly and she walked directly to him, taking the seat beside him. She ordered a grasshopper and the bartender mixed the drink in a hurry and brought it to her.

Baron paid for her drink.

"Thanks," she said, smiling at him. "Are you with the convention?"

He shook his head. "I'm working the C out of Philly," he said, deciding to fill her in right away so she could save her time. If she was a pro she'd know enough to make her pitch straight instead of playing games; if she was in the rackets she would leave him alone.

She didn't seem to have heard him. "I came down with my husband for the convention," she said. "You know, the auto merchants are having this convention. It started yesterday."

He nodded briefly.

"My husband had this meeting tonight," she said. "He won't be back until one or two in the morning. It gets boring for a girl, just sitting alone in a room."

He smiled; she didn't waste her time. He made her grift at once—it had to be the badger game the way she was planting her story. She would take him to her room and then her husband would come on with a gun, pretending to be furious. The hubby would threaten to kill him and settle for a cash settlement, and that would be that.

But she wasn't being very smooth about it. She should pretend to be more reluctant and make him do a little more of the work. Otherwise the mark wouldn't swallow the bait whole.

"What's your name?"

"Dick Baron," he said. "I just got finished working the rag in Dallas." Now she would have to realize he was in the know.

But she seemed totally oblivious to what he had said.

"I'm lonely," she said. "And I've got a bottle up in my room. Would you like to come up with me?"

He almost broke out laughing. Now he had the whole picture. She was working the badger game, all right, but she wasn't a professional at it. That's why her approach was so lousy and why she was missing the lines he was throwing at her. She was a crook, but an amateur crook.

And if there was one thing Baron couldn't stand it was an amateur crook. They didn't know the ropes and all they did was make things rough for the smart boys. Here was this blonde now, working like a slave to con a con man. How dumb could you get?

"Sure," he said, deciding to play along. "Let's go upstairs."

On the way to the elevator she took his arm, which was another mistake. She should let him do all the work—that way he'd believe she was a straight chick taking a first fling. It would make him hotter for her and at the same time scare him silly when her partner came on the scene.

"My name's Sally English," she said. "My husband and I are from Cedar Rapids."

He nodded and she tightened her grip on his arm. "I suppose you think I'm a tramp," she went on. "I'm not, not really. Don't you think I'm a tramp?"

"I think you're swell," he said, thinking that anybody who made such a mess out of a simple badger dodge ought to starve to death.

"I've never done this before," she said. "I mean, pick up somebody I never met before and take him to my room. But I get so lonely."

In the elevator she leaned against him and he could feel the warmth of her flesh through the thin cocktail dress. Hell, maybe he'd wind up making it with her if he played it right. She might be dumb, but she was certainly built for action. The top of her head was inches from his nose and he could smell her perfume. It was cheap stuff and she used a little too much of it. But there was no denying that it increased his desire for her.

Her room was on the floor beneath his. She led him inside and closed the door but didn't turn the lock, explaining that her husband couldn't possibly get home before one or two. Again, that was part of the pattern—but she shouldn't have bothered with the explanation. She was being too damned obvious about the whole thing.

She fished around in the dresser and came up with a fifth of blended rye, pouring tumblers full for each of them. He wondered idly whether she might be working it solo, planning on drugging him and picking his pocket. It was possible.

At any rate he had better things to do than swill cheap rye. When she wasn't looking he emptied his glass on the rug beneath the bed.

He slipped his arm around her and she turned to him, fastening her mouth on his. He kissed her and her tongue probed his mouth. Even if she played the rest of it wrong she knew what to do once she was in the bedroom, he decided. That one kiss had been enough to make him ache with desire for her.

Suddenly she stood up and reached behind her to unzip the dress. He stood up and helped, noting with approval that she wasn't wearing a bra. Everything under the dress was hers.

He had to draw in his breath. She had a superb body—firm and young and vibrantly alive.

He took a step toward her.

And then, right on schedule, a key turned in the lock, the door opened, and hubby walked in.

Baron was perfectly calm as he looked first at the man and then at the girl. The man should have had a gun; it would have made the situation more convincing. Outside of that the pair were effective actors. The girl was cringing against the wall. The man had fury blazing in his eyes and his hands were knotted into fists.

"Cut it," Baron snapped, suddenly angry at the amateur quality of the whole thing. "It doesn't work this time."

The man advanced on him, swearing.

Baron decided he had had just about enough of the whole thing. Besides, he wanted the girl, wanted her as he hadn't wanted a woman in a long time.

He meant to have her.

He met the man's rush neatly, blocking a punch and countering with a right to the chest. The man sagged and Baron chopped him savagely on the side of the neck.

Such a chop, properly done, kills a man. Baron had killed a man in just such a fashion several years back when he had to play it heavy for a change. This time he held back slightly with the blow. The man crumpled to the floor, alive but unconscious. He would remain unconscious for at least twenty minutes.

Baron turned to the girl. She was cowering against the wall, her eyes wide with terror that was quite probably genuine.

He laughed.

"Didn't expect that, did you? You ought to learn to tell who's a mark and who isn't."

"Please," she said. "Please."

"This time," he said, "you're going to have to go through with it. Maybe you'll learn better next time."

He took her by the shoulders and heaved her toward the bed. She stumbled for a few steps and sat down heavily. She didn't move.

Back in his own room Baron felt thoroughly relaxed for the first time in weeks. Sally English—or whatever her name might really be—was more woman than he had had in quite a while. She had one hell of a body and she knew what to do with it.

Baron smiled, remembering and enjoying the memory. At first she had fought, but after a while she quit fighting and started to enjoy what she was doing.

He laughed suddenly, wondering what the poor dope of a partner would think when he came to. The guy had been expecting a mark, not a guy who would knock him cold. It served him right for being such a damned amateur.

Well, maybe they would drop out of the rackets now. The badger game was a short con to begin with and not an especially good one at that, but that pair wasn't cut out for anything so professional. Maybe the girl would hustle and the guy would pimp for her. He decided that the guy wasn't much better than a pimp. And the girl would make a fine hustler.

Amateur crooks. They only got in the way, lousing things up for the boys who knew which end was up. They didn't know who to take and who to pass up.

And they always got caught. And when they got caught they didn't know what to do, and so they wound up in the tank. Which,

Baron reflected, was precisely where they belonged, the whole pack of them.

The professionals got caught too—but they didn't wind up in jail, not the smart ones. When they hit a town they found out who was the fixer and they established contact with the fixer before they started grifting. That way they stayed out of the jug.

If they got busted they either bought the cop right away or got word to the fixer, who bought whoever had to be bought. Sometimes the fixer would get to the mark and pay him off to get him to drop charges. That was the way most of the cannon mobs operated. If that failed, the fixer bought the judge. Almost any judge would square a small rap for the right price.

But amateurs! If a mark turned in Sally and her partner they would be lost. They might have the brains to get a lawyer, but if they did they'd still wind up doing a year or two apiece. Because the same judge who could be bought would go extra hard on an amateur, just to keep his record looking good.

The hell with them, Baron thought. They deserved whatever happened to them.

Mentally he went over all the ways the pair had played the game wrong. To begin with, Sally's whole approach was too heavy. She should have sat down a stool or two away from him instead of right next to him. She should have let him offer to buy her a drink—the second drink, not the first. She should have mentioned her husband right away and then left the rest of it up to Baron.

And, of course, she should have caught on to what he was talking about. The first words he spoke were, "I'm working the C out of Philly." This meant, quite simply, that he was a confidence man who started originally in Philadelphia. But she didn't even listen to him.

Then, later, he had told her he had just finished pulling off a rag, a phony stock con. Anybody but a damn fool would have caught that.

And her "husband" was just as stupid. He should have knocked first, then used the key. He was supposed to be expecting to find her in, so why in the hell didn't he knock? And he should have had a gun. Not loaded, of course. Not even a real gun, if he wanted to play extra safe. But as soon as he came in swinging he was making things hard for himself. Hell, even a mark might have gotten lucky and clipped him one.

Well, that was all over. In a day or two he'd get a wire from Lou and head either for Denver or the coast. And he would have happy memories of Tulsa.

There was a knock on the door.

Baron swung himself off the bed, wondering who was at the door. Maybe the telegram, he thought. Or maybe Sally, back for another round.

He walked to the door and opened it.

The "husband" was at the door. There was a gun in his hand.

"Inside," the man said. "Get inside."

Baron backed up, puzzled. The man followed him and closed the door behind him.

"Look," Baron said, "go home. You made me for a mark and you missed. Quit while you're ahead."

The man said, "I'm going to kill you."

"You tried to cop a score and you blew it."

The man's eyes were blazing. "I don't know what you're talking about," he said. "All I know is you were with my wife. I just finished beating the crap out of her. She won't be able to walk for a month. Now I'm going to kill you."

Baron just looked at him.

"She told me she was going to the movies," he went on dully. "I come back and she's with you. I always knew she was a tramp. I had to knock her silly before she'd tell me your name. And I had to give the clerk five bucks before he'd give me your room number.

"Now I'm going to kill you."

Baron started to laugh. No wonder their approach was so amateurish!

The man pointed the gun at him. Baron laughed again, thinking that it was really no time to laugh. But what the hell else could he do?

The man pulled the trigger.

Baron sat down heavily on the bed and began laughing once more. He couldn't help it. In a few seconds he stopped laughing because he was dead.

BARGAIN IN BLOOD

"YOU'VE GOT TO PROVE IT TO ME," she said.

He puffed nervously on his cigarette before answering her. She was a very beautiful girl, very well put together and very desirable, and it wasn't often that a girl like this even bothered to talk to him. He had to be very careful; he didn't want to say the wrong thing and maybe spoil everything before it even got off the ground.

"How do you mean?"

She took the cigarette from his fingers and dragged deeply on it. "You know," she said, talking through the smoke. "You say you want me, right?"

"Right."

"That's important, Benny. A guy's got to want me or he doesn't get me. Dig?"

He nodded. He wanted her, all right. He wanted her from the first time he saw her, before he even knew her name. He wanted her so much sometimes that he couldn't sleep and just lay in bed thinking about her, thinking about the way her blond hair curled around her face and the way her body could twist a sweater out of shape.

All the time he thought about her, but he never expected to get her. Not him. Not Benny Dix, the little kid with the pimples. The little kid with no dough and no car to drive around in, the little kid nobody paid much attention to at all.

She had class and he didn't; it was that simple. She was the type of chick who went with an important cat, a cat maybe like Moe. But she wasn't going with Moe now. She and Moe split, and now she was there for Benny. Maybe it didn't make sense, but it was nice. Real nice. She was so close to him now that he could reach out and touch her, and there was nobody else around the park, nobody to bother them.

"If you want me," she went on, "you got to show it. I need proof, Benny. You know why I broke with Moe?"

"Why?"

"No proof. Moe wanted me, but not enough to let me know it. You probably thought Moe was making it with me, didn't you?"

"I—"

"It's okay. Everybody thought so, but he wasn't. Not Moe or any-body else in this jerkwater town. Not because I'm cold, because I can be hot as a Nathan's hot dog for the right cat. But because I need proof. I could be hot for you, Benny."

He felt his hands starting to shake and struggled to control them. He'd give her the proof, whatever the hell it was. It didn't matter: he had to have her, and that was all there was to it.

"What kind of proof?" His voice sounded hollow to him, hol-low and nervous and tense, like when he was playing chickie and a cop car passed right by the hardware store, and then the cop car slowed down and he didn't know what to do, whether he should holler chickie or just wait for the cops to take off. Then the cops stepped on the gas and disappeared, and that came out the right way.

She was looking at him now, her eyes drilling holes in his, study-ing him very carefully. There was something so intense and direct about her gaze that he wanted to turn away, as if she were staring at him the way he did when he undressed a girl with his eyes. But this was deeper—she was undressing his insides, trying to decide about him.

"I want you to kill somebody."

"What?"

She smiled. "That's right, Benny. You heard me right. I want you to take a blade and slip it right into a cat's guts, understand? That's the kind of proof I want."

"Why, Rita? I mean—"

"To prove it. I'm nice stuff, Benny. I'm not easy, and I'll be worth it. Then we can do whatever you want whenever you want to."

His mind was racing in circles. He knew she was telling the truth. She'd be worth it, worth almost anything. But killing a guy was a big thing. If they caught you, you burned. And it wasn't like knocking over a candy store—they tried harder to catch you for murder.

Murder.

"Who's the cat? Anybody special?"

"You mean you'll do it?"

"Wait a minute. I just want to know who, that's all."

She took a breath. "Moe," she said.

"Moe?"

"That's right. You slip the shank in Moe and it's just you and me, Benny, for as long as you want it. What do you say?"

This was big. It was big enough shanking someone he didn't know, bad enough to slip steel into a cat he never met. But Moe was worse. Hell, he wasn't tight with Moe and he wouldn't miss him, not Moe with the short car with wire wheels and a girl in the back-seat whenever he wanted one. No, he could see Moe dead without crying about it. But killing him—

"It'll be easy," she went on, her voice husky and all excited. "It's about 9:30 now. I can go to his pad and pick him up. I'll tell him some lies so he thinks he's getting something now. Then we'll come walking over towards the park and you can get him about ten steps inside the North Entrance. Okay?"

He turned a little on the bench, looking off into the distance.

He was shook now. Killing— He couldn't pull a bit like that, not him.

And then he felt her small hand on his thigh.

"Okay," he said.

He saw them coming a long ways off. He heard them before he saw them, heard Moe's low, relaxed voice and Rita's, tense and shrill with anticipation. When they came into view he saw Moe's arm around her slender waist, his hand gently squeezing her flesh.

It made him mad, and he knew he'd be able to do it. He'd get even with Moe. He'd get even with him for all the girls he never had and the money he was never able to toss around.

They came closer. He took his knife from his dungarees pocket and clicked it open, fearing for a moment that Moe would hear the click of the blade and know what was going to happen. But Moe didn't notice. It was no wonder—Rita was leaning against him as they walked, and it would be tough for a cat to notice anything with a girl like her doing the leaning.

He rubbed his thumb nervously over the blade, feeling how sharp it was and wondering how it would go into Moe. It would go in nice and smooth, he decided. One push and that would be the end of Moe. And that little push would also serve as the beginning of Benny Dix.

They entered the park and stopped. They were just steps from him now, just steps from him and the knife and the murder. It was time now. He knew this, but he couldn't force himself to move for a moment, as if he were made of wood.

Now.

He stepped out from behind the tree and closed the gap between them in three quick strides, impatient to get it all over with as quickly as possible. Moe looked up and saw him, and he saw the total surprise in his eyes and the excitement and joy in Rita's. Then the expression in Moe's eyes changed to fear when he saw the knife, and he started to move but he couldn't move fast enough, couldn't dodge the knife that was coming up toward his soft belly, couldn't even scream when the knife went in and up into him, could only clutch at his gut as he fell back and crumpled to the pavement.

Rita came to him and stood next to him, and his arm went around her while she looked down at the body that a few minutes ago had been Moe. She was breathing hard now, hot and excited, staring as if she were hypnotized at the pool of blood below her. The blood looked almost purple in the light of the moon.

They stood in their tracks for several moments without either of them moving or saying a word. He felt torn in half, sick at the realization that Moe was dead and he had killed him, and hungry for Rita and knowing that he was going to get her now, that the loneliness and emptiness were over from here on in. She had the proof she wanted.

"Come on," she said at last. "Let's get out of here."

"Where to?"

"My pad. The folks are away for the weekend and nobody's going to bother us. You think you'll like that, Benny?"

"Yeah." His voice was hoarse and tight.

She slipped her hand in his and gave it a squeeze as they started walking swiftly out of the park. "I think you will, too," she said. "I think we'll both have a good time."

"Give me the knife," she said. "I'll wash it up so nobody can prove anything, okay?" She took the knife and walked off into the bathroom, and he kicked off his shoes and lay down on the bed to wait for her. He hadn't felt this way in a long time—wanting something so much that it was an ache instead of an ordinary hunger, and at the same time knowing that now he was going to get what he wanted, that she was in the next room and soon she would be in the same room with him, lying down on the bed beside him, and then he would have her.

Moe was dead. He killed Moe, but nobody was going to suspect him and no cops were going to prove anything even if they did figure it all out. Moe was dead in the park and he was in Rita's bed waiting for her, and even if killing was a bad thing there was nothing to do about it. It was all over—besides, it had to happen just the way it happened. He couldn't help it, not at all.

She was running water in the bathroom, washing the knife. Smart girl, he thought. The chick would figure all the angles. If the cops made noises, she could tell how the two of them were together all the time. It was clear.

She came back holding the knife in her hand and set it down on the little brown table at the head of the bed. "It's clean," she explained. "I'm leaving it open for now so it'll dry out, but there's no sweat now. Nobody saw a thing."

He nodded, and she sat down on the bed and kicked off her shoes. "You did it," she said. "You proved it to me, Benny. I knew you'd have the guts, and I knew you wanted me bad enough. That was the important part."

He didn't answer. She leaned back on the bed, resting her head on the pillow beside his. He could smell her perfume and the fragrance of her hair and he wanted to reach for her and take her right away without waiting for anything. He'd been with chicks before, but never one like Rita, never one who was made for this sort of thing, one that oozed sex with every step she took.

It was going to be good.

"I want you, too." She moved even closer to him and he turned so that their bodies pressed together tightly. He could feel every contour of her body and his arms went around her quickly, and then they were kissing. His heart was beating wildly and he couldn't control his breathing and he was no longer conscious of the room or the bed or the naked lightbulb hanging over the bed or the knife on the night table.

He was only conscious of his body and hers and nothing else mattered at all.

When it was over he lay motionless on the bed while she sat up and rearranged her clothing. He felt complete now for the first time in a long time, complete and whole and relaxed at last. She was even better than she'd promised, better than he had imagined.

He could almost forget Moe and the sick expression on his face when the knife tore into his stomach. Moe was something that couldn't be avoided, something in the way that had to be removed. It wasn't his fault for killing Moe, any more than it was his fault for being born or wanting Rita. It just happened that way.

And it was good for her, too. She loved every minute of it, every

second of the act. From here on in it was peaches and cream for
Benny Dix, with Rita whenever he wanted her. And he would want
plenty.

"You liked it," he said. "Didn't you?"

"Of course. Couldn't you tell?" There was a touch of amusement in her voice, a note of her knowing something that he was
missing.

"Yeah. I mean— You like doing that. You like it every time, don't
you?"

"Uh-huh."

Well, he'd give her plenty to like. He rolled over on one elbow
and looked at her, sitting silently on the edge of the bed. She looked
even prettier than before and it was hard to believe that he had
actually made love to her, that he had scored with such a good-
looking broad. But he could believe it. He could remember every
second of it as if it were still happening.

"I bet there's nothing you like better," he went on, talking
slowly. "You proved that you wanted me, just like I proved it to
you. Right?"

She nodded, and he could just make out the shadow of a smile
on her face.

"That's what I figured. A guy can tell if a chick's faking, you
know?"

"I wasn't faking."

"You don't have to tell me. You must like it better than anything
else in the world."

The smile grew wider. "Almost," she said, softly. "There's only
one thing in the world I like better, Benny. Just one thing." As she
spoke, it seemed to him as though she were playing some kind of a
game with him.

"Yeah?" he said, mildly curious. "What's that?"

"Something I just saw," she answered, and he still didn't know
what she was talking about. "It was fun to see it, Benny, and I bet
it's even better when you do it yourself!"

He opened his mouth to say something, and his mouth remained
uselessly open as he saw the knife in her hand, the knife he had

used on Moe. For one brief second he saw the answer to his question in her eyes; for one instant he knew what she really craved, what kind of excitement sent her blood racing. Just for that single second when he watched the insane stare in her eyes as she gazed at the blood gushing from the stab wound in his chest.

A second later his vision blurred and he saw nothing.

In another second he was dead.

BRIDE OF VIOLENCE

SHE DIDN'T SAY A WORD when I pulled the car off the road behind the clump of young poplars. I cut the motor and flicked off the lights. Then I pulled her to me and kissed her.

The kiss sent my blood racing. This was nothing new. Just being with Rita, just looking at her and running my eyes over the full curves of her body was enough to send me into a sweat.

I forced myself to pull away from her. "Come on," I said. "Let's get into the backseat."

She smiled, teasing me. "Why?"

"You know why."

"Tell me anyway."

I just looked at her. Her hair was long and golden and it spilled over her shoulders like a yellow waterfall. Her mouth was red with the lipstick I hadn't managed to kiss away yet. Her eyes were a sort of cornflower blue that deepened almost to purple in the dark.

I wanted her so much it was killing me.

"Quit playing games," I said.

"Games?" The eyes widened.

"Come on."

She smiled. "I just want you to tell me why we should get in the backseat, Jim. That's all."

"Don't you know?"

"I'm not sure," she said. "Maybe you have designs on my virtue. How should I know?"

"Rita—"

Her face softened. "I'm sorry, Jim," she said. "I don't like to tease you."

Not much, I thought. I didn't say anything.

"It's just that I don't want us to get too involved, Jim. Honey, every time we park the car and neck up a storm we go a little farther than we did last time. I'm afraid sometime we won't be able to stop."

"What's wrong if we don't?"

"Jim—"

"Well, what if we don't? God, Rita, I want you and you want me and that ought to be enough. Why in hell won't you let me make love to you?"

"I've already told you that."

"But it doesn't make any sense!"

She moved closer to me. I could feel her breasts pressing against my chest. My skin felt warm beneath my shirt where she was touching me. Her lips brushed my cheek.

"Not until we're married," she said. "I've told you a dozen times, darling."

More than a dozen times, I thought. *Closer to a hundred times.* I kissed her again, almost absently, thinking that this was just a repeat of a conversation the two of us went through almost every night.

But I had to keep going.

"We're going to be married," I said, "as soon as I get enough money saved up so that we won't have to pick through garbage cans when we want breakfast."

"I know."

"I'd marry you now," I went on. "Waiting was your idea, Rita. I—"

"You know it's the only sensible thing to do." She was closer to me now, so close I could feel every outline of her warm body. My arm slipped around her and stroked the firm flesh. I had a hard time getting the next sentence out; I wasn't much in the mood for conversation.

"Okay," I said. "Waiting to get married is sensible. But waiting to make love isn't."

"Suppose I got pregnant?" she demanded.

The same old arguments every damned night. "You won't," I said.

"You can't be sure about that, Jim. It happens, you know."

"Then we'd get married right away."

"And then we'd have everybody counting the months and snickering when the baby was born. I don't want that, Jim."

I didn't answer.

"But that's not the main thing. I'm an old-fashioned girl, honey. I want to wait until I'm married. That's all there is to it."

She seemed to be right—that was all there was to it. That was the trouble.

She snuggled up to me again. "I don't really feel like talking," she said. "Do you?"

"No," I said. "Of course not."

"We'll wait then? Until we're married?"

I nodded.

"Okay," she said. "Then let's get in the backseat."

I opened the door and helped her out and into the backseat. Then I reached for her and she came to me and our mouths met as they always did—hot and hungry and demanding. I kissed her again, savagely.

She purred like a kitten.

Then I was undoing the buttons on her blouse, and my arms were around her. I pressed her close to me and kissed her. My hands caressed her soft flesh. I fumbled with the catches of her bra.

"Here," she said. "Let me do that."

She broke away and reached behind her and the motion made her firm breasts strain against the bra until I thought it would break. Then the bra was off and she was in my arms again.

"Rita," I said. "God, I love you."

She started to say something but I stopped her mouth with mine. I held her and stroked her and kissed her and watched her turn from a beautiful girl into a hungry, passionate woman in my arms, her eyes burning like purple fires into mine.

Then I slipped my hand under her skirt and she froze.

"Stop," she said.

"Rita—"

"Stop!" She pushed my hand away and withdrew from me. "Jim, I told you—"

"I can't help it," I said. "I'm only human."

"But I *told* you."

I reached for her again, ready to tell her that I would try to control myself, loving her and hating her and wanting only to hold her close and love her.

Then the door opened.

He was about as tall as I am, but there the similarity ended.

He was built like an ox. His forearms were as thick as my legs and there wasn't an ounce of fat any place on him. It was all hard muscle.

His hair was clipped close to his scalp; his eyes were small and beady. His nose looked as though it had been broken once.

He was wearing clothing that looked familiar. It took me a minute to recognize it.

It was prison clothing.

There was a gun in his right hand that looked like a cannon.

"Out," he said. "Get out of the car." The words came out in a snarl.

I glanced at Rita. She was clutching her blouse around her, trying to button it but having a tough time. Her fingers were numb with fear.

His lips curled into a sneer. "Don't bother," he told her. "I'll just have to rip it off. Now get the hell out of the car."

We got out. There was nothing else to do.

"Over here," he said, motioning with the gun. We walked a few yards from the car into a clearing.

I said, "What do you want?"

He looked at me and smiled. Then he looked at Rita and the smile widened. She stiffened in terror. Her whole body shook.

"Guess," he said.

I guessed.

"I don't have much money," I said. "But you're welcome to it. And I suppose you'll want the car—it's not new by any means but it'll get you where you're going."

"Yeah," he said. He was still looking at Rita and I knew what he was thinking, what he was going to do.

He turned to me. "Chuck your wallet over here," he said. "And don't try anything. This thing works," he added, motioning with the gun.

I took the wallet from my inside jacket pocket and tossed it to him. He caught it easily with one hand and flipped it open, counting the money.

"Peanuts," he said. "Less than thirty bucks."

"It's all I have."

"With the heap you're driving, that'll hardly cover the gas. And I bet it burns oil by the gallon."

I didn't answer. His eyes went back to Rita and I wished he would stop looking at her, wished he would go away and leave us alone.

"You're nice," he said to her. "It's been a real long time."

She seemed to go limp. I think she probably knew what was happening all along, but as soon as he said those words the full impact of it hit her.

"A long time," he went on. "Too long. You got any idea what it's like?"

I looked at him.

"You," he said to me. "You know what it's like being without a woman for four and a half years? Huh?"

I almost started to laugh. I felt like asking him if he knew what it was like being with Rita and not making love to her.

But I didn't say anything.

"Naw," he said. "You wouldn't know. You wouldn't know what

it's like sitting in a goddamn cell every night and going crazy. Sitting there forever."

For a second his face seemed to relax. Then it went rigid again and he broke off.

"What did you do?" It was Rita talking this time. I wanted to tell her to shut up, to leave him alone and just pray he would go away without doing what I knew he was going to do. The words stuck in my throat.

"Huh?"

"What did you do that got you in jail?"

He smiled. It wasn't a pretty smile.

"Oh, I did lots of things."

"I mean—"

He walked over to her, keeping the gun trained on me as he did so. Neither of them said anything until he was standing inches away from her. He reached out a finger and chucked her under the chin as if she were a little girl.

"I took something," he said, "something that didn't belong to me."

"What was it?"

He chuckled. "It was a she. A broad. Looked something like you, come to think of it."

She said, "Oh." Her voice was flat and empty, almost lifeless.

"Not quite the same as you," he said. "Wore her hair long but it was a shade darker. Built a lot like you, though."

Without warning his hand snaked out and ripped her blouse all the way open, exposing her breasts. She took a step backward, drawing in her breath sharply as she did so.

He followed her.

"You're not going anywhere," he said. "Understand?"

She nodded dumbly.

He reached out and fastened a hand on her, and I could see how she shrank from his touch. For a moment I had a wild impulse to charge him. Maybe, with a little luck . . .

But I didn't move. Even if the gun wasn't loaded, even if he didn't manage to shoot me, I still didn't stand a chance. He could take me apart with his bare hands.

His hand tightened on her and she gasped.

"You're built better than she was," he said. "Bigger in the chest anyway. Let's see how your legs stack up against hers."

She didn't move.

"Come on," he said. "Get the skirt off."

It took her a moment to respond. Then she unhooked the skirt and stepped out of it. She wasn't wearing a slip—only a pair of black lace panties that matched the bra which was now in the backseat of the car.

I couldn't help staring at her. Even knowing what was going to happen to her, knowing that we would both be dead in an hour or two at most, I still couldn't help staring at her and realizing how breathtakingly beautiful she was. Her legs were long, with trim ankles and rounded calves leading up to swelling, full thighs.

"Nice," he murmured. "Very nice."

Her mouth opened and closed without any sounds coming out.

"The panties," he said suddenly. "Get 'em off."

"What—"

"Come on," he snapped. "I don't have time to waste."

"What are you going to do to me?"

The smile was back on his face, leering and open and ugly. "You damned little fool," he said. "Now what in hell do you *think* I'm going to do?"

She didn't say anything. I could see the tears welling up in the corners of her eyes.

"I'm going to make up for four and a half years," he said. "Now get the pants off."

"Wait a minute," I said.

He spun toward me and glared at me.

"Look," I said, "if you let us go I'll get you more money. I've got a few hundred at home. It'll get you out of the state."

He laughed. "Don't be a damn fool all your life," he said. "We couldn't even make it to your home, and we'd never make the state line. They got the roads blocked off all around."

"They know you escaped?"

"They sure as hell ought to," he said. "I broke out with half the prison watching me."

"But—"

He didn't let me finish. "I haven't got a chance in hell," he said. "By now they've got the whole area sealed off and they'll be closing in soon. They're going to get me."

"Look," I began. "If you let us alone and if you give yourself up maybe they'll go easy on you."

This time his laugh went through me like a cold wind. "Cut the crap," he said. "I was doing life for rape. You think they'll commute my sentence because I gave myself up?"

"But—"

He laughed again, even harsher this time. "I killed a guard on the way out. Shot another one in the gut and he's probably croaked by now. Still think I should give up? Or do you have any more bright ideas?"

I didn't say anything this time.

"I'm just out to get what I can," he said. "Right now I'm going to have some fun with your broad here. Then I'll probably kill the two of you, depending on how I feel. Then when the law comes I'll see how many of them I can take with me. And that's all—no more time in stir, no more nights in a cell. See?"

I saw.

He turned back to Rita. "The pants," he said. "In a hurry."

She took off her panties, slipping them down over her hips and thighs and stepping out of them. She was shaking like a leaf. It wasn't hard to figure out why.

"Please," she said suddenly. "Please—don't."

This got him mad. "You little bitch," he said. "I'm going to be dead in an hour or two—what the hell is it to you if I have some fun first? It's not like I was taking something away from you."

She hesitated. "I . . . I never did it before."

He stared at her. "Huh?"

"I'm a . . . a virgin."

"Sure," he said flatly. "Sure, so am I. We're all virgins. You and him—the two of you were just playing doctor in the backseat. Sure."

"I mean it," she protested. "Jim and I . . . we never went all the way."

He turned to me. "She telling the truth?"

I just nodded.

He looked at her again. Then he looked at me.

Then he started to laugh.

"You little punk," he said when he stopped laughing. "A guy like you, you wouldn't know what to do with a broad like this. What's the bit—just sit around necking?"

My cheeks were burning. But Rita was nodding very earnestly.

"Hell," he said. "I outgrew that when I was in junior high. I guess some people take awhile to grow up."

I still don't understand it exactly. When he touched her, when he told me what he was going to do to her, I was still able to stand still and not do anything about it. But now something snapped, as if his insult had hit home and I had to do something about it.

I rushed him.

I came in low and the gun sounded like a cannon when it went off. The shot missed and he pulled the trigger again when I was within a foot or two of him.

The hammer clicked on an empty chamber.

I crashed into him and he rolled over on his back. The gun dropped from his hand and I reached for it, managing to pick it up. Then he was on his feet again and coming at me.

Behind me Rita had started to scream.

"You punk," he snarled. "I'll kill you for that."

When he charged me I swung the gun like a club, putting everything I had into it. I had to nail him fast. If he got in one punch he could kill me.

The butt of the gun caught him on the side of the head and knocked him to the ground. It would have killed an ordinary man, or at least knocked him out. But he was shaking his head at once and on his feet a second later.

"Okay," he said. "Now you're going to get it."

I was still holding onto the gun as he came in for the kill. He was wary now, knowing that I had the gun and that I wasn't afraid to hit him with it.

Out of the corner of my eye I could see Rita. She was standing in the same place as before and she was stark naked, screaming her lungs out.

But there was no one around to hear her screams. I cursed myself mentally for parking so far away from town. I had wanted privacy—now I wished I had settled for a nice quiet spot on lover's lane by the river.

It was too late to wish. He stepped in closer, swinging his left like a meat cleaver. When I ducked it he threw the right.

I ducked under the punch and stepped out of the way. He had put his whole body into the blow, expecting it to connect, and now he couldn't stop. He went on right past me and I brought the gun down with all my might on the top of his head.

He dropped like a stone.

I knelt down next to him; he was unconscious. Then everything that had been bottled up inside me let loose and I rolled him onto his back. I brought the butt of the gun down on the bridge of his nose as hard as I could and I heard bone snap.

When somebody who knows judo does that with the side of his hand it can kill a man. I didn't know any more about judo than I had read in detective stories, but I wasn't using the side of my hand. I was using a gun butt.

I felt for a pulse. There was none.

He was dead.

When I straightened up she was in my arms, warm and sobbing and unconscious of her nakedness.

"Jim," she said. "Oh, God!"

I didn't feel anything. "Relax," I said. "He's dead. He can't do anything now."

"You were wonderful," she said. "You . . . you killed him."

I nodded.

"You knocked him out and you killed him."

I nodded again. My arms slipped around her and I stroked the smooth skin.

"He was horrible," she went on. "I . . . never met a man like that."

I mumbled, "He had a few good ideas."

"What did you say?"

I told her again.

She drew away from me. "What do you mean, Jim?"

I ignored her question. Instead I reached out a hand and took hold of her the way he had.

"He's right," I said. "You are nice."

She didn't know how to react. Finally she smiled. "I'm glad you think so."

I didn't smile. I tightened my grip on her the way I had seen him do it and she writhed in pain, staring at me.

"Does it hurt?"

"Yes," she gasped. "What—"

"If you weren't such a bitch," I said, "we wouldn't be here to-night. All this wouldn't have happened."

"I . . . let go, Jim."

I didn't let go.

"Jim—"

"We'd have been in bed, Rita. My bed. We never would have seen this guy."

She stared at me. I think she was beginning to catch on.

"Let go," she said. "I have to get dressed."

"Don't bother."

"I have to get some clothes on."

"I'll only rip them off again."

Her eyes opened wider. "Jim—"

"He had some good ideas," I said again. "I'm sick of necking, Rita. When I want something I'm going to take it."

She didn't answer.

"I want you," I said.

"Please," she said. It was the same tone of voice she had used before when he told her to take off her pants.

I managed to laugh. "Lie down," I said. "On the grass. It's not as good as a bed but I'm not going to wait anymore. I'm through with waiting, Rita."

She lay down in the grass, trying to cover her nakedness with her hands. Her eyes stared at me dully.

Very methodically I took off my jacket, folded it, and set it on the ground by the body. Then I removed the rest of my clothing.

When I knelt beside her she didn't try to resist me but her face was contorted in terror. I put my hand on her shoulder. She shivered.

"Relax," I told her. "It won't be that bad."

I added, "Someday you might even learn to like it."

THE BURNING FURY

HE WAS A BIG MAN with a rugged chin and the kind of eyes that could look right through a person, the piercing eyes that said, "I know who you are and I know your angle and I'm not buying it, so get out."

All of him said that—the solid frame without fat on it, the muscles in his arms, and even the way he was dressed. He wore a plaid flannel shirt open at the neck, a pair of tight blue jeans, and heavy logger's boots. Once the boots had been polished to a bright shine, but that was a long time ago. Now they were a dingy brown, scuffed and battered from plenty of hard wear.

He tossed off the shot of rot-gut rye and sipped the beer chaser slowly, wondering how much of the slop he would pour down his gullet tonight. Christ, he was drinking too much. At this rate he'd drink himself broke by the time the season was up and he'd have to go bumming a ride to the next camp. And then it would just start in all over again—breaking your back over the big trees in the day-time and pouring down the rye and beer every night.

The days off were different. On those days it was cheap wine, half-a-buck a bottle Sneaky Pete, down the hatch the first thing in the morning and you kept right on with it until you passed out. That was on your day off, and you needed a day off like you needed a hole in your head.

When he worked he stayed sober until work was through for the day. He didn't need a drink while he was working, not with the full flavor of the open air racing through him and the joy of swinging that double-bit axe and working the big saw, not then. Not when he was up on top, trimming her down and watching the axe bite through branches.

When he was working there was nothing to forget, no memories to grab him around the neck, no hungers to make him want to reach out and swing at somebody. Not when he had an axe in his hand.

But afterwards, then it was bad. Then the memories came, the Bad Things, and there had to be a way to forget them. The hunger came, stronger each time, and he couldn't sleep unless his gut was filled with whiskey or beer or wine or all three.

If only a man could work twenty-four hours a day . . .

He knew it would be bad the minute she came through the door. He saw her at once, saw the shape of her body and the color of her hair and the look in her eyes, and he knew right away that it was going to be one hell of a night. He took hold of the beer glass so hard he almost snapped it in two and tossed off the rest of the beer, calling for another shot with his next breath. The bartender came so slowly, and all the time he could see her out of the corner of his eye and feel the hunger come on like a sunset.

It was just like a sunset, the way his mind started going red and yellow and purple all at once and the way the hunger sat there like a big ball of fire nestling on the horizon. He closed his eyes and tried to black out the picture but it stayed with him, glowing and burning and sending hot shivers through his heavy body.

He told the bartender to make it a double, and he threw the double straight down and went to work on the beer chaser, hoping that the boilermakers would work tonight. Enough liquor would kill the sunset and put out the fire. It worked before. It had to work this time.

He watched her out of the corner of his eye, not wanting to but not able to help himself. She was small—a good head shorter than he was, and she couldn't weigh half of what he did. But the weight she had was all placed just right, just the way he liked a woman to be put together.

Her hair was blond—soft and fluffy and curling around her face like smoke. Her yellow sweater was just a shade deeper and brighter than her hair, and it showed off her body nicely, hugging and emphasizing the gentle curves.

The dark green skirt was tight, and it did things to the other half of her body.

He looked at her, and the ball of fire in his mind burned hotter and brighter every second.

Twenty or twenty-one, he guessed. Young, and with that innocent look that would stay with her no matter what she did or with whom or how often. He knew instinctively that the innocence was an illusion, and he would have known this if he saw her kneeling in a church instead of looking over the men in a logger's bar. But he knew at the same time that this was the only word for what she had: innocence. It was in the eyes, the way she moved, the half-smile on her full lips.

That was what did it: the youth, the innocence, the shape, and the knowledge that she was about as innocent as a Bowery flea-bag. That did it every time, those four things all together, and he thought once again that this was going to be one hell of a night.

Another double followed the beer. It was beginning to take hold now, he noticed with a short sigh of relief. He rubbed a callused finger over his right cheek and noted a sensation of numbness in his cheek, the first sign that the alcohol was reaching him. With his constant drinking it took a little more alcohol every night, but he was getting there now, getting to the point where the girl wouldn't affect him at all.

If only she'd give him time. Just a few more drinks and there would be nothing to worry about, a few more drinks and the numbness would spread slowly from his cheeks to the rest of his body and finally to his brain, quenching the yellow fire and letting him rest.

If only . . .

Out of the corner of his eye, he saw her eyes upon him, singling him out from the crowd at the bar. She took a hesitant step toward him and he wanted to shout "Go away!" at her. She kept on coming, and he wished that the stool on his right weren't empty, that with no place for her to sit she might leave him alone.

He finished the chaser and waved again for the bartender. Surely, inevitably, she walked to the bar and took the stool beside him. The dark green skirt caught on the stool and slithered up her leg as she sat, and the sight of firm white flesh heaped fresh fuel upon the mental ball of fire.

He tossed off the shot without tasting it or feeling any effect whatsoever. The beer followed the shot in one swallow, still bringing neither taste nor numbing peace. He winced as she tapped a cigarette twice on the polished surface of the bar and placed it between her lips.

The fumbling in her purse was, he knew, an act and nothing more. Christ, they were all the same, every one of them. He could even time the pitch—it would come on the count of three. One. Two. Thr—

"Do you have a match?"

Right on schedule. He ignored her, concentrating instead on the drink that had appeared magically before him. He hardly remembered ordering it. He couldn't remember anything anymore, not since she took the seat beside him, not since every bit of his concentration had been devoted to her.

"A match, please?"

He pulled a box of wooden matches from his shirt pocket without thinking, scratched one on the underside of the bar, and held it to her cigarette. She leaned toward him to take the light, moving her leg slightly against his, touching him briefly before withdrawing.

Right on schedule.

He closed the matchbox and stuffed it back into his shirt pocket, trying to force his attention back to the drink in front of him. His fingers closed around the shot glass. But he couldn't even seem to lift it from the bar, couldn't raise the drink that might save him for that night at least.

He wanted to turn to her and snarl: *Look, I'm not interested. I don't care if it's for sale or free for the taking, I'm not interested. Take your hot little body and get the hell out.*

But he didn't even turn around. He sat still, his heavy frame motionless on the stool, waiting for what had to come next.

"You're lonesome, aren't you?"

He didn't answer. Christ, even her voice had that sugary innocence, that mixture of sex and baby powder. It was funny he hadn't noticed it before, and he wished he hadn't noticed it now. It just made everything so much worse.

"You're lonesome." It was a statement now, almost a command.

"No, I'm not." Instantly he hated himself for answering at all. The words came from his lips almost by themselves, without him wishing it at all.

"Of course you are. I can tell." She spoke as if she were completely sure of herself, and as she talked her body moved imperceptibly closer to him, her leg inching toward his and pressing against it firmly, not withdrawing this time but remaining there, inflaming him.

His fingers squeezed the shot glass but it stayed on the bar, the rye out of his reach when he needed it so badly.

"Go away." He meant to snap the words at her like axe-blows, but instead they dribbled almost inaudibly from his lips.

"You're lonesome and unhappy. I know."

"Look, I'm fine. Why don't you go bother somebody else?"

She smiled. "You don't mean that," she said. "You don't mean that at all. Besides, I don't want to bother anybody else, can't you see? I want to be with you."

"Why?"

"Because you're big. I like big men."

Sure, he thought. It was like this all the time. "There's other big guys around."

"Not like you. You got that sad lonesome look, like I can see it a mile away how lonesome you are. And unhappy, you know. It sticks out."

It did; that much was true enough.

"Look," she was saying, "what are you fighting for, huh? You're lonesome and I'm here. You're unhappy and I can make you happy."

When he hesitated, she explained: "I'm good at making guys happy. You'd be surprised."

"I'll bet you are." Christ, why couldn't he just shut up and let her talk herself dry? No, he had to go on making small talk and feeling that hot little leg digging into his and listening to that syrupy voice dripping into his ear like maple syrup into a tin cup. He had to glance at her every second out of the corner of his eye, drinking in the softness of her. His nostrils were filled with the smell of her, a smell that was a mixture of cheap perfume and warm woman-smell, an odor that got into his bloodstream and just made everything worse than ever.

"I can make you happy."

He didn't answer, thinking how happy she would make him if she would just leave now, right away, if the earth would only open up and swallow her or him or both of them, just so long as she would leave him alone. There wasn't much time left.

"Look."

He turned his head involuntarily and watched her wiggle slightly in place, her body moving and rubbing against the sweater and skirt.

"It's all me," she explained. "Under the clothes, I mean."

He clenched his teeth and said nothing.

"I'll make you happy," she said again. When he didn't reply she placed her hand gently on his and repeated the four words in a half-whisper. Her hand was so small, so small and soft.

"C'mon," she said.

He stood up and followed her out the door, the glass of rye still untouched.

She said her place wasn't far and they walked in the direction she led him, away from the center of town. He didn't say anything all the way, and she only repeated her promise to make him happy. She said it over and over as if it were a magic phrase, a charm of some sort.

His arm went around her automatically and his hand squeezed the firm flesh of her waist. There was no holding back anymore—he knew that, and he didn't try to stop his fingers from gently kneading the flesh or the other hand from reaching for hers and enveloping it possessively. This act served to bring her body right up next to his so that they bumped together with every step. After a block or so her head nestled against his shoulder and remained there for the rest of the walk. The fluffy blond hair brushed against his cheek.

The cheek wasn't numb anymore.

It was cold out but he didn't notice the cold. It was windy, but he didn't feel the wind cut through the tight blue jeans and the flannel shirt. She had lied slightly: it was a long walk to her place, but he didn't even notice the distance.

She lived by herself in a little shack, a tossed-together affair of unpainted planks with nails knocked in crudely. Somebody had tried to get a garden growing in front but the few plants were all dead now and the weeds overran the small patch. He knew, seeing the shack, why she had fixed on the idea of him being lonely. She was so obviously alone, living off by herself and away from the rest of the world.

Inside, she closed and bolted the door and turned to him, her eyes expectant and her mouth waiting to be kissed. He closed his eyes briefly. Maybe he could open them and discover that she wasn't there at all, that he was back at the bar by himself or maybe out cold in his own cabin.

But she was still there when he opened his eyes. She was still standing close to him, her mouth puckered and her eyes vaguely puzzled.

"I'll make you happy." She said those four words as if they were the answer to every question in the universe, and by this time he thought that perhaps they were.

There was no other answer.

He clenched his teeth again, just as he had done when she squirmed before him on the barstool. Then he drove one fist into her stomach and watched her double up in pain, the physical pain of the blow more than matched by the hurt and confusion in her eyes.

He struck her again, a harsh slap on the side of her face that sent her reeling. She started to fall and he brought his knee up, catching her on the jaw and breaking several of her teeth. He hauled her to her feet and the sweater ripped away like tissue paper.

She was right. It was all her underneath.

The next slap started her crying. The one after that knocked the wind out of her and stopped her tears for the time being. His fingers ripped at the skirt and one of his nails dug at her skin, drawing blood. She crumpled to the floor, her whole body shaking with terror and pain, and he fell upon her greedily.

The bitch, he thought. The stupid little bitch.

Couldn't she guess there was only one way to make him happy?

THE DOPE

I'M NOT VERY BRIGHT. I've never been very smart, and even if I am four years older than Charlie, he's smarter than I am. It's been that way ever since I can remember. When we went to school, I was just one grade ahead of him. He skipped once and I flunked twice, because he's almost as much of a smart guy as I'm a dope. It used to bother the hell out of me, but I got used to it.

Then we both quit after a couple years of high school, and me and Charlie were a team. It was just the two of us. Charlie and Ben, the brains and the brawn. That's the way Charlie used to talk about it. I was lots bigger than him and stronger, but he had a brain like a genius. Let me tell you, we were a team.

Did he have a brain! That's what I used to call him—The Brain. And he used to call me The Muscle, 'cause I was so strong. Except when I did something stupid he would call me The Dope. He would be kidding when he said it, and he never did it when anyone was around, so I didn't mind too much.

We had it good—just me and Charlie, just the two of us. We

didn't stick around at home 'cause the folks were giving us a hard time ever since we left school. They wanted Charlie to graduate from Erasmus and go to college and be a doctor, but Charlie said the only college he'd ever get to was Sing Sing and he was in no hurry to get there. So we got the hell out of Brooklyn and took a room a ways off Times Square.

Let me tell you, that was the life. We bought some nice clothes, real fancy with sharp colors, and we ate all our meals in restaurants. There were loads of movie houses right around where we lived, and I'd see one or two shows a day. Charlie liked to stay in the room and read. He was a real brain, you see.

And once a week or so we'd pull a job. Charlie did all of the planning. He was a clever guy, let me tell you. One day he would go and case a store, and then he wouldn't do anything but plan for the next three or four days. He would sit in the room all by himself and think. He figured every angle.

We went mostly to candy stores. Charlie would get the low-down on how many people worked and what time the store would close, and he figured everything to the minute. Sometimes I wondered why he brought me along. The way he figured things out he could have done it all by himself.

But once in a while he would need me, and that's when I felt real good. Like for instance the time we hit a candy store in Yorkville—that's a German neighborhood uptown on the East Side. There was just this one old guy in the store, like Charlie figured. He was ready to close when we walked in. Charlie bought some candy and talked to the guy and the guy talked back in a thick accent as if he just got off the boat. Then Charlie had enough, and he pulled out his gun and told the guy to empty the cash register. The gun was another of Charlie's ideas. It looked just like a real gun, but all it would shoot was blanks. It's the kind you see advertised in magazines for when burglars come into your house. That way Charlie figured they couldn't pick us up for armed robbery, but we could scare a guy silly by shooting the gun into the air. Now let me ask you how many guys could have figured that out? He was a brain.

But to get back to the story, the old guy gave us a hard time. He started rattling off a mile a minute in German and he got real loud. So Charlie just turned to me and said, "Take him, Muscle."

That's all he had to say, and he said it just like that. That was what I was waiting for. I stepped right in and belted the guy one in the mush, but not too hard. He went out like a light, let me tell you. We emptied the cash box and got the hell out quick.

Those were the days. I was happy, you know. I didn't talk much, but I tried to tell Charlie how happy I was. Most of the time he just nodded, but one time he got mad.

"Happy?" he said. "What the hell are you happy about? We're a couple of small-time mugs living in a dump. What's to be happy about?"

I tried to tell him how nice it was, going to shows and just the two of us living together, but I don't talk too good.

"You dope," he said. "You'd be happy being a punk forever. That's not for me, Dope."

I couldn't see what he was getting at so I went out to a show. It was this picture where Jimmy Cagney wants to be the top man in the rackets so his mother will be proud of him and he winds up getting blown up in a factory. It was a damn good picture, except for the ending.

When I got back to the room Charlie was sitting on the bed writing something down. I got excited, 'cause I knew he was making notes for the next job. He always wrote everything out in detail, and burned his notes in the wastebasket. He didn't miss a trick.

I sat down next to him and gave him a smile. "What's new, Brain?" He didn't answer until he finished what he was writing, and then he smiled back at me. "A big one," he said. "No more candy store junk."

I didn't answer and he went on to explain it. I didn't get it all because I'm not too bright when it comes to that kind of thing, but there was some sort of office he knew about where they had the payroll set up at night and if we went in and robbed it we could get away with the whole payroll. He asked me didn't it beat knocking over candy stores and I told him it sure did. A guy like me never would have figured out something like that, but Charlie was sharp as a tack.

We pulled the job the next night. It was just a few blocks away from where we lived, and the place was all locked up. Charlie said there was a watchman on duty in the back, where the money was. Then he took a little hunk of metal and got the door open. I don't know where he learned how to do that, I really don't.

I started to walk right in but Charlie made me slow down. He whispered that the old guy could give an alarm unless we got him by surprise. We walked in on tiptoe, and we were practically on top of him before he looked up, and Charlie had the fake gun pointed right at him. I thought he'd have a heart attack then and there.

"Open the safe," Charlie said.

The old guy just stared for a minute, and then he stuck out his chin. "You boys better go home," he said. "I'll give you ten seconds before I call the cops."

Charlie knew how to put the screws on. He didn't say a word, but just kept standing there with the gun pointing right at the guy's head. It was so real that I almost started thinking it wasn't a phony gun with blank bullets.

Then the guy jumped. He fell right down off the chair, and Charlie yelled, "Get him, you goddamn dope!"

I went for him then, but he hit the alarm button before I could get him and the bells started ringing like mad. I was boiling then. I yanked him up off the floor and belted him all the way across the room, and his head hit the wall like Ted Williams hits a baseball.

I started across the room after him, I was so mad. But Charlie stopped me and we ran out. There were people all around, but they didn't know what was happening and we managed to get back to the room.

Charlie wouldn't even talk to me. He sat on the bed listening to the radio, and when the news came that the guy had died of a broken skull he looked at me like I was the stupidest guy in the world. Let me tell you, I felt horrible. It was just like me to swing too hard.

I thought we could still get away, but Charlie straightened me out. He told me how they saw us and they'd get us sooner or later. And he figured out the only way we could get out of it.

We wiped off his gun and got my fingerprints on it, and then we went to the police station. I told them the story just like Charlie told me to, about how I was the older brother and I was bigger than Charlie and made him come along and commit crimes, and how I beat up the guy and killed him. And then at the trial some doctor told how I was a dope and hardly knew what I was doing, and they shouldn't blame me for it. Charlie had to go to jail, but he got out in a year. Because I was such a dope they only gave me ten years for manslaughter.

It's not bad here, either. There are lots of nice guys to talk to, and the food's okay. And the best part of it is that Charlie's out now, and he comes to visit me once a month. He sends me money for cigarettes and everything, which is damn nice of him.

I'm just a dope, but I'm lucky. Most guys wouldn't pay any attention to me, especially if they were real smart. But Charlie comes every month, and he says, "Hi, Muscle," and I say, "Hiya, Brain."

We're still buddies, even after what I did.

He's a wonderful brother, let me tell you.

A FIRE AT NIGHT

HE GAZED SILENTLY INTO THE FLAME. The old tenement was burning, and the smoke was rising upward to merge against the blackness of the sky. There were neither stars nor moon in the sky, and the streetlights in the neighborhood were dim and spaced far apart. Nothing detracted from the brilliance of the fire. It stood out against the night like a diamond in a pot of bubbling tar. It was a beautiful fire.

He looked around and smiled. The crowd was growing larger, as everyone in the area thronged together to watch the building burn. They like it, he thought. Everyone likes a fire. They receive pleasure from staring into the flames, watching them dance on the tenement roof. But their pleasure could never match his, for it was his fire. It was the most beautiful fire he had ever set.

His mind filled with the memory of it. It had been planned to perfection. When the sun dropped behind the tall buildings and the sky grew dark, he had placed the can of kerosene in his car with the rags—plain, nondescript rags that could never be traced to him. And then he had driven to the old tenement. The lock on the cellar door was no problem, and there was no one around to get in the way. The rags were placed, the kerosene was spread, the match was struck, and he was on his way. In seconds the flames were licking at the ancient walls and racing up the staircases.

The fire had come a long way now. It looked as though the building had a good chance of caving in before the blaze was extinguished. He hoped vaguely that the building would fall. He wanted his fire to win.

He glanced around again, and was amazed at the size of the crowd. All of them pressed close, watching his fire. He wanted to call to them. He wanted to scream out that it was his fire, that he and he alone had created it. With effort he held himself back. If he cried out it would be the end of it. They would take him away and he would never set another fire.

Two of the firemen scurried to the tenement with a ladder. He squinted at them, and recognized them—Joe Dakin and Roger Haig. He wanted to call hello to them, but they were too far away to hear him. He didn't know them well, but he felt as though he did. He saw them quite often.

He watched Joe and Roger set the ladder against the side of the building. Perhaps there was someone trapped inside. He remembered the other time when a small boy had failed to leave the building in time. He could still hear the screams—loud at first, then softer until they died out to silence. But this time he thought the building had been empty.

The fire was beautiful! It was warm and soft as a woman. It sang with life and roared with joy. It seemed almost a person, with a mind and a will of its own.

Joe Dakin started up the ladder. Then there must be someone in the building. Someone had not left in time and was trapped with the fire. That was a shame. If only there were a way for him to warn them! Perhaps next time he could give them a telephone call as soon as the blaze was set.

Of course, there was even a beauty in trapping someone in the building. A human sacrifice to the fire, an offering to the goddess of Beauty. The pain, the loss of life was unfortunate, but the beauty was compensation. He wondered who might be caught inside.

Joe Dakin was almost to the top of the ladder. He stopped at a window on the fifth floor and looked inside. Then he climbed through.

Joe is brave, he thought. I hope he isn't hurt. I hope he saves the person in the building.

He turned around. There was a little man next to him, a little man in shabby clothes with a sad expression on his face. He reached over and tapped the man on the shoulder.

"Hey!" he said. "You know who's in the building?"

The little man nodded wordlessly.

"Who is it?"

"Mrs. Pelton," said the little man. "Morris Pelton's mother."

He had never heard of Morris Pelton. "Well, Joe'll get her out. Joe's a good fireman."

The little man shook his head. "Can't get her out," he said. "Can't nobody get her out."

He felt irritated. Who was this little jerk to tell him? "What do you mean?" he said. "I tell you Joe's a helluva fireman. He'll take care of it."

The little man flashed him a superior look. "She's fat," he said. "She's a real big woman. She must weigh two hundred pounds easy. This Joe's just a little guy. How's he gonna get her out? Huh?" The little man tossed his head triumphantly and turned away without an answer.

Another sacrifice, he thought. Joe would be disappointed. He'd want to rescue the woman, but she would die in the fire.

He looked at the window. Joe should come out soon. He couldn't save Mrs. Pelton, and in a few seconds he would be coming down the ladder. And then the fire would burn and burn and burn, until the walls of the building crumbled and caved in, and the fire won the battle. The smoke would curl in ribbons from the ashes. It would be wonderful to watch.

He looked up at the window suddenly. Something was wrong. Joe was there at last, but he had the woman with him. Was he out of his mind?

The little man had not exaggerated. The woman was big, much larger than Joe. He could barely see Joe behind her, holding her in his arms. Joe couldn't sling her into a fireman's carry; she would have broken his back.

He shuddered. Joe was going to try to carry her down the ladder, to cheat the fire of its victim. He held her as far from his body as he could and reached out a foot gingerly. His foot found the first rung and rested on it.

He took his other foot from the windowsill and reached out for the next rung. He held tightly to the woman, who was screaming now. Her body shook with each scream, and rolls of fat bounced up and down.

The damned fool, he thought. How could he expect to haul a fat slob like that down five flights on a ladder? He was a good fireman, but he didn't have to act like a superman. And the fat bitch didn't even know what was going on. She just kept screaming her head off. Joe was risking his neck for her, and she didn't even appreciate it at all.

He looked at Joe's face as the fireman took another halting step. Joe didn't look good. He had been inside the building too long. The smoke was bothering him.

Joe took another step and tottered on the ladder. Drop her, he thought. You goddamned fool, let go of her!

And then he did. The woman slipped suddenly from Joe's grip, and plummeted downward to the sidewalk. Her scream rose higher and higher as she fell, and then stopped completely. She struck the pavement like a bug smacking against the windshield of a car.

His whole being filled with relief. Thank God, he thought. It was too bad for the woman, but now Joe would reach the ground safely. But he noticed that Joe seemed to be in trouble. He was still swaying back and forth. He was coughing, too.

And then, all at once, Joe fell. He left the ladder and began to drop to the earth. His body hovered in the air and floated down like a feather. Then he hit the ground and melted into the pavement.

At first he could not believe it. Then he glared at the fire. Damn you, he thought. You weren't satisfied with the old woman. You had to take a fireman too.

It wasn't right.

The fire was evil. This time it had gone too far. Now it would have to suffer for it.

And then he raised his hose and trained it on the burning hulk of the tenement, punishing the fire.

FROZEN STIFF

AT TEN MINUTES TO FIVE the Mexican kid finished sweeping the floor. He stood by the counter, leaning on his broom and looking at the big white-faced clock.

"Go on home," Brad told him. "Nobody's going to want any lamb chops delivered anymore. You're through, go get some rest."

The kid flashed teeth in a smile. He took off his apron and hung it on a peg, put on a poplin windbreaker.

"Take it easy," Brad said.

"You stayin' here?"

"For a few minutes," Brad said. "I got a few things to see to." The kid walked to the door, then turned at the last moment. "You watch out for the freezer, Mr. Malden. You get in there, man, nobody can get you out."

"I'll be careful."

"I'll see you, Mr. Malden."

"Yeah," Brad said. "Sure."

The kid walked out. Brad watched the door close after him, then walked behind the meat counter and leaned over it, his weight propped up on his elbows. He was a big man, heavy with muscle, broad-faced and barrel-chested. He was forty-six, and he looked years younger until you saw the furrowed forehead and the drawn, anxious lines at the corners of his mouth. Then he looked fifty.

He took a deep breath and let it out slowly. He picked a heavy cleaver from a hook behind him, lifted it high overhead, and brought it down upon a wooden chopping block. The blade sank four inches into the block.

Strong, he thought. Like an ox.

He left the cleaver in the block. The freezer was in the back, and he walked through a sawdust-covered hallway to it. He opened the door and looked inside. Slabs of beef hung from the ceiling. Other cuts and sections of meat were piled on the floor. There were cleavers and hooks on pegs in the walls. The room was very cold.

He looked at the inside of the door. There was a safety latch there, installed so that the door could be opened from the inside if a person managed to lock himself in.

Two days ago he had smashed the safety latch. He broke it neatly and deliberately with a single blow of the cleaver, and then he told the Mexican kid what had happened.

"Watch yourself in the cold bin," he had told the kid. "I busted the goddamn latch. That door shuts on you and you're in trouble. The room's soundproof. Nobody can hear you if you yell. So make damn sure the door's open when you're in there."

He told Vicki about it that same night. "I did a real smart thing today," he said. "Broke the damn safety latch on the cold bin door."

"So what?" she said.

"So I got to watch it," he said. "The door shuts when I'm in there and there's no way out. A guy could freeze to death."

"You should have it fixed."

"Well," he had said, shrugging, "one of these days."

He stood looking into the cold bin for a few more moments now. Then he turned slowly and walked back to the front of the store. He closed the door, latched it. He turned off the lights. Then he went back to the cold bin.

He opened the door. This time he walked inside, stopping the door with a small wooden wedge. The wedge left the door open an inch or so. He took a deep breath, filling his lungs with icy air.

He looked at his watch. Five-fifteen, it read. He took another breath and smiled slowly, gently, to himself.

By eight or nine he would be dead.

It started with a little pain in the chest. Just a twinge, really. It hurt him when he took a deep breath, and sometimes it made him cough. A little pain—you get to expect them now and then when you pass forty. The body starts to go to hell in one way or the other and you get a little pain from time to time.

He didn't go to the doctor. What the hell, a big guy like Brad Malden, he should go to the doctor like a kid every time he gets a little pain? He didn't go to the doctor. Then the pain got worse, and he started getting other pains in his stomach and legs, and he had a six-letter idea what it was all about.

He was right. By the time he went to a doctor, finally, it was inoperable. "You should have come in earlier," the doctor told him. "Cancer's curable, you know. We could have taken out a lung—"

Sure, he thought. And I could breath with my liver. Sure.

"I want to get you to the hospital right away," the doctor had said.

And he asked, reasonably, "What the hell for?"

"Radium treatments. Radical surgery. We can help you, make the pain easier, delay the progress of the disease—"

Make me live longer, he had thought. Make it last longer, and hurt longer, and cost more.

"Forget it," he said.

"Mr. Malden—"

"Forget it. Forget I came to you, understand? I never came here, I never saw you, period. Got it?"

The doctor did not like it that way. Brad didn't care whether he liked it or not. He didn't have to like it. It wasn't his life.

He took a deep breath again and the pain was like a knife in his chest. Like a cleaver. Not for me, he thought. No lying in bed for a year dying by inches. No wasting away from two hundred pounds to eighty pounds. No pain. No dribbling away the money on doctors and hospitals until he was gone and there was nothing left for Vicki but a pile of bills that the insurance would barely cover. Thanks, doc. But no thanks. Not for me.

He looked again at his watch. Five-twenty. Go ahead, he told himself angrily. Get rid of the wedge, shut the door, lie down, and go to sleep. It was cold, and you closed your eyes and relaxed, and bit by bit you got numb all over. Go ahead, shut the door and die.

But he left the wedge where it was. No rush, he thought. There was plenty of time for dying.

He walked to the wall, leaned against it. This was the better way. In the morning they would find him frozen to death, and they would figure logically enough that the wedge had slipped and he had frozen to death. Vicki would cry over him and bury him, and the insurance policy would pay her a hundred thousand dollars. He had fifty thousand dollars of straight life insurance with a double indemnity clause for accidental death, and this could only be interpreted as an accident. With that kind of money Vicki could get a decent income for life. She was young and pretty, they didn't have any kids, in a few years she could remarry and start anew.

Fine.

The pain came, and this time it was sharp. He doubled over, clutching at his chest. God, he hoped the doctor would keep his mouth shut. Though it would still go as accidental death. It had to. No one committed suicide by locking himself in a cold bin. They jumped out of windows, they slashed their wrists, they took poison, they left the gas jets on. They didn't freeze themselves like a leg of lamb. Even if they suspected suicide, they had to pay the claim. They were stuck with it.

When the next stab of pain came he couldn't stand any longer. It had been hell trying not to wince, trying to conceal the pain from Vicki. Now he was alone; he didn't have to hide it. He hugged both hands to his chest and sank slowly to the floor. He sat on a slab of bacon, then moved the slab aside and sat on the floor. The floor was very cold. Hell, he thought, it was funny to sit in the cold bin. He'd never spent much time there before, just walked in to get some meat or to hang some up. It was a funny feeling, sitting on the floor.

How cold was it? He wasn't sure exactly. The thermostat was outside by the door; otherwise the suicide wouldn't have been possible, since he could have turned up the temperature. The damn place was a natural, he thought. A death trap.

He put his hand to his forehead. Getting cold already, he thought. It shouldn't take too long, not at this rate. And he didn't even have the door closed. He should close the door now. It would go a little faster with the door closed.

Could he smoke a cigarette? Sure, he thought. Why not?

He considered it. If they found the cigarette they would know he'd had a smoke before he froze to death. So? Even if it were an accident, a guy would smoke, wouldn't he? Besides, he'd make damn sure they'd think he tried to get out. Flail at the door with the cleaver, throw some meat around, things like that. They wouldn't make a federal case out of a goddamn cigarette.

He took one out, put it between his lips, scratched a match and lighted it. He smoked thoughtfully, wincing slightly when the pain gripped his chest like a vise. A year of this? No, not for him. The quick death was better.

Better for him. Better for Vicki, too. God, he loved that woman! Too much, maybe. Sometimes he got the feeling that he loved her too hard, that he cared more for her than she did for him. Well, it was only natural. He was a fatheaded butcher, not too bright, not much to look at. She was twenty-six and beautiful and there were times when he couldn't understand why she had married him in the first place. Couldn't understand, but remained eternally grateful.

The cigarette warmed his fingers slightly. They were growing cold now, and their tips were becoming numb. All he had to do was flip the wedge out. It wouldn't take long.

He finished the cigarette, put it out. He was on his way to get rid of the wedge when he heard the front door open.

It could only be Vicki, he thought. No one else had a key. He heard her footsteps, and he smiled quickly to himself. Then he heard her voice and he frowned.

"He must be here," she was saying. Her voice was a whisper. "In the back."

"Let's go."

A man's voice, that one. He walked to the cold bin door and put his face to the one-inch opening. When they came into view he stiffened. She was with a man, a young man. He had a gun in one hand. She went into his arms and he kissed her hard.

Vicki, he thought! God!

They were coming back now. He moved away, moved back into the cold bin, waiting. The door opened and the man was pointing a gun at him and he shivered. The pain came, like a sword, and he was shaking. Vicki mistook it for fear and grinned at him.

She said, "Wait, Jay."

The gun was still pointing at him. Vicki had her hand on the man's arm. She was smiling. Evil, Brad thought. Evil.

"Don't shoot him," she was saying. "It was a lousy idea anyway. Killed in a robbery—who the hell robs a butcher shop? You know how much dough he takes in during a day? Next to nothing."

"You got a better way, Vicki?"

"Yes," she said. "A much better way."

And she was pulling Jay back, leading him away from the door. And then she was kicking the wooden wedge aside, and laughing, and shutting the door. He heard her laughter, and he heard the terribly final sound the door made when it clicked shut, and then he did not hear anything at all. They were leaving the shop, undoubtedly making all sorts of sounds. The cold bin was soundproof. He heard nothing.

He took a deep, deep breath, and the pain in his chest knocked him to his knees.

You should have waited, he thought. One more minute, Vicki, and I could have done it myself. Your hands would be clean, Vicki. I could have died happy, Vicki. I could have died not knowing.

You're a bitch, Vicki.

Now lie down, he told himself. Now go to sleep, just the way you planned it yourself. Nothing's different. And you can't get out, because you planned it this way. You're through.

Double indemnity. The bitch was going to collect double indemnity!

No, he thought. No.

It took him fifteen minutes to think of it. He had to find a way, and it wasn't easy. If they thought about murder they would have her, of course. She'd left prints all over the cold-bin door. But they would not be looking for prints, not the way things stood. They'd call it an accident and that would be that. Which was the trouble with setting things up so perfectly.

He could make it look like suicide. That might cheat her out of the insurance. He could slash his wrists or something, or—

No.

He could cheat her out of more than the insurance.

It took awhile, but he worked it out neatly. First he scooped up his cigarette butt and stuck it in his pants pocket. Then he scattered the ashes around. Step one.

Next he walked to the rear of the cold bin and took a meat cleaver from the peg on the wall. He set the cleaver on top of a hanging side of beef, gave the meat a push. The cleaver toppled over and plummeted to the floor. It landed on the handle and bounced.

He tried again with another slab of meat. He tried time after time, until he found the piece that was just the right distance from the floor and found just the spot to set the cleaver. When he nudged the meat, the cleaver came down, turned over once, and landed blade-down in the floor.

He tried it four times to make sure it would work. It never missed. Then he picked the cleaver from the floor, wiped his prints from the blade and handle with his apron, and placed the cleaver in position on top of the hunk of meat. It was a leg of lamb, the meat blood-red, the fat sickly white. He sat down on the floor, then stretched out on his back looking up at the leg of lamb. Good meat, he thought. Prime.

He smiled, tensed with pain from his chest and stomach, relaxed and smiled again. Not quite like going to sleep this way, he thought. Not painless, like freezing. But faster.

He lifted a leg, touched his foot to the leg of lamb. He gave it a gentle little push, and the cleaver sliced through the air and found his throat.

HATE GOES COURTING

I SHOULD HAVE FIGURED IT the second day. By that time you have to see it unless you shut your eyes, and if you shut your eyes you just about deserve what happens.

It was the wind. It's that wind you get out on a plain or desert and almost nowhere else, the kind of wind that builds up miles away and comes at you and keeps on going right through you and on into the next county. Clothes don't help. If you're in the desert the sand goes right through your clothes, and if you put a wet handkerchief over your face the wind blows the sand right through the handkerchief.

When you're up north you freeze. The wind ices you right through.

And when you're in Kansas there's just the wind coming at you like a sword through a piece of silk, just the wind and nothing else. It's a sweeping wind, not the twister that blew Dorothy to Oz and knocks over a house now and then. The sky clouds up and the sun disappears and the damned wind is all over the place. Then it rains water by the pound and when it clears up the air is still and quiet.

That's how it usually happens, and that's why I couldn't have figured it out on the first day, not even with my eyes wide open. But the second day I should have known. On the second day there was still no rain, no storm at all, and the wind was blowing all over and harder than before.

It happens that way once in a while. It happens, with the wind holding up forever like it's never going to stop, and in Kansas they call it the bad wind. It blows forever, and it blows your tendons so tight you think they're going to snap on you.

And something happens. Something like a man dying or a house burning, something bad.

That's why I should have known—if I had my eyes open.

The afternoon of the second day we were out hunting jacks in the north field. The wind was coming from the west, bending the long grasses all the way over and holding them there. We were hunting into the wind; it didn't make too much sense that way, but it was late and we were headed back home, and back home meant walking into the wind.

"Bet she's been here," Brad was saying. "Not hunting—"

Lady let out a burst of good baying, sounding the way a good beagle sounds, and she cut off the rest of his sentence.

"You hear me, John?"

I nodded at him but he wasn't looking at me. He was about twenty yards ahead of me and it was no use talking into the wind. It just shoves the words right back into your mouth. You can shout at it, but I didn't much feel like shouting. I didn't feel like answering, when you come right down to it.

"You hear me? She's been out here plenty of times."

My cap was down over my ears but I could still hear him good and clear. We could have gone home right then. The bag was full of jacks, nice husky ones that Lady ran down like a champion, more rabbit than we could eat in the next year and a half. But going home wouldn't do any good. Brad was a tough guy to shut up.

"Nice soft grass out here. Her nice little body would fit real cozy in it, you know?"

I looked down at the grass without meaning to and my head started to ache.

"Know what we used to call a woman like that? Called them 'sweethearts of the fleet.' There's lots like her, Brother John. She's not the only little tramp in the—"

"Shut up."

"World. But you wouldn't know, would you? Old John stays on the farm through thick and thin. Doesn't let the glitter of the outside world knock his life apart. Sober Old John. You ever fixing to see the world, brother?"

"Maybe."

"Sure. I hear you went to Omaha once. Like it?"

"It was all right." I didn't want to answer him. I never wanted to answer him, but that didn't make much difference. It was always like that—him needling and pushing and prodding and me taking it and answering when I was supposed to.

When he was in the Navy it was nice. Pa and I made the farm run, coming out ahead in a good year and squeezing by in a bad one. Hunting with Lady and catching a movie in town now and then, and a long sleep at night and good food and plenty of it.

But with Brad around you don't sleep much. Ma died giving birth to him, and he's been killing the rest of us since then. Brad was a smart little brother, a real sharp little fellow.

Brad and I never got along.

"You like Omaha, huh? That's good—glad to hear it. But how does it stack up next to all the other big towns?"

This time I didn't answer.

"Did you really do the town or just go to the feed store? I hear they have a real fine feed store in Omaha. Lots of feed and all."

"Stop it."

He said something that I didn't catch, and then he said a little louder, "How does Margie stack up next to the Omaha chippies?"

I wanted to kill him. If he were right close instead of twenty yards off, I would have hit him. I could feel the bag slipping off my shoulder and my fist balling up and sinking into that soft belly of his. My fist would have gone through him like the wind was going through me right then.

I should have raised the gun and shot his head off.

Instead I clenched one fist and let it relax. I didn't say anything.

"She'd make a good one," he said. "It's her trade, all right. She's got the shape for it. And plenty long years of experience."

"Stop it, Brad."

"All she'd have to do," he went on, "is what they call relinquishing her amateur standing. Just sell it instead of giving it away. But maybe she likes it too much to set a price on it. Is it as good as I hear it is?"

"You never touched her."

It was out of me before I could stop it. It was part question even though I knew he hadn't. I had to make sure and I had to tell myself, and at the same time I didn't want to know if he had. It didn't matter. It didn't make any difference at all, but I just didn't want to hear about it.

"You sure about that, Brother John? Well, maybe yes and maybe no. But I guess I'm fixing to try her, all right. If she's as good as everybody says, I must be missing a hell of a lot. Is she that good?"

I closed my eyes and listened to the wind. His voice seemed to come over the wind, cutting and burning just like that wind, just as bad and holding up just as long.

"Or are you waiting until you're married? Is that it, Brother John? That's a good one—waiting it out on the town tramp!"

He started to laugh. His laugh was like the wind, ice cold and mean as a mad dog, cutting like a sword through a piece of silk. I gave a whistle for Lady and she came like she always did and I headed back toward home, walking away and leaving him laughing that laugh of his in the middle of the fields.

Ten minutes later I was still walking and I could still hear him laughing and the wind was as bad as ever.

He didn't understand.

Nobody understood the whole thing, but no one else got on my back the way Brad did. Everybody knew about Margie, but everybody else kept to their own business and let me mind my own.

Except for Brad.

The others knew about Margie, but they also knew that Margie was different, that she wasn't like any other woman who ever lived. It was something they could feel even if they didn't know just why.

She was beautiful. That was something all of them could see. It wasn't exactly hard to see; it jumped out at you until all you were conscious of was the beauty of her. Her hair was the color of corn and she wore it long, letting it flow down pure and golden and glowing. Her body was so smooth and rounded that she seemed to be made out of liquid. She looked like she was moving even when she was standing absolutely still.

When she slept, she looked like a big cat crouched and ready to spring.

Her skin was clear as a cameo. Her mouth was tiny and red and her eyes were a soft brown and her ears were little shells covered with a furry fuzz.

These were things that anybody could see—even Brad.

But nobody else could see inside. Nobody else could see her eyes when she cried because she never cried when anybody else was around. Most of her beauty was inside, and nobody else could see inside her. Their eyes stopped at the clear skin and the corn-colored hair and the gently curved body, and that is why I was the only person who ever knew Margie.

The others never knew how she felt in your arms when she was very happy or very sad. I don't give a damn how many arms she's been in; she's only happy or sad with me. With the others she crawled into a shell as thin and tight as skin, and the others think that shell is Margie.

But it isn't.

I felt sorry for the others, if you want to know the truth. I felt sorry for them because they never stayed all night with Margie and woke up with her tears matting the hair on their chests and her body warm and quiet.

When I asked her to marry me she cried more than ever and told me I was crazy and I didn't mean it. Then she said yes, and cried some more and we made love so beautifully that even thinking about it weeks later made me shake a little.

I finished cleaning the gun and set it up on the rack on the wall. I skinned the rabbits and dressed them and salted them down, and then I washed up and changed my shirt and headed towards Margie's place. She lived by herself in a little cabin on the outskirts of the town.

Days she clerked in the five-and-dime in town, but that was going to change. She'd be coming to my place and she'd be my woman, and then she wouldn't have to work anymore. She didn't have to do a thing she didn't want to. She could just lie around the house all day loving me.

That would be enough.

The moon was up by the time I got to her cabin. The moon was round and bright and golden and it floated like a California orange. When I opened Margie's door, the wind nearly tore it clear off its hinges.

The wind blew all night long, but I didn't hear it.

I think the wind set a record for our part of Kansas. It kept up day after day, each day a little worse than the last, and you could tell there was more than a storm brewing. You could smell it the way the wheat was bowed over so much it looked like it grew that way.

The wind was all over. There was a rush of accidents—a two-car head-on collision at the intersection of Mill Run and 68, a blowout just a mile from our house, a freak accident with a telephone pole dropping on a parked car.

Nobody walked away from those accidents. Five people died in the two-car deal and a salesman got sandwiched in the blowout when his car turned over. And there were two kids from the high school in the backseat of that parked car. You couldn't tell which was which, the way the telephone pole pressed their bodies together.

It sounded silly, but everybody knew it was the wind. And the wind kept blowing without a storm.

And the wind was in Brad, the way he kept up with his needling and prodding. He was getting through to me more often and my hand was sore from making a fist and relaxing it. He made up stories about Margie and who she went with and what they did and how many times and other crazy things. I just couldn't take it anymore.

"I'm telling you this for your own good," he would say. "Hell— get what you can. I don't blame you for that. But I have to keep you from marrying her. I've gotta look out for my older brother. You farmers don't know all the angles."

That got Pa mad. He started off how there was nothing wrong with being a farmer and how it wasn't as bad as the Navy where all you did was ride a tin boat or maybe kill some folk if there was a war on.

Every day was just that much worse than the last.

But when it happened I wasn't ready for it. I walked to her place in a harder and colder wind than ever, and when I got there she was all alone. She was sitting hunched up on her bed with her head almost touching her knees and her hair falling down over her face. I couldn't see her face. I pulled the door shut and walked over to her.

When I went to give her a kiss she turned her face to the wall and wouldn't look at me. I knew something was wrong, and I guess I knew just what it was, but I was hoping so hard that I wouldn't let myself believe it.

I sat down on the bed next to her and pulled her over to me. She didn't pull away. I let her head rest in my lap and ran my fingers through that long silky hair. I thought I could get her to cry it out but she wouldn't cry, not a single tear. Her whole body was shaking with something but she wouldn't open up and let it out. I just sat there stroking her hair and not saying a thing.

Then she looked at me and she started to cry. She cried for a long time, crying all the sickness and sadness out of her; when it was done she was better and I knew she would be all right.

It wouldn't leave a scar.

It was done.

The walk home was a long one even with the wind behind me. He was waiting for me, and when I came in he looked at me and he knew that I knew.

He said, "She was nice, Brother John. But I've had better."

I just looked at him. I didn't bother to tell him that he never had her, that I was the only man to have her, ever.

He wouldn't have known what I was talking about.

"You ought to get around more," he said. "Oughta see what the rest of the world's like. You know?"

The vein in my temple started throbbing just the way Margie's did before.

"There's other women. Bet you'll find some that's even better in the sack than she is, Brother John."

When you're up close a shotgun makes a big messy hole, big as a man's fist, but when I squeezed that trigger the shell went through him like a sword through a piece of silk, like the wind blowing outside. He let out a moan and put both hands over the hole in his stomach and sat down slowly. His eyes were staring like he couldn't believe it happened.

His eyes got glassy, but they stayed open that way, staring at me.

Outside the wind broke and it started to rain.

Fifteen months and I'll be out. The law's the law, but the people around here know me and they knew Brad, and the law can bend a little when it has to.

Margie will be waiting for me. I know she will.

I DON'T FOOL AROUND

FISCHER PULLED UP AT A CURB and we got out of the car in a hurry, heading for the black Chevy with the people standing around it. The precinct cop made room for us and we went on through. As far as I was concerned, this was just a formality. I knew who was dead and I knew who had killed him. Taking a good long look at the corpse wasn't going to change that.

The punk slumped over the wheel with holes in his head had lived longer than we had expected. He was a hood named Johnny Blue, a strongarm-weakbrain who crossed some of the wrong people. He'd been due for a hit for weeks, according to the rumbles that filtered through to Manhattan West. Now he'd been hit, and hard.

One slug in the side of the face. Another in the neck. Three more in the back of the head.

"Who is he?" Fischer asked. I told him.

"A messy way to do it," the kid went on. "Any of those shots would have killed him. Why shoot him up like that?"

My college cop. My new partner, my cross to bear ever since some genius switched Danny Taggert to Vice. My Little Boy Lost, who wanted murder to be a nice clean affair, with one bullet lodged in the heart and, if you please, as little blood as possible.

I said, "The killer didn't want to take chances."

"Chances? But—"

I was very tired. "This wasn't a tavern brawl," I told him. "This wasn't one guy hitting another guy over the head with a bar stool. This was a pro killing."

"It doesn't look so professional to me. A mess."

"That's because you don't know what to look for." I turned away, sick of the corpse and the killer, sick of Fischer, sick of West 46th Street at three in the morning. Sick of murder.

"It's a pro killing," I said again. "In a car, on a quiet street, in the middle of the night. Five bullets, any one of which would have caused death. That's a trademark."

"Why?"

"Because hired killers don't fool around," I said. "Let's get out of here."

The coffee was bitter but it was black and it was hot. I sipped it as I read through the file again. I knew everything in the file by heart. I read it automatically, then shoved it over to Fischer.

"Name," I said, "Frank Calder. First arrest at age 14, 1948, grand theft auto. Suspended. Arrested three months later, GTA again, six months in Elmira. Three years later he was picked up for assault with a deadly weapon. A knife. The victim refused to press charges and we dropped them."

I sipped some more of the coffee. "That was eight years ago. Since then he's been picked up fifteen times. Same charge each time. Suspicion of homicide."

"Innocent?"

"Guilty, of course. Fifteen times that we know about. Probably a dozen more that we don't know about. Fourteen times we let him go. Once we thought we had a case."

"What happened?"

"Grand jury disagreed with us. Indictment quashed."

Fischer nodded. "And you think he may have killed Blue?"

"No."

"Then why are we—"

"I don't *think* he *might* have killed Blue," I said. "I know damn well he killed Blue. Calder does most of his work in the Kitchen. A Hell's Kitchen boy from the start, grew up on 39th Street west of Ninth. Gun used was a .38. Calder always uses a .38. Likes to shoot people in cars."

"Still, you can't be sure that—"

"I can be sure," I cut in. I wished that Vice would send Danny back to me. Fischer was impossible. "Calder works for Nino Popo a lot of the time. Popo had a thing against Blue. Quit sounding like a public defender, will you? This was one of Calder's. Period."

"We pick him up now?"

"No."

"But you just said—"

"I know what I said. I know damn well what I said and I don't need a parrot to toss it back at me."

"But—"

"Shut up." I finished the coffee. "I told you Calder was a pro. You know what that means? You understand what that record says? He's a hired killer. You pay him and he shoots people. That's how he makes his living. A good living. He dresses in three-hundred-dollar suits. He wears gold cuff links. He lives in a penthouse overlooking Central Park. The west side of the park—he's not a millionaire. But he does well in his job."

I paused for breath. I just wanted to get home and go to bed. I was tired. "I told you about pros," I said. "They don't fool around. They don't leave loopholes. It's their business and they know it. They don't crack under pressure. If we pick up Calder he'll be out in no time at all. No witnesses. A cast-iron alibi. No holes at all."

"So what do we do?"

"We go home," I said. "We go home and take hot showers and go to bed. Tomorrow we pick him up."

I left him there to wonder what I was talking about. I went home and took a hot shower and fell asleep the minute I hit the bed.

Homicide is rugged. There are good things about it—we don't take bribes, we stay clean. There are also bad things.

Because there are only three types of murder, and of the three there is only one that we solve. There is the amateur killing with a motive, the husband who strangles his wife, the tavern brawl, the grudge murder. There you have your suspect at the start and you look around for the proof. And find it, no matter how clever a job they do of burying it. That is the kind that gets solved.

There is also the silly killing. The bum beaten to death on the Bowery. The hustler with a knife in her belly. The fag killed in his own apartment by a casual conquest. The mugging victim with a crushed skull. These we don't solve. Not without a break.

And there is the professional murder. And those we never solve.

I met Fischer at five in the afternoon. He was carrying a folded copy of an afternoon tabloid. The headline ran GANGLAND SLAY-ING IN HELL'S KITCHEN. I could have guessed it word for word. I took the paper from him and gave the story a quick run-through. It was about the same as the morning papers had it.

It didn't say we had nothing to work with. It didn't say we had anything to work with. It said that Johnny Blue had been found in a parked car with holes in him, and that he was dead. Then there were a few paragraphs trying to turn the career of a fourth-rater into something notorious, and then there was some nonsense to the effect that the cops were keeping mum.

Mum?

"We're on Calder," I told him. "No other assignment until we nail him. Got that?"

"Sure."

"I wanted it that way. I want to get Calder. I want to get him good."

"I thought you said it was impossible."

"It is."

"Then—"

"You talk too much," I said. I waited for him to get mad but he didn't. He was hurt—it showed in his face, in the way he wouldn't look at me. But he wouldn't get mad. And this made me like him that much less. He never got mad at anything. He didn't know how to hate.

I don't like college cops. I don't like people who are up to their ears in understanding and sympathy and sweetness and sunshine. I don't like people who don't know how to hate.

Maybe it's just the way a person is. If I were Calder I would hate cops. I'm a cop. I hate Calder. I hate him because he breaks laws and shoots people. I hate him because he gets away with it. I hated Johnny Blue. He used to get away with things too. Now he was dead and Calder had killed him and I hated Calder.

I was going to get him.

"Look it over again," I said, sliding Calder's file over to Fischer again. "Skip the record. Look at the picture."

Dark black hair. A flat face, not too bad-looking. Hard eyes, a long nose, a little scar on the chin. I don't know how he got the scar. Maybe he cut himself shaving.

"You said we pick him up today. Were you kidding?"

"I don't kid. I was serious."

"They found evidence?"

"No."

He looked at me. He was afraid to open his mouth. Gutless.

"We worry him a little. Don't bother your head about it. Go get the car and meet me out front. And wear a gun."

He didn't say anything, just went off for the car. I checked my gun, then stuck it back in the holster. I picked up Calder's file, and took a good long look at it. I let the face burn into my brain. I stood there for a minute or two and hated.

Then I went out to the car where Fischer was waiting.

The building was fancy. A uniformed doorman stood at attention out in front. I had to show him my shield before he let us inside. He was there to keep out undesirables. Unless they lived in the penthouse.

The carpet was deep in the lobby. The elevator rose in silence. I stood there and hated Calder.

He had the whole top floor. I got out of the elevator and took my gun out of its holster, wondering whether or not the doorman had called Calder yet. Probably.

I rang the bell.

"Yeah?"

A penthouse overlooking the park didn't get Hell's Kitchen out of his speech. Nothing would.

"Police."

"Whattaya want?"

"Open the door and shut up."

A few seconds later the door opened. He was short, five-six or five-seven. He was wearing a silk bathrobe and slippers that looked expensive. The apartment was well-furnished but for what he had paid he could have used an interior decorator. There was a shoddiness about the place. Maybe the shoddiness was Calder.

"Come on in," he said. "You use a drink?"

I ignored him. "You're under arrest," I told him.

"What for?"

"Murder."

"Yeah?" A wide smile. "Somebody got killed?"

"Johnny Blue."

"I'm covered," he said. No *I'm innocent* but *I'm covered*. "I was playing cards with some fellows."

"Uh-huh."

He shrugged heroically. "You want, we can go down to the station. My lawyer'll have me out right away. I'm clean."

"You're never clean," I said. "You were born filthy."

The smile widened. But there was uncertainty behind it. I was getting to him.

"You're cheap and rotten," I said. "You're a punk. You spend a fortune on cologne and it still doesn't cover the smell."

Now the smile was gone.

"Your sister sleeps with bums," I said. "Your mother was the cheapest whore on the West Side. She died of syphilis."

That did it. He was a few feet away—then he lowered his head and charged. I could have clubbed him with the gun. I didn't.

I shot him.

He gave a yell like a wounded steer and fell to his knees. The bullet had taken him in the right shoulder. I guess it hurt. I hoped so.

"You shot him." It was Fischer talking.

"Good thinking," I told him. "You're on the ball."

"Now what?"

I shrugged. "We can take him in," I suggested. "We can book him for resisting arrest and a few other things."

"Not murder?"

"You heard him," I said. "He's clean."

I looked at Fischer. That was the answer to my college cop, my buddy. Here was a murderer, a murderer with a shoulder wound. Now we would be nice to him. Get him to a hospital quick before he lost too much blood. Maybe drop the resisting arrest charge because, after all, he was a sick man.

I had my gun in my hand. I stepped back a few feet and aimed. I watched the play of expressions on Calder's face. He didn't know whether or not to believe it.

I shot him in the face.

I talked to Fischer while I found a gun in a drawer, picked it up in a towel, and wrapped Calder's fingers around it. It made it look good—he had drawn on me, I shot him in the shoulder, he went on and held onto the gun, and I shot him dead. It would look good enough—there wasn't going to be any investigation.

"Maybe thirty killings," I said. "That's what this animal had to his credit. He made beating the law a business. He didn't fool around. And there was no way to get him."

No answer from my partner.

"So this time he lost. He doesn't fool around. Well, neither do I."

I knew Fischer wasn't satisfied. He wouldn't blab, but it would worry him. He would feel uncomfortable with me. I don't fit into his moral scheme of things. Maybe he'll put in for a transfer.

I hope so.

JUST WINDOW SHOPPING

I CLIMBED OVER THE BACK FENCE and hurried down the driveway. They probably hadn't seen me at the window, but I couldn't afford to take chances. The police had caught me once. I certainly did not want to be picked up again.

It was horrible when the police caught me. I admitted everything but that wasn't enough for them. They put me in a chair with the light shining in my eyes so that I could barely see. Then they started hitting me. They used rubber hoses so there wouldn't be any marks. They hit me so much I nearly fainted.

The beating wasn't the worst of it, though. They called me names. They called me a sex fiend and a pervert. That hurt me more than the beatings.

Because I'm not a pervert, you see. All I want to do is watch people. There's no harm in that, is there? I don't hurt anyone, and I never really bother anybody. Sometimes someone sees me watching them, and they get frightened or angry, but that's only once in a great while. I've been very careful lately, ever since they caught me.

And if they think I am a pervert, you should see some of the things I've seen. You wouldn't believe the things some of these normal people do. It's enough to make you sick to your stomach. Yet they are normal, and they call me a pervert, a Peeping Tom. I can't quite understand it. All I do is watch.

Ever since they caught me I have been very careful. That is why I left the window when the man looked at me. I'm almost sure he didn't see me, but he glanced toward the window and I hopped the fence and got away from there. Besides, it wasn't much fun watching at his window. The woman with him was old and fat and I was getting bored with the whole thing. There was no sense in taking chances for that.

When I got out to the street I didn't know where to go. I used to have a perfect spot. A pretty young prostitute over on Tremont Avenue who saw at least ten men a night. I could spend night after night watching her. The backyard was dark and I had a perfect view. But one night she saw me watching.

She was nice about it and sensible, too. She didn't call me a pervert. But she said the men might notice me, that they wouldn't like it. She told me to stay away. It was a shame that I had to give up the spot, but at least she didn't call the police or anything.

But I couldn't watch there anymore, and I had to find a new spot. I walked down the street looking for a lighted window. I stopped at several places, but there was nothing much to see. There were just people sitting or reading or watching television.

Finally I found a house with a light on that looked promising. The backyard was dark, too, which was important. It's harder to see out from a lighted room when there is no light in the backyard.

I stood close to the window and watched. A man and woman were sitting on the bed, taking their clothes off. I watched them. The man wasn't bad looking but my attention was confined to the woman. I'm not queer, you understand.

She certainly wasn't beautiful. Better than average, though. Her face was nothing to write home about, her breasts were rather small, but she had beautiful legs and a generally nice shape all in all. I watched her undress and began to get excited. This was going to be a good night after all.

They undressed quickly, which is not the way I like it. It's better when they take a good long time about it. But they just pulled off their clothes and turned down the bedcovers. I guess they had been married for some time.

I was really excited by this time, and my eyes were practically glued to the window. Then the man stood up and walked over to the wall. He touched a switch, and the room was suddenly plunged into complete darkness. I was so mad I could have killed him. Why did he have to do a thing like that?

I stared through the window, but it was no use. The room was black as pitch. I couldn't understand it. How could he enjoy it with the lights out? He wouldn't be able to see a thing.

I was mad, and just about ready to go home and call it a night. But the little I had seen left me so excited that I could not stop there. I walked around looking for another window.

By this time it was late and I had no idea where to go. Most of the people in the neighborhood were asleep by now. But I continued walking around, hoping against hope that something would turn up.

I was just about ready to quit when I saw a lighted window on Bushnell Road. Never having been to that house before I decided to give it a try.

I approached the window and looked in. It was a bedroom window, with a woman reading there. She had her back to me, reading a magazine. She was all alone.

Ordinarily I would not have waited. Sometimes a woman will sit like that all night, just reading. But it was late and, having nowhere else to go, I waited. Besides, I had the feeling I would get a real show for my money.

As it turned out, I was right. She put down the magazine in less than five minutes, stood up, and turned toward me. I was stunned when I got a good look at her. She was beautiful.

She was wearing a flower-print dress that made her look like a schoolgirl, but one good look at her would tell you she was nothing of the sort. Her body was far too mature for a schoolgirl's with proud, full breasts that nearly ripped the dress apart. Her face was as pretty as a model's, and her hair was that soft reddish-brown that drives me crazy. I was ready to watch her forever.

She started to undress. I stared at her greedily. There was no one else around, and my eyes studied every detail of her body. She undressed slowly, tantalizingly, slithering out of her dress and hanging it up in the closet. Finally she stood there nude, and it was worth all the waiting, worth all the walking that I had done that night. She was like a vision, the most perfect woman I had ever seen.

I thought I would have to go home then. I expected she would turn off the light and go to bed, and if she had I would have been satisfied. It was enough for one night. Instead she walked to her mirror and began to examine herself.

It was the perfect view for me. I could see both her back and the mirror image of her front. She looked at herself, and I watched her. Then she began to dance.

It was not exactly a dance. She moved like a burlesque dancer, but there was nothing crude about it. She knew how beautiful she was, and she moved in rhythm, making a symphony of her body and watching herself as she did. It was something to watch.

Finally she stopped dancing. She slipped on a housecoat and stepped through a door. I guessed she was going to the bathroom, which meant it was the end of the show. I could have left then, but didn't. I wanted to get another glimpse of her. She had to come back.

I stood silently at the window, waiting for her.

Suddenly a door opened. I whirled around to find her standing there, in the doorway, pointing a gun at me. "Don't move," she said. "Don't move or I'll shoot."

I froze in terror, staring down the mouth of the gun, which looked like a cannon to me. "I wasn't doing anything," I stammered. "Just watching you. I didn't hurt you."

She didn't say a word.

"Look," I pleaded, "just let me go. I won't bother you anymore. I promise I'll stay away from here."

She ignored me. "I saw you in the mirror," she said. "Saw you watching me. I danced for you. Did you like the way I danced?"

I nodded dumbly, unable to speak.

"It was for you," she said. "I liked your eyes on me. I liked the way you looked at me."

She smiled. "Come inside."

I hesitated. Was this a trap? Had she called the police?

"Come here," she said. "Come inside. Don't be afraid."

I followed her into the house, into the bedroom. "I want you," she said. "I want you." She slipped out of the housecoat and tossed it over a chair.

"Come on," she said. "I know you want me. I could tell from the way you looked at me. Come here."

She set the gun on the dresser and motioned for me to step closer. "I want you to make love to me," she said.

I walked over to her, and she threw her arms around me. "Take me," she moaned.

I pushed her away. "No," I said. "I don't want *that*. I just wanted to watch you. I wouldn't do *that*."

She pressed against me again. "I want you," she insisted. She opened her arms and I felt her hot breath on my face.

There was only one way to stop her. I picked up the gun from the dresser. "Don't come any closer," I warned. "Leave me alone."

"Don't be silly." She smiled. "You want me and I want you." She kept coming closer as I retreated.

That's when it happened—when the gun went off. The noise resounded in the small bedroom, and she crumpled and fell. "Why?" she moaned. Then she died.

The police beat me. They beat me harder than last time, and they called me a pervert. They think I tried to rape her, but that's not true. I wouldn't do a thing like that.

LIE BACK AND ENJOY IT

IT WAS THE AFTERNOON, and the sun was beginning to dip to the level of the horizon. Frank pressed down heavily on the accelerator, gunning the car smoothly along the highway. Just a few more miles, he thought. Just a few more miles and he'd be home, if you could call an empty room in a run-down hotel home. Just a few more miles and he could take a hot bath and drink himself to sleep.

Then he saw the girl. At first glance he took her for just another hitchhiker, and speeded up to pass her by. Then his eyes took in the long hair and the swell of the breasts, and his foot found the brake pedal and slowed the car to a stop. He reached across the front seat and opened the door.

"Hop in," he said.

She climbed into the car and sat down beside him. He took a good look then, and he liked what he saw.

She was wearing a pair of faded blue dungarees and a man's shirt, open at the throat, but even the shapeless clothing couldn't conceal the shapeliness of her figure. Her breasts were large and full, and they pressed against the flannel fabric of the shirt. Her hair was long and jet black; her face very attractive, with high cheekbones and large brown eyes. As he looked at her, Frank felt the blood surging through his veins. He'd been a long time without a woman.

"Going to Milford?" she asked, naming a town a few miles the other side of Frank's destination.

"Sure," he said. She leaned back in the seat and closed the door, setting her small black purse on her lap.

He put the car in gear and eased back onto the highway again, watching her out of the corner of his eye. Pretty, he thought. Almost beautiful. And so very young, too—she couldn't be over nineteen.

"Been waiting long?" he asked.

"Not too long. About fifteen minutes or so."

"Funny how some guys won't stop for a person, isn't it?"

"Yes," she said. "They read about people getting robbed and all, and they just drive on by."

He stole another glance at her. It took a lot for a girl to look like that in men's clothes. He pictured her in a dress, in a bathing suit, and finally in nothing at all. He turned his eyes back to the road as the perspiration began to form on his forehead.

If only he could have a girl like that! Then he wouldn't mind those damned trips all over the country, not if he had something like that back at his room, waiting for him to come home. But he couldn't have luck like that, not him. He never had.

He was forty-one, and his hair was starting to go. Slowly but surely, his life was slipping by, without anything real or important ever happening to him. The only love he ever had he bought for three dollars in a little room over Randy's Bar. And he knew that he would go on like that, coming home every night to an empty room and passing three dollars to a prostitute every Saturday. And someday he would die without ever doing anything.

"Mind if I smoke?" Her voice broke into his reverie and stopped his train of thought.

"Go right ahead," he said. He took a lighter from his pants pocket and turned toward her, offering her the flame.

She leaned forward to take the light. The shirt fell away from the front of her body, and Frank got a quick glimpse of smooth white skin and rounded flesh.

Again the desire surged through him. He replaced the lighter in his pocket and gripped the wheel as tight as he could in his large hands. He was breathing fast, almost panting.

"Thanks," she said, softly.

The sun dipped lower, and he passed a sign which indicated that his town was only two miles further on down the road. Just two more miles, then three or four to Milford, and she would be gone from his life. She would leave, and he would be left with her memory and nothing more.

He looked at her again. She seemed so soft, so warm and peaceful. She yawned and stretched her lush body before him. And then he decided that he was going to have her.

The decision came in a flash. He couldn't let his whole life disappear without doing something about it. He would take her, swiftly and violently; and the freshness of her would let him live again like a full man.

The realization of what he was going to do calmed him. At the same time, he was tense with anticipation. He could practically feel the soft pressure of her body against his, could picture her nude in his arms.

"Just a few more miles," she said.

"Won't be long now." He turned and smiled at her.

"I really appreciate this. It'd be terrible out on the road at night."

I'm glad you appreciate it, he thought. You'll get a chance to show just how grateful you are. A good chance.

He didn't really want to hurt her. He glanced over at her again. Hell, he thought, she was no virgin. It wasn't as though he were taking something away from her. She might even like it. He chuckled inwardly, remembering the old saying, "If rape is inevitable, lie back and enjoy it."

Well, it was inevitable. He was going to take her, and nothing was going to stop him. He wouldn't hurt her anymore than he had to, of course. Maybe she would tell the police, but he was willing to take the chance. He couldn't stop himself now, even if he wanted to.

Besides, there was little chance that she would tell. He had read somewhere that ninety percent of the rape cases were never reported, because the girls involved were ashamed of it. And he could always say that she let him—no one could prove otherwise.

"It's a nice day," he said.

"Very nice."

He spotted a turnoff, a rutted, two-lane road that went nowhere and was rarely used by anyone. He slowed down the car and cut over onto it.

"Where are we going?" she asked. There was a touch of alarm in her voice.

"A shortcut," he replied.

"I never went this way before."

"It cuts out Herkinsburg. Not many people know about it."

He was amazed to hear himself lie so easily. He had always had difficulty in lying, but now he was so set on his goal that the words came from his lips with no trouble at all. Evidently she believed him, for she relaxed in the seat.

After a few hundred yards on the turnoff, he cut the motor and pulled the car over to the shoulder of the road. It was time, now. No one would disturb them.

"Why are we stopping?" There was panic in her voice now, as she sat up rigidly and gripped the black purse tight in both hands.

He didn't answer. His right hand encircled both her wrists in a tight grip; his left shoved the car door open. Then he forced her out of the car. The purse flew from her hands as he sent her sprawling to the ground and flung himself upon her.

"No!" she pleaded. "Don't!" His face was so close to hers that he could feel her breath against his cheek, just as he could feel the warmth of her body through the thin shirt.

"You can't stop me," he said. "No one'll hear you if you scream." He smiled. "You might as well lie back and enjoy it."

At last it was over. The girl remained motionless.

"There," he said. "That wasn't so bad, was it?"

She didn't answer. He walked slowly back to the car, taking deep breaths of air and savoring the taste of it in his lungs.

He had one hand on the door handle when he heard her say, "Stop!" There was something in her voice that compelled him to release the door handle and turn around.

She was holding the small black purse in one hand and a small black automatic in the other. The gun was trained on him.

"You bastard," she said. "I was just going to take your car, I would even have left you a little money to get home on, but not now."

His mouth dropped open in shock. "Wait," he stammered. "Wait a minute."

"You can't stop me," she said, levelly. "I'm going to kill you. You might as well lie back and enjoy it."

The bullet made a small, round hole in his stomach. He fell on the ground and lay there moaning while she straightened her clothes and took the wallet and keys from his pockets. He watched her get into the car, blow him a kiss, and drive away down the road.

It took him twenty minutes to die.

LOOK DEATH IN THE EYE

SHE WAS BEAUTIFUL.

She was, and she knew that she was—not only by the image in her mirror, the full and petulant mouth and the high cheekbones, the silkiness of the long blond hair and the deep blue color of her eyes. The image in her mirror at home told her she was beautiful, and so did the image she saw now, the image in the mirror in the tavern.

But she didn't need the mirrors. She was made aware of her beauty by the eyes, the eyes of the hungry men, the eyes that she felt rather than saw upon her everywhere she went. She could feel those eyes caressing her body, lingering too long upon her firm ripe breasts and sensuous hips, touching her body with a touch firmer than hands and making her grow warm where they rested. Wherever she went men stared at her, and the intensity of their stares undressed their passions and hungers just as thoroughly as the stares attempted to strip her body.

She sipped at her drink, hardly tasting it but knowing that she had to drink it. It was all part of the game. She was in a bar, and the hungry men were also in the bar, and now their eyes were wandering over her. But for the moment there was nothing for her to do. She had to drink her drink and bide her time, waiting for the men—or one of them, at least—to get up the courage to do more than stare.

Idly, she turned a few inches on the barstool and glanced at the other customers. Several men were too busy drinking to pay any attention to her; another was busy in a corner booth running his hand up and down the leg of a slightly plump redhead, and it was easy to see that he wouldn't be interested in her, not that night.

But the other three customers were fair game.

She regarded them thoughtfully, one at a time. Closest to her was a young one—no more than twenty-one or twenty-two, she guessed, and hungry the way they are when they're that age. He was short and slim, dressed in a dark suit and wearing a conservative bow tie. She noticed with a little amusement the way he was embarrassed to stare at her but at the same time was unable to keep his eyes off her lush body. Twice his eyes met hers and he flushed guiltily, turning away and nervously flicking the ashes off his cigarette.

And each time the eyes returned to her, hungry and desperate in their hunger. Mr. Dark Suit couldn't keep away from her, she thought, and she wondered if he would be the one for the evening. It was always difficult to predict, always tough to calculate which pair of eyes would get up enough courage to make the pass. It might be Mr. Dark Suit, but she doubted it. He had the hunger, all right, but he probably lacked the experience he'd need for hero.

Mr. Baldy was two stools further from her. She named him easily since his baldness was his outstanding feature in a face that had no other memorable features. His head was bare except for a very thin fringe around the edges and the light from the ceiling shined on it.

Next, of course, she noticed his eyes. They were hungry eyes, too—but hungry in a way that was different from Mr. Dark Suit. Mr. Baldy was a good-twenty-five years older, and he was probably used to getting his passes tossed back into his lap. He wanted her, all right; there was no mistaking the intensity of his gaze. But the possibility of a refusal might scare him away.

For a half-second she considered flashing him a smile. No, she decided, that wouldn't be fair. Let them work it out themselves. Let the hungriest assert himself and the others forever hold their peace.

And there was no hurry. It was rather a pleasant feeling to be caressed simultaneously by three pairs of eyes, and though the sensation was hardly a new one, it was one she never tired of.

And the third man. He was seated at the far end of the bar, seated so that he could study her without turning at all. But, strangely, his eyes were not glued to her body the way Mr. Dark Suit's and Mr. Baldy's were. Instead he was relaxing, biding his time, and occasionally letting his eyes wander from his beer glass to her and back to his beer.

He was somewhere in his thirties, with a strong and vaguely handsome face and jet-black hair. Mr. Bright-Eyes, she named him, laughing inwardly at the glow of assurance and confidence in his eyes.

Mr. Bright-Eyes wouldn't be afraid or stumbling about it. At the same time, she wondered whether or not he would care enough to make an approach. He wanted her; that much she knew. But he might need a little shove in the right direction.

A rock-and-roll tune was playing noisily on the jukebox. *Not yet,* she thought. *Wait until everything is just right, with soft music and all the trimmings. Let the eyes stay hungry for a few minutes.*

She studied them again, the three of them. Mr. Dark Suit's eyes, she noticed, were brown. Mr. Baldy's eyes were a watery blue, a bit bloodshot and sick-looking. But Mr. Bright-Eyes had, happily, bright blue eyes. They seemed to gleam in his powerful face.

She wondered who it would be. Another night, another pair of eyes—but who would it be tonight? Which eyes were the hungriest? Which eyes wanted her, wanted her enough to hurry up and make a pass?

Mr. Dark Suit finished his drink and signaled the bartender for another. He sipped at it nervously when it arrived, then set it down on the bar and stole another glance at her, drumming his fingers on the bar all the while.

He's so nervous, she thought. *If I made the first move he'd come running. But he's scared silly.*

Mr. Baldy, his drink forgotten, stared at her quite openly. He didn't seem shy at all, and the watery blue eyes moved up and down her body without the slightest embarrassment.

He can watch, she thought. *A looker, but not much for action. What's the matter, Mr. Baldy?*

Mr. Bright-Eyes looked up from his beer and saw her studying him. For a moment a shadow of a smile passed over his face; then it was gone, and he was gazing once again into the glass of beer.

Although she wanted to be perfectly fair, she felt herself hoping that it would be Mr. Bright-Eyes. She always played perfectly fair, always went with the first one, but this time she felt a decided preference. There was something about those eyes, something about the way they looked at her so openly . . .

The rock-and-roll tune came to a noisy finish. She waited on her stool, fluffing her hair into place and taking another short sip of her drink.

The next record was a slow one.

Now, she thought. First she stretched a little, throwing her shoulders back so that her two perfect breasts stood out in bold relief as they pressed against the thin fabric of her blouse. Then she crossed one leg over the other, letting her skirt fall away as she did so and giving Mr. Dark Suit and Mr. Baldy a quick glimpse of milk-white skin.

Unfortunately, Mr. Bright-Eyes couldn't see her legs from where he sat. It was a pity.

Then, with her breasts jutting and her legs crossed, she tossed off the rest of her drink and leaned forward on her stool, hesitating a moment before ordering a refill. This was the crucial moment, the time when one of the three had to be ready for a game of drop-the-handkerchief. Somebody had to pick up the cue.

"Another beer for me, and one more for the lady."

She started, turned her head, and discovered happily that it was Mr. Bright-Eyes. He certainly was smooth, she marveled, the way he was right at her side the minute she was ready for another drink.

A moment later the beer was poured, the drink made, and Mr. Bright-Eyes seated on the stool beside her. She noticed the sad looks in the eyes of Mr. Baldy and Mr. Dark Suit, sad because they realized the chance they had missed.

Too bad, she thought. *You had your chances. Why, you had a better chance than Mr. Bright-Eyes, what with looking at my legs and all.*

"You're a lovely woman," Mr. Bright-Eyes was saying, and she was pleased to note that he had a fine manner of speaking, spacing his words nicely and pronouncing all the consonants the way they belonged. Why, that man a few nights ago didn't talk very well at all, mumbling the way he did. Of course it was partly the drinking, but she was glad Mr. Bright-Eyes could speak so clearly and nicely.

But she didn't pay much attention to what he was saying. It wasn't too important, and besides she was far too busy looking into his blue eyes and enjoying the way they traveled so gently over her body. She could feel them on her, and when his gaze traveled down her body and caressed her hips she almost shivered.

He continued to talk to her and she continued to answer him and the jukebox continued to play, but she spent most of her time looking into his eyes and loving the feeling they gave her. He told her his name, which she promptly forgot because Mr. Bright-Eyes suited him so much better, and she told him that her name wasn't especially important, since it really wasn't.

Mr. Bright-Eyes said something about a rose by another name and she laughed politely, but it was his eyes that really held her interest. Even when his hand moved down to rest gently on her thigh, she was more aware of the hunger in his eyes than the gradually more insistent pressure of his hand.

Slowly his hand moved up and down her thigh, gently caressing her flesh, and all the while Mr. Bright-Eyes was talking earnestly, his voice just a little louder than a whisper and his eyes deliciously lustful and hungry.

But it wouldn't do to ignore the hand. Keeping her gaze rooted to Mr. Bright-Eye's face, she gently placed her own hand on top of his. At first he seemed taken aback, thinking that she wished him to remove his hand from her thigh. That, of course, was not what she intended at all.

Reassuringly, she moved his hand over her thigh, pressing it gently and tenderly. She was pleased to notice Mr. Bright-Eyes get an even hungrier gleam in his eyes and begin to breathe a slight bit heavier than before. It was all part of the game, but the game could be very pleasant for her.

". . . one of the most exciting women I've ever met," he was saying, and as he spoke the words his hand closed possessively around her knee. His eyes were glued to her breasts. She knew that they would leave any moment now, that he was almost ready and almost convinced that she would now follow him to the ends of the earth if he were only to ask.

And indeed she would.

"Honey?"

She smiled expectantly.

"Would you like to have the next one up at my place?"

"Of course," she said.

His bright blue eyes gleamed more than ever. How bright they were! She was actually in love with him now, in love with his eyes and the hunger and beauty in them.

As they stood up, she saw Mr. Baldy shake his head sadly. Mr. Dark Suit's jaw fell slightly and he looked quite awkward, sitting precariously on his stool with his mouth half-open. Then Mr. Bright-Eyes slipped his arm easily around her waist and walked her to the door. She could feel their eyes watching her every step of the way, and it wasn't hard at all to imagine the regret in their eyes— regret mixed with admiration for Mr. Bright-Eye's technique.

He was smooth, all right. So very smooth, and while it was a shame that Mr. Dark Suit and Mr. Baldy were doomed to sadness for the evening, it simply couldn't be helped.

And besides, wasn't there a book about survival of the fittest or something? If they had Mr. Bright-Eyes' finish they wouldn't be sitting by themselves, with their eyes all afraid and beaten.

It was dark out, and Mr. Bright-Eyes seemed to be in a hurry, and as a consequence they were walking very swiftly toward his apartment. He said something about wasn't it dark out, and she agreed that it was, and his arm tightened around her waist.

She leaned a little against him and rubbed her body against his. Walking as they were and with the night as dark as it was, it was hard for her to see his eyes. Each time when they passed a streetlamp she leaned forward a bit and glanced into his face, as if to reassure herself that his eyes still wanted her as much as they had.

In his apartment everything went very well. He told her how beautiful she was and she thanked him quite modestly, and they went to the bedroom and he took her in his arms and kissed her very expertly.

Then, after she had been expertly kissed, he bent over to remove the spread from the bed. It was at just that moment that she took the knife from her purse and plunged it into his back, right between the shoulder blades. One jab was enough; he crumpled up on the bed and lay very still, without a scream or a moan or any sound at all.

Afterwards, back in her own apartment, she put his eyes in the box with the others.

MAN WITH A PASSION

HE SET HIS SUITCASE DOWN on the floor in front of the desk, then unslung the leather bag from his shoulder and placed it beside the suitcase. He smiled across the desk at the clerk, an easy, automatic smile. "I'd like a room," he said. "With bath."

The clerk nodded wordlessly and passed the hotel register to the man. He uncapped a pen and began filling in the blanks. *Jacob Falch,* he wrote. *Free-lance photographer.* He hesitated a moment before the last blank, then quickly scrawled *No permanent address.* He paid in advance, took a key from the clerk, and carried his luggage up the steep staircase to his room.

He was a short man, with broad shoulders and a rough, craggy face. He walked swiftly and purposefully, carrying the bag with ease despite its weight. He reached his room, turned the key in the lock, and seated himself heavily on the bed.

The room was drab and colorless. There was the bed, a straight-backed chair that looked as though it would buckle if he sat on it, and a dull-brown dresser studded with cigarette burns. In short,

Falch reflected, it was a crummy room in a cheap hotel. But it would do for the time being.

He started to lie down for a nap, then changed his mind and began to unpack the suitcase. His camera supplies—flashbulbs, filters, chemicals, and film—he placed in the bottom drawer of the dresser. He hung his suit in the small closet, noting with satisfaction that the pants still held a crease. His shirts and other clothing went into the middle bureau drawer. Only one small package remained in the suitcase, and he took it out and held it lovingly in his large hands. It was a very important package. It contained ten thousand dollars.

Ten thousand dollars, he thought, and he chuckled softly. He'd had to work hard for the money. Any hack photographer could plaster a composite picture together, but it took skill to make one that would stick. It took plenty of skill to come up with a batch of shots that put the mayor's wife in a compromising position. A very compromising position, he reflected, and chuckled once again.

The mayor had paid through the nose, but the mayor could afford it. And the mayor could definitely not afford to have his opponents get hold of those pictures. His wife seemed to be doing things that a mayor's wife shouldn't do. Very interesting things.

Falch chuckled again, and patted the packet of money tenderly. Of course he'd had to leave town, but Tarleton was a dull town anyway. And with ten thousand in his suitcase he could go far.

No more portraits, he thought. No more squirming brats in family groups, no more dirty pictures for backroom boys, no more publicity shots of fertilizer plants. For once in his life Jake Falch could do what he damn well wanted.

And Jake Falch knew what he wanted. Plenty of relaxation, for one thing. Decent food, and a woman now and then. His tastes were inexpensive enough, and he could be very happy in the dumpy hotel, with his battered coupe parked outside.

Oh, he'd take pictures now and then. A little cheesecake, if there was a decent-looking broad in the town. And, when the money ran out . . . well, every town had a mayor, and every mayor had a wife. Or a daughter. Or a sister.

He looked around the room for a hiding place for the money. No, he realized, that was senseless. It would be hard hiding a toothpick in that place, let alone a nice thick wad of bills. And, since he was staying in town, he might as well bank his dough, like a respectable businessman. He chuckled again, and left the room.

The desk clerk stopped him on the way out. "You a photographer, Mr. Falch?"

Falch nodded.

"Figure on staying in town?"

Falch nodded again, impatiently.

"You'll need a studio, a darkroom. Brother of mine has a place . . ."

"No," said Falch, cutting him short. "I won't be working for a while. Came into some money and I feel like taking it easy." He smiled again, the same easy smile he had flashed to the mayor, and walked out the door. The bank was across the street, on the corner.

Five minutes later he strode out of the bank, with $9500 in a checking account. He breathed deeply and headed across the street again to a restaurant. He felt good.

It was then that he saw the girl. She was walking toward him on the other side of the street, and even a half-block away he could see that she was beautiful. She was young—eighteen or nineteen, he guessed—and she had soft, shining blond hair that fell to her shoulders and framed her face perfectly. Automatically, Falch placed her face inside a mental picture frame.

By the time he reached the restaurant, the girl was within twenty yards of him. He saw that her body was a perfect match for her face. It was the kind of body he liked, with full, round curves. It was a lush body, a young body.

Just as he had placed her face inside a frame, he mentally undressed her. He let his eyes run over her body, lingering on the firm, jutting breasts and the rounded hips. Guiltily, he tried to turn away and enter the restaurant, but before he could move she had walked right up to him.

"Hi," she said. "You're new in town, aren't you?" Her voice was as soft and as fresh as the rest of her. She'd make a good model, he thought. She had a face and a figure, and that was a rare combination.

He smiled then, the wide, friendly smile that came so easily to him. "That's right. My name's Jake Falch."

"Mine's Saralee Marshall. Are you the photographer?"

He blinked. "How did you know?"

"Jimmy at the hotel told my ma, and Ma told me. I figured you must be the photographer, because not many strangers ever come to Hammondsport." She made the name of the town sound like a dirty word.

He smiled again. "You don't like this town?"

"Oh," she said, "I guess it's okay. But it's so awful dull. Nothing ever happens, hardly."

"Where would you like to live?"

She shrugged her shoulders, and her breasts rose and fell with the motion. "New York, maybe. Or Hollywood."

"You want to be an actress, huh?"

"No," she said. "I want to be a model."

He had to catch his breath, and before he could get a word out she was off a mile a minute. "I wonder if you need a model? I'd work hard, Mr. Falch. Honest I would. There's no school all summer and I could work whenever you wanted me to and I know I don't have any experience but I can learn real well and . . ."

"Hold on a minute!" He laughed and held up his hand. "I don't know how much I could pay you . . ."

"You don't have to pay me. Just for the experience, it would be worth it." Her eyes pleaded with him, and it was all he could do to keep from laughing out loud. He'd pay ten bucks an hour for a gal like her, any day of the week.

"Well," he said, forcing himself to hesitate, "I guess we could give it a try. But you might not like modeling; I mean, you might not like to pose for, well . . ."

She smiled. "You mean cheesecake? I don't mind. Whatever you want."

Whatever he wanted! If only she knew what he wanted, what

plans he had for her. He looked over her body again, drinking in the vibrance of it. Paula must have been like that, once. It had been good with Paula, and he could almost feel the way it would be with Saralee.

"Saralee," he said, aloud, "where would you like to work? I don't have a studio yet."

"How about outside? There is a little stream down the road, no good for swimming or fishing. Nobody goes there, so it's a perfect spot. Nice scenery too. Kind of wild, like."

"Fine," said Falch. "I'll pick you up tomorrow morning, in front of the hotel. Eleven-thirty okay?"

"Wonderful. Oh, I can hardly wait!" She turned, then, and half-ran, half-walked down the street. Falch stood rooted to the spot watching her.

When he left the hotel the next morning, his camera bag over his shoulder, she was waiting for him. She wore a gray skirt that hugged her hips and a tight yellow sweater that threatened to burst any minute. He led her to the car, and they drove off down the road to the spot she had picked out.

It was, as she had said, a perfect spot. The tough wooden bridge and thick-trunked oak provided a rustic touch, which contrasted sharply with the green of the grass and the blue water. Falch wished fleetingly that he had brought color film.

He was a good photographer, and he worked swiftly. He posed her in a variety of spots—leaning lazily against the bridge, sitting at the base of the tree, staring moodily into the water. He taught her how to pose, how to smile, and she was a good pupil. Falch was surprised to discover that his interest in the pictures was almost as great as his desire for Saralee.

He was careful not to try any real cheesecake that first day. He did take a few leg shots, but he kept her fully clothed and avoided the more provocative poses. Saralee attracted him more than any girl he could remember, and he didn't want to spoil things at the start. She was so young and inexperienced, he'd have to play things very slowly. And he had all the time in the world.

Getting into the car for the ride back, she brushed against him accidentally, and the softness of her skin startled him and sent his pulse up. He wanted to reach for her, then and there, but he forced himself to bide his time.

At night, he covered the cracks and light openings in his room with masking tape and developed the pictures. They were better than he had expected. The girl could project herself, could endow the pictures with real vitality. He thought how she would be in his arms, with her blond hair spread over a pillow.

Gradually, day by day, he took increasingly sexier pictures of her. He taught her to bring her body into harmony with the camera. He photographed her in a skimpy bathing suit, with the sun glistening on her flawless skin. He posed her in a low-cut gown that he bought just for that purpose, and with her blouse open part way down the front, so that it barely hid her breasts. That time he could barely stand it, and beads of sweat dotted his forehead.

Saralee took it all in stride. She never faltered, accepting it all as part of the job of becoming a model. She showed more and more of her legs and breasts, and never so much as blushed.

"Don't you have a boyfriend?" he'd asked one day.

"I used to go with Tom Larson, but not anymore. He's too young for me. Maybe you met him," she'd added. "He works at the drugstore."

Falch remembered the boy—thin, with pimples on his face. He would be no problem at all.

And then one day, when the curves of her breasts and belly and thighs filled him with a desire he couldn't suppress, he knew that the time had come. "Saralee," he said, "I think we ought to try something a little bit different. Unless you'd rather not."

She looked at him. "Nudes? Is that what you mean, Jake?"

"Well . . ."

"I think that would be nice," she said, smiling sweetly. "I mean, all the top models did nude shots first, didn't they?"

He nodded, breathing heavily. "I'd love to," she said. "But we can't do that *here*, Jake. Somebody might see, and besides, there's a law against it."

"Maybe at my room, in the hotel."

"Wait," she said. "I have a better idea. How about my house?"

He stared at her incredulously. "Your house? But your folks . . ."

"They're out of town for the weekend. Could you come up about nine?"

It was better than he'd dared to hope for. The clerk might be nosy at the hotel, and if she got rough it might be noisy. But at her house there'd be no worries. "Nine," he said. "I'll be there."

He was there early, and when she stood nude before him he felt that he had never seen anything so beautiful in his life. There was not a hint of shyness about her, just pride and pleasure in her own loveliness. He began taking pictures.

After he'd shot a roll of film, he took a pint of whiskey from his camera bag. "This calls for a celebration," he explained. "Your first nude shots. We have to have a few drinks."

She protested weakly that she had never had whiskey before, but gave in without much argument. They had a drink each, then shot another roll, and then had another round of drinks.

It was easy to see that she was unaccustomed to alcohol. A glow came into her cheeks and her eyes became even brighter than usual. They went on drinking and taking pictures, and he knew that he was almost ready to take her.

When he posed her, he let his hands linger longer than necessary upon her smooth skin, and he felt the heat building up within her. She breathed faster, deeper. It was time.

He said nothing; he didn't have to. He set down the camera, switched off the lights, and took her by the hand. His right arm encircled her waist, his hand stroking the soft flesh of her belly. He led her down the hall, to the darkened bedroom, and disrobed swiftly. His hands raced over her body, he pressed a long hard kiss upon her lips, and then he took her.

When the morning sunlight filtered through the venetian blinds, Falch rolled over and swore softly. His mind filled with memories of the night and he chuckled to himself. God, she had been good! Fresh and new and hot as a stove. And she had enjoyed it as much as he had.

He turned over to look at her, but the bed was empty. Must

be cooking up some breakfast, he thought, chuckling. Breakfast in bed.

It had taken a lot of hard work, but you didn't get things like that easily. And she had been worth it. He had a good life to look forward to now, with no more fooling around. He'd have her whenever he wanted.

"Saralee!" he called. "Saralee!"

Seconds later the door opened. But it was not Saralee. It was a boy.

"Who the hell are you?" Falch demanded. Then he took a closer look, and he recognized him. It was Tom Larson, the boy from the drugstore.

The boy smiled, and it was a smile very much like Falch's. "Shut up," he said. "You just keep quiet there, Mr. Falch."

Falch gaped at him, unable to utter a sound.

"Got a surprise for you," said Tom. He reached into a pocket of his jeans and pulled out a picture, passing it to Falch.

Falch stared at the picture and his mouth fell open. "Got lots more like that," the boy said. "Took 'em last night, a whole mess of pictures. They're going to cost you, Mr. Falch."

The boy tapped the picture significantly. "Nice and clear, huh? Saralee's a good little model, Mr. Falch. And only seventeen, too. A nice respectable girl like that, it's going to cost you plenty. They're rough on guys like you in this state."

He pulled the picture from Falch's hand and studied it, grinning with satisfaction.

"Came out perfect, the whole batch of 'em. Used infra-red film and a fast shutter. Just stood in the closet and snapped 'em off. Didn't need a drop of light."

The boy laughed. "But I don't need to explain all that to you, Mr. Falch. Hell, I bet you're an old hand at this sort of thing!"

MURDER IS MY BUSINESS

I LIVE IN A POORLY FURNISHED ROOM a block off the Bowery. I used to live there because I couldn't afford anything better. But times have changed. I live there now because I like it. It's almost cozy, once you get used to it. The smells stop bothering you after the first week or so, and the people down there never bother anybody. The other tenants are upper-caste prostitutes. The winos are always drunk and the prostitutes are always available. I like the setup.

It's also a good business location. I live in my room, and I run my business from the bar a few doors down the street. Some of my clients don't like the neighborhood, but they manage to come here anyhow. They need me more than I need them. Business has been good this year.

I was sitting in the bar at my usual table in the back looking at a beer and watching it get warm. It was the middle of the afternoon, and I never drink before dinner. Eddie doesn't like me to sit without drinking, so I usually buy a beer or two during the afternoon and watch it go flat. I was reading a book of Spanish poetry when she came in.

I knew right off she was a prospective client. Women like her don't hang out in Skid Row bars. They were either kept in pent-houses or married to Scarsdale millionaires. You could tell from one look at her.

It wasn't just that she was beautiful, but that was a part of it. The women who live here have used up their best years on Eighth Avenue, and all the flavor has gone out of them. They all drank too much, and most of them have scars on their faces from men who drank too much. And they walk with a what-the-hell shuffle. The women on the Bowery aren't beautiful, and this one was.

She had blond hair, and not the kind that comes out of a bottle. It was cut short, and curled around a very passable face. She was wearing a suit, but it couldn't hide her body. It was a more than passable body.

But as I said, it was more than her beauty. She had class, and that is something which never winds its way to the Bowery. It's some-thing you can't pin down, but it's the visible difference between Nashua and the horse that pulls Benny's peanut wagon. This babe had class.

She walked in as though she had every right to be there, and every eye in the place turned to her. They didn't watch her for long, though. The people who hang out in Eddie's Bar are only interested in wine, and a woman is something which just stirs up memories.

She looked around for a minute, and finally met my stare. She came over and I pointed to a chair. She sat down, and we stared at each other for a while.

"Are you the man?"

It was a hell of an opener, so I played it cool and asked her just what man she was talking about.

"The man who . . . does jobs for people."

"That depends," I said. "What kind of job?" I was enjoying this.

"Couldn't we go someplace more private?"

I shook my head. "Nobody listens here," I said. "And if they do, they won't remember. And if they remember, they won't care. So speak up."

"A man told me you . . . killed people." It was an effort for her to get the words out.

I asked her what man, and she described Al. That meant a quick ten percent for Al, and it also meant that the chick was an honest customer.

"Did he tell you my fee?"

"He said five hundred dollars."

I nodded. "Do you have it?" This time she nodded. "Well," I said, "whom do you want taken care of?"

"My husband," she said. "He found out I was playing around and he's cutting me out of his will."

That was standard enough. "Okay," I said. "When do you want the job done?"

"Is tonight too soon?"

"Tonight is fine," I said. "Give me the address." She did and it wasn't Scarsdale, but Riverside Drive came to about the same thing. I memorized it quickly.

"Okay," I said. "I'll be up about nine-thirty."

"Fine," she said. "I'll go out."

I shook my head. "Stay home. What do you usually do nights?"

She nearly blushed. "Watch television," she said. "My husband is old."

I could see why she wanted to kill him. A woman like her needed to be loved plenty. She was wasted on an old guy.

I got back to business. "Stay home tonight," I said. "Watch television. I'll make like a burglar and take care of him, then you give me time to get away and call the cops. That way if I should get picked up, you can say I wasn't the murderer. Get it?"

She nodded. I asked for the cash, and she passed it to me under the table. I gave it a quick count and pocketed it.

"Fine," I said. "I'll see you tonight." I waited for her to get up and leave, but she didn't move.

"You're young for this business, aren't you?" I almost broke out laughing.

"Not that young," I said. "It beats petty larceny."

She kept looking at me. "What's your name?" she asked.

"I haven't got one," I said. It was the truth. I had had ten names in the past year and a half, and I was between aliases at the moment.

She was still staring at me. "Do you live around here?"

"Yes."

"Take me to your room."

I hadn't expected it, but it wasn't a shock. I stood up, threw a dime on the table for the beer, and led the way. She didn't say a word.

When we reached my room I discovered I had been right—the suit couldn't hide her perfection.

When she left, still without a word, I lay on my back staring at the cracks in the ceiling. Tonight would be a pleasure. Bodies like that should not be wasted on rich old men. I felt like a public servant.

I dressed again and went back to the bar, reclaiming my table and watching another beer get flat. I read some more of the Spanish poetry, but it was anticlimactic. I had made love to a poem, and the printed page cannot compete with that.

Then he came in, and I saw he was another client. He looked no more at home in Eddie's Bar than she had. He looked a little like my uncle Charlie, and I liked him right off. He didn't hesitate, but came right over and sat down.

"I have a job for you," he said. "Al sent me. Here's your fee and the address of the party in question." He slipped an envelope under the table, and I pocketed it.

"I'll be home," he said. "In case they ever pick you up, I'll refuse to identify you. Force an entrance, do your job, and leave."

He was one hell of a guy, businessman right down the line. I don't normally enjoy people telling me the way to operate, but I didn't mind it coming from him. He was sharp.

I nodded, and asked him when he wanted the job done.

"Tonight," he said.

I shook my head. "I can't make it," I said. "How's tomorrow?"

"Tonight," he said. "It has to be tonight."

I thought for a minute. I didn't relish the idea of two jobs in one night. It just doubled the chances of getting caught. But I could use the money, and I knew I couldn't stall him. "All right," I said. "I'm not sure on the time, but I'll make it tonight."

He didn't waste any time. He stood up and left. The heads in the bar followed him until he reached the door, then returned to their glasses of port. I returned to the Spanish poetry.

I read for about an hour, threw another dime on the table, and left. I walked up to my room, placed the money in a strongbox, and put two hundred dollars into my wallet. I'd need two guns tonight, one for each job. I hoped that Sam had them on hand.

Then I glanced at the address and flushed the slip of paper and the envelope down the hall toilet. I walked downstairs, and I got all the way to Sam's hockshop before it hit me.

I bought one gun. I bought a Luger with a silencer, and loaded it. It cost one hundred dollars across the counter, with no record of sale.

Sam was a good businessman himself. I could be sure that the gun would never be traced to me, and that was important. I made it back to my room and ate dinner.

Dinner was the usual—three fried eggs and two cups of black coffee. I live on eggs and coffee. It's cheap and nourishing, and I like it. I suppose I could afford caviar if I wanted it, but I'd rather let the money accumulate in the strongbox.

You see, a real businessman never worries about the money. He doesn't care about spending it, and he doesn't count up the pennies. The money's just the chips in the poker pot, just something to keep score with. A real businessman is interested in running a straight business, and he gets his kicks out of the business itself. A real businessman is along the lines of an artist. And I am a businessman. I do a clean job. It's the way I like to live.

I finished the meal and washed up the dishes. I didn't feel much like reading, so I sat around thinking. I had come a long way from the days when I used to steal food and swindle hockshops for a couple of bucks at a time. I was established in business, and the competition was nothing to speak of. I could raise my prices sky-high, and I'd still have more work than I could handle. There's a remarkable shortage of free-lance gunmen in town.

I sat around till 8:30 and then caught the subway to Times Square. I transferred to the Broadway IRT train there, and got off at 96th Street. It was a short walk to Riverside Drive.

The elevator was a self-service one, which cut down the chances of an identification. I rode to the top floor and rang the bell.

He answered it with a smile on his face. I walked in, and noticed that the television was on good and loud. He hadn't realized that I used a silencer.

I closed the door, took the gun from my pocket, and shot him. The bullet caught him in the side of the head and he didn't have time to be surprised. He fell like an ox.

She jumped up and came to me. She was wearing a skirt and sweater this time, and I could see every bit of that body. She was the kind of woman I could fall in love with, if I believed in love. But in my business I can't afford to.

I leveled the gun again and squeezed the trigger. Her eyes opened in horror before the bullet hit her, but she didn't have time to scream. I shot her in the head, and she died immediately.

It was a shame I had to kill her. But I had made an agreement, and I stick to my word even if my client is a corpse. Business is business.

NOR IRON BARS A CAGE

THE FIRST ALTHEAN SAID, "Well, the tower is completed."

The second Althean smiled. "Good. It is all ready for the prisoner, then?"

"Yes."

"Are you sure he'll be quite comfortable? He won't languish and die in such a state?"

"No," said the first Althean. "He'll be all right. It's taken a long time to build the tower, and I've had ample opportunity to study the creature. We've made his habitat as ideal for him as possible."

"I suppose so." The second Althean shuddered slightly. "I don't know," he said. "I suppose it's nothing more than projection on my part, but the mere thought of a *prison* . . ." He broke off and shuddered again.

"I know," said the other, sympathetically. "It's something none of us have ever had to conceive of before. The whole notion of locking up a fellow being is an abominable one, I'll admit. But for that matter, consider the creature itself!"

"It wouldn't do for him to be loose."

"Wouldn't do! Why, it would be quite impossible. He actually murders. He killed three of our fellow beings before we were able to subdue him."

The second Althean shuddered more violently than before, and it appeared for a moment as though he was about to become physically ill. "But *why*? What type of being is he, for goodness' sake? Where does he come from? What's he doing here?"

"Ah," said the first, "now you've hit upon it. You see, there's no way of knowing any of those answers. One morning he was discovered by a party of ten. They attempted to speak to him, and what do you think his rejoinder was?"

"He struck out at them, the way I heard it."

"Precisely! Utterly unprovoked assault, with three of their number dead as a result. The first case of murder on record here in thirty generations. Incredible!"

"And since then . . ."

"He's been a prisoner. No communication, no new insights, nothing. He eats whatever we feed him—he sleeps when the darkness comes and wakes when it goes. We have learned nothing about him, but I can tell you this for a fact. He is dangerous."

"Yes," said the second Althean.

"Very dangerous. He must be kept locked up. Of course, we wish him no harm—so we've made his prison as secure as possible, while keeping it as comfortable as possible. I daresay we've done a good job."

"Look," said the second, "perhaps I'm squeamish. I don't know. But are you sure he can never escape?"

"Positive."

"How can you be sure?"

The first Althean sighed. "The tower is one hundred thirty feet high. A drop from that distance is obviously fatal. Right?"

"Right."

"The prisoner's quarters are at the top of the tower, and the top is wider than the base—that is, the sides slope in. And the sides are very, very smooth—so climbing down is quite impossible."

"Couldn't he come down the same way he'll go up? It only stands to reason."

"Again, quite impossible. He'll be placed in his quarters by means of a pneumatic tube, and the same tube will be used to send him his food. The entire tower is so designed that it can be entered via the tube, and can only be left by leaping from the top. The food that he doesn't eat, as well as any articles which he tires of, may be thrown over the side."

The second Althean hesitated. "It *seems* safe."

"It should. It *is* safe."

"I suppose so. I suppose it's safe, and I suppose it's not cruel, but somehow . . . Well, when will the prisoner be placed in the tower? Is it all ready for his occupancy?"

"It's ready, all right. And, as a matter of fact, we're taking him there in just a few minutes. Would you care to come along?"

"It might be interesting at that."

"Then come along."

The two walked in silence to the first Althean's motor car and drove in silence to the tower. The tower was, indeed, a striking structure, both in terms of size and of design. They stepped out of the motor car and waited, and a large motor truck drew up shortly, pulling to a stop at the base of the tower. Three Althean guards stepped out of the truck, followed by the prisoner. His limbs were securely shackled.

"See?" demanded the first Althean. "He'll be placed in the tube like that, and he'll discover the key to his shackles in his quarters."

"Clever."

"We've worked it out carefully," the first explained. "I don't mean to sound boastful, but we've figured out all the angles."

The prisoner was placed in the tube, the aperture of which was located at the very base of the tower. Once inside, it was closed securely and bolted shut. The three Althean guards hesitated for several moments until a red light at the base indicated that the prisoner had entered his quarters. Then they returned to the motor truck and drove off down the road.

"We could go now," said the first. "I'd like to wait and see if he'll throw down the shackles, though. If you don't mind."

"Not at all. I'm rather interested now, you know. It's not something you see every day."

They waited. After several minutes, a pair of shackles plummeted through the air and dropped to the ground about twenty yards from the two Altheans.

"Ah," said the first. "He's found the key."

Moments later, the second pair of shackles followed the first, and the key followed soon thereafter. Then the prisoner walked to the edge of the tower and leaned over the railing gazing down at them.

"Awesome," said the second Althean. "I'm glad he can't escape."

The prisoner regarded them thoughtfully for several seconds. Then he mounted the railing, flapped his wings, and soared off into the sky.

ONE NIGHT OF DEATH

IT WAS JUST SEVEN O'CLOCK. I heard the bells ring at the little church two blocks down Mercer Street, and the bells set me on edge.

Seven o'clock.

In five hours they would kill my father.

They would take him from his cell and walk slowly to a little room at the end of the corridor. It would be a long walk, but it would end with him inside the little room, alone, with the door closed after him. Then he would sit or stand or wait.

At precisely twelve o'clock, they'd open the gas vents. The cyanide gas would rush into the chamber. Maybe he'd cough; I didn't know. But whether he did or not, the gas would enter his lungs when he breathed. Oh, he'd try to hold his breath as long as he could. My dad's a fighter, you see, but there are some things you can't fight.

The gas would kill him. Then they would draw the gas back into the tanks to save it for the next one, and they'd take my father's body out of the room. It would be buried somewhere.

I couldn't stay in the house another minute. I couldn't sit watching my mother try to dull the pain with glass after glass of cheap muscatel, couldn't listen to her crying softly. I wanted to cry, too—but I didn't know how anymore.

I slipped on my jacket and left the house, closing the door softly. It was cool outside. The air was crisp and fresh, with a breeze blowing and the fallen leaves skittering along the pavement.

It could have been a beautiful night, but it wasn't.

My father was a murderer, and tonight they were going to kill him.

Murderer. The picture that word makes isn't right at all. Because my dad's not a cruel or a vicious man or a money-hungry man. He was a cutter in a dress shop, not too long ago, and he saved his money so that he could go into business for himself in the Seventh Avenue rat-race.

It was no place for him, a mild, easy-going guy. The law of the Avenue is kill or be killed, screw the competition before they screw you. But Dad didn't want to hand anyone a raw deal. He just wanted to make pretty dresses and sell them. And Seventh Avenue isn't like that, not at all.

He managed to stomach it. It kept us eating good and he managed to make the kind of dresses he wanted. A man can learn to adjust to almost anything, he told me once. A man does what he has to do.

Dad's partner was a man named Bookspan, and he handled the business end while Dad took care of production. Bookspan was a crook, and the one thing Dad couldn't adjust to was a crooked partner, a partner who was cheating him.

When Dad found out, he killed him.

Not impulsively, with the anger hot and fresh in him, because he's not an impulsive sort of man. He bided his time and waited, until he and Bookspan took a business trip to Los Angeles. He picked up a pistol in a hockshop in L.A. and blew out Bookspan's brains.

And they caught him, of course. The poor guy, he didn't even try to get away. It was an open-and-shut case, premeditated and all. He was tried in L.A. where the murder took place, and he was sentenced to death at San Quentin.

I walked around aimlessly, just thinking about it. Here I was in New York, and my father was going to die on the other side of the continent. In less than five hours.

Then, of course, I realized that it would be eight hours. There's a time difference of three hours between New York and California. He had eight hours to live, and I had eight hours before it was time to mourn him.

How do you wait for a person to die? What do you do, when you know the very minute of death? Do you go to a movie? Watch television, maybe? Read a magazine?

I hadn't even noticed where I was, and I looked up to discover that I'd drifted clear over to Saint Mark's Place. It was natural enough. I used to spend most of my time on that little street, just east of Third Avenue and north of Cooper Square. I used to spend my time with Betty, who used to be my girl.

Before the murder.

Murders change things, you see. They turn things upside down, and suddenly Betty wasn't my girl anymore. Suddenly, she wasn't speaking to me any longer. I was a murderer's son.

Dan Bookspan wasn't a murderer's son, though. He was the same rotten, smooth-talking, crooked kind of a bastard as his old man, but his old man was dead now. So Dan Bookspan had my girl.

I got the hell away from Saint Mark's Place. I walked south to an old joint on the corner of Great Jones Street and the Bowery. I sat down on a stool in the back and ordered rye and soda. I sat down there with bums stinking and babbling on either side of me, in a Bowery bar where no one cared that I was just seventeen and too young to drink, and I poured the rye in.

The time passed, thank God. The television was going but I didn't look at it, and there were a few brawls but I didn't watch or participate. I just wanted to get loaded and watch the hours go by until it was three in the morning and my father was dead.

I didn't get drunk. I drank slowly, for one thing. More important,

I had too much of a fire going inside of me to get tight. I burned the alcohol up before it could get to me, I guess.

By midnight I couldn't stand it any longer. I wanted to be with someone, and being alone was impossible. I couldn't go home, for I knew how important it was to Mom that she be by herself. She had a lot of crying and drinking to do, and I didn't want to get in her way.

There was no one I wanted to see. No one but Betty.

It would have been so good to be with her then, to have her in my arms, holding me close and telling me that everything was going to be all right. What the hell, I thought. I walked over to the phone booth and gave her a ring.

The phone rang ten times without an answer. If I'd had anything better to do, I'd have given up. But I didn't so I stayed in the booth listening to the phone ring. And after ten rings, she answered it.

She couldn't have been sleeping, for there was a tension in her voice that showed she'd been busy. Her voice was tight and husky.

"Betty," I said "Betty, I want to come over."

There was a pause. "You can't."

"Look, I won't bother you. It's ... it's a bad night, Betty. I need someone, you know? Let me come over."

Again a pause, and a boy's voice in the background. Bookspan's. I gritted my teeth and banged the phone down on the hook. I needed another drink, and I had one. And then I had another, and another.

I left the joint at one, and I walked home. I felt fine, in spite of the liquor I'd had. I walked a straight line and my head was clear as crystal. I tiptoed up the stairs, past the living room where Mom was drinking and crying.

I found what I was looking for in Dad's bureau drawer. He'd tried to kill Bookspan before, you see. Once he bought a gun at a Third Avenue hockshop, but he never used it, never even pulled its trigger. When he finally shot the bastard, he was in California and the gun was still in the bureau drawer. It was almost as though he had left it there for me.

I left the house as silently as I had entered it, the gun snug and comfortable in my jacket pocket. At one-thirty, I climbed the stairs to the apartment house on Saint Mark's Place.

She didn't let me in, because she didn't have to. They'd left the door open, and I walked in without knocking. I walked through the familiar kitchen to the equally familiar bedroom. I knew that I'd find them there.

I flung open the bedroom door and I saw them lying there, in each other's arms. My girl. My girl, with the guy I hated most in the world. I'd expected it, but it was a hard thing to watch.

Her lips parted for a scream, but she stopped instantly when she saw the gun in my hand. Her face froze in terror, and she looked like a very little girl just then, a little girl trying to pretend she was a woman.

Bookspan just looked scared. I enjoyed the fear in his eyes, as much as I could have enjoyed anything at the time. I let them look at the gun for several minutes, without saying a word.

Then I told them to close their eyes, and then I walked to the side of the bed and struck each of them on the head with the barrel of the gun. I just used enough force to knock them unconscious. I didn't want to kill them; I couldn't do that.

I tore a bedsheet into strips of cloth and tied them up. I put their arms tight around each other, tying his hands around her back and her hands around his. Then I gagged them, and I waited.

When they came to, they struggled helplessly while their bodies pressed together. It could have been funny, if the circumstances had been different.

But I didn't laugh. I just watched them for a while, waiting. I put the gun back in my pocket, because I didn't need it anymore.

Later, I walked around the apartment, making sure that all the windows were closed tightly. It was precisely three o'clock when I opened all the gas jets full blast and left, shutting the door behind me.

But it was midnight in California.

PACKAGE DEAL

"IF I WERE YOUNGER," John Harper said, "I would do this myself. One of the troubles with growing old. Aging makes physical action awkward. A man becomes a planner, an arranger. Responsibility is delegated."

Castle waited.

"If I were younger," Harper went on, "I would kill them myself. I would load a gun and go out after them. I would hunt them down, one after another, and I would shoot them dead. Baron and Milani and Hallander and Ross. I would kill them all."

The old man's mouth spread in a smile.

"A strange picture," he said. "John Harper with blood in his eye. The president of the bank, the past president of Rotary and Kiwanis and the Chamber of Commerce, the leading citizen of Arlington. Going out and killing people. An incongruous picture. Success gets a man, Castle. Removes the spine and intestines. Ties the hands. Success is an incredible surgeon."

"So you hire me."

"So I hire you. Or, to be more precise, we hire you. We've had as much as we can take. We've watched a peaceful, pleasant town taken over by a collection of amateur hoodlums. We've witnessed the inadequacy of a small-town police force faced with big-town operations. We've had enough."

Harper sipped brandy. He was thinking, looking for the right way to phrase what he had to say. "Prostitution," he said suddenly. "And gambling. And protection—storekeepers paying money for the right to remain storekeepers. We've watched four men take control of a town which used to be ours."

Castle nodded. He knew the story already but he wasn't impatient with the old man. He didn't mind getting both the facts and the background behind them. You needed the full picture to do your job properly. He listened.

"I wish we could do it ourselves. Vigilante action, that type of thing. Fortunately, there's also a historical precedent for employing you. Are you familiar with it?"

"The town-tamer," Castle muttered

"The town-tamer. An invention of the American West. The man who cleans up a town for a fee. The man who waives legality when legality must inevitably be abandoned. The man who uses a gun instead of a badge when guns are effective and badges are impotent."

"For a fee."

"For a fee," John Harper echoed. "For a fee of ten thousand dollars, in this instance. Ten thousand dollars to rid the world and the town of Arlington of four men. Four malignant men, four little cancers. Baron and Milani and Hallander and Ross."

"Just four?"

"Just four. When the rats die, the mice scatter. Kill four. Kill Lou Baron and Joe Milani and Albert Hallander and Mike Ross. Then the back of the gang will be broken. The rest will run for their lives. The town will breathe clean air again. And the town needs clean air, Mr. Castle, needs it desperately. You may rest assured of that. You are doing more than earning a generous fee. You are performing a service for humanity."

Castle shrugged.

"I'm serious," Harper said. "I know your reputation. You're not a hired killer, sir. You are the twentieth-century version of the town-tamer. I respect you as I could never respect a hired killer. You are performing an important service, sir. I respect you."

Castle lit a cigarette. "The fee," he said.

"Ten thousand dollars. And I'm paying it entirely in advance, Mr. Castle. Because, as I have said, your reputation has preceded you. You'll have no trouble with the local police, but there are always state troopers to contend with. You might wish to leave Arlington in a hurry when the job is finished. As I understand it, the customary method of payment is half in advance and the remaining half upon completion of the job at hand. I trust you, Mr. Castle. I am paying the full sum in advance. You come well recommended."

Castle took the envelope, slipped it into an inside jacket pocket. It made a bulge there.

"Baron and Milani and Hallander and Ross," the old man said, "four fish. Shoot them in a barrel, Mr. Castle. Shoot them and kill them. They are a disease, a plague."

Castle nodded. "That's all?"

"That is all."

The interview was over. Castle stood up and let Harper show him to the door. He walked quickly to his car and drove off into the night.

Baron and Milani and Hallander and Ross.

CASTLE HAD NEVER MET THEM but he knew them all. Small fish, little boys setting up a little town for a little fortune. They were not big men. They didn't have the guts or the brains to play in Chicago or New York or Vegas. They knew their strengths and their limitations. And they cut a nice pie for themselves.

Arlington, Ohio. Population forty-seven thousand. Three small manufacturing concerns, two of them owned by John Harper. One bank, owned by John Harper. Stores and shops, doctors and lawyers. Shopkeepers, workers, professional men, housewives, clerks.

And, for the first time, criminals.

Lou Baron and Joe Milani and Albert Hallander and Mike Ross. And, as a direct result of their presence, a bucketful of hustlers on Lake Street, a handful of horse drops on Main and Limestone, a batch of numbers-runners, and a boatload of muscle to make sure everything moved according to plan. Money being drained from Arlington, people being exploited in Arlington, Arlington turning slowly but surely into the private property of four men.

Baron and Milani and Hallander and Ross.

Castle drove to his hotel, went to his room, put ten thousand dollars in his suitcase. He took out a gun, a .45 automatic which could not be traced farther than a St. Louis pawnshop, and slipped the loaded gun into the pocket which had held the ten thousand dollars. The gun made the jacket sag a bit too much and he took out the gun, took off the jacket, and strapped on a shoulder holster. The gun fit better this way. With the jacket on, the gun bulged only slightly.

Baron and Milani and Hallander and Ross. Four small fish in a pond too big for them. Ten thousand dollars.

He was ready.

EVENING.

A warm night in Arlington. A full moon, no stars, temperature around seventy. Humidity high. Castle walked down Center Street, his car at the hotel, his gun in its holster.

He was working. There were four to be taken and he was taking them in order. Lou Baron was first.

Lou Baron. Short and fat and soft. A beetle from Kansas City, a soft man who had no place in Kerrigan's K.C. mob. A big wheel in Arlington. A man employing women, a pimp on a large scale.

Filth.

Castle waited for Baron. He walked to Lake Street and found a doorway where the shadows eclipsed the moon. And waited.

Baron came out of 137 Lake Street a few minutes after nine. Fat and soft, wearing expensive clothes. Laughing, because they took good care of Baron at 137 Lake Street. They had no choice.

Baron walked alone. Castle waited, waited until the small fat man had passed him on the way to a long black car. Then the gun came out of the holster.

"Baron—"

The little man turned around. Castle's finger tightened on the trigger. There was a loud noise.

The bullet went into Baron's mouth and came out of the back of his head. The bullet had a soft nose and there was a bigger hole on the way out than on the way in. Castle holstered the gun, walked away in the shadows.

One down.

Three to go.

MILANI WAS EASY. Milani lived in a frame house with his wife. That amused Castle, the notion that Milani was a property owner in Arlington. It was funny.

Milani ran numbers in St. Louis, crossed somebody, pulled out. He was too small to chase. The local people let him alone.

Now people ran numbers for him in Arlington. A change of pace. And Milani's wife, a St. Louis tramp with big breasts and no brains, helped Milani spend his money that stupid people bet on three-digit numbers.

Milani was easy. He was home and the door was locked. Castle rang the bell. And Milani, safe and secure and self-important, did not bother with peepholes. He opened the door.

And caught a .45-caliber bullet over the heart.

Two down and two to go.

HALLANDER WAS A GUN MAN. Castle didn't know much about him, just a few rumbles that made their way over the coast-to-coast grapevine. Little things.

A gun, a torpedo, a zombie. A bodyguard out of Chi who goofed too many times. A killer who loved to kill, a little man with dead eyes who was nude without a gun. A psychopath. So many killers were psychopaths. Castle hated them with the hatred of the businessman for the competitive hobbyist. Killing Baron and Milani had been on the order of squashing cockroaches under the heel of a heavy shoe. Killing Hallander was a pleasure.

Hallander did not live in a house like Milani or go to women like Baron. Hallander had no use for women, only for a gun. He lived alone in a small apartment on the outskirts of town. His car, four years old, was parked in his garage. He could have afforded a better car. But to Hallander, money was not to be spent. It was chips in a poker game. He held onto his chips.

He was well protected—a doorman screened visitors, an elevator operator knew whom he took upstairs. But Hallander made no friends. Five dollars quieted the doorman forever. Five dollars sealed the lips of the elevator operator.

Castle knocked on Hallander's door.

A peephole opened. A peephole closed. Hallander drew a gun and fired through the door.

And missed.

Castle shot the lock off, kicked the door open. Hallander missed again.

And died.

With a bullet in the throat.

The elevator operator took Castle back to the first floor. The doorman passed him through to the street. He got into his car, turned the key in the ignition, drove back to the center of Arlington.

Three down.

Just one more.

"WE CAN DEAL," Mike Ross said. "You got your money. You hit three out of four. You can leave me be."

Castle said nothing. They were alone, he and Ross. The brains of the Arlington enterprise sat in an easy chair with a slow smile on his face. He knew about Baron and Milani and Hallander.

"You did a job already," Ross said. "You got paid already. You want money? Fifteen thousand. Cash. Then you disappear."

Castle shook his head.

"Why not? Hot-shot Harper won't sue you. You'll have his ten grand and fifteen of mine and you'll disappear. Period. No trouble, no sweat, no nothing. Nobody after you looking to even things up. Tell you the truth, I'm glad to see the three of them out of the way. More for me and no morons getting in the way. I'm glad you took them. Just so you don't take me."

"I've got a job to do."

"Twenty grand. Thirty. What's a man's life worth? Name your price, Castle. Name it!"

"No price."

Mike Ross laughed. "Everybody has a price. Everybody. You aren't that special. I can buy you, Castle."

Ross bought death. He bought one bullet and death came at once. He fell on his face and died. Castle wiped off the gun, flipped it onto the floor. He had taken chances, using the same gun four times. But the four times had taken less than one night. Morning had not come yet. The Arlington police force still slept.

He dropped the gun to the floor and got out of there.

A PHONE RANG IN CHICAGO. A man lifted it, held it to his ear.

"Castle," a voice said.

"Job done?"

"All done."

"How many hits?"

"Four of them," Castle said. "Four off the top."

"Give me the picture."

"The machinery is there with nobody to run it," Castle said. "The town is lonely."

The man chuckled. "You're good," he said. "You're very good. We'll be down tomorrow."

"Come on in," Castle said. "The water's fine."

PROFESSIONAL KILLER

HE WAS SITTING ALONE in a hotel room.

He was, possibly, the most average man in the world. His clothes were carefully chosen to pass in a crowd—dull brown oxfords, a brown gabardine suit, a white shirt, and a slim brown tie. On his head he usually wore an almost shapeless brown felt hat, but the hat now rested on a chair in a corner of the room. He was neither short nor fat nor tall nor thin.

Even his face was uninteresting. His features were unimpressive in themselves, and they didn't add up to a distinctive face. He had the usual number of noses, eyes, mouths, and so on—but somehow each feature seemed to be lifted from another dull face, so that he himself possessed no facial character whatsoever.

In many professions such a lack of individuality would be a handicap. A salesman without a face has a difficult time making a living. An executive, a merchant—almost anyone has a better chance of success if people remember his face and take notice of him. But the man in the hotel room was very pleased with his nondescript appearance, and did what he could to make himself even less noticeable. In his business it was an asset—perhaps the most important asset he possessed.

The man in the hotel room was named Harry Varden. He lived with his wife in a small house in Mamaroneck, in lower Westchester County. He had no children and no close friends.

He was a professional killer.

His office was a hotel room, and the location of this particular hotel room was of little importance. His office changed every week, and when he moved from one hotel to another, his phone number was placed in the classified section of the *New York Times*. A customer could always find him.

He was reading. He read a good deal, since there was nothing else to do while he waited for the phone to ring. Most days he spent morning and afternoon reading, and most afternoons and mornings were quite barren of phone calls. At $5000 a killing, he didn't need too large a volume of business.

This afternoon, however, the phone rang.

He closed his book, walked to the edge of the bed, sat down, and lifted the receiver. "Hello," he said, in a voice that was as unimpressive as his appearance.

"Hello." The voice on the other end of the line was a woman's.

He waited.

"I . . ." the woman began. "Who is this?"

"Whom do you want?"

The woman hesitated. "Are . . . are you the man?"

Harry Varden sighed to himself. He despised the hesitation and ineptness on the part of some clients, the clients who wouldn't open their mouths, the ones who were so terribly unsure of themselves. Professionals were different. Some of his clients, the ones who used him three or four times a year, had no trouble coming to the point at once.

"What man do you want?" he asked.

"The man who . . . the man with the number in the paper."

Coward, he thought. *Come on and speak your piece.* And aloud he said, "Yes, I'm the man."

"Will you do a job for me?"

Suddenly he was angry. The fee became of little importance now; his whole mind was set on forcing this woman to talk, on opening her up and making her say the words she didn't want to say.

"Don't be coy," he snapped. "What the hell do you want?"

After a long pause, the woman said, "I want you to murder my husband."

"Why?"

"I . . . what do you mean?"

"Look," he said, tiredly, "you want me to kill your husband. I want to know why."

"But I thought I just told you what you should do and sent you the money and that was all. I mean . . ."

"I don't care what you thought. You can open up or find another boy."

And he hung up.

He waited for the phone to ring again, knowing for certain that it would ring and that this time she would talk. It occurred to him that this was the first time he had acted in such a manner, the first time he had even pretended to care any more about a job than the name and the location of the victim. But there was some familiar whine in the woman's voice, some peculiar nagging quality that made him think he had heard it before. For some reason he disliked the owner of the voice intensely.

The phone rang, and the woman said at once, "I'm sorry. I don't understand."

"Okay. Give me the story."

She paused for a second and began. "I don't love my husband," she said. "I don't think I ever really loved him, and now there's somebody else, if you know what I mean. That is, I've met this other man and he and I are in love with each other, so naturally . . ."

Once she got started she didn't seem able to stop. Harry Varden listened half-heartedly, wondering why in the name of the Lord he had started her going. He couldn't care less why he was earning his $5000 (which by this time only a strict sense of professionalism kept him from raising to $7500) and he cared even less about the woman's married life.

But she kept right on. Her husband was dull and boring. He never talked to her, never paid any attention to her, never told her what was on his mind. She didn't even know for certain where he worked or what he did for a living.

Oh, he was a good provider, but there were more important things in a woman's life. She needed to feel that she was an important and distinctive woman with an equally important and distinctive man to love her. And her husband was dull and not the least bit important or distinctive or at all interesting, and . . .

The voice was one he had heard a million times in the past. For a moment it seemed that he had indeed heard this same voice before, but he decided that it was only the routine nature of the sentiments expressed which made the voice seem familiar.

Besides, Harry Varden never remembered a voice and rarely recalled a face. He himself was neither noticed nor remembered, and he retaliated unconsciously by means of a poor memory.

And she had met a man, a dashing, romantic man who sold brushes from door to door, and if her husband were dead she would have all his money, because he did seem to have a great deal of money although she wasn't quite sure how he came by it, and with the money she could marry the brush salesman, and they could live happily, albeit not forever, and besides there was the insurance if he had insurance and she supposed again that he did although again she wasn't sure, and for all she knew he *sold* insurance, but at any rate for all these reasons she wanted to pay Harry Varden $5000, in return for which payment he was to shoot her husband in his own home, some evening at eight o'clock or thereabouts, at which time she would be home and would be most willing to swear that Harry Varden was not the murderer, in the event that Harry Varden was ever caught, which was improbable from what she had heard.

By the time she had finished, Harry Varden was almost as tired as she was. The woman was a colossal bore, and he felt a considerable amount of sympathy for her uninteresting and opaque husband. He could easily understand why such a man didn't spend much time talking to such a woman.

In fact he felt that it was a shame he had to shoot the man, with whom he felt some sympathy, rather than the woman, whom it would be a genuine pleasure to shoot. But business, sadly, was business.

"I'll want the money in advance, of course," he said.

"I see," she said. "But why does the money have to be in advance?"

"That's the way I do business."

"I see. But then . . . I mean, you could just take the money and then never do the job for me, I mean . . ."

And, of course, he hung up for the second time.

When he answered the phone the third time she began talking quickly even before he had time to put the receiver to his ear, saying that she was very sorry and would he please forgive her since of course he was honest and she should have known better than to say such a thing, or even to think such a thing, but $5000 was a large sum of money, wasn't it?

He agreed that it was.

"Look," he said, tiring of the game, "I want you to put $5000 in tens and twenties in a bag or something. Lock it in a Grand Central locker and mail the key to PO Box 412. In the envelope with the key put the time you want the job done, the name of the party, and the address. Get that key in the mail today and the job will be done tomorrow night. Okay?"

"I guess so."

"You got the box number?"

"Box 412," she said.

"Excellent," he murmured, and he replaced the receiver on the cradle. He waited for a moment, wondering whether she might call back for some strange reason. Then, after a moment had passed without the phone ringing, he picked up his book and began reading once again.

It took him a moment to recapture the line of thought in the book, but he reread a paragraph and immersed himself once again in the text and read for the remainder of the afternoon without interruption.

The following day was routine. Lesser men than Harry Varden might have considered it a rut, but he was content with his lot. Out of the "office" at five, a quick walk to Grand Central, the 5:17 to Mamaroneck, a slightly longer walk to his home, dinner, and a good book in his hands while Mary washed the dishes and turned on the television set.

It was a good life—well-ordered, intelligently planned, more money in the bank than either he or Mary could ever spend, and all the comforts that anyone could want in a home.

When he bedded down for the night at a few minutes after eleven, he went to sleep easily. There was a time, long ago when he was new in the trade, when sleeping had been a problem. Time, however, healed all wounds, and routine removed whatever scruples might once have been involved in his profession.

He did his job, and when his job was done he slept. It was simple enough, certainly nothing to lose any sleep over.

In fact, it was a rare occasion when he took any interest in his work greater than the interest in doing a clean and workmanlike job. Today, for example, he had become far too involved with that woman. A client should never even begin to become a person. A client should be no more than a voice on a telephone, just as a victim should be merely a name scrawled (more often, for some obscure reason, typewritten or hand-printed) on a piece of paper. When either became a real person, the job became several times as difficult.

An ideal job was totally impersonal. It was much easier to erase a scrap of paper than to obliterate a human life. One time he had followed a potential victim long enough to gain some insight into the other's personality. It was infinitely more difficult to pull the trigger, and he had almost bunged that particular job.

For one moment he found himself almost dreading tomorrow's job, almost hoping that the money would not be at the locker, that the key would not arrive at his post office box.

Then he told himself that he was being foolish, and a moment later he was asleep.

His breakfast, on the table when he descended the staircase in the morning, was the same breakfast he'd eaten for a good many years—orange juice, cinnamon toast, and black coffee. As usual, he was out the door by 7:53 and on the 8:02 to Grand Central. He permitted himself the luxury of a taxi to the post office, leaning back in the backseat of the cab and enjoying the first cigarette of the day.

He studied the cabdriver's face in the mirror, wondering idly whether he had taken this cab before, whether he had met this very driver somewhere else. At times his lack of memory for people disturbed him; at other times, he recognized it as a double blessing.

For one thing, if his memory were good he would be constantly hailing people whom he had met and who, since he himself was so inconspicuous, would not remember him at all.

And, of course, there was the matter of conscience. While he didn't consciously feel any remorse over a murder, he was intelligent enough to realize that he was unconsciously beset with periodic visitations of guilt.

When the faces and voices of clients and victims were reduced by time to a vague blur, the guilt was diminished through his own removal from a vivid recollection of the entire affair.

The envelope was in his box. He removed it, closed the box, and took another cab back to Grand Central. He removed the key from the envelope without troubling to glance at the slip of paper, only noticing that the name and address were typewritten.

He located the locker, opened it, and removed $5000, which he pocketed at once. Then he took a room at another hotel in the area.

Once in the hotel, his whole mind and body slipped into the role of the killer, the comfortable and familiar role of the hired murderer.

He had become a machine. The money was in his pocket; in a short while it would be in his bank account. He would now have to purchase a fresh gun from the pawnbroker on Third Avenue, pick up a silencer for the gun, place an ad in the *Times* announcing the change of address, and prepare himself for the job.

The gun cost him $100. The silencer, purchased in another pawnshop a block further down Third Avenue, set him back another $25. The ad, which stated simply that Acme Services was located at 758 Grosvenor, cost very little. The ad meant, of course, that Harry Varden was now in room 758 at the Grosvenor. To avoid any confusion it was placed in the SITUATIONS WANTED, MALE column—the clients knew where to look.

The next stop was the bank. The money was deposited to his account, quickly and easily. He walked out with a gun in his shoulder holster, a silencer in an inside jacket pocket, a slip of paper still in the envelope in his pants pocket, and the brown felt hat riding easily on his head. He was walking on familiar ground.

The attack of nerves which the book said was inevitable at such a moment was entirely absent, and this worried him at times. Perhaps he ought to feel more. Perhaps the work should revolt him. But it didn't, and he resolved that this was really something to be thankful for. Perhaps that was the secret of Harry Varden's happiness; he invariably managed to mentally convert every apparent liability into an asset.

He ate lunch before opening the envelope once again. He did this on purpose; experience had taught him that the longer he waited before learning even the victim's name, the easier the whole process became.

Lunch finished, he returned to the hotel room, sat down on the bed, and pulled the envelope from his pocket. He opened it, pulled out the small slip of paper, and unfolded the slip methodically.

For a moment he was angry. For a moment the anger burned in him like a blue flame, but this was only for a moment, and the emotion passed quite rapidly. With it, the thought of a possible course of action vanished from his mind. He remembered the old maxim about a lawyer who tried his own case having a fool for a client.

He picked up the receiver and asked for a number. When the phone was answered a soft voice said, "Hello," in a guarded fashion.

"Pete?" he said. "This is Harry. Look, I've a job for you—more work than I can handle. It's got to be tonight. Okay?"

"Right."

He smiled to himself. "Tonight at eight," he said. "The mark's a woman living at forty-three Riverton, in Mamaroneck. It's exactly eight minutes' walking time from the railroad station."

PSEUDO IDENTITY

SOMEWHERE BETWEEN FOUR AND FOUR-THIRTY, Howard Jordan called his wife. "It looks like another late night," he told her. "The spot TV copy for Prentiss was full of holes. I'll be here half the night rewriting it."

"You'll stay in town?"

"No choice."

"I hope you won't have trouble finding a room."

"I'll make reservations now. Or there's always the office couch."

"Well," Carolyn said, and he heard her sigh the sigh designed to reassure him that she was sorry he would not be coming home, "I'll see you tomorrow night, then. Don't forget to call the hotel."

"I won't."

He did not call the hotel. At five, the office emptied out. At five minutes after five, Howard Jordan cleared off his desk, packed up his attaché case, and left the building. He had a steak in a small restaurant around the corner from his office, then caught a cab south and west to a four-story redbrick building on Christopher Street. His key opened the door, and he walked in.

In the hallway, a thin girl with long blond hair smiled at him. "Hi, Roy."

"Hello, baby."

"Too much," she said, eyeing his clothes. "The picture of middle-class respectability."

"A mere facade. A con perpetrated upon the soulless bosses."

"Crazy. There's a party over at Ted and Betty's. You going?"

"I might."

"See you there."

He entered his own apartment, tucked his attaché case behind a low bookcase improvised of bricks and planks. In the small closet he hung his gray sharkskin suit, his button-down shirt, his rep-striped tie. He dressed again in tight Levi's and a bulky brown turtleneck sweater, changed his black moccasin toe oxfords for white hole-in-the-toe tennis sneakers. He left his wallet in the pocket of the sharkskin suit and pocketed another wallet, this one containing considerably less cash, no credit cards, and a few cards identifying him as Roy Baker.

He spent an hour playing chess in the back room of a Sullivan Street coffeehouse, winning two games of three. He joined friends in a bar a few blocks away and got into an overly impassioned argument on the cultural implications of Camp; when the bartender ejected them, he took his friends along to the party in the East Village apartment of Ted Marsh and Betty Haniford. Someone had brought a guitar, and he sat on the floor drinking wine and listening to the singing.

Ginny, the long-haired blonde who had an apartment in his building, drank too much wine. He walked her home, and the night air sobered her.

"Come up for a minute or two," she said. "I want you to hear what my analyst said this afternoon. I'll make us some coffee."

"Groovy," he said, and went upstairs with her. He enjoyed the conversation and the coffee and Ginny. An hour later, around one thirty, he returned to his own apartment and went to sleep.

In the morning he rose, showered, put on a fresh white shirt, another striped tie, and the same gray sharkskin suit, and rode up-town to his office.

IT HAD BEGUN INNOCENTLY ENOUGH. From the time he'd made the big jump from senior copywriter at Lowell, Burham & Plescow to copy chief at Keith Wenrall Associates, he had found himself working late more and more frequently. While the late hours never bothered him, merely depriving him of the company of a whining wife, the midnight train to New Hope was a constant source of ag-gravation. He never got to bed before two-thirty those nights he rode it, and then had to drag himself out of bed just four and a half hours later in order to be at his desk by nine.

It wasn't long before he abandoned the train and spent those late nights in a midtown hotel. This proved an imperfect solution, substituting inconvenience and expense for sleeplessness. It was often difficult to find a room at a late hour, always impossible to locate one for less than twelve dollars, and hotel rooms, however well appointed, did not provide such amenities as a toothbrush or a razor, not to mention a change of underwear and a clean shirt. Then too, there was something disturbingly temporary and mar-ginal about a hotel room. It felt even less like home than did his split-level miasma in Bucks County.

An apartment, he realized, would overcome all of these objec-tions while actually saving him money. He could rent a perfectly satisfactory place for a hundred dollars a month, less than he pres-ently spent on hotels, and it would always be there for him, with fresh clothing in the closet and a razor and toothbrush in the bath-room.

HE FOUND THE LISTING IN THE CLASSIFIED PAGES—*Christopher St, 1 rm, bth, ktte, frnshd, util, $90 mth.* He translated this and decided that a one-room apartment on Christopher Street with bathroom and kitchenette, furnished, with utilities included at ninety dollars per month, was just what he was looking for. He called the landlord and asked when he could see the apartment.

"Come around after dinner," the landlord said. He gave him the address and asked his name.

"Baker," Howard Jordan said. "Roy Baker."

After he hung up he tried to imagine why he had given a false name. It was a handy device when one wanted to avoid being called back, but it did seem pointless in this instance. Well, no matter, he decided. He would make certain the landlord got his name straight when he rented the apartment. Meanwhile, he had problems enough changing a junior copywriter's flights of literary fancy into something that might actually convince a man that the girls would love him more if he used the client's brand of gunk on his hair.

The landlord, a birdlike little man with thick metal-rimmed glasses, was waiting for Jordan. He said, "Mr. Baker? Right this way. First floor in the rear. Real nice."

The apartment was small but satisfactory. When he agreed to rent it the landlord produced a lease, and Jordan immediately changed his mind about clearing up the matter of his own identity. A lease, he knew, would be infinitely easier to break without his name on it. He gave the document a casual reading, then signed it "Roy Baker" in a handwriting quite unlike his own.

"Now I'll want a hundred and eighty dollars," the landlord said. "That's a month's rent in advance and a month's security."

Jordan reached for his checkbook, then realized his bank would be quite unlikely to honor a check with Roy Baker's signature on it. He paid the landlord in cash, and arranged to move in the next day. He spent the following day's lunch hour buying extra clothing for the apartment, selecting bed linens, and finally purchasing a suitcase to accommodate the items he had bought. On a whim, he had the suitcase monogrammed "R.B." That night he worked late, told Carolyn he would be staying in a hotel, then carried the suitcase to his apartment, put his new clothes in the closet, put his new toothbrush and razor in the tiny bathroom and, finally, made his bed and lay in it. At this point Roy Baker was no more than a signature on a lease and two initials on a suitcase.

Two months later, Roy Baker was a person.

THE PROCESS BY WHICH ROY BAKER'S BONES were clad with flesh was a gradual one. Looking back on it, Jordan could not tell exactly how it had begun, or at what point it had become purposeful. Baker's personal wardrobe came into being when Jordan began to make the rounds of Village bars and coffeehouses, and wanted to look more like a neighborhood resident and less like a celebrant from uptown. He bought denim trousers, canvas shoes, bulky sweaters; and when he shed his three-button suit and donned his Roy Baker costume, he was transformed as utterly as Bruce Wayne clad in Batman's mask and cape.

When he met people in the building or around the neighborhood, he automatically introduced himself as Baker. This was simply expedient; it wouldn't do to get into involved discussions with casual acquaintances, telling them that he answered to one name but lived under another, but by being Baker instead of Jordan, he could play a far more interesting role. Jordan, after all, was a square, a Madison Avenue copy chief, an animal of little interest to the folksingers and artists and actors he met in the Village. Baker, on the other hand, could be whatever Jordan wanted him to be. Before long his identity took form: he was an artist, he'd been unable to do any serious work since his wife's tragic death, and for the time being he was stuck in a square job uptown with a commercial art studio.

This identity he had picked for Baker was a source of occasional amusement to him. Its expedience aside, he was not blind to its psychological implications. Substitute *writer* for *artist* and one approached his own situation. He had long dreamed of being a writer, but had made no efforts toward serious writing since his marriage to Carolyn. The bit about the tragic death of his wife was nothing more than simple wish fulfillment. Nothing would have pleased him more than Carolyn's death, so he had incorporated this dream into Baker's biography.

As the weeks passed, Baker accumulated more and more of the trappings of personality. He opened a bank account. It was, after all, inconvenient to pay the rent in cash. He joined a book club and promptly wound up on half the world's mailing lists. He got a letter from his congressman advising him of the latest developments in Washington and the heroic job his elected representative was doing to safeguard his interests. Before very long, he found himself heading for his Christopher Street apartment even on nights when he did not have to work late at all.

Interestingly enough, his late work actually decreased once he was settled in the apartment. Perhaps he had only developed the need to work late out of a larger need to avoid going home to Carolyn. In any event, now that he had a place to go after work, he found it far less essential to stay around the office after five o'clock. He rarely worked late more than one night a week—but he always spent three nights a week in town, and often four.

Sometimes he spent the evening with friends. Sometimes he stayed in his apartment and rejoiced in the blessings of solitude. Other times he combined the best of two worlds by finding an agreeable Village female to share his solitude.

He kept waiting for the double life to catch up with him, anticipating the tension and insecurity which were always a component of such living patterns in the movies and on television. He expected to be discovered, or overcome by guilt, or otherwise to have the error of his dual ways brought forcibly home to him. But this did not happen. His office work showed a noticeable improvement; he was not only more efficient, but his copy was fresher, more inspired, more creative. He was doing more work in less time and doing a better job of it. Even his home life improved, if only in that there was less of it.

Divorce? He thought about it, imagined the joy of being Roy Baker on a full-time basis. It would be financially devastating, he knew. Carolyn would wind up with the house and the car and the lion's share of his salary, but Roy Baker could survive on a mere fraction of Howard Jordan's salary, existing quite comfortably without house or car. He never relinquished the idea of asking Carolyn for a divorce, nor did he ever quite get around to it—until one night he saw her leaving a nightclub on West Third Street, her black hair blowing in the wind, her step drunkenly unsteady, and a man's arm curled possessively around her waist.

His first reaction was one of astonishment that anyone would actually desire her. With all the vibrant, fresh-bodied girls in the Village, why would anyone be interested in Carolyn? It made no sense to him.

Then, suddenly, his puzzlement gave way to absolute fury. She had been cold to him for years, and now she was running around with other men, adding insult to injury. She let him support her, let him pay off the endless mortgage on the horrible house, let him sponsor her charge accounts while she spent her way toward the list of Ten Best-Dressed Women. She took everything from him and gave nothing to him, and all the while she was giving it to someone else.

He knew, then, that he hated her, that he had always hated her and, finally, that he was going to do something about it.

What? Hire detectives? Gather evidence? Divorce her as an adulteress? Small revenge, hardly the punishment that fit the crime. No. No, *he* could not possibly do anything about it. It would be too much out of character for him to take positive action. He was the good clean-living, midtown-square type, good old Howie Jordan. He would do all that such a man could do, bearing his new knowledge in silence, pretending that he knew nothing, and going on as before.

But Roy Baker could do more.

From that day on he let his two lives overlap. On the nights when he stayed in town he went directly from the office to a nearby hotel, took a room, rumpled up the bed so that it would look as though it had been slept in, then left the hotel by back staircase and rear exit. After a quick cab ride downtown and a change of clothes, he became Roy Baker again and lived Roy Baker's usual life, spending just a little more time than usual around West Third

Street. It wasn't long before he saw her again. This time he followed her. He found out that her lover was a self-styled folksinger named Stud Clement, and he learned by discreet inquiries that Carolyn was paying Stud's rent.

"Stud inherited her from Phillie Wells when Phillie split for the Coast," someone told him. "She's got some square husband in Connecticut or someplace. If Stud's not on the scene, she don't care who she goes home with." She had been at this, then, for some time. He smiled bitterly. It was true, he decided; the husband was really the last to know.

He went on using the midtown hotel, creating a careful pattern for his life, and he kept careful patterns on Stud Clement. One night when Carolyn didn't come to town, he managed to stand next to the big folksinger in a Hudson Street bar and listen to him talk. He caught the slight Tennessee accent, the pitch of the voice, the type of words that Clement used.

Through it all he waited for his hatred to die, waited for his fury to cool. In a sense she had done no more to him than he had done to her. He half-expected that he would lose his hatred sooner or later, but he found that he hated her more every day, not only for cheating but for making him an ad man instead of a writer, for making him live in that house instead of a Village apartment, for all the things she had done to ruin every aspect of his life. If it had not been for her, he would have been Roy Baker all his life. She had made a Howard Jordan of him, and for that he would hate her forever.

Once he realized this, he made the phone call. "I gotta see you tonight," he said.

"Stud?"

So the imitation was successful. "Not at my place," he said quickly. "One-nine-three Christopher, Apartment one-D. Seven-thirty, no sooner and no later. And don't be going near my place."

"Trouble?"

"Just be there," he said, and hung up.

His own phone rang in less than five minutes. He smiled a bitter smile as he answered it.

She said, "Howard? I was wondering, you're not coming home tonight, are you? You'll have to stay at your hotel in town?"

"I don't know," he said. "I've got a lot of work, but I hate to be away from you so much. Maybe I'll let it slide for a night—"

"No!" He heard her gasp. Then she recovered, and her voice was calm when she spoke again. "I mean, your career comes first, darling. You know that. You shouldn't think of me. Think of your job."

"Well," he said, enjoying all this, "I'm not sure—"

"I've got a dreary headache anyway, darling. Why not stay in town? We'll have the weekend together—"

He let her talk him into it. After she rang off, he called his usual hotel and made his usual reservation for eleven-thirty. He went back to work, left the office at five-thirty, signed the register downstairs, and left the building. He had a quick bite at a lunch counter and was back at his desk at six o'clock, after signing the book again on the way in.

At a quarter to seven he left the building again, this time failing to sign himself out. He took a cab to his apartment and was inside it by ten minutes after seven. At precisely seven-thirty there was a knock on his door. He answered it, and she stared at him as he dragged her inside. She couldn't figure it out; her face contorted.

"I'm going to kill you, Carolyn," he said, and showed her the knife. She died slowly, and noisily. Her cries would have brought out the National Guard anywhere else in the country, but they were in New York now, and New Yorkers never concern themselves with the shrieks of dying women.

He took the few clothes that did not belong to Baker, scooped up Carolyn's purse, and got out of the apartment. From a pay phone on Sheridan Square he called the air terminal and made a reservation. Then he taxied back to the office and slipped inside, again without writing his name in the register.

At eleven-fifteen he left the office, went to his hotel and slept much more soundly than he had expected. He went to the office in the morning and had his secretary put in three calls to New Hope. No one answered.

That was Friday. He took his usual train home, rang his bell a few times, used his key, called Carolyn's name several times, then made himself a drink. After half an hour he called the next door neighbor and asked her if she knew where his wife was. She didn't. After another three hours he called the police.

Sunday a local policeman came around to see him. Evidently Carolyn had had her fingerprints taken once, maybe when she'd held a civil service job before they were married. The New York police had found the body Saturday evening, and it had taken them a little less than twenty-four hours to run a check on the prints and trace Carolyn to New Hope.

"I hoped I wouldn't have to tell you this," the policeman said. "When you reported your wife missing, we talked to some of the neighbors. It looks as though she was—uh—stepping out on you, Mr. Jordan. I'm afraid it had been going on for some time. There were men she met in New York. Does the name Roy Baker mean anything to you?"

"No. Was he—"

"I'm afraid he was one of the men she was seeing, Mr. Jordan. I'm afraid he killed her, sir."

Howard's reactions combined hurt and loss and bewilderment in proper proportion. He almost broke down when they had him view the body but managed to hold himself together stoically. He learned from the New York police that Roy Baker was a Village type, evidently some sort of irresponsible artist. Baker had made a reservation on a plane shortly after killing Carolyn but hadn't picked up his ticket, evidently realizing that the police would be able to trace him. He'd no doubt take a plane under another name, but they were certain they would catch up with him before too long.

"He cleared out in a rush," the policeman said. "Left his clothes, never got to empty out his bank account. A guy like this, he's going to turn up in a certain kind of place. The Village, North Beach in Frisco, maybe New Orleans. He'll be back in the Village within a year, I'll bet on it, and when he does we'll pick him up."

For form's sake, the New York police checked Jordan's whereabouts at the time of the murder, and they found that he'd been at his office until eleven-fifteen, except for a half hour when he'd had a sandwich around the corner, and that he had spent the rest of the night at the hotel where he always stayed when he worked late.

That, incredibly, was all there was to it.

After a suitable interval, Howard put the New Hope house on the market and sold it almost immediately at a better price than he had thought possible. He moved to town, stayed at his alibi hotel while he checked the papers for a Village apartment.

He was in a cab, heading downtown for a look at a three-room apartment on Horatio Street, before he realized suddenly that he could not possibly live in the Village, not now. He was known there as Roy Baker, and if he went there he would be identified as Roy Baker and arrested as Roy Baker, and that would be the end of it.

"Better turn around," he told the cabdriver. "Take me back to the hotel. I changed my mind."

He spent another two weeks in the hotel, trying to think things through, looking for a safe way to live Roy Baker's life again. If there was an answer, he couldn't find it. The casual life of the Village had to stay out of bounds.

He took an apartment uptown on the East Side. It was quite expensive but he found it cold and charmless. He took to spending his free evenings at midtown nightclubs, where he drank a little too much and spent a great deal of money to see poor floor shows. He didn't get out often, though, because he seemed to be working late more frequently now. It was harder and harder to get everything done on time. On top of that, his work had lost its sharpness; he had to go over blocks of copy again and again to get them right.

Revelation came slowly, painfully. He began to see just what he had done to himself.

In Roy Baker, he had found the one perfect life for himself. The Christopher Street apartment, the false identity, the new world of new friends and different clothes and words and customs, had been a world he took to with ease because it was the perfect world for him. The mechanics of preserving this dual identity, the taut fabric of lies that clothed it, the childlike delight in pure secrecy, had added a sharp element of excitement to it all. He had enjoyed being

Roy Baker; more, he had enjoyed being Howard Jordan playing at being Roy Baker. The double life suited him so perfectly that he had felt no great need to divorce Carolyn.

Instead, he had killed her—and killed Roy Baker in the bargain, erased him very neatly, put him out of the picture for all time.

Howard bought a pair of Levi's, a turtleneck sweater, a pair of white tennis sneakers. He kept these clothes in the closet of his Sutton Place apartment, and now and then when he spent a solitary evening there he dressed in his Roy Baker costume and sat on the floor drinking California wine straight from the jug. He wished he were playing chess in the back room of a coffeehouse, or arguing art and religion in a Village bar, or listening to a blues guitar at a loft party.

He could dress up all he wanted in his Roy Baker costume, but it wouldn't work. He could drink wine and play guitar music on his stereo, but that wouldn't work, either. He could buy women, but he couldn't walk them home from Village parties and make love to them in third-floor walk-ups.

He had to be Howard Jordan.

Carolyn or no Carolyn, married or single, New Hope split-level or Sutton Place apartment, one central fact remained unchanged. He simply did not like being Howard Jordan.

RIDE A WHITE HORSE

ANDY HART STARED UNBELIEVINGLY at the door of Whitey's Tavern. The door was closed and padlocked, and the bar was unlighted. He checked his watch and noted that it was almost 7:30. Whitey should have opened hours ago.

Andy turned and strode to the candy store on the corner. He was a small man, but his rapid walk made up for his short legs. He walked as he did everything else—precisely, with no wasted motion.

"Hey," he asked the man behind the counter, "how come Whitey didn't open up yet?"

"He's closed down for the next two weeks. Got caught serving minors." Andy thanked him and left.

The news was disturbing. It didn't annoy him tremendously, but it did break up a long-established routine. Ever since he had started working as a bookkeeper at Murrow's Department Store, eleven years ago, he had been in the habit of eating a solitary meal at the Five Star Diner and drinking a few beers at Whitey's. He had just finished dinner, and now he found himself with no place to go.

Standing on the street corner, staring at the front of the empty bar, he had a vague sensation that he was missing something. Here he was, thirty-seven years old, and there was nowhere in the city for him to go. He had no family, and his only friends were his drinking companions at Whitey's. He could go back to his room, but there he would have only the four walls for company. He momentarily envied the married men who worked in his department. It might be nice to have a wife and kids to come home to.

The thought passed as quickly as it had come. After all, there was no reason to be brokenhearted over a closed bar. There was undoubtedly another bar in the neighborhood where the beer was as good and the people as friendly. He glanced around and noticed a bar directly across the street.

There was a large neon sign over the doorway, with the outline of a horse and the words "White Horse Cafe." The door was a bright red, and music from a jukebox wafted through it.

Andy hesitated. There was a bar, all right. He had passed it many times in the past, but had never thought to enter it. It seemed a little flashy to him, a little bit too high-tone. But tonight, he decided, he'd see how it was on the inside. A change of pace wouldn't hurt him at all.

He crossed the street and entered. A half-dozen men were seated at the bar, and several couples occupied booths on the side. The jukebox was playing a song which he had heard before, but he couldn't remember the title. He walked to the rear, hung his coat on a peg, and took the end seat.

He ordered a beer and sat nursing it. He studied his reflection in the mirror. His looks were average—neatly combed brown hair, brown eyes, and a prominent chin. His smile was pleasant, but he didn't smile too often. He was, all in all, a pretty average guy.

The time passed slowly. Andy finished his beer and ordered another, and then another. Some of the people left the bar and others entered, but he saw no one he recognized. He was beginning to regret coming to the White Horse. The beer was fine and the music was nice enough, but he had no more company than the four walls of his room provided.

Then, while he was drinking his fourth beer, the door opened and she entered. He saw her at once. He had glanced to the door every time it opened in the hope of seeing an acquaintance, and each time he had turned back to his glass. This time, however, he couldn't turn his eyes away from her.

She was tall, very pretty, with long blond hair that fell to her shoulders. She took off her coat and hung it up and Andy could see that she was more than just pretty. Her skirt clung to her hips and hugged her thighs, and her breasts threatened to break through the tight film of her sweater. Andy couldn't stop looking at her. He knew that he was staring, but he couldn't help himself. She was the most beautiful woman he had ever seen.

He was surprised when she walked over and sat down on the stool beside him. Actually, it was natural enough. There were only two other empty stools at the bar. But to Andy it seemed like the rarest of coincidences.

He was glad that she was sitting next to him but at the same time he was embarrassed. He felt a desire for her which was stronger than anything he had experienced in years. He had neither needed nor wanted a woman in a long while, but now he felt an instantaneous physical craving for her.

The girl ordered a sidecar and sipped at it, and Andy forced himself to drink his beer. He wanted desperately to start a conversation with her but couldn't think of a way to begin. He waited, listening to the music, until she finished her drink.

"Miss," he said nervously, "could I buy you another?"

She turned and looked at him for a long moment, and he felt himself flush. "Yes," she said at last. "Thank you."

He ordered a sidecar for her and another beer for himself, and they began talking. He was amazed to discover that he was able to talk freely and easily to her, and that she in turn seemed interested in everything that he had to say. He had wanted to talk to anybody in the world, and talking to her was almost the answer to a prayer.

He told her everything about himself—his name, his job, and the sort of life he led. She didn't have much to say about herself.

Her name was Sara Malone and she was twenty-four, but that was all she volunteered.

From that point on the time flew by, and Andy was thankful that Whitey's had been closed. He wanted the evening to pass more slowly. He was happy, and he dreaded returning to his empty bed in his tiny room.

Finally she glanced at her watch, then smiled up at him. "I have to go," she said. "It's getting late."

"One more drink," he suggested.

"No," she said. "We've had enough. Let's go."

He helped her on with her coat and walked outside with her. He stood there on the sidewalk, awkwardly. "Sara," he said, "when can I see you again?"

She smiled, and it was a warm, easy smile. "You could come home with me. If you'd like to."

They walked quickly, with the blackness of the night around them like a blanket. And when they reached her apartment they kissed and they held each other. He took her, and lying there in her arms, with her firm breasts warm against his chest, he felt complete and whole again.

When he woke up the next morning she was already awake, and he smelled food cooking. He washed and dressed, then went into the kitchen for breakfast. It was a fine breakfast, and so very much better than toast and coffee at the Five Star Diner. He had to keep looking across the table at her to make sure that he was really awake and that she was really there. He couldn't believe what had happened, but the memory of last night was too vivid to leave room for doubt.

They didn't talk much during breakfast. He couldn't talk, afraid that he might do something to spoil it all. When he finished his second cup of coffee, he stood up regretfully.

"I have to go now," he said. "I have to be at work by nine."

"When will you be home? I'll have dinner ready."

"Right after work," he said. "About five-fifteen or so. Don't you have to work?" He remembered that she hadn't mentioned it last night.

"No. I have enough money for a while, so I don't work." She smiled. "Would you do me a favor?"

"Of course."

"I checked a package at the public library yesterday and forgot to pick it up on the way out. You work across the street from the library, don't you?"

He nodded.

"Here," she said. She took a ticket from her purse and handed it to him. "Will you get it for me?"

"Sure." He put the ticket in his pocket and slipped on his overcoat. He walked slowly to the door, and when he turned she was in his arms suddenly, kissing him. "I love you," he said. He walked lightly down the street, and she closed the door softly behind him.

His work went easily and quickly that day. He was anxious for five o'clock to roll around, but the memory of last night and the promise of the coming one made the time pass. At noon he picked up her parcel at the library, a small box wrapped in brown wrapping paper. He brought it home to her that night, and she put it on the top shelf in the closet.

Sara cooked him a good dinner, and he helped her with the dishes. They sat in the living room, listening to records, until it was time for bed. Then they made love, and he knew that he could never live without her again, that he could never sleep without her beside him.

Days passed and the nights. Andy had never been so happy and contented in his life. He settled into a routine once again, but it was a groove rather than a rut. His life before had lacked only a woman like Sara to make it complete, and now nothing was missing.

From time to time he thought of asking her to marry him. But, for some reason, he was afraid to. Everything was so perfect that he was hesitant to chance changing the arrangement. He let things remain as they were.

He knew very little about her, really. She seemed reluctant to talk about her past life. She didn't say how she was able to afford the luxurious apartment they lived in, or what she did during the days while he was at the office. He didn't press her. Nothing mattered, just so long as she was there for him when he arrived home.

She had him pick up packages frequently—about twice a week or so. They were always the same type—small boxes wrapped in brown wrapping paper. Sometimes they were in a locker at the bus depot, sometimes at the library, sometimes in a safety deposit box at the bank. He wondered idly what the boxes contained, but she wouldn't tell him, and he suspected it was some sort of medicine which she didn't want to mention. The question nagged at him, though. It bothered persistently. He didn't care about her earlier life, for that was beyond her now. But he wanted to know every- thing about her as she was now, wanted to share all of her life.

Inevitably, one evening he brought home a package and she was not home. He sat waiting for her, the package in his lap. He stared at the package, turning it over and over in his hands, as though he were trying to burn a hole in the wrapping paper with his eyes. Five, ten minutes passed, and he couldn't stand it any lon- ger. He untied the string, removed the wrapping paper, and opened the box.

The box was filled with a white powder. He looked at it, smelled it, and tasted a flake of it. It was nothing that he could recognize. He was wondering what the devil it could be when he heard a key in the lock, and he began guiltily to rewrap the package. Sara en- tered the room while he was still fussing with the string.

"Andy!" she cried. "What are you doing?"

"The package came undone," he said lamely. "I was rewrapping it for you."

She looked at him accusingly. "Did you see what was inside?"

"Yes," he said. "What was it, Sara?"

She took the box from him. "Never mind," she said. "Just some powder."

But this time he would not be put off. He had to know. "What is it? I'll find out anyway."

She let out a sigh. "I guess you had to find out. I . . ."

He waited.

"It's . . . horse, Andy."

"What!"

"Horse. Heroin."

"I know what 'horse' is," he said. "But what are you doing with it? You're not an addict, are you?" He couldn't believe what she had told him, but he knew from the expression on her face that she was telling the truth. Still, it was hard to believe, and he did not want to believe it.

"No," she said. "I'm not an addict. I'm what they call a pusher, Andy. I sell the heroin to addicts."

For a moment he could not speak. Finally he managed to say, "Why?"

She hesitated. "Money," she said. "I make lots of money. And it costs money for an apartment like this, and for good clothes and steak for dinner."

"You'll stop. I'm making enough money for us both, and you'll stop before you get caught. We'll get a smaller place somewhere and . . ."

"No," she cut in. "I won't get caught, Andy. And I want to keep on like this. I like steak, Andy. I like this place."

He stared at her. His mouth dropped open and he shook his head from side to side. "No! Sara, I won't let you!"

"I'm going to."

"I . . . I can't pick up any more packages for you."

She smiled. "Yes, you can. And you will, because you need me." She threw back her shoulders so that her breasts strained against the front of her dress. "We need each other, don't we?"

He stood up, and the package fell to the floor. He reached for her and lifted her in his arms, carrying her to the bedroom. And they came together fitfully and fiercely, as though the force of their bodies could erase everything else.

Later, when he was lying still beside her, she said, "In a way, it's better that you know. I'll need help with the business, and you can quit your job and help me. I guess it's better this way."

At that moment Andy began to distrust her. His love slowly dissolved, eventually to be replaced by an ever-increasing hatred.

The following morning he quit his job. It had never been an especially exciting job, but he had liked it. He liked the office and the people he worked with. He hadn't wanted to quit.

But he could never give up Sara. He couldn't live without her, couldn't sleep again in an empty bed. She had become a habit, a part of his routine, and he had to have her no matter what.

The days that followed were hell for him. Sara taught him the business step by step, from pickups and deliveries to actual sales. He learned how to contact an addict and take his money from him. He watched feverish men cook the heroin on a spoon and shoot it into a vein. And he watched Sara refuse a shot to an addict without money, and watched the man beg and plead while his hands twitched and his knees shook.

He thought he would lose his mind. He argued with Sara, telling her what a rotten thing she was doing, but he couldn't sway her. He saw her for what she was—cold, mercenary, and ruthless. And in her arms at night, he couldn't believe that she was the same woman.

Bit by bit, piece by piece, he learned the business. It became a routine after a while, but it was a routine which he hated. He settled into it, but he had trouble sleeping nights. Time after time he tried to leave her, but it was impossible.

One night he was siting in the living room, trying to read a magazine. She came over and sat beside him, taking the magazine from his hands. She handed him a brown cigarette, loosely packed. "Here," she said, smiling. "Smoke this."

"What! This is marijuana, isn't it?"

"That's right. Smoke it."

"Are you crazy?"

She smiled slowly and ran her hand up and down his thigh. "Don't be silly. I've been smoking pot for a long time now, and it doesn't hurt you. It makes you feel real fine. Try it?"

He drew away from her, his eyes searching hers. "I don't want to become an addict, Sara. I've seen the poor fish suffer, and I don't want it."

She laughed. "It's not habit-forming. I've been smoking since I was seventeen, and I just have a joint whenever I want one. You want to stay clear of horse, but this won't hurt you."

He drew a deep breath. "No," he said, firmly. "I don't want it."

Her hand worked on his thigh, and with her other hand she toyed with the buttons on her blouse. "You want me, though," she said, huskily. "Don't you, Andy?"

She put the cigarette between his lips and lit it, and made him smoke it quickly, drawing the pungent, acrid smoke deep into his lungs. At first he was dizzy; then his stomach churned and he was sick. But she only made him smoke another, and this time the smoke took hold of him and held him, and the room grew large and small and large again, and he made love to her with a thousand voices shrieking warning inside his brain.

And so marijuana, too, became a part of Andy's routine. He smoked as an alcoholic drank, losing his worries in the smoke. It was more a habit with him than it was with Sara. He grew to depend upon it, mentally if not physically.

And he learned things, too. He learned to smoke the joint down to a "roach," or butt, in order to get the maximum charge from it. He learned to hold as much smoke as he could in his lungs for as long as possible, in order to intensify the effect. He learned to smoke two or three joints in a row.

At the same time, he learned his business from start to finish. He bargained with contacts and squeezed the last cent from customers, burying his conscience completely. He gained an understanding of the operations of the narcotics racket, from the Big Man to the small-time pusher. Everything he did became part of him, and part of his routine.

He sat alone in the apartment one day, just after selling a cap of heroin to an addict. He opened a glassine envelope and idly poked the powder with the point of a pencil.

Horse, he thought. White Horse, the same as the bar where they had met. Valuable stuff. People killed for it, went through hell for it.

He sat looking at it for a long time, and then he folded a slip of paper and poured some of the powder on it. He raised the paper to his nose, closed his eyes, and sniffed deeply. He drew the flakes through his nostrils and into his lungs, and the heroin hit home.

It was a new sensation, a much bigger charge than marijuana had given him. He liked it. He threw away the slip of paper, put the heroin away, and leaned back to relax. Everything was pink and fuzzy, soft and smooth and cool.

He started sniffing heroin daily, and soon he noticed that he was physically aware of it when it was time for a fix. He began increasing the dosage, as his body began to demand more of the drug. And he didn't tell Sara anything about it.

His hate for her had grown, but it too became habitual. He learned to live with it. However, when they had a disagreement over the business, he realized that she was standing in the way.

Andy wanted to expand operations. He saw that, with a little effort and a little muscle, he and Sara could move up a notch and have a crowd of pushers under them. He explained it to her, step by step. It couldn't miss.

"No," she said, flatly. "We're doing fine right where we are. We make good money and nobody will want us out of the way."

"We could make more money," he said. "Lots more. The cops wouldn't be able to touch us."

"It's a risk."

He shrugged. "Everything's a risk. Walking across the street is a risk, but you can't stay on your own block forever. It's a chance we've got to take."

She refused, and once again she used her body as a bargaining point. At last he gave in, as always, but the hate was beginning to boil in him.

A few days later an addict came whining for a shot. Andy saw the way he trembled and twitched, but the spectacle didn't bother him any longer. He had seen it time and time again, until it was just a part of the day's work.

"Sorry, junkie," he said. "Come back when you raise the dough."

The man begged, and Andy started to push him out the door when a thought came to him. He opened the door and let the man in.

"C'mere," he said. "You got a spike?"

The addict nodded dumbly and pulled a hypodermic needle from his pocket. Andy took it from him and inspected it, turning it over and over in his hand. "Okay," he said at length. "A shot for your spike."

The man sighed with relief, then demanded, "How am I gonna take the shot without a spike?"

"Take it first; then get out."

Andy followed the addict into the bathroom and watched him heat the powder on a spoon. Then he filled the syringe and shot it into the vein in his arm. It hit immediately, and he relaxed.

"Thanks," he said. He handed the syringe to Andy. "Thanks."

"Get out." The addict left, and Andy closed the door after him.

He washed the syringe in hot water, then put some heroin on a spoon. He deftly filled the syringe and gave himself a shot in the fleshy part of his arm.

It was far more satisfying than sniffing the powder. It was stronger and faster. He felt good.

As the heroin became more and more a part of his life, he switched to the mainline, shooting it directly into the vein. It was necessary to him now, and he itched to build up his trade until he controlled narcotics in the town. He knew he could handle it. Already, he had virtually replaced Sara. She was the messenger now, while he handled the important end. But she still called the shots, for she still held the trump card. And no matter how he argued, she would simply rub herself up against him and kiss him, and the argument would be finished. So he could do nothing but wait.

And, at last, he was one day ready.

He took a long, sharp knife from the kitchen drawer and walked slowly to the bedroom, where she lay reading. She looked up from the magazine and smiled at him, stretching languorously.

"Hi," she said. "What's up?"

He returned the smile, keeping the knife behind his back. "I have news for you," he said. "We're expanding, like I suggested. No more small-time stuff, Sara."

She sighed. "Not again, Andy. I told you before . . ."

"This time *I'm* telling *you*."

"Oh," she said, amused. "Do you think you can get along without me?"

"I know I can."

"Really?" She threw back the bedcovers and smiled up at him. "You need me, Andy."

He forced himself to look at her. He ran his eyes over the firm breasts, the soft curves of her hips. He looked at her carefully, waiting for the familiar stir within him. It didn't come.

"I don't need you," he said, slowly. "Look."

He held out his right hand, the hand that held the knife. He unbuttoned the sleeve and rolled it down slowly, showing her the marks of the needle. "See? I'm a junkie, Sara. I only care about one thing, baby, and it isn't you. You don't show me a thing."

But her eyes were not on the marks on his arm. They were on the knife in his hand, and they were wide with fear.

"I don't need you at all," he went on. "I don't need liquor, I don't need sex, I don't need you. You're just dead wood, Sara."

She rose from the bed and moved toward him. "Andy," she cooed. "Andy, honey." Her whole body seemed to reach out for him, hungrily.

He shook his head. "Sorry," he said. "It just won't work anymore. I don't care about it. Just the horse is all that matters."

She looked into his eyes, and they were flat and uncaring. "Wait," she said. "We'll play it your way, Andy. We'll expand, like you said. Anything you say."

"You don't understand. I don't *need* you."

"Please!" she moaned. "Please!"

"Sorry. It's time for my shot." And he lowered the knife.

He moved toward her and she tried to back away, but he kept coming, the knife pointed at her. "No!" she shrieked. And she started to say something else, but before she could get the words out the knife was in her heart.

A SHROUD FOR THE DAMNED

SIGMUND OPENED THE DOOR SLOWLY and tiptoed inside. The door squeaked shut behind him as he headed for his room. The night was still and dark and Sigmund was very tired. He wanted to sleep.

"Sigmund!" He started at the voice.

She was sitting in the red armchair. At least it had been red once, many years and several owners ago. With the passage of time the color had faded almost entirely away, and in the dim lamplight the chair was an unimaginative gray. And she looked gray in the lamplight, with her hands so busy and her eyes so still. She looked as gray and as shop-worn as the old armchair.

"Hi, Ma," he said. "I thought you'd be sleeping." He smiled automatically and started once again for his room.

"Sigmund!" The voice caught him, halted him in his tracks, and turned him toward her once more.

"Come here, Sigmund."

He tiptoed at first, until he realized that she was awake and that she had seen him, and he had no reason to walk softly. He crossed to the side of the old armchair and stood there awkwardly, looking down at her, waiting for her to speak.

"Sit down," she said. "In the other chair. Sit down so your mother can talk to you. You're so tall I can't talk to you when you stand up. You grew fast this last year, Sigmund."

He started to protest, started to tell her how tired he was, then gave it up and took the seat across from her. He sat, watching her, and if her hands had not been moving all the while he would have thought that she was sleeping. But her hands moved, quick and sure, and they were as much alive as her eyes were dead.

"Sigmund," she said at last, "you were out late."

He looked away. "It's not so late."

"Late," she said, firmly. "You should come home early and be with your mother. Then maybe you could wake up mornings. It's not good you should sleep so late in the mornings." He didn't say anything. He started to tap his foot on the floor, slowly and rhythmically, but after a few experimental taps the foot stopped by itself.

"You know what I'm doing?"

"Knitting," he said.

"Smart boy. And do you know what I'm knitting?"

He shook his head, desiring only to end the conversation and crawl into his warm bed. But she had no one else to talk to, and she seemed so horribly alone, always looking desperately and methodically for something which was no longer present.

"You don't know," she said, accusingly. "In the old country you would know, but here . . ." She shrugged briefly and left the sentence dangling, unfinished.

Here we go, he thought. The old country bit again. You'd think she was still living there.

"It's a shroud," she said. "You know what's a shroud for?"

"Yeah. It's for when someone dies."

She nodded. "To wrap them. In the old country, when a person died he was wrapped in a shroud before they buried him. It was to keep out the spirits."

He looked at her hands and watched the long knitting needles flash back and forth. All right, he thought. But so what?

"Not here," she continued. "Not in this country, where they bury a man in a suit. Does it make sense? A suit? This will keep out spirits?"

He didn't answer, nor did she wait for an answer. "Your father once said that a person who made shrouds and grew food would never grow hungry. You understand?"

He didn't, but nodded anyway.

"Because," she said triumphantly, "if people lived, he sold food, and if they died, he sold shrouds. You understand?"

"Sure. I understand."

"But not in this country. Here they bury men in suits. Here a boy sixteen years old thinks just because he's tall he can stay out all night. It isn't right that children should come home so late."

He sighed. "Look, Ma. Listen a minute, will you? People don't buy shrouds here and you can't grow food in a crack in the sidewalk. You know what I mean?" His voice rose involuntarily and he lowered it.

"Ma, we have to eat. You can't sell your shrouds, and we have to eat. I brought money for you." He pulled some bills from his pocket and held them out to her.

She closed her eyes and silently refused the money. "Where did you get it, Sigmund?"

He looked away. "I got it. What's the difference where?"

She darted a look at him, and for an instant there was life again in her eyes. Then they were dull once more, dull and flat and tired. "You stole it," she said. "You are a thief."

He tightened his hands into fists and remained silent.

"My son is a thief. My son Sigmund stole money. A thief." And then she too was silent . . .

The silence came over him like a dark woolly blanket, more accusing than anything she could say. He had to break it. "Ma," he said at last, "don't you understand? Don't you?"

"I understand only that you are a thief."

"We need the money to live. You won't let me quit school and get a job . . ."

"A boy should go to school," she said.

"And you won't let me take a job on Saturdays . . ."

"No son of mine will work on the Sabbath."

"And you won't take the relief money . . ."

"Charity," she broke in. "Charity I don't want."

"And you don't have a job. So I have to steal, Ma. What else can I do?"

She didn't seem to hear his question. "I would work," she said slowly. "I would have a job. No one will hire me, not in this country."

Her eyes closed then, and only her hands moved. It was the same argument, the same words that Sigmund had heard a hundred times in the past. Either he would be a thief or she would go hungry, it was that simple.

He stood up and walked quietly to the kitchen. He took the lid from the cookie jar and noted that only a handful of change remained. She could spend it well enough, even if she never took it directly from him or acknowledged the source of the money. He grinned sadly and placed the bills in the jar.

He slept well that night. There were dreams, unpleasant ones, but he was tired enough to sleep anyway and he didn't hear the alarm clock in the morning. And once again he was almost an hour late for school.

SCHOOL ENDED, FINALLY. The classes were dull and the teachers were something of a nuisance, but Sigmund clenched his hands into fists and lived through it, just as he lived through the flight from Poland long ago. He would clench his hands into tight little fists, and sometimes lower his eyelids, and everything passed in time.

Lucci was waiting for him after school. Lucci was the same age but not as tall as Sigmund. But Lucci's mother was dead and Lucci's father drank red wine all day, so Lucci did not go to school.

"Tonight," Lucci said. "We'll go out tonight, okay?"

Sigmund hesitated. "It's cold out. It'll be cold as ice tonight."

"So what? You can use the gold, can't you?"

Sigmund nodded.

"So we'll go out then. Want to shoot some pool?"

"I can't," said Sigmund. "No money."

Lucci shrugged. "What the hell, we're buddies, aren't we? I'll treat."

They were buddies, and they went to the small poolroom on Christie Street where the cigar smoke was thick and warm in the air. They played two games of eight-ball and one game of straight and one game of Chicago, and they each smoked two of Lucci's cigarettes, and Lucci paid for all the games. Then it was time to go. They shook hands warmly because they were buddies and Sigmund walked home for his dinner. It was so cold on the street that he could see his breath in front of his eyes, hovering in the air like the cigar smoke in the poolroom. He shuddered.

When he opened the door he could smell food cooking on the stove, but otherwise he would not have known that his mother had moved at all since the previous night. She was sitting again in the red armchair, her fingers flying as they skillfully manipulated the slender needles. She looked up as he came in.

"It is cold out," she said. "You are almost blue from the cold, Sigmund."

He rubbed his hands together. "It's not that bad." He took off his jacket and hung it on a peg on the wall. When he turned around she was holding her knitting up proudly.

"Look," she said. "It's almost finished. Weeks I have worked on it, and it's almost finished."

He forced himself to smile. "That's good. That's real good, Ma."

"Tonight it will be done." She stood up slowly and beckoned to him. "Come, let us eat."

The food was good. There was tender boiled cabbage and lamb stew and milk, and Sigmund enjoyed the meal. He ate quickly despite her frequent injunctions to chew his food more thoroughly, and he stood up from the table as soon as he was finished.

"That was a good meal, Ma."

She frowned at him. "Where are you going? You're not going out, Sigmund?"

"Yeah. There's a guy I have to meet."

"No," she said. "Not one of your hoodlum friends, not in this weather. It's too cold for your hoodlum friends."

"I've got to go out," he said, uncomfortably. "It's not that cold."

"All night you'll be out. All night you'll be freezing in the cold with your hoodlums. Don't go, please."

He leaned over and pecked at her forehead. "Good-bye, Ma. I'll try to be home early." He grabbed his jacket from the peg and hurried out the door, managing to escape her final words.

THE NIGHT WAS COLD and the wind blew through the thin jacket. But Lucci was waiting at the corner, a smile playing on his thin lips, a light dancing in his eyes. "It's too early," Lucci said. "Let's have a game of pool."

They played two games of eight-ball and a game of Chicago at the place on Christie Street. Sigmund lost all three games, as he always lost when they played, and Lucci paid for all three, as he always paid. Then Lucci said it was time enough, and they set the cue sticks on the tabletop and hurried into the night.

They walked west, through the cold clutter of the streets toward the Bowery. "This is the ticket," Lucci explained. "You just give a drunk a tap on the head and he's out for the night. Just a little tap and we take his gold. But don't tap too hard, 'cause they get soft in the head from drinking, and you'll squash their heads like a melon."

Sigmund saw a drunk, weaving back and forth along the sidewalk. "Him?"

"No, too seedy. You got to pick a guy with money."

They walked on, passing up some as too run-down and others as too sober, until Lucci saw a victim. They surrounded the man and Lucci chopped him across the temple and the man went to the ground without protest. It was very easy.

But the drunk's pockets yielded only seven dollars and change, so they kept on looking. The wind grew colder and colder, and few men were on the streets, but they didn't give up.

They saw the man then, out of place on the Bowery. They walked up behind him and Sigmund hit him hard on the head, but the man did not lose consciousness as the other had. Instead he stared up from the sidewalk and opened his mouth to scream.

Lucci kicked him, a short, hard kick in the side of the head. The man's head rolled slightly on the pavement, his eyes closed, and he died.

"Christ!" said Lucci. He grabbed for the man's wallet and they ran in panic down the street. At the corner they divided the money and split up.

Sigmund's share for the night was sixty dollars. It was more money than he had ever had before, more money than he had seen in a long time. But the man was dead and cold on the cold sidewalk, and the icy wind could not stop the sweat from forming steadily on Sigmund's brow.

The man was dead. The thought was colder than the wind, and the wind was very cold.

HE OPENED THE DOOR and tiptoed inside, softly. The door squeaked shut behind him and she looked up across the room from the faded red armchair. Although her eyes were flat and lifeless, they seemed to look right through him.

"Sigmund," she said.

He rubbed his hands together to warm them. He was cold, very cold. He took off his jacket and hung it on the peg.

"You're cold," she said. "On a night like this you had to go out. Stealing, on a night like this."

She looked into his eyes then, and he returned the look. For a moment her eyes were alive again, burning into him. But the life vanished as suddenly as it had appeared.

"I want to go to sleep," he said. "Ma, I . . . I want to go right to sleep."

She took a deep breath and released it slowly, almost as though she were reluctant to let go of it. Then she stood up, slowly, lifting the black garment and holding it in front of her. "Sigmund, tonight you'll be cold. It's a cold night, this one."

He was shivering. "I know. That's why I want to go to bed now."

"Do me a favor. Wear this." She reached out her hands, offering the shroud to him. "Do it for your mother."

"What for?"

"It's warm. Believe me, it's a warm thing."

"But it's a shroud, Ma."

"So? In this country, it's just something else to wrap in. They don't have shrouds, not in this country."

He started to back away. "I don't need it. Honest."

"Take it," she said. "Tight stitching it's got, so it should be warm. Please."

He shrugged and took the shroud from her, then hurried to his room. He undressed rapidly, wrapped himself in the shroud, and got into bed. It was warm, anyhow, and it was a very cold night.

She stayed for a long time in the red armchair. She sat very still, and now even her hands were motionless. Time passed slowly.

She stood up at last and walked to his room. The door was slightly ajar. She pushed it open and entered.

"Sigmund," she whispered. "Are you asleep?"

There was no answer. He lay very still, not tossing as much as he had done on recent nights. The shroud was wrapped neatly around him, almost covering his face.

"Sigmund," she repeated, and again there was no response.

She looked then, at the knitting needle that she held in her right hand. She looked at it for several minutes, and she knew what had to be done. She would do it swiftly, just as her husband had done to the German many years ago.

Carefully she lifted the blanket back, exposing the shrouded form. Then, in one motion, she jabbed the long slender needle through the shroud and into the body at the base of the spine. The boy twitched once, as the German had done, and then lay still.

She pulled out the knitting needle and washed it in the sink. Then she returned to the faded red armchair and sat in it, thinking. He would be warm now. The shroud would keep him warm.

And he would be good, for the shroud would keep the evil spirits from him.

After some time she picked up the needles and her ball of yarn. She began to knit again, and at first her fingers moved very slowly. Gradually they picked up speed, and her hands moved faster and faster.

SWEET LITTLE RACKET

THE NEWSPAPER SEEMED TO OPEN by itself to the classified ads. You get that way after a while. You get so used to fumbling through the paper every morning, hunting for a job, then folding the paper up and throwing it against the wall. It's a regular routine—not the greatest bit in the world—but one that sort of grows on you when you go long enough without working.

I was sick of it. I ran my eyes down the column but there was nothing, nothing worth wasting my time on. I folded the paper methodically and flung it against the wall. It didn't help; I still felt lousy.

If I were just a punk I wouldn't mind it, but I wasn't used to wasting my time sitting around a crummy room. I was never rich, but I used to have a red-hot little liquor store that made nice money.

I cut prices and did a volume business until they brought in Fair Trade and knocked the business to hell. Then the heavy taxes on small businesses made things just that much worse. Bit by bit the business fell apart.

Five months. Five months without working, five months doing nothing, and all because the big boys had things rigged against the little man. I could have gone out and grabbed a two-bit job, but there's no sense working for somebody else. You never get any place that way.

I stood up, ready to go down the street for a beer before the landlady came around and yelled for the rent, when the idea hit me. I just couldn't go on like this anymore. And I hit on a way to set up a handy little business all my own, a business the big boys couldn't pull out from under me.

The big boys had the world nicely wrapped around their pinkies. But when everything stacks up so perfectly for you, that's the time you have to be careful. You scare easy. You hedge your bets and quit taking the chances that brought you to the top.

All I needed was a couple of big boys who were afraid. If I could scare five of them to the tune of fifty bucks a week, I would be set up with a little business pulling down two and a half yards per. And that was handy money to a loner like me. No wife and kids to feed—no folks to support—it could be big dough. And the big boys can afford fifty a week with no headaches.

The first big boy I wanted to get was Gargan. James Gargan of Gargan Motors, the fat slob who repossessed my buggy when I fell a few months back in the payments. He could afford the fifty, that was certain enough. And I'd like to be sitting on his payroll.

I drafted a letter to Gargan and read it over. It looked good—simple and to the point. He was to mail fifty dollars a week to me, or one of his kids might get hit by a car. Nice and simple. I could picture his face while he read the letter. First he'd think it was a bluff. Then he'd start wondering. And finally he'd decide it didn't matter whether it was a bluff or not. Hell, he couldn't chance anything happening to one of his kids, could he?

And the next thing he knew, he'd be slipping a brand-new fifty in an envelope and addressing it to me.

You know I almost mailed that letter. I was halfway down the street to the mailbox before I realized what a stupid play that would be. I remembered reading somewhere that there were two kinds of blackmail, the only difference being whether the threat came by letter or in person. By letter was a felony; in person was only a misdemeanor. Sending that letter would have been one of the dumbest things ever.

Instead, I walked into Mr. Gargan's office that afternoon. I gave him the pitch, laying it right on the line. Then I leaned back in my chair and stared at him.

For several minutes he didn't say anything, but I could hear his mind working it out. Then he blew a cloud of cigar smoke at the ceiling and said, "I suppose you know this is blackmail."

I just smiled in his face.

"I could have you arrested," he went on. "I could call a policeman and have you arrested immediately."

"How would you prove it?"

"They'd take my word for it."

I shrugged. "You're a smart man, Mr. Gargan. You don't figure I'm working this all by myself, do you? If you lock me up, your kid'll get it just the same."

He chewed on the cigar and I wondered whether he'd have the guts to call my bluff. But he didn't.

"Fifty dollars?"

I nodded.

"I'm to send it to you?"

I shook my head. "No," I said. "I'll pick it up every Monday afternoon, and you can start the ball rolling this afternoon. Just put me on your payroll for fifty bucks."

"You bastard," he said. He considered for another moment and stood up, reaching in his pocket for his wallet. He slipped me two twenties and a ten and swore at me again.

"It's just a business," I told him. "Don't take it so hard, Mr. Gargan." Before he could answer I turned around and walked out.

One time at the liquor store I jabbed a hypodermic needle through the corks in half a dozen bottles of imported Scotch, drained them dry, and filled them again with a cheap blend. That had been easy money, but the fifty bucks I had in my pocket right now was the easiest money ever. And it was steady: Gargan would kick in with fifty every Monday, without even whimpering from here on in.

I paid off the landlady and bought a couple shirts. I took a girl to my room for the evening. That damn near shot the fifty, but I wasn't figuring on living the rest of my life on fifty dollars per; $250 would be a lot more like it.

I picked another customer Tuesday, a guy named Theodore Sims. He ran a big insurance agency on Wilkin Street, and I came on telling him I wanted to sell him some insurance. He tried to hustle me out the door, but by the time I finished my spiel he was sitting down again and doing some heavy thinking. I walked out of there ten minutes later with another fifty in my pocket and another client on my list.

Choosing my customers was the most important part. If I picked a guy who couldn't drop fifty a week without noticing it, I'd get in trouble eventually. If I tabbed a muscle boy with more guts than brains, my bluff wouldn't stand a chance.

But I was careful.

I added my name to another payroll on Wednesday and another on Thursday. Both times I spruced up my pitch a little, starting off with the insurance salesman bit and moving right into the regular routine. I got smoother and smoother, until by Friday I had myself believing that they were in for trouble if they didn't come across.

Of course, no matter what they did they were safer than a virgin in a roomful of eunuchs. I wasn't going to take a swipe at anybody's kid, and I didn't even have a car to run a kid down with if I felt like it. But the big boys don't have to take chances, and that's why I cleared two hundred bucks the first week.

Friday was a day of rest. I had plenty of time to find a fifth sucker, and besides it was a good day to go to the beach. I took a quick dip in the water and spread out a blanket on the sand, letting the sun burn down on me and thinking what a nice little business I had. The nicest thing was the absence of competition. There was no heavy operator to push me out of the catbird's seat.

On Monday, Gargan started to make noises until I reminded him that I could always raise the ante if he didn't behave himself.

The others were respectfully quiet. Another week, another two hundred for me—and with no taxes to pay. Who could ask for a better setup?

Two hundred was enough, when you came right down to it. I'm not a guy with expensive tastes. Sure, I like a drink when I'm dry and a woman now and then, and I like expensive Scotch and high-priced women, but two hundred a week will buy plenty of liquor and sex. I'm not a pig.

It went on that way for about two months. It was a regular routine: Gargan on Monday, Sims on Tuesday, Lon Butler on Wednesday, and David Clark on Thursday. I had regular working hours, and my wages came to something like fifty bucks an hour.

It even became a routine for my customers. After a while we didn't even bother to talk to each other. I walked into the office, picked up my money, and walked out. That was all there was to it.

My landlady was thrilled. She got her rent right on the button without asking twice, and she never had it so good. She must have wondered where the hell I was getting the dough, but that was none of her business and she had enough sense to keep her nose out. She was strictly business. As long as I paid on time, she kept her eyes closed and her mouth shut.

That was the main reason I kept on living in my little dump. But I found other things to spend the money on. I picked up an Italian silk suit and some decent shoes, bought a radio for the room, and even got some pictures for the walls. I gave one of my broads a silk nightgown and she was extra-good to me from that point on.

I even bought a car. With a steady income, it was no headache keeping up payments. I latched onto a little foreign job with wire wheels and plenty of speed. It was nice, sitting behind the wheel of the car and opening her up. It was particularly nice when I stopped to think how the car was being paid for.

Nice, huh?

But after a while the idea of another half a yard a week began looking better and better. I could get along without it all right, but fifty bucks more wouldn't hurt. I took my time, trying to pick the perfect mark. I was set up so perfectly that there was no point in risking everything unless I had a sure thing. I took my time and waited.

And I found my mark.

He was a doctor, a rich man's doctor by the name of Alfred Sanders. He had a good-looking wife and a little boy named Jerry. He loved his wife, he loved his kid. It looked pretty perfect.

I called Dr. Sanders during the week and made an appointment for Friday afternoon. He had a spot open, and that struck me as funny. My only open afternoon, and he could fit me in!

His layout on Middlesex Road was something to see—brick front, a lawn like a putting green, and rugs on the floor that you could get lost in. His nurse showed me into the office and I took a seat.

"I'm selling insurance," I began.

He smiled. "I wish you had told me over the phone," he said. "I'm sorry, Mr. Boyle, but I have all the insurance I need. As a matter of fact, I'm probably overinsured as it stands. You see—"

"Not this kind of insurance." And then I let him have it from beginning to end.

"I see," he said when I finished. He stood up and began pacing the floor slowly, swinging his arms as he walked. "Could you give me a quick run-down on your proposition again? I missed some of the details."

I gave it to him again. Hell, I had all the time in the world.

When I got through he asked me a few questions, and I fed him the answers. I tried to sound as tough as I could. It wasn't hard; I had the whole business down pat by now.

"That should do it," he said suddenly, grinning. "I want you to hear something, Mr. Boyle. I believe you'll find it interesting."

He walked over to a cabinet on the wall that he had passed while pacing the floor. He opened the cabinet, and I saw a tape recorder with the spools revolving slowly. My eyes almost fell out of my head.

His grin widened. "Do you understand, Mr. Boyle? Or should I play it back for you?"

I started sweating. "Okay," I said. "So what does it get you? You can't call copper or my associate will play rough with Jerry. So where are you, Doc?"

"That's true," he said. "But you don't get your pound of flesh, do you? Not while I have this on tape. Fifty dollars a week would hardly send me to the workhouse, Mr. Boyle. But I don't like blackmailers and I don't plan on paying blackmail. Get out!"

I got out. I got out in a hurry, not wasting time to get in a last word. I was lucky to get out, for that matter. He had me by the throat, and the baloney about an "associate" was the only thing that saved me from a blackmail rap.

What the hell, $200 was plenty. I still had enough to pay for the car and the liquor and the women and the rent, and I didn't need the extra fifty, not really. It would have been nice but I learned a lesson from it. I wouldn't get greedy anymore.

I stayed in my room all night, thinking how lucky I was and how I nearly shot everything to hell. At one point I started to shake. Here I was with a perfect racket, and a stupid try for fifty bucks I didn't even need nearly bollixed up the works.

That was yesterday. Today was Saturday, and it was another good day for the beach. I thought of calling up a woman but I figured it would be a good day to be alone. A few minutes after noon I hopped into the sportscar and headed for the beach. I found a little spot all to myself and took it easy, getting through the whole day without bumping into anyone I knew or starting a conversation with anybody.

I was feeling good by the time I got back from the beach. The afternoon all by myself did it. That and the sun and the water got my mind off Dr. Sanders and the way I had balled things up. It was dark out by the time I parked the car out in front and walked up the stairs to my room.

I chalked up yesterday's goof to profit and loss. Hell, the best small business in the world can't come out ahead every time.

I stretched out on the bed and turned on the radio. It came on in the middle of a newscast, and I reached for the dial to try and get some music. News always bores the hell out of me, and after lying in the sun all day I just wanted to listen to some music and relax.

I got my hand on the dial and was ready to turn it, but the news item got through to me just in time. My fingers let go of the dial as if it was red hot.

It was a fairly ordinary news item, about some kid who got gunned down by a car that afternoon while I was at the beach.

It seems the kid's name was Jerry Sanders.

It seems the car was a little foreign job with wire wheels.

The radio's going now. I can't concentrate on the music too well, because all I can think of is how no matter how good a business you set up, something's going to pull it out from under you.

The cops should be here any minute.

THE WAY TO POWER

HE OPENED THE DOOR IN HIS BATHROBE and motioned me inside. "Have a seat, Joe," he said. "Relax a little."

I took a seat, and it was easy to relax in the soft, plush cushions. I looked around the room and the familiar feeling of awe hit me. I had been to his house maybe a thousand times, but I never missed feeling the lushness of the place.

"Drink?"

I nodded, and went on filling my eyes while he went for drinks. I took it all in, from the Mexican jade on the mantel to the ivory-and-ebony chess table. He had done well. Damned well.

He brought the drinks, and I forced myself to sip mine, rather than throw it straight down. It was Scotch, and straight from Scotland. Nothing but the best for him, ever.

I looked up at him from my drink. He had taken a seat in an equally plush chair across from me, and was waiting expectantly. I played the game.

"Thanks, Chief. What's up?"

"Lucci. He doesn't understand."

I knew what he was talking about, but I also knew how he liked to play it. "What do you mean, Chief?"

"Phil Lucci," he said. "Remember I mentioned him?"

"I remember."

His eyes narrowed, until I could hardly see the red veins that mapped them. "He's making book, still. Three weeks ago he was told to pay off or lay off, one or the other. He wouldn't join the mob, and he wouldn't quit taking bets. You know what that means, Joe."

I knew, of course. The Chief was about as subtle as a Coney Island prostitute. But the Chief ran every racket in Central City, and he had the town in his pocket. So when the Chief wanted to tell me something, I let him tell me.

"He's gotta lose," he said. "He has to lose all the way, the big loss." He paused for effect, but I was so used to the gesture that it was lost on me. "Joe, Lucci's gotta die."

I could have dropped it there, but he would have missed all his fun. He was all keyed up for his big speech, and I couldn't afford to let him down. His eyes were waiting, expectant. So I let him have his kicks.

"Why, Chief? All he's costing us is maybe ten bucks a day. Why do we rub him out?"

He stood up then. He stood up and threw what was left of the imported Scotch straight into his stomach, and his eyes were shining. "Power," he said, and the word seemed to come from the inside of a bass drum. "Power," he repeated.

"Joe," he went on, "the money doesn't matter. Oh, it's nice to have, but if you worry about it you're through. The money is just the chips in the pot, just a way to keep score. The thing is, you have to be on top. You have to have power.

"There was this German guy named Nietzsche who figured it all out, and for a Square-head he made a lot of sense. He said the important thing, the thing that makes a man superior, is his Will to Power. A man who wants to be on top, just for the hell of it, he's the guy to be."

He paused for a breath, and I finished my drink. "A smart guy," he said. "I read every one of his books."

He had told me this at least twenty times. "Every one?" I marveled.

"Every one. Every goddamned one." He sat down heavily in his seat and let out a deep sigh. Evidently the performance had exhausted him.

"Joe," he said, "I can't let anyone get in the way. I gotta stay on top. I gotta keep every bit of my power, and that's why Lucci has to die. Does that make sense?"

"Damn good sense."

"You said it, boy. You said it." He seemed almost relieved, as if he had expected me to argue with him.

"Look, Chief," I said, when he didn't say anything, "what do you expect from me? I mean, you don't want me to gun him, do you? I will if you want, but I'm not a torpedo."

"No, I don't want you for that. I got a million guns. But I don't want him gunned at all. Dammit, Joe, we can't risk another shooting. We've had five already this year."

"I don't get it," I said, because I didn't. "Chief, you have the whole force in your pocket. If you give the word, every cop in town buries his head in the sand and stuffs cotton in his ears. What's the worry over a shooting?"

He shook his head. "Sure I've got the cops. But the citizens don't know this. The citizens don't understand how the ball bounces. When there are enough unsolved homicides, they get upset. They switch mayors. They switch cops. They switch everything. And then where the hell am I?"

I nodded slowly. He was no moron. He had used his head to get where he was.

"I want to nail him sort of indirect," he said. "But I'm not sure how. That's why I called you. Figure a way."

I closed my eyes and began stroking my chin with my left hand. This was one of the big reasons he tolerated me—he was convinced I was a thinker. He would have me come to his house and think until I told him what he had already said, and he knew then that I must be a genius.

I made him feel powerful, and he liked that. That's the only reason he tolerated anyone. Ruthie made him feel powerful too. She would crawl on her belly to him, begging him to take her. The last girl he had didn't crawl to him one night, and he got irritated and broke her back. So Ruthie crawls, and I can't really blame her.

But she didn't always crawl for him. There was a time when she would have crawled to me, and not because she was afraid of getting a broken back. But that was a long time ago.

So I stroked my chin like a baboon and thought. It was more difficult than usual, since I didn't have the slightest idea what he wanted me to suggest. He seemed to want me to come up with an idea all on my own.

And I did. It was strange, for it was about the first idea I had ever had all by myself, at least since I started working for the Chief. But I had an idea, and the more I thought about it the better it sounded. I opened my eyes and looked up at him. He was waiting.

"I got it," I said. "We'll frame him."

The Chief got a happy look in his eyes. He liked new gimmicks, and this sounded like a fairly new way to take a boy for a ride. "Go on," he said. "Go on, Joe."

"We'll frame him for murder," I said. "We'll knock off someone, some Skid Row bum, and we'll tie it to him. The cops will pick him up right away, because you'll tell them to. And we'll have thirty guys swear they saw Lucci kill the guy. And you'll tell the judge to hang him, and he will."

He hesitated, and I gave him the clincher. "You've got the power," I said, reverently. "You can pull something like this off perfectly."

That did it, of course. *Power* was the magic word to the Chief. "Yes," he said, sliding the word over his tongue. "I could do it. And it would be perfect, wouldn't it?"

I nodded.

"Yes," he repeated. "Perfect." He smiled a big, oily smile. "When do you want to pull it off?"

"Tonight!" I practically shouted the word. His enthusiasm was suddenly contagious, and this time it was *my* idea. I was all caught up in the beauty of it.

"Tonight?" He smiled. "Okay, Joe. Who do you think ought to gun the tramp?"

I thought a moment, and although I didn't want to come up with the answer I couldn't help myself. "I'll do it," I said, calmly. "The less people on to this caper, the better it is. I'll fix it."

He smiled wider this time. "Now you're talking," he said. "You're starting to understand what power means, Joe. I'll get you a gun."

He vanished and came back in a minute. "Here you go," he said, handing me a lightweight .38 automatic. "It's clean, Joe. No registration, no nothing. Just wipe it off and drop it, and it might as well be Lucci's as anyone else's."

I took it from him and fitted it to my grip. It felt good. I pocketed it and stood up. "Okay," I said. "I'll be right back, by nine-thirty at the latest. Wait up for me and we can talk over the next part, huh?"

"That's the ticket," he said. "I'll be waiting right here. Of course," he added, "I may have to go upstairs and spend a few minutes with Ruthie." He winked. "She'd go nuts otherwise."

I smiled nervously, shook hands with him, and walked down the long driveway to my car. It was a fine car, a new Pontiac, and while it didn't measure up to his Caddy, it got me wherever I was going. It was one of the benefits of being the Chief's lieutenant.

That, and a good apartment, and money in the bank. The only loss involved had been Ruthie, and I stopped caring about her after the first month or so. She was just a woman, and the world is full of them. There were other things that were much more important. Power, perhaps. The Chief and Nietzsche had something there.

I drove onto Clinton Street and down toward the waterfront. It was only a little way to Skid Row, the street of broken dreams and broken men. It was the place where nobody really cared about anything, and where everyone waited hopefully for death. Killing a wino would hardly seem like murder. The poor sonofabitch would neither know nor care what happened to him.

I drove slowly once I hit Halsey Street. I didn't want to park the car and chase around on foot. I wanted one good shot from the front window. Then I would drive like hell for two blocks, then slow down and head back to the Chief's home. It would be simple enough.

I circled up and down the Row a good four or five times, and I never managed to get off a shot. There were either too many lights or not enough light to see by, either a crowd of bums or no bums at all.

I was almost ready to give up for the night when I got another idea, an original idea. It was my second original idea of the evening, and I just couldn't pass it up. It was a good idea too. So I drove partway back on Clinton and made a phone call at a drugstore.

I returned to the Chief's place at 9:30, right on the dot. I rang the bell and waited for him. He took a long time answering, and he was panting slightly when he opened the door. It was easy to guess where he had been, but he had to spell it out for me.

"What a woman!" he oozed. "She goes crazy for me."

I nodded and walked into the house. I sat down in the chair without waiting for an invitation.

"Joe," he said, "I really didn't expect you back so soon. How did it go, boy?"

"Fine," I said. "Smooth as silk, Chief."

"Good," he said. "You've got a head on your shoulders, Joe." He left the room, and came back with another pair of drinks. I took one, only this time I didn't bother to sip it. I threw it right down.

"Now what?" he asked. "Do we just wait till a prowl cop tumbles to it?"

"Relax," I said. "It's all taken care of, Chief."

He gave me a puzzled look, and I stole a glance at my watch: 9:45.

Just then the doorbell rang. He was right on time. The Chief started to stand up, but I beat him to it. "Stay there," I said. "I'll get it." I went to the door and let him in.

He walked in almost apologetically, holding his hat in his hands. "Okay," he said. "I'll deal. Start talking."

The Chief nearly hit the ceiling. "Lucci!" he screamed.

Lucci shrugged. "That's the name," he said. "You wanted to deal, right? Wanted to straighten everything out?"

I couldn't wait much longer. I was afraid the Chief would have an apoplectic fit. I drew the .38 automatic from my pocket and pointed it at the Chief. I fired it three times, and the slugs hit him solidly in the stomach, chest, and head. He was dead in almost no time at all.

And just before he died he didn't look powerful at all. He looked weak as a kitten.

I turned to Lucci, and he was utterly dumbfounded. I wiped off the .38 and tossed it on the floor. He looked from the gun to me and back to the gun. The fear danced crazily in his eyes.

"You'd better run," I said. "You'd better run, Lucci."

He ran. I drew slowly, and I fired my .45 just as he reached the door. I shot him three times, too. He died quickly.

Then I sat back and waited. I didn't have long to wait. The prowl cop was right around the corner, and he heard the shots and came running. He took a look at the two men and let out a whoop.

"What happened?"

I pointed to Lucci. "He shot the Chief," I said. "And I shot him."

"Gosh," said the cop. He was a new boy, and this was his first homicide.

"The Chief was cracking down on him," I explained, "and this crumb tried to even things up a little."

"Gosh," repeated the cop. "It's good you shot him. Nice shooting."

"It was an easy shot," I said. "Nothing to it."

"Sure," he said. "But it was a good thing you had your gun."

"We're all required to carry them twenty-four hours a day."

He shrugged. "Not everyone does, though. It was still good work, Lieutenant."

I smiled at the kid. "Thanks," I said. "But it doesn't bring back the Chief, does it?"

I smiled again, sadly. I felt almost like a father to the cop. He was young, but he'd learn.

I wondered if Ruthie was still awake.

I felt powerful as all hell.

YOU CAN'T LOSE

ANYONE WHO STARVES IN THIS COUNTRY deserves it. Almost anybody who is dumb enough to want to work can get a job without any back-breaking effort. Blindies and crips haul in twenty-five bucks an hour bumming the Times Square district. And if you're like me—able-bodied and all, but you just don't like to work, all you got to do is use your head a little. It's simple.

Of course, before you all throw up your jobs, let me explain that this routine has its limitations. I don't eat caviar, and East Third Street is a long way from Sutton Place. But I never cared much for caviar, and the pad I have is a comfortable one. It's a tiny room a couple blocks off the Bowery, furnished with a mattress, a refrigerator, a stove, a chair, and a table. The cockroaches get me out of bed, dress me, and walk me down to the bathroom down the hall. Maybe you couldn't live in a place like that, but I sort of like it. There's no problem keeping it up, 'cause it couldn't get any worse.

My meals, like I said, are not caviar. For instance, in the refrigerator right now I have a sack of coffee, a dozen eggs, and part of a fifth of bourbon. Every morning I have two fried eggs and a cup of coffee. Every evening I have three fried eggs and two cups of coffee. I figure, you find something you like, you should stick with it.

And the whole thing is cheap. I pay twenty a month for the room, which is cheap anywhere and amazing in New York. And in this neighborhood food prices are pretty low too.

All in all, I can live on ten bucks a week with no trouble. At the moment I have fifty bucks in my pocket, so I'm set for a month, maybe a little more. I haven't worked in four months, haven't had any income in three.

I live, more or less, by my wits. I hate to work. What the hell, what good are brains if you have to work for a living? A cat lives fifty, sixty, maybe seventy years, and that's not a long time. He might as well spend his time doing what he likes. Me, I like to walk around, see people, listen to music, read, drink, smoke, and get a dame. So that's what I do. Since nobody's paying people to walk around or read or anything, I pick up some gold when I can. There's always a way.

By this I don't mean that I'm a mugger or a burglar or anything like that. It might be tough for you to get what I'm saying, so let me explain.

I mentioned that I worked four months ago, but I didn't say that I only held the job for a day. It was at a drugstore on West 96th Street. I got a job there as a stock and delivery boy on a Monday morning. It was easy enough getting the job. I reported for work with a couple of sandwiches in a beat-up gym bag. At four that afternoon I took out a delivery and forgot to come back. I had twenty shiny new Zippo lighters in the gym bag, and they brought anywhere from a buck to a buck-seventy-five at the Third Avenue hockshops. That was enough money for three weeks, and it took me all of one day to earn it. No chance of him catching me, either. He's got a fake name and a fake address, and he probably didn't notice the lighters were missing for a while.

Dishonest? Obviously, but so what? The guy deserved it. He told me straight off the Puerto Ricans in the neighborhood were not the cleverest mathematicians in the world, and when I made a sale

I should short-change them and we'd split fifty-fifty. Why should I play things straight with a bum like that? He can afford the loss. Besides, I worked one day free for him, didn't I?

It's all a question of using your head. If you think things out carefully, decide just what you want, and find a smart way to get it, you come out ahead, time after time. Like the way I got out of going to the army.

The army, as far as I'm concerned, is strictly for the sparrows. I couldn't see it a year ago, and I still can't. When I got my notice I had to think fast. I didn't want to try faking the eye chart or anything like that, and I didn't think I would get away with a conscientious objector pitch. Anyway, those guys usually wind up in stir, or working twice as hard as everybody else. When the idea came to me it seemed far too simple, but it worked. I got myself deferred for homosexuality.

It was a panic. After the physical I went in for the psychiatric, and I played the beginning fairly straight, only I acted generally hesitant.

Then the doc asks, "Do you like girls?"

"Well," I blurt out, "only as friends."

"Have you ever gone with girls?"

"Oh, no!" I managed to sound somewhat appalled at the idea.

I hesitated for a minute or two, then admitted that I was homosexual. I was deferred, of course.

You'd think that everybody who really wanted to avoid the army would try this, but they won't. It's psychological. Men are afraid of being homosexual, or of having people think they're homosexual. They're even afraid of some skull doctor who never saw them before and never will see them again. So many people are so stupid, if you just act a little smart you can't miss. After the examination was over I spent some time with the whore who lives across the hall from me. No sense talking myself into anything. A cat doesn't watch out, he can be too smart, you know.

To get back to my story—the money from the Zippos lasted two weeks, and I was practically broke again. This didn't bother me though. I just sat around the pad for a while, reading and smoking, and sure enough, I got another idea that I figured would be worth a few bucks. I showered and shaved, and made a half-hearted attempt at shining my shoes. I had some shoe polish from the drugstore. I had had some room in the gym bag after the Zippos, so I stocked up on toothpaste, shoe polish, aspirins, and that kind of junk. Then I put on the suit that I keep clean for emergencies. I usually wear dungarees, but once a month I need a suit for something, so I always have it clean and ready. Then, with a tie on and my hair combed for a change, I looked almost human. I left the room, splurged fifteen cents for a bus ride, and got off at Third Avenue and 60th Street. At the corner of Third and 59th is a small semi-hockshop that I cased a few days before. They do more buying and selling than actual pawning, and there aren't too many competitors right in the neighborhood. Their stock is average—the more common and lower-priced musical instruments, radios, cameras, record players, and the cheap stuff—clocks, lighters, rings, watches, and so on. I got myself looking as stupid as possible and walked in.

There must be thousands of hockshops in New York, but there are only two types of clerks. The first is usually short, bald, and over forty. He wears suspenders, talks straight to the customers, and kowtows to the others. Most of the guys farther downtown fit into this category. The other type is like the guy I drew: tall, thick black hair, light-colored suit, and a wide smile. He talks gentleman-to-gentleman with his upper-class customers and patronizingly to the bums. Of the two he's usually more dangerous.

My man came on with the Johnny-on-the-spot pitch, ready and willing to serve. I hated him immediately.

"I'm looking for a guitar," I said, "preferably a good one. Do you have anything in stock at the moment?" I saw six or seven on the wall, but when you play it dumb, you play it dumb.

"Yes," he said. "Do you play guitar?" I didn't, and told him so. No point in lying all the time. But, I added, I was going to learn.

He picked one off the wall and started plucking the strings. "This is an excellent one, and I can let you have it for only thirty-five dollars. Would you like to pay cash or take it on the installment plan?"

I must have been a good actor, because he was certainly playing me for a mark. The guitar was a Pelton, and it was in good shape, but it never cost more than forty bucks new, and he had a nerve asking more than twenty-five. Any minute now he might tell me that the last owner was an old lady who only played hymns on it. I held back the laugh and plunked the guitar like a nice little customer.

"I like the sound. And the price sounds about right to me."

"You'll never find a better bargain." Now this was laying it on with a trowel.

"Yes, I'll take it." He deserved it now. "I was just passing by, and I don't have much money with me. Could I make a down payment and pay the rest weekly?"

He probably would have skipped the down payment. "Surely," he said. For some reason I've always disliked guys who say "Surely." No reason, really. "How much would you like to pay now?"

I told him I was really short at the moment, but could pay ten dollars a week. Could I just put a dollar down? He said I could, but in that case the price would have to be forty dollars, which is called putting the gouge on.

I hesitated a moment for luck, then agreed. When he asked for identification I pulled out my pride and joy.

In a wallet that I also copped from that drugstore I have the best identification in the world, all phony and all legal. Everything in it swears up and down that my name is Leonard Blake and I live on Riverside Drive. I have a baptismal certificate that I purchased from a sharp little entrepreneur at our high school back in the days when I needed proof of age to buy a drink. I have a Social Security card that can't be used for identification purposes but always is, and an unapproved application for a driver's license. To get one of these you just go to the Bureau of Motor Vehicles and fill it out. It isn't stamped, but no pawnbroker ever noticed that. Then there are membership cards in everything from the Captain Marvel Club to the NAACP. Of course he took my buck and I signed some papers.

I made it next to Louie's shop at 35th and Third. Louie and I know each other, so there's no haggling. He gave me fifteen for the guitar, and I let him know it wouldn't be hot for at least ten days. That's the way I like to do business.

Fifteen bucks was a week and a half, and you see how easy it was. And it's fun to shaft a guy who deserves it, like that sharp clerk did. But when I got back to the pad and read some old magazines, I got another idea before I even had a chance to start spending the fifteen.

I was reading one of those magazines that are filled with really exciting information, like how to build a model of the Great Wall of China around your house, and I was wondering what kind of damn fool would want to build a wall around his house, much less a Great Wall of China type wall, when the idea hit me. Wouldn't a hell of a lot of the same type of people like a Sheffield steel dagger, twenty-five inches long, an authentic copy of a twelfth-century relic recently discovered in a Bergdorf castle? And all this for only two bucks postpaid, no COD's? I figured they might.

This was a big idea, and I had to plan it just right. A classified in that type of magazine cost two dollars, a post office box cost about five for three months. I was in a hurry, so I forgot about lunch, and rushed across town to the Chelsea Station on Christopher Street, and Lennie Blake got himself a post office box. Then I fixed up the ad a little, changing "25 inches" to "over two feet." And customers would please allow three weeks for delivery. I sent ads and money to three magazines, and took a deep breath. I was now president of Comet Enterprises. Or Lennie Blake was. Who the hell cared?

For the next month and a half I stalled on the rent and ate as little as possible. The magazines hit the stands after two weeks, and I gave people time to send in. Then I went west again and picked up my mail.

A hell of a lot of people wanted swords. There were about two hundred envelopes, and after I finished throwing out the checks and requests for information, I wound up with $196 and sixty-seven 3¢ stamps. Anybody want to buy a stamp?

See what I mean? The whole bit couldn't have been simpler. There's no way in the world they can trace me, and nobody in the post office could possibly remember me. That's the beauty of New

York—so many people. And how much time do you think the cops will waste looking for a two-bit swindler? I could even have made another pickup at the post office, but greedy guys just don't last long in this game. And a federal rap I need like a broken ankle.

Right now I'm one hundred percent in the clear. I haven't heard a rumble on the play yet, and already Lennie Blake is dead-burned to ashes and flushed down the toilet. Right now I'm busy establishing Warren Shaw. I sign the name, over and over, so that I'll never make a mistake and sign the wrong name sometime. One mistake is above par for the course.

Maybe you're like me. I don't mean with the same fingerprints and all, but the same general attitudes. Do you fit the following general description: smart, coldly logical, content with coffee and eggs in a cold-water walk-up, and ready to work like hell for an easy couple of bucks? If that's you, you're hired. Come right in and get to work. You can even have my room. I'm moving out tomorrow.

It's been kicks, but too much of the same general pattern and the law of averages gets you. I've been going a long time, and one pinch would end everything. Besides, I figure it's time I took a step or two up the social ladder.

I had a caller yesterday, a guy named Al. He's an older guy, and hangs with a mob uptown on the West Side. He always has a cigar jammed into the corner of his mouth and he looks like a holdover from the twenties, but Al is a very sharp guy. We gassed around for a while, and then he looked me in the eyes and chewed on his cigar. "You know," he said, "we might be able to use you."

"I always work alone, Al."

"You'd be working alone. Two hundred a night."

I whistled. This was sounding good. "What's the pitch?"

He gave me the look again and chewed his cigar some more. "Kid," he said, "did you ever kill a man?"

Two hundred bucks for one night's work! What a perfect racket! Wish me luck, will you? I start tonight.

THE LOST CASES OF ED LONDON

Introduction
CALLING ED LONDON

HE SHOULD PROBABLY STAY LOST.

In fact, you can argue that he never should have existed in the first place. I didn't set out to write about him. His first appearance was in a book originally called (albeit not by me) *Death Pulls a Doublecross*, and I was writing about another fellow named Roy Markham.

That wasn't my idea, either. The idea originated with someone at a paperback house called Belmont Books, where they'd arranged with some TV people to do a novel that would tie in with *Markham*, an episodic television series about a private eye with that name, played by Ray Milland.

TV tie-ins were standard paperback fare at the time. God knows why. The notion, I suppose, was that people who already knew the character from television would want to read more about him. The books were what you'd expect—uninspired and uninspiring.

At this point I'd written and sold one crime novel, *Mona*, slated for publication by Fawcett Gold Medal. I got the assignment to write about Roy Markham, and I wrote the book, and by the time I was done I found myself thinking that it was too good to waste on a Belmont TV tie-in for a $1,000 advance. I showed it to Henry Morrison, who was representing me at the time, and he agreed; he showed it to Knox Burger at Gold Medal, who had recently bought *Mona*, and he agreed, too.

I met Knox in his office on West 44th Street next to the Algonquin, and we talked about what it would take to change Roy Markham into somebody else. I recall that he took exception to the name Roy, maintaining that it brought to mind a lot of crackers who gave him a hard time in the service.

I went home and turned Roy Markham into Ed London, and made a couple of other changes that Knox suggested, and that I no longer recall. (This was in 1960. There is much of 1960 that I do not recall, and it's probably just as well.) The book went in, and the book came out, and that was that.

Except that I owed Belmont a TV tie-in, which I then had to write. I knocked it out, and they published it as *Markham*, and subtitled it *The Case of the Pornographic Photos*. (It has since been republished as *You Could Call It Murder*, even as *Death Pulls a Doublecross* has since been republished as *Coward's Kiss*. These are better titles, but I don't know that they're enough to transform this pair of sows's ears into silk purses, or even plastic ones.) Poor Belmont. The network pulled the plug on Ray Milland well before the book came out, so they had nothing to tie in with.

Meanwhile, I had a private eye. Ed London, private eye.

Lucky me.

THING IS, I'd been figuring all along that what I needed was a series character. I liked reading about the same character over and over, and figured I'd like writing about one, too. So, having published one book about Ed London, I thought the thing to do was write more of them.

Turned out I couldn't. Blame it on my youth, or on my low estimate of self, but in those years I only managed to hit a mark if I was deliberately aiming below it. *Mona* started out as a pseudonymous sex novel for one of my regular crap publishers; a few chapters in I thought it might have potential, and changed its direction. Ed London's first appearance started out as a TV tie-in. But when I aimed high in the first place, I froze. There were a couple of abortive first chapters for a second Ed London novel, but that's as far as it got.

Except for these three novelettes.

I have precious little recollection of the circumstances of writing them. I believe they were all produced while I was living in a suburb of Buffalo in 1962–63, but who knows? I think, too, that they were all initially published in *Man's Magazine*, and at least some of them were reprinted a couple of years later by the same publisher in *Guy Magazine*.

When it came time to assemble the stories for *One Night Stands*, the three Ed London stories were nowhere to be found. I knew I'd written at least one and it seemed to me I'd written two, but I didn't have copies, and none had turned up, so that was that.

Then, after *One Night Stands* came out, the other stories began to turn up, thanks especially to Terry Zobeck and Lynn Munroe. It turned out there were three of them. Three! How did that happen?

And here they are. I can't delude myself for a moment with the notion that the literature of crime fiction is riched for their reappearance. I, however, will be a few dollars richer, and, crass bastard that I am, that strikes me as reason enough for bringing them out in this extremely attractive format. (It's a handsome volume, isn't it? Satisfying to pick up and hold in the hand, a pleasure to see on the bookshelf. Hey, nobody says you've got to *read* the damn thing.)

Enjoy!

Lawrence Block
Greenwich Village
2001

THE NAKED AND THE DEADLY

ONE

The wind was right and I could smell the polluted waters of Brooklyn's Jamaica Bay a few blocks to the east. It was a warm night in August, and I was in the Canarsie section getting ready to meet a blackmailer. I puffed on my pipe, turned around, looked at the bar again. A neon sign—*Johnny's.* A picture of six would-be Miss Rheingolds, chastely flat-chested and smiling buoyantly. I opened the door and went inside.

The bar had a small-town feel, like the neighborhood. It was a place for men who wanted to get away from their wives and kids and installment-plan television sets long enough for a couple of beers. There were two booths in the back, both empty. Seven or eight men sat at the bar and drank beer. They all wore gabardine slacks and open-necked sports shirts. Two others were playing a shuffle-bowler near the booths. I walked to the furthest booth and sat down.

A Budweiser clock rotated hypnotically over the bar. Nine-thirty. My blackmailer was late.

The bartender came over. It looked like the wrong bar for cognac but that's all I drink. I asked for Courvoisier.

"You want the Three-Star or the VSOP?"

Life is filled with surprises. I asked for the good stuff and he went away. When he came back, he brought the cognac in a little snifter. I paid for the drink and sipped it.

At 9:55 my glass was emptier than the Rheingold girls' bras and my man was still missing. I was ready to take the subway home and tell Rhona Blake to save her money. The bartender came over, his eyes hopeful, and I started to shake my head when the door opened and a little man entered.

"Give me a refill," I said.

The little man had cagy eyes and he used them on the whole room before he got around to me.

He came up the aisle, stopped at my booth, sat down across from me. "You gotta be Ed London," he said.

"That's right."

"You got the dough, London?"

I patted the left side of my jacket and felt my .38 snug in a shoulder rig. I patted the right side and touched the roll of bills Rhona Blake had given me. I nodded.

"Then we're in business, London. This is a place to meet and not a place to do business. Too many distractions."

He waved one hand at the bowling machine. I told him I had a drink on the way and he was willing to humor me. The bartender brought the drink. I paid for it. The little man didn't want anything and the bartender went back to tend the bar.

I studied the little man over the brim of my glass. He was a few years too old for the Ivy League shirt and tie. He had a low forehead to fit Lombrosi's theories of criminal physiognomy and a pair of baby-blue eyes that didn't fit at all. His nose was strong and his chin was weak and a five o'clock shadow obscured part of his sallow complexion.

"The broad could of come herself," he said.

"She didn't want to."

"But she could of. She didn't need a private cop. Unless she's figuring on holding out the dough."

I didn't answer him. I'd have liked to play it that way, but Rhona Blake wouldn't go for it. You can pay a blackmailer or you can push him around, and if you pay him once you pay him forever. And the little man looked easy to push around. But I was just a hired hand.

"You almost done, London?"

I finished my drink and got up. I walked to the door and the little man followed me like a faithful dog.

"Your car here, London?"

"I took the subway."

"So we use mine. C'mon."

His car was parked at the curb, a dark blue Mercury two or three years old. We got in, and he drove up Remsen Avenue through the Canarsie flatlands. A few years back the area had been all swamps and marshes until the developers got busy. They put up row on row of semi-detached brick-front houses.

There was still plenty of marshland left. Canarsie by any other name was still Canarsie. And it didn't smell like a rose.

"This is private enough," I said. "Let's make the trade."

"The stuff ain't with me. It's stashed."

"Is that where we're going?"

"That's the general idea."

He took a corner, drove a few blocks, made another turn. I looked over my shoulder. There was a Plymouth behind us . . . It had been there before.

"Your friends are here," I said. "In case you hadn't noticed."

"Huh?"

"Your protection. Your insurance."

He was looking in the rear-view mirror now and he didn't like what he saw. He swore under his breath and his hands tightened on the steering wheel. He leaned on the accelerator and the big car growled.

He said: "How long?"

"Since we left Remsen."

He grunted something obscene and took a corner on less wheels than came with the car. The Plym picked up speed and cornered like a wolverine. A good driver might have beaten them—the Merc had enough under the hood to leave the Plymouth at the post. But the little man was a lousy driver.

We took two more corners for no reason at all and they stayed right with us. We ran a red light at Flatlands Avenue and so did they. The little man was sweating now. His forehead was damp and his hands were slippery on the wheel. They chased us for two more blocks and I dug the .38 out and let my finger curl around the trigger. I wasn't sure what kind of party we were going to, but I wanted the right costume.

The Plymouth came alongside and I pointed the gun at it. There were three of them, two in front and one in back. I had a clear shot but I held it back—for all I knew they were police. They've got a strict law for private detectives in New York State: shoot a cop and you lose your license.

But he wasn't a cop. Cops don't tote submachine guns, and that's what the boy by the window was holding. The Plym cut us off and the little man hit the brakes, and then the submachine gun cut loose and started spraying lead at us.

The first burst took care of the little man. A row of bullets plowed into his chest and he slumped over the wheel like the corpse he was.

And that saved my life.

Because when he died his foot slid off the brakes and came down on the accelerator, and we went into the Plymouth like Grant into Vicksburg. The tommy-gun stopped chattering and I hit the door hard and landed on my feet. I didn't make like a hero. I ran like a rabbit.

The field had tall swamp-grass and broken beer bottles. I zigged and zagged, and I was maybe twenty yards in before the tommy-gun took up where it had left off. I heard slugs whine over my shoulder and took a dive any tank fighter would have been proud of, landing on my face in a clump of tall grass. I turned around so that I could see what was happening and crawled backwards so that it wouldn't be happening to me.

The tommy-gun threw another spasmodic burst at me, way off this time. I got the .38 steadied and poked a shot at one of the three silhouettes by the roadside. It went wide. They answered with another brace of shots that didn't come any closer.

Some more of the same. Then the tommy-gun was silent, and I raised my head enough to see what was happening. The hoods were off the road and in their car, and their car was leaving.

So was the blackmailer's Mercury. Evidently the collision hadn't damaged it enough to ground it, because it was following the Plymouth down the road and leaving me alone.

I waited until I was sure they were gone. Then I waited until I was sure they wouldn't be back. I got up slowly and dragged myself back toward the road. The .38 stayed in my hand. It gave me a feeling of security.

A car came down the road toward me and I hit the dirt again, gun in hand. But it wasn't the Mercury or the Plymouth, just a black beetle of a Volkswagen that didn't even slow down. I got up feeling foolish.

There were skid marks on the pavement, a little broken glass as an added attraction. There was no dead little man, not on the street and not in the field. There was no blood. Nothing but glass and skid marks, and Brooklyn is full of both. Nothing but a very tired private cop with a very useless gun in his hand, standing in the road and wishing he had something to do. Wishing he was home on East 83rd Street in Manhattan with a glass of Courvoisier in one hand and something by Mozart on the record player.

I stuck the gun back where it belonged. I found a pipe in one pocket and a pouch of tobacco in the other. I filled the pipe, got it going, headed over toward Flatlands Avenue.

The third cab I stopped felt like making a run to Manhattan. I got into the backseat and pulled the door shut. The cabby threw the flag down and the meter began ticking up expenses to be charged to the account of a girl named Rhona Blake.

I sat back and thought about her.

TWO

I saw her for the first time that afternoon. It was too hot to do much but sit in an air-conditioned apartment. I'd spent the morning waking up and writing checks to creditors, and in another hour it would be four o'clock and I could add brandy to my coffee without feeling guilty about it. For the time being I was feeling guilty.

The door must have been open downstairs because she rang my bell without hitting the downstairs buzzer first. I opened the door and she came inside.

"You're Edward London," she said. "Aren't you?"

I admitted it. I would have admitted to being Judge Crater or Ambrose Bierce or Martin Bormann. She had that kind of effect.

"May I sit down, Mr. London?"

I pointed at the couch. She went over and sat on it, crossing one leg very neatly over the other. I sat down across from her in my leather chair and finished my coffee.

She was beautiful. Her hair was ash blond, wrapped up tight in a French roll, and if there were any dark roots they were well hidden. She was tall, close to my own height, and built along Hollywood lines. Her mouth was a dark ruby wound and her eyes were a jealous green. She was wearing a charcoal business suit but the thrust of her breasts made you wonder what business it was.

Thirty, maybe. Or twenty-five. The really beautiful ones are ageless. I watched her open a black calf purse, find a cigarette, light it with a silver lighter. She smiled at me through smoke.

"I hate to barge in on you like this," she said. "But this was the only listing I could find for you. I thought it was your office."

"I work here," I said. "It's a good-sized apartment. And I live alone, so there are no distractions."

"You're not married?"

"No."

She nodded thoughtfully, filing the information away somewhere in that beautiful head. "I don't know where to start," she said suddenly. "My name is Rhona Blake. And I want to hire you."

"Why?"

"Because I'm being blackmailed."

"When did it start?"

"Yesterday. With a letter and a telephone call. The letter came in the morning mail and told me I would have to pay five thousand dollars for . . . certain things."

"Do you have the letter?"

"I threw it away."

I frowned. "You shouldn't have."

"I thought it was a joke. Or maybe I was just mad, and I tore up the note. A few hours later I got a phone call. It was the same thing again. A man told me to meet him in a bar in Brooklyn with the money."

I asked her what she wanted me to do.

"Meet him and pay him. Then bring the goods to me. That's all."

I told her she was crazy. "Blackmailers operate on the install-ment plan," I said. "If you pay him once you'll have to pay him again. He'll bleed you white."

"I can't help it."

"You can't go to the cops?"

"No," she said quietly. "I can't."

"Why not?"

"Because I can't. Let's leave it at that, Mr. London."

So we left it at that. "Then call his bluff," I said. "Tell him to go to hell for himself. Chances are he'll throw the stuff away if he can't get anything out of it."

"No. He'll . . . sell it elsewhere."

"What's it all about, Miss Blake?"

"I can't tell you."

"Look—"

Her eyes were hard now. "You look," she said. "You don't have to know. To be perfectly frank, it's none of your business. I want you to do an errand for me. That's all. I want you to meet this man and pay him five thousand dollars and bring the goods to me. That's simple enough isn't it?"

"It's too simple."

"He won't go on blackmailing me. He'll give the material to you. I'm sure of it."

"Then maybe I'll do the blackmailing. Ever think of that?"

"I've heard about you." She laughed. "I don't think I have to worry."

I knocked the dottle out of my pipe and set it down in the ash-tray. I started to tell her I was a private cop, not a messenger service. But the words didn't come out. She was getting on my nerves, being cool and competent and stepping all over my masculine pride, and that was a pretty silly reason to turn down a fee.

And a pretty silly reason to send Rhona Blake out of my life.

I said, "All right."

"You'll take the case?"

"Uh-huh. But I have to know more."

"Like what?"

"You could start with the identity of the blackmailer. From there you could tell me what he's got on you, and what he's going to do with it if you can't pay, and why you're over a barrel. Then you can tell me a few things about yourself. Like who you are, for a starter."

"I'm sorry. I want to keep this matter a secret, Mr. London."

"Even from me?"

"From everyone."

I went over to my desk, picked up a pencil and pad. I wrote *Rhona Blake* on the pad and looked up.

"Address," I said.

"I can't tell you."

"Phone number, then."

She shook her pretty head. "I can't tell you that either, Mr. London."

"*Mr. London.* Look," I said, "if we're going to be such close friends you really ought to call me Ed."

I didn't get a smile. I said: "How in hell am I going to get in touch with you?"

"You aren't, Ed. I'll call you."

She opened her purse again and took out an envelope filled with new money.

"Five thousand dollars," she said.

"To waste on a blackmailer?"

"To invest in my peace of mind. And how much do you want, Ed?"

"I get a hundred a day plus expenses. And if all I know is your name, I'm afraid your credit rating isn't too good. I'll take two hundred for a retainer."

She gave it to me in two bills. Brand new ones. I started to write out a receipt for $5,200 but her hand touched mine and stopped me. Her fingers were cool and soft. I looked up into the crisp green of her eyes.

"I don't need a receipt."

"Why not?"

"Because I trust you, Ed."

There were at least a dozen answers to that one. They all chased their tails in my brain, and I looked at Rhona and didn't say a word. Her hair looked as though Rumpelstiltskin had spun it out of gold. She stepped closer to me and her perfume came on like gangbusters.

"Ed—"

It was like this raw wet wind that comes just before the rain. Her hand held mine, and her eyes turned soft, and her body flowed up against mine. She came into my arms and our mouths met and that fine body of hers was taut against me and the world did a somersault.

My bed wasn't made. She didn't seem to mind. We went into the bedroom and I kicked the door shut. She kissed me, lips warm with the promise of hurried lust. She stepped back neatly and her hands made the charcoal suit melt from her body. I helped her with her bra and her breasts leaped into my hands. She gave a little shiver of animal joy and small sounds of passion tore from her throat.

It was a moment torn from Time. And we were on the bed, and her head was tossed back and her eyes were tightly shut, and her big beautiful body was a Stradivarius and I was Fritz Kreisler and Menuhin and Oistrakh and everybody else, stroking the world's sweetest music out of her.

"Oh, Ed. Oh, yes!"

She was a life-size doll who cried real tears. The room rocked. Someone took the earth out from under us and we took a Cook's tour through a brand-new world. At the end there was a monumental crescendo, and the finale came with a shake and a shudder and a sob.

HER VOICE CAME THROUGH A FILTER. "I'll call you later, Ed. I've got to go now. The blackmailer said he would call me late this afternoon and make the arrangements for the meeting. I'll tell him you'll be coming as my agent, then call you and give you the details. You can meet him tonight, can't you?"

I grunted something. She leaned over the bed and her lips brushed my face. I didn't move. She left, and I could hear her feet on the stairs. A door closed. I still didn't move.

Later, I got up and showered. I washed the sweet taste of her body from my skin and told myself it didn't mean a damned thing. She was playing Lady of Mystery, and in that department she could give the Mona Lisa cards and spades and chuck in Little Casino. The interlude in bed was no love affair, no meeting of soul mates. It was a way to seal a bargain, a quick little roll in the hay to ensure my cooperation, an added bonus tacked onto the 200-buck retainer.

I could tell myself this. It was hard to believe it.

So I showered and got dressed and went into the living room to build myself a drink. Later she would call me. Then I would run out to Brooklyn to do the job for her.

I poured more cognac. There was a girl I was supposed to meet that night, a dark-eyed brunette named Sharon Ross. A publisher's Gal Friday, a warm and clever thing. I picked up the phone and tried to find the right way to explain why I couldn't take her to the theater that night.

"You've got a nerve," she told me. "We made that date two weeks ago. What's the matter, Ed?"

"Business," I said. "How's tomorrow night?"

"It's out." She clicked the receiver in my ear.

So I drank the drink and crossed another Sweet Young Thing off my mental list of Things to Be Physical With. I was already giving up a lot for Rhona Blake.

She called around six. "This is Rhona," she said. "I talked to . . . to the man. He wanted me to come personally but agreed to meet with you."

"Sweet of him."

"Don't growl. You're supposed to meet him at nine-thirty at a place called Johnny's. It's out in Canarsie on Remsen Avenue near Avenue M. Give him the money and get the goods, Ed."

"Maybe I could get the goods without giving him the money."

"No. The money doesn't matter. Don't do anything silly, like getting rough with him. Just . . . just follow orders."

"Yes, ma'am."

"Ed—"

"What?"

A long pause. "Nothing," she said, finally. "I'll . . . I'll call you tonight, Ed."

THREE

My cabby came off the Manhattan Bridge at Canal Street, then found the East Side Drive and headed uptown. It was close to eleven and the traffic was thin. We made good time. The meter was a few ticks past $5 when he pulled up in front of my brownstone. I gave him a five and two singles and waved him away.

It was still too damned hot out. I went inside, took the stairs two at a time, unlocked my door, and pulled it shut after me. I poured a stiff drink and drank it.

It was getting cute now. My client had given me five grand, and I still had that. But the little blackmailer was dead and gone, and the stuff he had on her was nowhere to be found. It was time for me to call my client, of course. Time to fill her in on all the novel developments. But I couldn't get in touch with her. She was willing to sleep with me but she wouldn't let me know where she lived.

A few minutes after twelve, the phone rang.

"Rhona, Ed. Everything go all right?"

"No," I said.

"What happened?"

I gave it to her in capsule form, telling her how I met the little man, how they waylaid us, how they killed him and tried to kill me. She let me talk without an interruption, and when I stopped she was silent for almost a minute.

Then: "What now, Ed?"

"I don't know, Rhona. I've got five thousand bucks you can have back. I guess that's about all."

"But I'm in trouble, Ed."

"What kind of trouble?"

A pause. "I can't tell you over the phone."

"Then come over here."

"I can't, Ed. I have to stay where I am."

"Then I'll come over there."

"No."

I was getting sick of the whole routine. "Then give me a post-office box and I'll mail you five grand, Rhona. And we can forget the whole thing. Okay?"

It wasn't okay. She got nervous and stuttered awhile, then told me she would call me in the morning. I told her I was sick of phone calls.

"Then meet me," she said.

"Where?"

She thought it over. "Do you know a place called Mandrake's?"

"In the Village? I know it."

"I'll meet you there at two in the afternoon."

"Are they open then?"

"They're open. Will you meet me?"

I thought about that red mouth, those green eyes. I remembered the poetry of her body. "Sure," I said. "I'll meet you."

Hanging up, I hauled the .38 out of its resting place and broke it open. I wanted a full gun handy. It looked as though it was going to be that kind of a deal.

It was too early for sleep. I thought about the girl I'd broken my date with: dark hair, soft curves, a sulky mouth. Right now we'd have been out of the theater. We'd be sitting in a cozy club some-where on the East Side, listening to atonal jazz and drinking a little too much. And then homeward, for a nightcap and maybe a cup of kindness. But a date with a blackmailer had made me break my date with Sharon Ross. And now she was mad at me.

For the hell of it, I called her. The phone rang and rang and rang and nobody answered it.

I went into the kitchen and made instant coffee and thought about Canarsie. A tommy-gun—that was something to mull over. Only prison guards have them. They've been illegal in the States since the Dillinger era, and a hood who wants one has to shell out two or three grand for the thing. And needs good connections.

It sounded pretty complex for an ordinary blackmail dodge, and made me wonder what kind of league Rhona Blake was playing in. Triple-A, anyway. They don't use choppers in the bush leagues.

It was late by the time I got into bed. I wedged a stack of records on the hi-fi and crawled under the covers. They played and I thought about things, and I fell asleep before the stack was finished.

THE MORNING WAS RAW AND RAGGED. I'd gone to sleep without flip-ping on the air-conditioner, and when I woke up the blankets were sticking to my skin. I pried them loose and took a long shower.

I was through with breakfast by 10:30. I wasn't supposed to meet Rhona until two, but my apartment was beginning to feel like a jail cell. I looked through the bookcases for something to read and didn't come up with anything. I plucked the *Times* off my doormat, glanced through it, and tossed it into the wastebasket.

I left the apartment wearing slacks, a sport jacket, and a gun. I locked my door and headed down the stairs, and was on my way through the vestibule just as a man was leaning on my bell. I saw his index finger pressing a button next to a strip of plexiglas with *E. London* inscribed thereon. He didn't look like anyone I wanted to meet, but it was a hot day and I had a few hours to kill. I tapped him on the shoulder.

"You won't get an answer," I said.

"No?"

"No. I'm E. London, and there was nobody home when I left."

He didn't smile. "Carr," he said. "Phillip Carr, attorney at law." He handed me a card. "I want to talk to you, London."

I didn't really want to talk to him. We went upstairs anyway, and I unlocked my door again and led him inside. We sat down in the living room. He offered me a cigar and I shook my head. He made a hole in the end with an elaborate cigar cutter, wedged it in his mouth, lit it, blew foul smoke all over my apartment. I hoped it wouldn't clog the air-conditioner.

"I'll come to the point," he said.

"Fine."

"I'm here representing a client," Carr said, "who wants to remain nameless. He's a wealthy man, a prominent man."

"Go on."

"His daughter's missing. He wants her located."

"That's interesting," I told him. "The Missing Persons Bureau is at Headquarters, on Centre Street. They have a lot of personnel and they don't charge anything. You go down there, make out a report, and they'll find your man's daughter a damn sight faster than I will."

He chewed his cigar thoughtfully. "This isn't a police matter," he said.

"No?"

"No. We . . . my client needs special talents. He's prepared to pay ten thousand dollars as a reward for his daughter's return."

"Ten grand?"

"That's right."

"I don't work that way," I said. "I'm not a bounty hunter, Carr. I don't chase rewards any more than a decent lawyer chases ambulances to nail negligence cases. I get a hundred a day plus expenses. The price is the same whether I find your missing person or not."

"That's not how my client wants it."

"Then your client can find himself another boy."

"You're not a patient man," Phillip Carr said.

"Maybe not."

"You should be. Can't you use ten grand, London?"

"Anybody can."

"Then be patient. Let me show you a picture of my client's errant daughter; then you can decide whether or not you want to work for a reward. For ten grand, I'd be willing to chase an ambulance, London."

It was early in the day and it was hot as hell and my head wasn't working too well. I let him dig a thin wallet from his hip pocket. He pulled a picture from it and passed it to me.

Well, you guessed it. And I should have, but it was that kind of a day. The daughter-reward bit was as nutty as a male Hershey bar and the picture told me everything I had to know. Just a head-and-shoulder shot, the kind that made you want to see what the body looked like. A beautiful girl. A familiar face.

Rhona Blake, of course.

Carr was looking at me, a supercilious smile on his lips. I wanted to turn it inside out. But I could be as cute as he. I handed the picture back to him and waited.

"A familiar face?"

"No."

"Really?"

I stepped closer to him. "I've never seen the girl," I lied. "And the reward couldn't interest me less. I think you ought to go home, Carr."

He pointed the cigar at me. "You're a damn fool," he said.

"Why?"

"Because ten thousand dollars is a healthy reward any way you look at it."

"So?"

He made a pilgrimage to the window. I felt like walking behind him and kicking him through it. He was a smooth little bastard who wanted me to sell out a client to him, and he didn't even have the guts to lay it on the line. He had to be cute about it.

"The girl is in over her head," he said levelly. He still had his back to me. "You're working for her. You don't have to. You can be cooperative and pick up a nice package in the process. What's wrong with that?"

"Get out of here," I said.

He turned to face me. "You damn fool."

"Get out, Carr. Or I'll throw you out."

He sighed. "My client's a great believer in rewards," he said. "Rewards and punishments."

"I'd hit you, Carr, but you'd bleed all over my carpet."

"Rewards and punishments," he said again. "I don't have to draw you pictures, London. You're supposed to be a fairly bright boy. You think it over. You've got my card. If you change your mind, you might try giving me a ring."

He left. I didn't show him the door.

I looked at his card for a few minutes, then went to the phone. I dialed Police Headquarters and asked for Jerry Gunther at Homicide. It took a few minutes before he got to the phone.

"Oh," he groaned. "It's you again."

Jerry and I had bumped heads a few times in one squabble or another. We wound up liking each other. He thought I was a bookish bum who liked to live well without working too hard and I thought he was a thorough anachronism, an honest cop in the middle of the twentieth century when honest cops were out of style. We had less in common than Miller and Monroe, but we got along fine.

"What's up, Ed?"

"Phillip Carr," I said. "Some kind of a lawyer. You know anything about him?"

"It rings a bell," he said. "I could find out if this was a vital part of police routine. Is this a vital part of police routine, Ed?"

"No."

"What is it?"

"An imposition on your friendship."

"What I figured," he said. "Next time we have a vital conference, you buy."

"That could be expensive. You've got a hollow leg."

"Better than a hollow head, crumb. Hang on."

Finally, Jerry Gunther came back. "Yeah," he said. "Phillip Carr. Sort of a mob lawyer, Ed. A mouthpiece type. He takes cases for the kind of garbage that always stays out of jail. He's been on the inside of some shady stuff himself, according to the dope we've got. Nothing that anybody could ever make stick. Bankrolling some smuggling operations, stuff like that. Using his connections to make an illegal buck."

I grunted.

"That your man, Ed?"

"Like a glove," I said. "He wears sunglasses and he's oily. He's the type who goes to the barbershop and gets the works."

"Like Anastasia," Jerry said. "It should happen to all of them. What's it all about, Ed?"

"I don't know yet."

"Nothing for Homicide, is it?"

"Nothing, Jerry."

"Then the hell with it. I only get into the act when somebody dies, fella."

I thought about the corpse in Canarsie. But he never got into the files. The boys in our little poker game were too professional for that. By now he was sleeping in a lime pit in Jersey or swimming in Jamaica Bay all wrapped in cement.

"Remember," Jerry Gunther was saying, "you buy the liquor. And don't play rough with this Carr. He's got some ugly friends."

"Sure," I said. "And thanks."

I put down the phone, got out of the building, and grabbed a pair of burgers at the lunch counter around the corner. As I ate, I thought about a corpse in Canarsie and a man named Phillip Carr and a blond vision named Rhona Blake. Life does get complicated, doesn't it?

FOUR

I picked up my car from the garage on Third Avenue where I put it out to pasture. The car's a Chevy convertible, an antique from the pre-fin era. I drove it down to the Village, stuck it in a handy parking spot, and looked around for a bar called Mandrake's.

Rhona was right. Mandrake's was open at two in the afternoon, even if I couldn't figure out why. It was a sleek and polished little club with a circular bar, and at night the Madison Avenue hippies came there to listen to a piano player sing dirty songs. They paid a buck and a quarter for their drinks, patted the waitresses on their pretty little bottoms, and thought they were way ahead of the squares at P.J. Clark's.

But in the afternoon it was just another ginmill, empty, and its only resemblance to Mandrake's-by-nightfall was the price schedule. The drinks were still a buck and a quarter. I picked up Courvoisier at the bar and carried it to a little table in the back. The barmaid was the afternoon model, hollow-eyed and sad. I was her only customer.

I nursed my drink, tossed a quarter into the chrome-plated jukebox, and played some Billie Holliday records. They were some of her last sides, cut after the voice was gone and only the perfect phrasing remained, and Lady Day was sadder than Mandrake's in the daylight. I waited for Rhona and wondered if she would show.

She did. She was a good three drinks late, waltzing in at three o'clock and glancing over her shoulder to find out who was following her. Probably the whole Lithuanian Army-in-Exile, I thought. She was that kind of a girl.

"I'm late," she said. "I'm sorry."

We were still the bartender's only customers. I asked her what she was drinking. She said a Rob Roy would be nice. She sipped at it, and I sipped at the cognac, and we looked at each other. She asked me for the story again and I gave it to her, filling in more of the details. She hung on every word and gave me a nod now and then.

"You're positive he was killed?"

"Unless he found a way to live without a head. They shot it off for him."

"I don't know what to do next, Ed."

"You could tell me what's happening."

"I'm paying you a hundred a day. Isn't that enough?"

This burned me. "I could make ten grand in five minutes," I said. "That's even better."

She looked at me. "What do you mean?"

"Nothing at all," I said. I finished my drink, put the empty glass on the table in front of me. "I had a visitor today, Rhona. A lawyer named Phillip Carr. He told me a client of his was missing a daughter. This client was willing to shell out ten grand if I dug her up and brought her around."

"So?"

"He showed me your picture, Rhona."

For a moment she just stared. Then her face cracked like ice in the springtime. She shuddered violently, and she spilled most of her Rob Roy on the polished tabletop, and her stiff upper lip turned to jello.

She said: "Oh, hell."

"Want to talk now, Rhona?"

She stared at the top of the table, where her hands were shaking uncontrollably in a Rob Roy ocean. I walked to the jukebox, threw away another quarter, and sat down again. She was still shaking and biting her lip.

"You'd better tell me, Rhona. People are playing with tommy-guns and talking in ten-grand terms. You'd better tell me."

She nodded. On the jukebox, Billie was singing about strange fruit. Husky, smoky sounds shrieked out of a junked-up dying throat. The barmaid came over with a towel and wiped up the Rob Roy.

Rhona looked up at me. The veneer of poise was all gone. She wasn't ageless anymore. She looked very young, very scared. A scared kid in over her head.

"Ed," she said. "They want to kill me."

"Who does?"

"The man who came to see you. The same men who killed my blackmailer in Canarsie last night."

"Who are they?"

"Gamblers. But not real gamblers. Crooked ones. They run a batch of rigged games. They have some steerers who send over suckers, and the suckers go home broke. The lawyer who saw you works for a man named Abe Zucker. He's the head of it. And they're all looking for me. They want to kill me."

"Why?"

"Because of my father."

"Who's your father?"

I don't think she even heard the question. "They killed him," she said quietly. "Slowly. They beat him to death."

I waited while she took the bits and pieces of herself and tugged them back together again. Then I tried again. I asked her who her father was.

"Jack Blake," she said. "He was a mechanic."

"He fixed cars?"

She laughed humorlessly. "Cards," she corrected. "He was a card mechanic. He could make a deck turn inside out and salute you, Ed. He could deal seconds all night long and nobody ever tipped. He was the best in the world. He had gentle hands with long thin fingers—the most perfect hands in the world. He could crimp-cut and false-shuffle and palm and . . . He was great, Ed."

"Go on."

"You ought to be able to figure the rest of it," she said. "He quit the crooked-gambling circuit years ago when my mother died. He went into business for himself in Cleveland, ran a store downtown on Euclid Avenue and went straight. I worked for him, keeping the books and clerking behind the counter. The store was a magic shop. We sold supplies to the professional magicians and simple tricks to the average Joes. Dad loved the business. When the pros came in he would show off a little, fool around with a deck of cards and let them see how good he was. It was the perfect business for him."

"Where did Zucker come in?"

She sighed. "It happened less than a year ago. We came to New

York. Part business and part pleasure. Dad bought his supplies in New York and liked to get into town once or twice a year to check out new items. It was better than waiting for the salesman to come to him. We were at a nightclub, a cheap joint on West Third Street, and the busboy asked Dad if he was looking for action. Poker, craps, that kind of thing. He said he wouldn't mind a poker game and the busboy gave him a room number of a Broadway hotel. I went back to the place where we were staying and Dad went to the game."

Billie's last record ended and the juke went silent. I was tired of wasting quarters—and we didn't need music.

"He told me about it later," Rhona said, "when he got back to our room. He said he sat down and played two hands, and by that time he knew the game was rigged. He was going to get up and leave, he said, but they were so sloppy it made him mad. So he beat them at their own game, Ed. He played tight on the hands unless he was dealing, and on his deal he made sure things went his way.

"He was careful about it. He threw every trick in the book at them and they never caught on. It was a big game, Ed. Table stakes with a heavy takeout. Dad walked out of the game with twenty thousand dollars of their money."

I whistled. The rigged games are usually pretty small—when you get in the high brackets, nobody trusts anybody and the games are generally honest. It's easier to rake cheap suckers over the coals than to pick the big-money boys.

"Who played in the game?"

"Two or three of the sharps. And Dad. And some oil and cattle-men."

It figured. Texans with too much money and too much faith.

"Even the oilmen didn't do badly," she said. "Dad took the money straight from the crooks. He had the time of his life. And then . . . then they must have figured out what happened. For a few weeks everything was fine. Then we got a note in the mail. It wasn't signed. It said Jack Blake better give back the twenty grand he won or he would get what was coming to him. He just laughed it off, Ed. He said he was surprised they had figured it out but he wasn't going to let it worry him."

"And then they killed him?"

"Yes." She finished her drink. "I was over at a friend's house. I got home and found him lying on the living-room floor. There was blood all over. I went to him and touched him and . . . and he was still warm—"

I picked up her hand and held on to it. Her skin was white. She took a quick breath and squeezed my hand. "I'm all right, Ed."

"Sure."

We sat there. It was pushing 4:30 and the bar was starting to draw lushes. A tough little dyke in tight slacks strode over to the jukebox and played something noisy. I looked at Rhona again.

"How do you fit in?" I asked.

"They want to kill me."

"Why?"

"They want their money back."

I shook my head. "I won't buy it. You're in New York, not Cleveland. You were busy paying off a blackmailer who caught a load of lead in Canarsie. I don't buy it at all, Rhona. They wouldn't chase you that hard just because your father took them with a few fancy cuts and shuffles. They might run him down and kill him, but they wouldn't bother you."

"It's true, Ed."

"It is like hell. Where does the blackmailer fit?"

"He was blackmailing me. I told you."

"How? Why? With what?"

She thought about it. The juke was still too noisy and the bar was filling up. I was beginning to dislike the place.

She said: "All right."

I waited.

"I'm Jack Blake's daughter," she said. "I'm not a weeper and I don't throw in the towel when somebody hits me. I'm pretty tough, Ed."

I could believe it. She looked the part. Her green eyes were warm enough to throw sparks now.

"I came to New York to get them," she said. "They killed my father, Ed. Those rotten bastards killed him. They beat him and he died, and I'm not the kind of girl who can sit on her behind in

Cleveland and write it off to profit and loss. I flew to New York to get something good on Abe Zucker, something good enough to put him on death row at Sing Sing. That's why they want me out of the way, Ed. Because they know I won't give up unless they kill me."

"And the blackmailer?" I asked. "How did he fit in?"

"Klugsman," she corrected. "Milton Klugsman. He got in touch with me, told me he could prove that Zucker had my dad killed. I . . . I guess I let you think he was blackmailing me just to make things simpler. He called me and told me he had evidence to sell. The price was five grand."

"He might have been conning you, Rhona."

She raised an eyebrow. "Don't you think I thought of that? He could have been looking for some easy money or he could have been setting me up for Zucker. That's why I wouldn't meet him myself, why I hired you. I decided it was worth risking five grand, Ed. Five grand was just an ante in a game this size—"

She stopped, shrugged. "I guess Klugsman was telling the truth. Whatever he had, I won't get it now. He's dead. They killed him, and now they want to kill me. If I had any sense I'd get out of town until they forgot all about me."

"Why don't you?"

"Because I'm Jack Blake's daughter. Because I'm a stubborn girl. I always have been. Well, where do we go from here, Ed?"

I put a dollar on the table for the barmaid. "For a starter," I said, "we get the hell out of here."

FIVE

We took my Chevy. I drove uptown on Eighth Avenue as far as Twentieth, then cut east. There was a parking spot in front of a swanky five-story brick building on Gramercy Park. I coaxed the Chevy into it, with a Caddy in front of us and a Lincoln behind.

The Chevy felt outclassed. We got out of the car, walked past a stiff doorman and into a self-service elevator.

"I didn't want a hotel room," she said as we entered her place. "I thought it would be too easy for them to find me. This apartment was listed in the *Times*. It's a sublet, all furnished and ready. It costs a lot of money but it's worth it."

"What name did you rent it under?"

"I don't remember," she said. "Not mine."

She said there was scotch if I wanted a drink. I didn't. I wandered around the living room, a brazenly modern room. Rhona sat down on an orange couch and crossed her legs.

"What do we do next, Ed?"

"Go back to Cleveland."

"And forget about it?"

"Uh-huh."

She looked away. I studied her legs, then let my eyes move slowly up her body. I remembered last afternoon, in my apartment, in my bedroom. I took a quick breath, then crammed some tobacco into a pipe and scratched a match on a box.

"He was my father, Ed."

"I know."

"I can't quit."

"Hell," I said, "you absolutely can't do anything else. You know how Zucker took care of your father? Zucker didn't go there himself, Rhona. He picked up a telephone—or he hired somebody to pick up a phone. And then a bunch of hired muscle from Detroit or Chicago or Vegas got on a plane to Cleveland and beat your father to death and flew back on the next plane. You couldn't pin something like that to Zucker in a hundred years. All you can do is take a gun and shoot a hole in his head."

"That's not such a bad idea, is it?"

I didn't answer her.

"No," she said finally. "You're wrong, Ed. Why is he scared of me? Why can't he just ignore me? He had this lawyer offer you ten thousand dollars? If he's in the clear, why am I worth that kind of money to him?"

"You must have him scared."

She swung a small fist into the palm of her other hand. A startling gesture from a girl, especially a feminine one like her. "You are goddamned right. I've got him scared," she said. "I've got the son of a bitch turning green. And there has to be evidence, Ed. Klugsman had evidence."

"Unless he was conning you."

"Then why did they kill him?"

She was right. Abe Zucker was in enough trouble to work up a sweat, enough to make him spray Canarsie with machine-gun slugs and paper Manhattan with ten-grand rewards. It didn't quite mesh yet. Something was wrong somewhere, something didn't ring true. But for the time being she was right and I had to ride with her.

I drew on my pipe. "What do you know about Klugsman?"

"Nothing but his name. And that he's dead."

"You never met him?"

"No."

"You know where he lives?"

She shook her head. "He called me on the phone, Ed. He said his name was Milton Klugsman and he told me he had the information I needed. He said he could prove who killed my father. He didn't give his address or his phone number or anything."

"The phone. Is it in your name?"

"No, it's in the name of the people I'm subletting from."

"Then how did he reach you?"

"I have no idea."

We kept running into walls and up blind alleys. I wondered if she was lying to me. So far she'd fed me enough nonsense to earn her a Pathological Liar Merit Badge, but the latest version had a plausible ring to it.

"Somebody knew you were in town. Who?"

"I don't know."

"Phillip Carr showed me a picture of you. Any idea where he got it?"

"None."

"It was a head-and-shoulder shot, Rhona. You had your hair swept back and you were smiling, but not too broadly."

Her face clouded. "That . . . sounds like a picture Dad carried in his wallet. They could have stolen it when they killed him." She bit her lip. "But that doesn't make sense, does it?"

It didn't. I poked at my memory, brushed the snapshot away, and brought a different picture into focus. A face I'd seen a day ago in Canarsie. I described Klugsman as well as I could, told her how tall he was and what kind of a face he had and what clothes he was wearing. The description rang no bells for her.

I stood up, leaned over to knock the dottle from my pipe, and walked over to her. "We have to start with Klugsman," I said. "Klugsman may have had some evidence. Without it we're no-where. I can try getting a line on him. Maybe I can find out who he was, where he lived, and who his friends were. If he had anything around the house, it's probably gone by now. But maybe he's got a friend or a relative who knows something. It's worth a try."

"You're going now?"

She seemed sad about it. She was standing just a few feet from me, her hands at her sides, her shoulders back, her breasts in sharp relief against the front of her dress. Her mouth was pouting a little and her eyes were unhappy. I looked at her and didn't want to go anywhere. I wanted to stay awhile.

"I'd better get going," I said.

"Wait a few minutes, Ed."

The voice was soft as a pillow. Her eyes were moist. She took a short step toward me, stopped. I put out my hands and caught her shoulders and she pressed against me, hard.

"Ed—"

I kissed her. Her mouth tasted of Rob Roys and cigarettes and she put her arms around me and clung to me like a morning glory on a wire fence. Her body was on fire. I kissed her eyes, her cheeks, her throat.

"I'm all alone," she said. "All alone and afraid. Stay with me, Ed."

"Sure," I said, leading her into the bedroom, decorated in various shades of green. She stood there like a statue, but who likes statues dressed? I took off her clothes and ran my hands over her body. She vibrated like a tuning fork, purred like a kitten.

The mattress was firm. I put a pillow under her head and spread that ash blond hair over it. I touched her, kissed her. She breathed jaggedly and her eyes were wild.

"Ed—"

To hell with Klugsman. He was dead. He could wait awhile . . .

I LEFT HER IN BED, face pressed to pillow, eyes closed, body curled like a fetus. I told her not to leave the apartment, not to answer the door, not to pick up the telephone unless it rang once, stopped, then rang again. That would be my signal.

"One if by land," she mumbled. "Two if by sea."

I kissed her cheek. She smiled like a Cheshire cat, happy and contented. I dressed and left her apartment.

The first stop was my own apartment. I got on the phone, cursed myself once, quietly, and called the Continental Detective Agency in Cleveland. The voice that answered sounded two years out of an expensive college. I told him to run a brief check on a man named Jack Blake, supposed to be a homicide victim within the past couple of months, and to ring me back on it.

It was simple stuff and it only took him half an hour. Jack Blake, he revealed, was a card sharp who ran a magic shop on Euclid Avenue, got beaten to death in his own home, and had a daughter named Rhona. It was she who reported all this to the police. So far it was unsolved. Did I want to know more?

I didn't. I told him to bill me and got off the phone. *I'm sorry, Rhona*, I said softly. *This time I should have believed you. I'm sorry.*

Then I got out of there and headed for the Senator, a cafeteria on Broadway at 96th, downstairs from Manny Hess's pool hall and across the street from a Ping-Pong emporium. They serve good food and run a clean place, and every small-time operator on Upper Broadway drops in for coffee-and. I went inside and got a cup of coffee and carried it to the table where Herbie Wills was sitting.

Wills, a small, gray man of forty-five, was eating yogurt and buttered whole wheat toast. There was a glass of milk standing on the table.

"Ulcers," he said. "I went to this doctor because of my stomach, he said I have ulcers. I have this very sensitive stomach, Mr. London. There are certain foods I can't eat. They disagree with me, you know."

"Sure," I said.

"Now," he said, spooning in a teaspoon of yogurt. "Can I help you, Mr. London?"

"I need some information."

"Sure, Mr. London."

Information was Herbie's livelihood. He wasn't exactly a stool pigeon, just a little man who kept his ears open and filed away everything into separate compartments of his mind. When the information market was weak he ran errands for bookies. He was a hanger-on, living in a clean but shabby room in a 98th Street hotel.

"Milton Klugsman," I said.

Herbie pursed his bloodless lips, tapped three times on the table with his index finger. "So far," he said, "nothing. More?"

I gave him a quick description. "I make him in Canarsie, Herbie. At least he's familiar with the area out there. A Brooklyn or Queens boy, then. Any help?"

"Miltie," he said. I looked at him. "Miltie Klugsman, Mr. London. This is what throws me for a moment; you said Milton Klugsman, I start thinking in terms of Milton or Milt. But I knew a Miltie Klugsman. This is all he gets called. Miltie."

"Go on."

Another spoon of yogurt, bite of toast, deliberate sip of milk. I watched him and hoped I would never get ulcers. He wiped his mouth again and shrugged.

"I do not know much," he said carefully. "Miltie Klugsman. I think he works for himself, Mr. London. I think maybe selling things, like a fence. But this is just a guess because I hardly know him at all."

"Who are his friends?"

Herbie shrugged. "This I don't know. As a matter of fact, I hardly know Miltie Klugsman at all. You were right about Brooklyn. He lives somewhere in East New York near the Queens line."

"Married?"

"He could be. I see him once with a dark-haired girl. She was wearing a mink stole. But this doesn't mean she is his wife, Mr. London."

That sounded logical enough. "I have to find Miltie," I said. "Where does he hang out?"

He thought about it, through another spoon of yogurt, bites of toast, two sips of milk. "Now wait a minute," he said. "Sure."

"What?"

"A diner in Brooklyn!" he said. "On Livonia Avenue near Avenue K. I don't know Brooklyn too well. The diner is one of those old trolley cars but like remodeled. I don't know the name."

"Probably something like 'Diner'."

"That might be it," he said seriously. "Try there, ask around. You might even find Miltie himself."

I doubted it. Miltie Klugsman wouldn't be there unless they had plastered him under the basement floor. But I didn't tell this to Herbie.

He was a stool pigeon with a conscience. He wouldn't take the ten I gave him, insisting it was too much for the sort of information he had given me. I gave him a five finally and got out of there.

I went back to the Chevy. Some juvenile delinquent had relieved me of my radio aerial—in the morning he would go to shop class and make a zip gun out of it. Deprived of music, I headed dolefully for Brooklyn.

SIX

Livonia Avenue was filled with people. I parked two blocks from the diner—which was named Diner after all—and stopped in a drugstore to see if Miltie Klugsman had had a phone. He did, plus an address on Ashford Street. The pharmacist told me how to get to

Ashford Street. I started in that direction, then decided to try the diner first.

It wasn't much. A ferret-faced counterman was pressing a hamburger down on a greasy grill. He turned to look at me when I walked in. An antique whore sat at the counter near the door drinking coffee with cream.

I took a stool halfway between the old girl and a trio of young punks in snap-brim hats, all of them trying to look like latterday Kid Twists. I was in Reles country, Murder Inc.'s old stamping grounds not far from the heart of Brownsville.

The counterman decided that the hamburger was cooked enough to kill the taste. He surrounded it with a stale roll, slapped it onto a chipped saucer, slid it down the counter to the snap-brim set. He came over to me and leaned on the counter. His face didn't change expression when he saw the bulge the .38 made in my jacket. He looked at me, deadpan, and waited.

"Black coffee," I said.

"No trouble. Not in here."

He talked without moving his lips. It's a trick they teach you in Dannemora and other institutions of higher learning. I asked him if I looked like a troublemaker. He shrugged.

"I just want coffee," I said.

The counterman nodded. He gave me the coffee and I handed him a dime for it. He walked away to trade a story or two with the old hooker. I waited for the coffee to cool. The snap-brim triplets were looking me over.

The coffee tasted like lukewarm dishwater that some fool had rinsed a coffee cup in. I left it alone. The counterman came back, leaned over me like the Tower of Pisa.

"You want anything else besides coffee?"

"A plain doughnut."

He gave me one. "That all?"

"Maybe not."

"What else?"

I sat for a moment or two trying to look like a hood trying to think. My eyes were as wary as I could make them.

"I'm looking for a guy," I said. "I was told I could find him here."

"Who is he?"

"A guy named Klugsman," I said. "Miltie Klugsman. You know him?"

Not a flicker of expression. Just a nod.

"You know where I can find him?"

"He ain't around much. What do you want with him?"

"It's private."

"Yeah?"

I pretended to do some more thinking. "I hear he buys things. I got a thing or two for sale."

"Like what?"

I shook my head. "No," I said.

"You might get a better price from somebody else," the counterman said. "Depending on what you got to sell. Miltie, now he can be cheap. You got something for sale, you want all you can get."

"I was given orders to see Miltie," I said. The hell with it—let him think I was only a hired hand. I didn't care that much about the prestige value of the bit.

"Miltie," he said. "Miltie Klugsman."

"Yeah."

"You hang on a minute," he said. "I think that guy there wants more coffee. You just hang on."

He filled a cup with coffee and took it over to the young punks. The one he gave it to had his hat halfway over his eyes. The counterman said something unintelligible without moving his lips. The kid answered.

The counterman came back. He asked me my name. I told him it didn't matter. He asked me who I worked for and I said that didn't matter either.

"I'll tell it to Klugsman," I said.

"He could be hard to find."

"So maybe I came to the wrong place." I started to slide off the stool, got one foot on the floor before his hand settled on my shoulder. I stood up and turned to face him again.

"Don't be in a hurry," he said.

"I got things to do."

"Miltie used to come in a lot. He ain't been around much. I was talking to a guy"—he nodded toward the triplets—"over there."

"I figured."

"One of 'em hangs with Miltie now and then. He says maybe he can help. If you want."

"Sure."

"Danny," he said, "c'mere."

Danny c'mered. He was almost my height but his posture concealed the fact neatly. His fingers were yellow from too many cigarettes and not enough soap. His suit must have been fairly expensive and his shoes had a high shine on them, but nothing he wore could take the slob look away from him. It came shining through.

"You want Miltie," he said.

"That's the idea."

"He's a little hot right now," Danny said. "He's holed up a few blocks from here. I could show you."

We left the diner. Danny lit a cigarette in the doorway. He didn't offer me one. We turned right and walked to the corner, turned right again and left Livonia for a side street. The block was darker, more residential than commercial. We walked the length of the block in silence and took another right turn.

"You ever meet Miltie?"

"No," I said.

"You from New York?"

"The Bronx. Throg's Neck."

"Long way from home," he said.

I didn't answer him. We kept walking. At the corner we made another right turn.

"This is a hell of a way to go," I said.

"Yeah?"

"We just go around the block," I said. "There must be a shorter way to do it."

"This is easier."

"Yeah?"

"It gives 'em time," he said.

It took a minute. Time? Time to make a phone call, time to take the short route and come around the block to meet us. I went for my gun. I was too slow. Danny was on my left, a foot or so behind me. His gun dug into my rib cage and the muzzle felt colder than death.

"Easy," he said.

My hand was three or four inches from the .38. It stopped in midair and stayed there.

"Take out the piece," he said. "Do it slow. Very slow. Don't point it at me. I'd just as soon shoot you now and find out later who the hell you are."

I took out the gun and I did it slowly. There was a warehouse across the street, dark and silent. On our side was a row of brownstones filled with people who didn't report gunshots to the police. I let the gun point at the ground.

"Drop it."

I dropped it. It bounced once on the pavement and lay still.

"Kick it."

"Where?"

"Just kick it."

I kicked it. The .38 skidded twenty feet, bounced into the gutter. His gun was still on my ribs and he kept poking me as a reminder.

"Now we wait," he said. "It shouldn't be long."

IT WASN'T LONG AT ALL. They came down the block from Livonia, walking fast but not quite running. They had their hands in their pockets and their hats down over their foreheads. They were in uniform. I stood there with Danny's gun in my ribs and waited for them.

"He's a cop," one of them said.

Danny dug at me. "A cop?"

"A private cop. His name is London and he's sticking his nose into things he shouldn't. They tried to buy him off but he wouldn't be bought."

"It's good we checked."

"Well," the punk said. "They said anybody comes nosing for Miltie, we should call. So I called."

I looked at my gun. It was three miles away from me in the gutter. I wanted it in my hand.

"What's the word, man?"

"The word is we got a contract."

"At what price?"

"Three yards apiece," the punk said. He was thinner than Danny, maybe a year or two older. His face was pockmarked and his eyes bulged when he stared, as though he needed glasses but he was afraid they wouldn't fit the hard-guy image.

"Cheap," Danny said.

"Hell, it's an easy hit. We just take him and dump him. Nothing to it, Danny."

"Yeah."

"It's three quick bills. And it sets us up, man. It makes us look good and it gives us an in."

They would need all the ins they could get. Danny was sloppy, strictly an amateur. You don't stand next to a person when you're holding a gun on him. You get as far away as you can. The gun's advantage increases with distance. The closer you are, the less of an edge you've got.

"We take him for a ride," Danny was saying. "Take him the same place they gave it to Miltie. Ride him around Canarsie, hit him in the head, then drive back."

"Sure, Danny."

"We use his car," he went on. "Which is your car, buster?"

"The Chevy."

"The red convertible?"

"That's the one."

"Gimme the keys."

He was much too close. He should have backed off four or five steps, more if he was a good enough shot. He was making my play too easy for me.

"The keys."

The other two were in front of us. They both had their hands in their pockets. They were heeled, but one had his jacket buttoned and the other looked slow and stupid.

"The keys!"

I let him nudge me with the gun. I felt the muzzle poke into me, then relax.

I dropped. I fell down and I fell toward him, and I snapped his arm behind his back and took the gun right out of his hand. One punk was trying to reach through his jacket button to his own gun. I gave the trigger a squeeze and the bullet hit him in the throat. He took two steps, clapped both hands to his neck, fell over, and died.

The other one—the slow-looking one—wasn't so slow after all. He drew in a hurry and he shot in a hurry, but he didn't stop to remember that I was using Danny as a shield. He had time to get off two shots. One went wide. The other caught Danny in the chest. The punk was getting ready for a third shot when I snapped off a pair that caught him in the center of the chest. Danny's gun was a .45. The holes it made were big enough to step in.

I dropped Danny just as he was starting to bleed on me. He was still alive but didn't figure to last more than a few seconds. He blacked out immediately.

I wiped my prints off his .45 and tossed it next to him on the pavement. I ran over to the curb, scooped my .38 out of the gutter, and wedged it into my shoulder rig. That made it easy for the cops. Three punks had a fight and killed each other, and to hell with all of them. Nobody would shed tears for them. They weren't worth it.

The gunshots were still echoing in the empty streets. I looked at three corpses for a second or two, then ran like hell. I kept going for two blocks, turned a corner, slowed down. I was digging a pipe out of a pocket when the sirens started up.

I filled the pipe, lit it. I walked down the street smoking and taking long breaths and telling my nerves they could unwind now.

But my nerves didn't believe it . . . I couldn't blame them.

Brooklyn was cool, quiet, and dark, with only the police siren cutting through the night. I got back on Livonia, skirted the diner, got into the Chevy.

Behind the wheel, I dumped out my pipe, put it away. Then I

drove along, trying to remember the directions to Ashford Street. I got lost once, but I found the place—Klugsman's address.

The building was like all the others. He must have been small-time, I thought. Otherwise he would have found a better place to live. I walked into the front hallway. A kid, twelve or thirteen, was sprawled on the stairs with a Pepsi in one hand and a cigarette in the other. He watched me lean on Klugsman's bell.

"The bell don't work," he said. "You looking for Mrs. Klugsman?"

I hadn't known there was one, but I was looking for her now. I told the kid so.

"Upstairs," he said. "Just walk right up. Third floor, apartment three-C."

I thanked the kid, he shrugged, and I went up two flights of rickety stairs. The building smelled of age and stale beer. I stood in front of the door marked 3-C. The apartment was not empty. Gutbucket jazz boomed through the door, records playing too loudly on a lo-fi player. I knocked on the door. Nothing happened. I knocked again.

"C'mon in, whoever in hell it is!"

The voice was loud. I turned the knob and went into the apartment where Miltie Klugsman had once lived. It was a railroad flat, three or four rooms tied together by grim little hallways. The furniture was old and the walls needed paint. The place had the general feel of a cheap apartment which someone had tried to hold together until, recently, that someone had stopped caring.

The someone was sitting on a worn-out couch. She could have been beautiful once. She may have been attractive, still; it was hard to tell. There was a pint of blended rye in her hand. The pint was about three-quarters gone and she was about three-quarters drunk. She was a thirty-five-year-old brunette with lines at the corners of her eyes and mouth.

She was wearing a faded yellow housedress that was missing a button or two in front and had floppy slippers on her feet. She waved a hand at me and took another long drink that killed most of the pint of rye.

"Hiya," she called. "Who in hell are you?"

I closed the door, walked over, sat on the couch.

"My name's Shirley. Who're you?"

"Ed," I said.

"You lookin' for Miltie? He doesn't live here anymore. You know the song? 'Annie Doesn't Live Here Anymore'?" Her eyes rolled. "Miltie doesn't live here anymore," she said sadly. "Miltie's dead, Ed. That rhymes. Dead, Ed."

I walked over to the record player and turned off something raucous. I went back to the couch. She offered me a drink of the blend. I didn't want any.

"Poor Miltie," she said. "I loved him, you believe it? Oh, Miltie wasn't much. Me and Miltie, just a couple of nothings."

"Shirley—"

"That's me," she said. Her face clouded, and for a moment I thought she was going to start crying. She surprised me by laughing instead. She tossed her head back and her body shook with laughter. She couldn't stop. I reached over and slapped her, not too hard, and she sat up and rubbed the side of her face and nodded her head vigorously.

"Shirley, Miltie was murdered," I said. "You know that, don't you?"

She looked at me and nodded. The tears were starting now. I wanted to go away and leave her alone. I couldn't.

"Murdered, Shirley. He had some . . . evidence that some man wanted. Do you know where it is?"

She shook her head.

"He must have talked about it, Shirley. He must have told you something. Think."

She looked away, then back at me, cupped her chin with one hand, closed her eyes, opened them. "Nope," she said. "He never told me a thing. Not Miltie."

"Are you sure?"

"Uh-huh." She reached for the bottle again. I took it away from her. She came at me, sprawled across me, fingers scrabbling for the bottle. I gave it to her and she killed it. She held it at arm's length, reading the label slowly and deliberately. Then she heaved it across the room. It bounced off the record player, took another wild bounce, and shattered.

"Poor Miltie," she said.

"Shirley—"

"Jussa minute," she said. "What's your name again? Ed? I'm gonna tell you something. Ed, I'll tell you about Miltie Klugsman. Okay?"

"Sure."

"Miltie was just a little guy," she said. "Like me, see? Before I met him I used to work the clubs, you know, do a little stripping, get the customers to buy me drinks. I was never a hooker, Ed. You believe me?"

"I believe you."

She nodded elaborately. "Well," she said. "Lots of guys, you say you were a stripper, they figure you were a whore. Not me. Some girls, maybe. Not me."

She was standing now, swaying a little but staying on her feet. She picked a pack of cigarettes from a table, shook one loose, and put it in her mouth. I scratched a match for her and she leaned forward to take the light. Her dress fell away from her body. She wasn't wearing a bra. I looked away and she laughed hysterically.

"See something you shouldn't, Ed?" I didn't say anything. "Oh," she said, continuing her story. "So I met Miltie at the club. He was a good guy, you know? Decent. Oh, he did some time. You live like this, this kind of life, you don't care if a man did time. What's the past, Ed? Huh? It's the present, and what kind of guy a guy is, and all. Right?"

"Sure."

"He wanted to marry me. Nobody else, they always wanted, oh, you know what they wanted. He wanted to marry me. So what the hell. Right, Ed?"

"Sure."

"He was just a little guy. Nobody important. But we stuck with each other and we made it. We stuck together, we ate steady, we lived okay. This place is a mess now. When it's fixed up it looks better."

She pranced around the room like a hostess showing off her antiques. Something struck her funny and she started laughing again, reeling around the room and laughing hysterically. Her voice caught on a snag and the laughter changed abruptly to tears. She cried as she laughed, putting all of herself into it. I got up to catch her and she sagged against me, limp as a dishrag. I held on to her for a few seconds. Then she got hold of herself and pulled away from me.

"Poor, poor poor Miltie," she said. "I was afraid, I knew he was getting in over his head. Listen, I was just a lousy dime-store stripper, you know? I knew enough not to try to play the big-time circuit. I stuck to my own league. You know what I mean?"

"Sure, Shirley."

"But Miltie didn't know this. He wanted to do something big. I was afraid, I knew he was getting mixed up, getting in over his head. He was all tangled up in something too big for him. He was a *good* guy but he wasn't a *big* guy. I knew something like this was going to happen. I knew it."

The cigarette burned her fingers. She dropped it and squashed it beneath one of the floppy slippers. She kicked off the slippers, first one and then the other. Her toenails were painted scarlet and the paint was chipped here and there.

"He was going to get out. He was going to stick to his own league. And then—"

She didn't break. She came close, but she didn't. The last of the liquor was taking hold of her now and she was staggering. She stepped into the center of the room, walked to the record player, put on something slow and jazzy. I stayed where I was. "I'm still good-looking," she said. "Aren't I?"

I told her she was.

"Not a kid anymore," she said. "But I'll get by."

The music was strip-club jazz. She took a few preliminary steps to it, tossing her hips at me in an almost comical bump-and-grind, and grinned.

Then, slowly, she went into her act. We weren't in a strip joint and she wasn't wearing a ball gown. She was wearing a faded yellow housedress that buttoned down the front, and she undid it a button at a time. Her fingers were clumsy with blended rye but she got the dress open and shrugged it away. It fell to the floor bunched around her long legs. She took a step and kicked the dress away.

No bra. Just thin black panties. She had a fine body, slender waist, trim hips, full breasts with just the slightest trace of age to them. She kept dancing, moving with the music, flinging her breasts at me, grinding her loins at me.

"Not bad, huh? Not bad for an old broad, huh, Ed? Still lively, huh?"

I didn't answer her. I wanted to get up and go away but I couldn't do that either. I watched while she peeled off the panties and tossed them away. She had trouble with them but she got them off and danced her wicked dance in blissful nudity.

"Ed," she said.

She came at me, threw herself at me. Her flesh, warm with drink, was soft as butter in my arms. She looked into my eyes, her face a study in alcoholic passion mixed in equal parts with torment. She looked at me, and she squirmed against me, and then her eyes closed and she passed out cold.

There was a double bed in the bedroom. She had to sleep alone in it now. Some men with machine guns had killed the man who used to share it with her. I drew back the top sheet, put her down on the bed. I covered her with the sheet, tucked a pillow under her head.

Then I got out of there.

SEVEN

The ride back to Manhattan was a long one. Every traffic light was red when I got to it.

I told myself that the picture was refusing to take shape, and then I changed my mind—it was taking shape, all right. It was taking a great many shapes, each conflicting with the other. Nothing made much sense.

Shirley Klugsman was a widow because her husband had tried to sell evidence to Rhona Blake. A man named Zucker wanted Rhona dead. He also wanted me dead, and three punks in East New York had tried to carry it off for him. And they were dead now.

I GOT THE CHEVY BACK TO MY GARAGE and walked halfway home before I changed my mind. Then I jumped in a cab.

Rewards and punishments—Phillip Carr's phrase. They were at the punishment stage now. They wanted me dead, and they had tried once already that night, and maybe my apartment wasn't the safest place in the world.

Besides, Rhona was alone . . .

The doorman barely looked at me. I let the elevator whisk me up to her floor, went to her door, and jabbed at the bell. Nothing happened. I remembered our signal, rang once, waited a minute, then started ringing. Nothing happened. I called out to her, told her who it was. And nothing happened.

She was out, of course. At a show, having a drink, catching a bite to eat. I got halfway to the elevator and my mind filled with another picture, a less pleasant one in which she was lying facedown on the wall-to-wall carpet and bleeding. I went back to her door.

On television I would have given the door a good hard shoulder, wood would have splintered, and that would have been that. This is fine on television, where they have balsa doors. But every time I hit a door with my shoulder I wind up with a sore shoulder and an unimpaired door. In Manhattan, apartment doors are usually reinforced with steel plates. You just can't trust television.

I took out the little gimcrack I use to clean my pipe. It had a penknife blade. I opened it and played with the lock. It opened. I went inside.

She wasn't there. So I sat down in the living room to wait for her, first checking the bar to see if there was any cognac. There wasn't. There was scotch, but cognac is all I drink.

Hell. This was a special sort of situation. I poured a lot of scotch into a glass and sat down to work on it.

After half an hour, I was worried. She was in too deep, playing way over her head, and she wasn't around. The room was beginning to get to me. I kept smelling her perfume and the furniture kept glaring at me.

Where the hell was she?

I remembered the afternoon, and the green eyes warming very suddenly, and her body close to mine. Bed, and whispers, and passion, and the happy drowsiness afterwards. And now she was gone. It was the sort of magic trick Jack Blake would have gone wild over. You just make love to this girl, see, and she disappears.

After ten more minutes of this I was morbid. I started combing the apartment in a cockeyed search for help notes or struggle signs or bullet holes. I got down on hands and knees and peered owlishly under the bed. There was a single slipper there, and a pair of stockings that had run for their lives, and a respectable quantity of dust. I checked out the closet in the bedroom. Her clothes, and not many of them. A suitcase, streamlined and airplane-gray. She had been traveling light. She was Jack Blake's daughter, coming from Cleveland with a single suitcase and a bellyful of determination, and that wasn't going to be enough.

I went back to the living room. The bedroom closet had been a disappointment from an aesthetic standpoint. You're supposed to open a closet door and watch a body fall out. That was how they did it on television. And all I got was a suitcase and some clothing.

There was still a closet in the front hall. I gave the knob a twist, yanked open the door, and stepped ceremoniously aside so that the body wouldn't hit me when it fell.

No body fell.

Instead there was a noise like a shotgun blast at close quarters, and there was a wind like Hurricane Zelda, and I flew up in the air and bounced off one wall into another. Then the lights went out.

EIGHT

It was timeless. There was the lifting sensation, the spinning, the impact, the blackness. Then I was on my back on that orange couch and my eyes were open. I saw ash blond hair, a red mouth.

Rhona.

She was saying: "Lie still, Ed. Relax, lie still, don't try to move. My God, I came in and found you. I thought you were dead. The whole hallway was a mess. It looked as though someone fired a cannon in here. Are you all right, Ed?"

She was leaning over me, stroking my forehead with one soft hand. Her eyes were wide, concerned. Sensation was starting to come back now, with pain leading the procession. My whole body ached. I ran hands over myself to find out what was broken. Surprisingly, everything seemed to be intact. I started to sit up. There was dizziness, and I fell back on the couch and closed my eyes for a minute.

I must have blacked out again. Then I came back to life and she was lighting a cigarette for me, putting it between my lips. I smoked. I started to sit up, saw the worry in her eyes. I told her I was all right now.

"What happened, Ed?"

"A bomb."

"Where?"

"In your closet," I said. "I opened the door and it went off."

"What were you doing in the closet?"

"Looking for bodies."

"Huh?"

"Forget it." I closed my eyes, remembering the cute little sidestep I'd executed, a nutty bit of business designed to permit the mythical corpse to fall out of the closet without hitting me. Corny, but damn fortunate. The sidestep had taken me out of the way of the blast. If the full force had gotten me, I'd have found a body, all right.

My own.

"Ed—"

I took a breath. "Rhona, somebody had it set up for you. You were supposed to walk into the apartment and hang your coat in the front closet. They must have rigged it with a wire running to the door handle, something like that. Open the door and you yank the wire and the thing blows."

"God."

"Uh-huh. When did you leave, Rhona? Why the hell didn't you stay put?"

She was chewing on her lower lip and her eyes were focused on the floor. She said: "I got a phone call."

"You weren't supposed to answer the phone."

"I know. But it rang and rang and rang . . . I picked it up."

"Who was it?"

"A man. He didn't give me his name. He just said he was calling for you."

"For me?"

She nodded. "I didn't know whether to believe him or not. But he said you were in trouble and couldn't call yourself, and I thought you were the only person who knew the telephone number here—"

"Klugsman knew it, didn't he?"

"Oh," she said. "I forgot that, Ed—"

"When did he call?"

"Around midnight."

"And you left right away?"

"That's right."

I put out the cigarette. "Then I missed you by less than half an hour," I said. "They must have had a man stationed right out front, ready to drop up and install the bomb the minute you left the building. It's easy enough to get into this place. The doorman is so busy being proper and distant that he doesn't pay any attention to what's going on. So the guy came in, set up shop, and left. Then I got here and waited for you." I looked at her. "Where the hell were you, anyway?"

"Times Square."

"Huh?"

"I took a taxi to Times Square, Ed. That's what the man on the phone said I was supposed to do. I went to a place called Hector's, a big cafeteria. I took a table and waited for you."

"For how long?"

"A little over an hour, I guess. It was a bore and I was scared stiff and I didn't know what was going to happen next. Then finally a man came over to me and handed me a note. He was gone almost before I knew what was going on. The note said you wouldn't be able to meet me but everything was all right and I was supposed to go back to my apartment. I got here just in time to find you."

I got up, dragged myself over to the front hall, what was left of it. There was a gaping hole in the wall directly opposite the closet door. If I hadn't stepped aside, the blast would have made a similar hole in me.

It was something to think about.

I dropped to my hands and knees and poked around in the closet. There wasn't much to look at, just enough to confirm my diagnosis of the blast. It was a simple sort of booby-trap, the kind even a child could put together. A few sticks of dynamite, evidently touched off with a blasting cap. A piece of thin copper wire was attached to the cap and to the doorknob. There was still a trace of the wire around the knob.

"God, Ed."

I got up, put an arm around her. We walked to the kitchen. She put water on for coffee. While it cooked, I gave her a quick rundown on my part of the evening. I left out the call to the Continental agency in Cleveland. She didn't have to know that I hadn't trusted her.

SHE WAS SMOKING TOO MANY CIGARETTES too quickly. She was nervous and it showed. Why not? She had a lot to be nervous about. Half the world was trying to kill her. That sort of thing tends to get on your nerves.

"It doesn't add," I said.

"What doesn't?"

"The whole thing. This morning they didn't know where to find you, Rhona. Zucker's lawyer was ready to pay ten thousand bucks just to get hold of you. A few hours later they know where you are and all they want to do is kill us both. They hand out contracts on the two of us. I'm supposed to get shot in East New York and you're supposed to get blown up in your own apartment."

"Maybe they had us followed. Or maybe somebody tipped them off."

"Who?" I shrugged. "But there's more. Why should they play around with a bomb? They could decoy you with a phone call, then drop you with a bullet on the street. Why get so fancy? Why send you on a wild goose chase to Hector's? That's the kind of play an amateur might use. A pro would be more direct. And we're up against professionals."

The coffee finished dripping. She poured out a pair of cups. I sweetened mine with a shot of scotch and let it cool a little.

"Look," I said. "Let's suppose they wanted to search the apartment. They still didn't have to get cute about it. Did you have anything here?"

"Nothing they would be interested in."

"Well, they might not have known that. But they still could have shot you down on the street and then sent a man upstairs. Or they could break in, kill you, then search. It just doesn't make any sense."

"I guess not," she said.

We sat there drinking our coffee, tossing it all back and forth and getting nowhere in particular. She started to relax. God knows how. I decided that a card mechanic has to have a sound nervous system, and she was a card mechanic's daughter. Maybe that's the sort of thing that passes down a family tree.

I told her to go to sleep.

"Is it safe?"

"Nothing's safe," I said. "I don't think they'll be around tonight. It's late and we're both half-dead. I am, anyway, and you must be."

"I'm kind of tired, Ed."

"Sure. We'll get some sleep and see what happens tomorrow. It's been their play all along now. Maybe I can start something for our side, set some wheels in motion."

"I'm scared, Ed."

"So am I. But I'm tired enough to sleep. How about you?"

She shrugged. "I guess I'm all right," she said. "Uh . . . you'll sleep on the couch tonight, won't you?"

"No."

"Ed," she said. "Ed, listen, don't be silly. You're exhausted and you almost got killed tonight and—"

"No."

"Ed, you're crazy. Oh, you nut. Ed, Ed, you *will* sleep on the couch, won't you?"

I didn't—not on the couch . . .

SHE FELL ASLEEP RIGHT AWAY. I tossed and turned and listened to her measured breathing, and I wondered how the hell she managed it. I closed my eyes and counted fences jumping sheep, and things like that, and nothing worked. I hadn't expected it to.

It was still too tangled up to make any appreciable sort of sense. There were just too damned many inconsistencies. I couldn't figure them out.

Sleep on it, I told myself. Sleep on it, stupid. And, eventually, I did just that.

The morning wasn't too bad. She woke up first, and by the time I opened my eyes she was busy frying bacon and eggs in the kitchen. I showered and got dressed and went in for breakfast. There was fresh coffee made and the food was on the table. She even looked pretty in the morning. It seemed impossible, but she did.

The bacon was crisp, the eggs were fine, the coffee was perfect. I told her so and she beamed. "I had plenty of practice," she said. "I used to cook for Dad all the time, since my mother died."

It was around ten by the time I got out of there. First we had to go over the ground rules. This time, dammit, she would stay in the apartment. This time, dammit, she wouldn't answer the phone unless it was my signal. Same for the door.

"Ed—"

I was at the door. I turned. Her mouth came up to me and her lips brushed mine.

"Be careful, Ed."

Outside, the sun was shining. There was a different doorman on duty. He ignored me—he knew the ground rules there, by George, and the rules said that the doorman took no notice of anyone. They were strictly ornamental.

I hauled out my wallet, dug out the card I'd gotten a day ago. Just a day? It seemed much longer. I studied the card—*Phillip Carr. Attorney at Law. 42 East 37ᵗʰ Street.*

I walked to the corner to save the doorman the trouble of hailing me a cab, and to save myself the tip I'd have had to give him. I got into a taxi and told the driver to take me to Fifth and 37th.

It was time to get rolling. Carr and Zucker and the rest of the crooked-card-game set had dealt every hand so far. Rhona and I were just throwing our chips in the center and calling every bet.

You can do that for just so long. Then it's time to deal a hand yourself.

I sat in the backseat and gnawed on a pipestem while the cabby fought his way uptown through mid-morning traffic. Phillip Carr, Attorney at Law. Okay, shyster, I thought. Let's see what happens.

NINE

The cab dropped me in front of Carr's building about midway between Fifth and Madison on 37th Street. I took an express elevator to the twentieth floor, walked along a chrome-plated hallway to a door with Carr's name on it. I walked in.

The secretary's desk was kidney shaped. The girl behind it wasn't. Her bright red hair had been painfully spray-netted until it had the general consistency of plastic. Her smile was metallic. Her sweater bulged nicely, giving a hint of flesh that the hair and the smile tried to conceal. I told her I wanted to see Carr.

"Your name, please?"

"Ed London," I said.

She got up gracefully, wiggled her well-girdled hips on the way through a door marked PRIVATE. The door closed behind her. I picked up a magazine from a table, glanced at it, tossed it back. The door opened and the girl came out again.

"He'll see you," she said.

"I thought he would."

Phillip Carr's office had framed diplomas on the wall from every college but Leavenworth. He stood up, smiled at me, and stuck out his hand for a handshake. I didn't take it, and after a few seconds he fetched it back again.

"Well," he said. "I'm damn glad to see you, London. You were pretty hostile yesterday. I guess you've thought things over."

"Something like that."

"Cigar?"

"No thanks."

"Well," he said.

"I thought it all over. Especially what you said about rewards and punishments."

"And?"

"I've got a reward for you."

He didn't get it until I hit him in the face. He'd stood there, hands at his sides, waiting patiently for me to tell him what the reward was, while I curled one hand into a fist, and aimed it at his jaw. It was a nice punch. It picked him up and sent him sailing over his desk, and it dropped him in an untidy pile on the floor.

He came up cursing. He made a grab for a desk drawer, probably to get a gun. I kicked him away from it. He crouched, snarling like a tiger at bay, and lunged for the button that would summon the secretary. I caught him by the lapels and gave him a little push that turned his lunge into a full-blown charge. He didn't slow down until he bounced off a wall and collapsed onto the high-pile carpet.

"Take it easy," I said. "You'll have a heart attack."

"You son of a—"

I picked him up and hit him a few times. It wasn't a particularly nice thing to do. At the moment, I wasn't an especially nice guy. Try to kill someone often enough and he's bound to get riled.

I hit him in the nose, and some of the cartilage melted down and readjusted itself. I hit him in the mouth and heard a tooth or two snap. He spat them out and stared at them. I hauled him to his feet again and gave him another heave and watched him fall all over the floor.

The secretary never got in the way. Good Old Miss Girdled-Hips—she only came running when someone pressed the little buzzer. She was the soul of discretion. You could murder her boss in his office and she'd never leave her desk.

I picked him up again. He was breathing raggedly and bleeding profusely. I held him by the lapels and gave him my nastiest glare.

"Had enough?"

"Yes," he panted, fear in his eyes.

I felt a little foolish. Then I remembered the dynamite blast in Rhona's apartment, the tommy-gun in Canarsie, the three punks in East New York. I started to get mad again. That was dangerous—I didn't want to kill the bastard. I dumped him in an armchair and let him catch his breath.

"This time I'll talk about rewards and punishments," I told him. "You've got a client and I've got a client. Your client is trying to kill mine."

He didn't say anything.

"Your client is a man named Abe Zucker," I said. "He runs a rigged card game and fleeces heavy-money marks. He was doing fine. Then a man named Jack Blake came along and tried a few tricks of his own."

And, like a proud little schoolboy reciting the preamble to the Constitution, I read the whole bit to him. First he just sat there. Then he looked amused, and then he started to laugh.

I asked him what was so funny.

"London," he smirked. "You're a panic. A detective? You couldn't find sand in a desert."

"What are you getting at?"

"What am I getting at?" He laughed some more. "Abe Zucker running a card game," he said. "That's a wild one, London. Don't you know who Zucker is? Abe Zucker is so damned big he wouldn't waste his time on all the poker games in the country. That's not his line, London. It never was."

"What is?"

"Nothing just now. He got out of the heavy stuff a long time ago. He put his dough in legit stuff and kept it there. Abe Zucker is cleaner than you are, London. Card games!" He laughed again.

I kept my eyes on his face, trying to see what I could read there. If he was putting on an act he was good enough for Broadway . . . I believed him.

"Card games," he repeated. "Card games."

"Then straighten me out, Carr."

He looked at me, the smile gone now. "I wouldn't tell you the right time, London. Now get out of here—"

I started to leave when he added, " . . . you punk."

I picked him up, shook him like a rat. "Talk," I said.

"Let go of me."

"Carr—"

"You'll wind up in the river," he whined. "One word from me and every gun in the city will have you in his sights."

"I'm terrified."

"London—"

We weren't getting anywhere. He wasn't scaring me and I wasn't going to get anything more out of him. I didn't need him anymore, not now.

But he could get in the way.

I put him out with a good, clean shot to the jaw. It landed right and I got vibrations all the way up my arm to the shoulder. He sagged and went limp. I lowered him back into the chair, folded his hands in his lap for laughs. Then I opened the door and slipped through it.

The secretary was sitting in her swivel chair. I winked at her and she smiled her metallic smile at me. I wanted to reach over and pinch the place where her sweater bulged. I suppressed the impulse. I had enough problems.

THERE WAS A DRUGSTORE on the corner of Madison and 36th with a raft of phone booths. I ducked into an empty one, switched on the overhead fan, and dialed Centre Street. I asked the cop who answered to give me Jerry Gunther.

"I'm in a rush," I told him. "Just want some fast information. Know anything about a man named Abe Zucker?"

"I know the name."

"And?"

"Just a second. Lemme think . . . Yeah."

"Go on."

"He's an old-timer," Jerry said. "Was mixed up in everything big. Junk, numbers, women. He was one of the boys who managed to stay out of the papers, not just out of jail. But he was big."

"What's he doing now?"

"Nothing."

"Nothing he talks about?"

"Nothing at all," Jerry said. "He doesn't have to, Ed. He did what they've all been doing, made the money illegally and then sank it into legitimate business. He owns a piece of three hotels in Miami Beach and a couple of points in one of the big Vegas casinos. Plus God knows what else. I remember him now, Ed. I saw him once years ago—we had him up on the carpet for something. But that's ancient history now."

"Is he in New York?"

"Who knows, Ed. He's clean and nobody cares about him anymore. I think he's got a big place somewhere in Jersey. I wouldn't swear to it."

"Thanks."

"That all you wanted?"

"For the time being," I said. "I may have something for you later on."

I got off the phone, went to the counter, and picked up a couple of dollars worth of small change and a fresh pouch of tobacco. I had to wait for a booth—some fat old lady ducked into mine and she had enough dimes in front of her to talk all day and all night. Another booth emptied and I grabbed it. I dropped a fortune in silver into the phone and called the Continental agency in Cleveland.

It took a few minutes before I was connected with the op I'd talked to before. I didn't remember his name, and that had slowed things down. But I managed to get him on the line.

"London," I said. "You did a job for me yesterday. Remember?"

"I remember, Mr. London."

"Good. I want the same thing but in depth. I want you to check out Jack Blake and his magic shop. Find out what kind of business the shop was doing, what scale Blake was living on, if he was spending more than he was earning, everything. Run a line on his daughter. Find out what you can about her. Not just a surface job. The works."

"When do you want it, sir?"

"Yesterday," I said.

He laughed politely.

"I mean—"

"I know what you mean." I checked my watch—it was a shade past noon. "When can you have it?"

"Hard to say. Two hours, three hours, four hours—"

"Give me an outside time. I don't know where I'll be. I want to be able to call you and find out what you've got."

He thought a moment. "Call between five and six," he said. "We'll have the works by then."

That left me with five or six hours to kill. I didn't want to go back to my apartment. A man's home is his castle, but mine might very well be under siege by now. Carr was undoubtedly conscious and undoubtedly sending up a hue and cry, shrieking mightily for the bloody scalp of some private eye named London. For the next five or six hours I wanted to get away from the world. My own place seemed like a ridiculous place to hide.

I settled on a movie. I sat in the balcony of a 42nd Street movie house, puffed on my pipe, munched popcorn, and watched *Ma Barker's Killer Brood* and *Baby Face Nelson*. I saw both pictures twice, and if you think that's a pleasant way to spend an afternoon, it's only because you've never tried it.

It was five when I left the show. I had a quick dinner at a cafeteria and used their phone to make another call to Cleveland. My op was on hand and he told me everything I wanted to know. I listened quietly, thoughtfully. At the end he said he would send me a bill and I told him that was fine.

Nothing was fine, though.

I stayed in the phone booth, sitting, thinking. I made two more calls, local ones. I talked a little, listened a little, hung up. I went on sitting in that booth until a stern-faced man came over and rapped on the door. I apologized to him and left.

The sun was dying outside, dropping behind the Jersey mud flats. The air was still too warm. I walked for a block or two, checking now and then to see if anybody was following me. Nobody was.

I thought about the way things can sneak up behind you from out of nowhere and slip you a rabbit punch. I thought about the way you can walk around wearing blinders, and then you can take the blinders off and still not believe what you see. But you see it, and sooner or later it sinks in and your world falls apart.

I hailed a cab and took a ride to a certain posh apartment house. I walked past a doorman, into an elevator. I rode up in silence. I got out and went to a door. I stood in front of it for a long time. Finally, I rang . . . I waited . . . I rang again.

TEN

She had never looked better. Even nude, with a white sheet under that flawless full-blown body and a pillow beneath that ash blond head, she had never looked better wearing a skirt and sweater. She flowed toward me like a hot river and she came into my arms and stayed there.

I let her kiss me. I ran my hands over her back, felt the firmness of her body, and I waited for something to happen inside me, some-thing I was afraid of: a shadow of response, a flicker of desire.

It never came.

"Oh, Ed," she was saying. "I was so worried. You didn't call me all day. I was afraid. I thought something had happened to you; I didn't know what to think."

I didn't say anything.

"I tried calling you. You weren't at your apartment. I must have called you a dozen times but you weren't there."

"No. I wasn't."

She turned coy, twisting in my arms and looking up at me. "You weren't with another girl, were you? I'll scratch her eyes out, Ed."

And then she turned kittenish again, burrowing her head in my chest and making little sounds.

I put my hands on her shoulders. I pushed, gently, easing her away. She looked at me, a question in her eyes.

They must have heard the slap in Canarsie. I hit her that hard, open-palmed, my hand against the side of her face. She stumbled and went down, started to get up, tripped, fell, then finally scram-bled to her feet again. Her eyes said she didn't believe it.

"You dirty little liar," I snapped.

"Ed—"

"Shut up. I know the whole bit now, Rhona. All of it, from top to bottom. I got some of it here and some of it there and figured out the rest myself. It didn't take too much thinking on my part. It was all there. All I had to do was look for it."

"Ed, for heaven's sake—"

"Sit down." She looked at me, thought it over, plopped down on the orange couch.

"Jack Blake," I said, pacing like a caged tiger. "He was a card sharp, all right. And he stopped being a card sharp. Not to go straight, though. Just to change his line of work. He stopped cheat-ing at cards but he found other ways to cheat.

"He opened a magic shop. It was a front, nothing more. I had a detective agency in Cleveland check the place out. Oh, the store was completely open and aboveboard, all right. Only the place ran at one hell of a loss. Blake never made a nickel out of it."

I wanted a drink. Courvoisier, a lot of it, straight and in a hurry.

"So the shop lost money," I continued, "and Blake lived high off the hog. A big house out in Shaker Heights. Trips to Vegas and Hawaii. You don't pull that kind of money out of a successful magic shop, let alone a losing proposition like the one on Euclid Avenue.

"So Blake had another source of income. It's not hard to figure out what it was, Rhona. The record of deposits to Jack Blake's checking account makes it obvious. The two of you were working a string of blackmail dodges. You were on a dozen different payrolls for anywhere from a hundred to five hundred bucks a month. It was a sweet little setup. And you weren't his daughter, either. That was another little lie, wasn't it?"

"You can't be serious—"

"The hell I can't. Jack Blake was never married. He never had a wife and he never had a kid. You were his mistress and his partner. His private whore."

She started to get up. She saw my eyes, and she must have guessed what I would do to her the minute she got to her feet. So she stayed where she was.

"His private whore." I liked the sound of it. "And his partner. The two of you were doing fine. Then you got hold of something that made all the little swindles look like small potatoes in comparison. You latched on to the prize pigeon of them all. You hooked a man named Abe Zucker."

I took a breath. "Five months ago Miltie Klugsman got in touch with Blake and told him he had the goods on Zucker. Zucker's been straight for years so he must have had something big on him, a rap the statute of limitations wouldn't cover. Something like murder.

"It doesn't much matter what it was. It was too big for Klugsman and he was scared to work it on his own. He knew Blake was doing a land-office business in blackmail. They worked out a split. Klugsman couldn't have done too well with it—his widow isn't exactly living in style. But that's how it went. Klugsman held on to the evidence and Blake set up the blackmail gambit and Zucker paid. There was a healthy deposit to your father's—pardon me, your keeper's account five months ago. The first payment from Zucker was something like ten thousand dollars.

"Zucker must have thought it was a one-shot deal. When it happened a second time he figured out that it would be cheaper to arrange an accident for Blake than to pay him that kind of money for any length of time. And that was the end of Jack Blake, at least as far as this world is concerned.

"You told that part of it straight enough, Rhona. A few thugs went to Cleveland and beat Jack Blake to death."

I took another deep breath and looked at her, all prim and proper on the bright orange couch, all schoolgirl-lovely in green sweater and black skirt, and I tried to make myself believe it. It was true, all of it. But it still seemed impossible.

"JACK BLAKE WAS DEAD," I went on. "But this didn't faze you much. You could live without him, but you weren't going to let a big fat fish like Zucker wiggle off the hook. He was too profitable a source of income.

"Klugsman was anxious to give up. When Blake was rubbed out, Klugsman got nervous. He didn't want to play blackmail games anymore. He wanted out. So you got in touch with him and offered him a fast five grand for the evidence on Zucker. That would put Klugsman out of the picture and give him a healthy piece of change for his trouble. He went for it. It looked like easy money.

"But it wasn't," I said. "Zucker's hirelings were already onto Klugsman. They picked us up when I met him in Canarsie and they shot a million holes in Miltie Klugsman. They didn't kill me. Maybe they didn't care much at that point. They just wanted Klugsman.

"That left you in a bind. Zucker wanted to see you dead, too, because as long as you were alive he had a murder rap hanging over his head like a Sword of Damocles. You had to stay away from him and you had to get me to dig up Miltie's package of evidence. You were too damned greedy to take your life and run with it. You couldn't let go of that pile of dough."

"It wasn't like that—" she started.

"The hell it wasn't. It was like that all across the board. And you never came close to leveling with me. You started out as the woman-of-mystery and when that fell in you shifted gears as smooth as silk and turned yourself into the damsel-in-distress.

"You let me go to Brooklyn last night and almost get killed. You let me go up against Phillip Carr this morning. You never put your cards on the table and you never gave up the idea of bleeding that money out of Zucker." I paused. "You look great in a sweater. You look great out of one. And you put on one hell of an act in bed. But you're just another deceitful crook, Rhona. Nothing more."

Then it was quiet. Neither of us said a word. Finally, she blurted: "Ed—what now?"

"Now I call the police," I said. "I don't care what happens after that."

She uncoiled from the couch like a serpent. She flowed toward me again, and her eyes were radiating sex once more. She turned the stuff on and off like a faucet.

"Ed," she cooed. "Ed, I'm sorry."

"Stow it," I said.

"Ed, listen to me. I didn't trust you. I should have, I know it. And I'm sorry. But you don't have to call the police."

I stared at her.

"Listen to me, Ed. I didn't . . . didn't hurt anybody. I never mur-dered anyone. It's not my fault Klugsman was shot and I wasn't the murderer. It was Zucker and the men he hired. I just thought I could find a way to make a quick dollar.

"Don't you understand? Ed, I never killed anyone. I never hurt you—I lied to you but I never hurt you. And, Ed, when we were in bed together I wasn't acting. I don't care what you think of me. Maybe I deserve it—"

"Maybe?"

"I know I deserve it. But I wasn't acting. Not in bed, not when we were making love—"

I wish someone had filmed all this. She would have won the Oscar in a walk.

"You could let me go," she pleaded. "You could call the police and give them everything you want on Zucker and Carr and the rest of them. I'll even help you. I'll tell you what I know. With that much, the police won't need Klugsman's evidence. You can even tell them about me, Ed, if it will make you feel better. Just give me a few hours' head start. In a few hours I can be out of town and they won't ever find me. Just a few hours, Ed," she pleaded.

"Ed, you owe me that much. We meant that much to each other, Ed."

She was as persuasive as a loaded gun. "I'd have given you that much," I told her. "Except for one thing."

"What?"

"The dynamite," I said. "Did you forget the dynamite, Rhona? You tried to kill me!"

That time I didn't slap her. It would have been superfluous. She reacted as though someone had belted her but good.

"The dynamite," I said. "It didn't make any sense at the time. I couldn't figure out why Zucker would use a cockeyed routine like that to get you out of the way, or how he knew where you were, or any of it. The dynamite had to be all your idea. Maybe you were afraid I would sell you out for Carr's ten-grand reward. Maybe you thought I was guessing too much about you.

"Anyway, you decided to get rid of me. And you were cute about it, too. You knew I'd come over here sooner or later. You left the apartment, figuring I'd eventually wander over to the closet. Then the dynamite would go off and I'd be out of your hair.

"And you would be in the clear. You were subletting the place under a phony name, and once I blew myself to hell you would just disappear, rent another apartment somewhere else. Nobody could tie you to me. You'd be all alone in the clear."

"Ed, I must have been crazy—"

"You still are if you think you can talk your way out of this, Rhona."

"Ed, I'm sorry. Ed—"

She was making sexy movements, slithering toward me. But I saw what she was really doing, moving toward the table next to the couch, heading toward her purse. I could have stopped her then and there, but I wanted to give her more rope to hang herself.

She got her hands on the purse. She was talking but I wasn't listening to a word she was saying. I watched her hands move behind her back, opening the purse, dipping inside.

She never managed to point her gun at me. My timing was too good. She dragged it out of the purse and I slapped it out of her hand and it sailed across the room and bounced around on the carpet. A .22, a woman's gun. They can kill you too.

Then she was beaten, and she knew it. I took out my own gun and pointed it at her, but I didn't even need it. She stayed put while I picked up the phone. It was too late to get Jerry Gunther at Headquarters. I called him at his home.

"Call downtown," I said. "Tell them to get a pickup order out for Phillip Carr and Abe Zucker. And get over here"—I gave him the address—"and make an arrest of your own."

He whistled softly.

"This is going to get a lot of unsolved ones off your books," I said. "Maybe I'll let you do the buying during our next vital conference."

He said something unimportant. I hung up. Then I stood pointing the gun at Rhona while we waited for him.

ELEVEN

It was Thursday, and I was having dinner at McGraw's, a favorite steakhouse of mine. I wasn't eating alone. There was a girl across the table from me, a girl named Sharon Ross.

She chewed a bit of steak, washed it down with a sip of Beaujolais, and looked up at me with wide eyes.

"The girl," she said. "Rhona. What's going to happen to her, Ed?"

"Not enough."

"Will she go to jail?"

"Probably," I said. "It's hardly a sure thing, though. She was a blackmailer, and there's a law against that sort of thing, but she's in a position to turn state's evidence and help them nail the lid on Zucker and his buddies. And, as she said, she never killed anyone. Only tried."

I shrugged. "And she's a girl. A pretty one. That still makes a difference in any case where you have trial by jury. The worst she can look forward to is a fairly light sentence. She could even get off clean, if she has an expensive lawyer."

"Like Phil Carr?"

"Like him, but not Carr. He won't be practicing much law anymore. He'll be in jail for everything the D.A. can make stick. And Zucker will stand trial, too."

I'D CALLED SHARON A DAY OR TWO after the whole thing was wrapped up, and after she had cooled off from the broken-date routine. And, over our steaks, I had filled her in on most of the story. Not all of it, of course. She got the expurgated version. You never tell one girl about the bedroom games you played with another girl. It's not chivalrous. It's not even especially intelligent.

"I guess I forgive you," she said.

"For what?"

"For breaking our date, silly. Brother, was I mad at you! You didn't sound like a man with business on his mind, not when you called me. You sounded like a man who had just crawled out of bed with someone pretty. And I was steaming."

I looked away. Hell, I thought. When I called her I *had* just crawled out of bed with something pretty. But I didn't know you could tell over the phone.

"Ed?"

I looked up.

"Where do you want to go after dinner?"

"A little club somewhere on the East Side," I said. "We'll listen to atonal jazz and drink a little too much."

She said it sounded good. It did. We would listen to atonal jazz and drink a little too much, and then we would go back to her place for a nightcap. She wouldn't be a secretive blackmailer with a closet full of dynamite. She would just be a soft warm girl, and that was enough.

There might be explosions. But dynamite wouldn't cause them, and I wouldn't mind them at all.

STAG PARTY GIRL

ONE

Harold Merriman pushed his chair back and stood up, drink in hand. "Gentlemen," he said solemnly, "to all the wives we love so well. May they continue to belong to us body and soul." He paused theatrically, "And to their husbands—may they never find out!"

There was scattered laughter, most of it lost in the general hubbub. I had a glass of cognac on the table in front of me. I took a sip and looked at Mark Donahue. If he was nervous, it didn't show. He looked like any man who was getting married in the morning—which is nervous enough, I suppose. He didn't look like someone threatened with murder.

Phil Abeles—short, intense, brittle-voiced—stood. He started to read a sheaf of fake telegrams. "Mark," he intoned, "don't panic—marriage is the best life for a man. Signed, Tommy Manville" . . . He read more telegrams. Some funny, some mildly obscene, some dull.

We were in an upstairs dining room at McGraw's, a venerable steakhouse in the East Forties. About a dozen of us. There was Mark Donahue, literally getting married in the morning, Sunday, tying the nuptial knot at 10:30. Also Harold Merriman, Phil Abeles, Ray

Powell, Joe Conn, Jack Harris, and a few others whose names I couldn't remember, all fellow wage slaves with Donahue at Darcy & Bates, one of Madison Avenue's rising young ad agencies.

And there was me. Ed London, private cop, the man at the party who didn't belong. I was just a hired hand. It was my job to get Donahue to the church on time, and alive.

On Wednesday, Mark Donahue had come to my apartment. He cabbed over on a long lunch hour that coincided with the time I rolled out of bed. We sat in my living room. I was rumpled and ugly in a moth-eaten bathrobe. He was fresh and trim in a Tripler suit and expensive shoes. I drowned my sorrows with coffee while he told me his problems.

"I think I need a bodyguard," he said.

In the storybooks and the movies, I show him the door at this point. I explain belligerently that I don't do divorce or bodyguard work or handle corporation investigations—that I only rescue stacked blondes and play modern-day Robin Hood. That's in the storybooks. I don't play that way. I have an apartment in an East Side brownstone and I eat in good restaurants and drink expensive cognac. If you can pay my fee, friend, you can buy me.

I asked him what it was all about.

"I'm getting married Sunday morning," he said.

"Congratulations."

"Thanks." He looked at the floor. "I'm marrying a . . . a very fine girl. Her name is Lynn Farwell."

I waited.

"There was another girl I . . . used to see. A model, more or less. Karen Price."

"And?"

"She doesn't want me to get married."

"So?"

He fumbled for a cigarette. "She's been calling me," he said. "I was . . . well, fairly deeply involved with her. I never planned to marry her. I'm sure she knew that."

"But you were sleeping with her?"

"That's right."

"And now you're marrying someone else."

He sighed at me. "It's not as though I ruined the girl," he said. "She's ... well, not a tramp, exactly, but close to it. She's been around, London."

"So what's the problem?"

"I've been getting phone calls from her. Unpleasant ones, I'm afraid. She's told me that I'm not going to marry Lynn. That she'll see me dead first."

"And you think she'll try to kill you?"

"I don't know."

"That kind of threat is common, you know. It doesn't usually lead to murder."

He nodded hurriedly. "I know that," he said. "I'm not terribly afraid she'll kill me. I just want to make sure she doesn't throw a monkey wrench into the wedding. Lynn comes from an excellent family. Long Island, society, money. Her parents wouldn't appreciate a scene."

"Probably not."

He forced a little laugh. "And there's always a chance that she really may try to kill me," he said. "I'd like to avoid that." I told him it was an understandable desire. "So I want a bodyguard. From now until the wedding. Four days. Will you take the job?"

I told him my fee ran a hundred a day plus expenses. This didn't faze him. He gave me $300 for a retainer, and I had a client and he had a bodyguard.

From then on I stuck to him like perspiration.

Saturday, a little after noon, he got a phone call. We were playing two-handed pinochle in his living room. He was winning. The phone rang and he answered it. I only heard his end of the conversation. He went a little white and sputtered; then he stood for a long moment with the phone in his hand, and finally slammed the receiver on the hook and turned to me.

"Karen," he said, ashen. "She's going to kill me."

I didn't say anything. I watched the color come back into his face, saw the horror recede. He came up smiling. "I'm not really scared," he said.

"Good."

"Nothing's going to happen," he added. "Maybe it's her idea of a joke ... maybe she's just being bitchy. But nothing's going to happen."

He didn't entirely believe it. But I had to give him credit.

I don't know who invented the bachelor dinner, or why he bothered. I've been to a few of them. Dirty jokes, dirty movies, dirty toasts, a lineup with a local whore—maybe I would appreciate them if I were married. But for a bachelor who makes out there is nothing duller than a bachelor dinner.

This one was par for the course. The steaks were good and there was a lot to drink, which was definitely on the plus side. The men busy making asses of themselves were not friends of mine, and that was also on the plus side—it kept me from getting embarrassed for them. But the jokes were still unfunny and the voices too drunkenly loud.

I looked at my watch. "Eleven-thirty," I said to Donahue. "How much longer do you think this'll go on?"

"Maybe half an hour."

"And then ten hours until the wedding. Your ordeal's just about over, Mark."

"And you can relax and spend your fee."

"Uh-huh."

"I'm glad I hired you," he said. "You haven't had to do anything, but I'm glad anyway." He grinned. "I carry life insurance, too. But that doesn't mean I'm going to die. And you've even been good company, Ed. Thanks."

I started to search for an appropriate answer. Phil Abeles saved me. He was standing up again, pounding on the table with his fist and shouting for everyone to be quiet. They let him shout for a while, then quieted down.

"And now the grand finale," Phil announced wickedly. "The part I know you've all been waiting for."

"The part Mark's been waiting for," someone said lewdly.

"Mark better watch this," someone else added. "He has to learn about women so that Lynn isn't disappointed."

More feeble lines, one after the other. Phil Abeles pounded for order again and got it. "Lights," he shouted.

The lights went out. The private dining room looked like a blackout in a coal mine.

"Music!"

Somewhere, a record player went on. The record was "The Stripper," played by David Rose's orchestra.

"Action!"

A spotlight illuminated the pair of doors at the far end of the room. The doors opened. Two bored waiters wheeled in a large table on rollers. There was a cardboard cake on top of the table and, obviously, a girl inside the cake. Somebody made a joke about Mark cutting himself a piece. Someone else said they wanted to put a piece of this particular wedding cake under their pillow. "On the pillow would be better," a voice corrected.

The two bored waiters wheeled the cake into position and left.

The doors closed. The spotlight stayed on the cake and the stripper music swelled.

There were two or three more lame jokes. Then the chatter died. Everyone seemed to be watching the cake. The music grew louder, deeper, fuller. The record stopped suddenly and another—Mendelssohn's "Wedding March"—took its place.

Someone shouted, "Here comes the bride!"

And she leaped out of the cake like a nymph from the sea.

She was naked and beautiful. She sprang through the paper cake, arms wide, face filled with a lipstick smile. Her breasts were full and firm and her nipples had been reddened with lipstick.

Then, just as everyone was breathlessly silent, just as her arms spread and her lips parted and her eyes widened slightly, the whole room exploded like Hiroshima. We found out later that it was only a .38. It sounded more like a howitzer.

She clapped both hands to a spot between her breasts. Blood spurted forth like a flower opening. She gave a small gasp, swayed forward, then dipped backward and fell.

Lights went on. I raced forward. Her head was touching the floor and her legs were propped on what remained of the paper cake. Her eyes were open. But she was horribly dead.

And then I heard Mark Donahue next to me, his voice shrill. "Oh, no!" he murmured. " . . . It's Karen, it's Karen!"

I felt for a pulse; there was no point to it. There was a bullet in her heart.

Karen Price was dead.

TWO

Lieutenant Jerry Gunther got the call. He brought a clutch of Homicide men who went around measuring things, studying the position of the body, shooting off a hell of a lot of flashbulbs, and taking statements. Jerry piloted me into a corner and started pumping.

I gave him the whole story, starting with Wednesday and ending with Saturday. He let me go all the way through once, then went over everything two or three times.

"Your client Donahue doesn't look too good," he said.

"You think he killed the girl?"

"That's the way it reads."

I shook my head. "Wrong customer."

"Why?"

"Hell, he hired me to keep the girl off his neck. If he was going to shoot a hole in her, why would he want a detective along for company?"

"To make the alibi stand up, Ed. To make us reason just the way you're reasoning now. How do you know he was scared of the girl?"

"Because he said so. But—"

"But he got a phone call?" Jerry smiled. "For all you know it was a wrong number. Or the call had been staged. You only heard his end of it. Remember?"

"I saw his face when he took a good look at the dead girl," I said. "Mark Donahue was one surprised hombre, Jerry. He didn't know who she was."

"Or else he's a good actor."

"Not that good. I can't believe it."

He let that one pass. "Let's go back to the shooting," he said. "Were you watching him when the gun went off?"

"No."

"What were you watching?"

"The girl," I said. "And quit grinning, you fathead."

His grin spread. "You old lecher. All right, you can't alibi him for the shooting. And you can't prove he was afraid of the girl. This is the way I make it, Ed. He was afraid of her, but not afraid she would kill him. He was afraid of something else. Call it blackmail, maybe. He's getting set to make a good marriage to a rich doll and he's got a mistress hanging around his neck. Say the rich girl doesn't know about the mistress. Say the mistress wants hush money."

"Go on."

"Your Donahue finds out the Price doll is going to come out of the cake."

"They kept it a secret from him, Jerry."

"Sometimes people find out secrets. The Price kid could have told herself. It might have been her idea of a joke. Say he finds out. He packs a gun—"

"He didn't have a gun."

"How do you know, Ed?"

I couldn't answer that one. He might have had a gun. He might have tucked it into a pocket while he was getting dressed. I didn't believe it, but I couldn't disprove it either.

Jerry Gunther was thorough. He didn't have to be thorough to turn up the gun. It was under a table in the middle of the room. The lab boys checked it for prints. None. It was a .38 police positive with five bullets left in it. The bullets didn't have any prints on them, either.

"Donahue shot her, wiped the gun, and threw it on the floor," Jerry said.

"Anybody else could have done the same thing," I interjected.

"Uh-huh. Sure."

He grilled Phil Abeles, the man who had hired Karen Price to come out of the cake. Abeles was also the greenest, sickest man in the world at that particular moment.

Gunther asked him how he got hold of the girl. "I never knew anything about her," Abeles insisted. "I didn't even know her last name."

"How'd you find her?"

"A guy gave me her name and her number. When I . . . when we set up the dinner, the stag, we thought we would have a wedding cake with a girl jumping out of it. We thought it would be so . . . so corny that it might be cute. You know?"

No one said anything. Abeles was sweating up a storm. The dinner had been his show and it had not turned out as he had planned it, and he looked as though he wanted to go somewhere quiet and die.

"So I asked around to find out where to get a girl," he went on. "Honest, I asked a dozen guys, two dozen. I don't know how many. I asked everybody in this room except Mark. I asked half the guys on Madison Avenue. Someone gave me a number, told me to call it and ask for Karen. So I did. She said she'd jump out of the cake for $100 and I said that was fine."

"You didn't know she was Donahue's mistress?"

"Oh, brother," he said. "You have to be kidding."

We told him we weren't kidding. He got greener. "Maybe that made it a better joke," I suggested. "To have Mark's girl jump out of the cake the night before he married someone else. Was that it?"

"Hell, no!"

Jerry grilled everyone in the place. No one admitted knowing Karen Price, or realized that she had been involved with Mark Donahue. No one admitted anything. Most of the men were married. They were barely willing to admit that they were alive. Some of them were almost as green as Phil Abeles.

They wanted to go home. That was all they wanted. They kept mentioning how nice it would be if their names didn't get into the papers. Some of them tried a little genteel bribery. Jerry was tactful enough to pretend he didn't know what they were talking about. He was an honest cop. He didn't do favors and didn't take gifts.

By 1:30, he had sent them all home. The lab boys were still making chalk marks but there wasn't much point to it. According to their measurements and calculations of the bullet's trajectory, and a few other scientific bits and pieces, they managed to prove conclusively that Karen Price had been shot by someone in McGraw's private dining room.

And that was all they could prove.

Four of us rode down to Headquarters at Centre Street. Mark Donahue sat in front, silent. Jerry Gunther sat on his right. A beardless cop named Ryan, Jerry's driver, had the wheel. I occupied the backseat all alone.

At Fourteenth Street Mark broke his silence. "This is a nightmare. I didn't kill Karen. Why in God's name would I kill her?"

Nobody had an answer for him. A few blocks further he said, "I suppose I'll be railroaded now. I suppose you'll lock me up and throw the key away."

Gunther told him, "We don't railroad people. We couldn't if we wanted to. We don't have enough of a case yet. But right now you look like a pretty good suspect. Figure it out for yourself."

"But—"

"I have to lock you up, Donahue. You can't talk me out of it. Ed can't talk me out of it. Nobody can."

"I'm supposed to get married tomorrow."

"I'm afraid that's out."

The car moved south. For a while nobody had anything to say.

A few blocks before police Headquarters Mark told me he wanted me to stay on the case.

"You'll be wasting your money," I told him. "The police will work things out better than I can. They have the manpower and the authority. I'll just be costing you a hundred a day and getting you nothing in return."

"Are you trying to talk yourself out of a fee?"

"He's an ethical bastard," Jerry put in. "In his own way, of course."

"I want you working for me, Ed."

"Why?"

He waited a minute, organizing his thoughts. "Look," he sighed, "do you think I killed Karen?"

"No."

"Honestly?"

"Honestly."

"Well, that's one reason I want you in my corner. Maybe the police are fair in these things. I don't know anything about it. But they'll be looking for things that'll nail me. They have to—it's their job. From where they sit I'm the killer." He paused, as if the thought stunned him a little. "But you'll be looking for something that will help me. Maybe you can find someone who was looking at me when the gun went off. Maybe you can figure out who did pull that trigger and why. I know I'll feel better if you're working for me."

"Don't expect anything."

"I don't."

"I'll do what I can," I told him.

Before I caught a cab from Headquarters to my apartment, I told Mark to call his lawyer. He wouldn't be able to get out on bail because there is no bail in first-degree murder cases; but a lawyer could do a lot of helpful things for him. Lynn Farwell's family had to be told that there wasn't going to be a wedding.

I don't envy anyone who has to call a mother or father at 3 A.M. and explain that their daughter's wedding, set for 10:30 that very morning, must be postponed because the potential bridegroom has been arrested for murder.

I sat back in the cab with an unlit pipe in my mouth and a lot of aimless thoughts rumbling around in my head. Nothing made much sense yet. Perhaps nothing ever would. It was that kind of a deal.

THREE

Morning was noisy, ugly, and several hours premature. A sharp, persistent ringing stabbed my brain into a semiconscious state. I cursed and groped for the alarm clock . . . turned it off. The buzzing continued. I reached for the phone, lifted the receiver to my ear, and listened to a dial tone. The buzzing continued. I cursed even more vehemently and stumbled out of bed. I found a bathrobe and groped into it. I splashed cold water on my face and blinked at myself in the mirror. I looked as bad as I felt.

The doorbell kept ringing. I didn't want to answer it, but that seemed the only way to make it stop ringing. I listened to my bones creak on the way to the door. I turned the knob, opened the door, and blinked at the blonde who was standing there. She blinked back at me.

"Mister," she said. "You look terrible."

She didn't. Even at that ghastly hour she looked like a toothpaste ad. Her hair was blond silk and her eyes were blue jewels and her skin was creamed perfection. With a thinner body and a more severe mouth she could have been a *Vogue* model. But the body was just too bountiful for the fashion magazines. The breasts were a perfect 38, high and large, the waist trim, the hips a curved invitation.

"You're Ed London?"

I nodded foolishly.

"I'm Lynn Farwell."

She didn't have to tell me. She looked exactly like what my client had said he was going to marry, except a little better. Everything about her stated emphatically that she was from Long Island's North Shore, that she had gone to an expensive finishing school and a ritzy college, that her family had half the money in the world.

"May I come in?"

"You got me out of bed," I grumbled.

"I'm sorry. I wanted to talk to you."

"Could you sort of go somewhere and come back in about ten minutes? I'd like to get human."

"I don't really have anyplace to go. May I just sit in your living room or something? I'll be quiet."

There are a pair of matching overstuffed leather chairs in my living room, the kind they have in British men's clubs. She curled up and got lost in one of them. I left her there and ducked back into the bedroom. I showered, shaved, dressed. When I came out again the world was a somewhat better place. I smelled coffee.

"I put up a pot of java." She smiled. "Hope you don't mind."

"I couldn't mind less," I said. We waited while the coffee dripped through. I poured out two cups, and we both drank it black.

"I haven't seen Mark," she said. "His lawyer called. I suppose you know all about it, of course."

"More or less."

"I'll be seeing Mark later this afternoon, I suppose. We were supposed to be getting married in"—she looked at her watch—"a little over an hour."

She seemed unperturbed. There were no tears, not in her eyes and not in her voice. She asked me if I was still working for Donahue. I nodded.

"He didn't kill that girl," she said.

"I don't think he did."

"I'm sure. Of all the ridiculous things . . . Why did he hire you, Ed?"

I thought a moment and decided to tell her the truth. She probably knew it anyway. Besides, there was no point in sparing her the knowledge that her fiancé had a mistress somewhere along the line. That should be the least of her worries, compared to a murder rap.

It was. She greeted the news with a half-smile and shook her head sadly. "Now why on earth would they think she could blackmail him?" Lynn Farwell demanded. "I don't care who he slept with . . . Policemen are asinine."

I didn't say anything. She sipped her coffee, stretched a little in the chair, crossed one leg over the other. She had very nice legs.

We both lit cigarettes. She blew out a cloud of smoke and looked at me through it, her blue eyes narrowing. "Ed," she said, "how long do you think it'll be before he's cleared?"

"It's impossible to say, Miss Farwell."

"Lynn."

"Lynn. It could take a day or a month."

She nodded thoughtfully. "He has to be cleared as quickly as possible. That's the most important thing. There can't be any scandal, Ed. Oh, a little dirt is bearable. But nothing serious, nothing permanent."

Something didn't sound right. She didn't care who he slept with, but no scandal could touch them—this was vitally important to her. She sounded like anything but a loving bride-to-be.

She read my mind. "I don't sound madly in love, do I?"

"Not particularly."

She smiled kittenishly. "I'd like more coffee, Ed . . ."

I got more for both of us.

Then she said, "Mark and I don't love each other, Ed."

I grunted noncommittally.

"We like each other, though. I'm fond of Mark, and he's fond of me. That's all that matters, really."

"Is it?"

She nodded positively. Finishing schools and high-toned colleges produce girls with the courage of their convictions. "It's enough," she said. "Love's a poor foundation for marriage in the long run. People who love are too . . . too vulnerable. Mark and I are perfect for each other. We'll both be getting something out of this marriage."

"What will Mark get?"

"A rich wife. A proper connection with an important family. That's what he wants."

"And you?"

"A respectable marriage to a promising young man."

"If that's all you want—"

"It's all I want," she said. "Mark is good company. He's bright, socially acceptable, ambitious enough to be stimulating. He'll make a good husband and a good father. I'm happy."

She yawned again and her body uncoiled in the chair. The movement drew her breasts into sharp relief against the front of her sweater. This was supposed to be accidental. I knew better.

"Besides," she said, her voice just slightly husky, "he's not at all bad in bed."

I wanted to slap her well-bred face. The lips were slightly parted now, her eyes a little less than half lidded. The operative term, I think, is *provocative*. She knew damned well what she was doing with the coy posing and the sex talk and all the rest. She had the equipment to carry it off, too. But it was a horrible hour on a horrible Sunday morning, and her fiancé was also my client, and he was sitting in a cell, booked on suspicion of homicide.

So I neither took her to bed nor slapped her face. I let the remark die in the stuffy air and finished my second cup of coffee. There was a rack of pipes on the table next to my chair. I selected a sandblast Barling and stuffed some tobacco into it. I lit it and smoked.

"Ed?"

I looked at her.

"I didn't mean to sound cheap."

"Forget it."

"All right." A pause. "Ed, you'll find a way to clear Mark, won't you?"

"I'll try."

"If there's any way I can help—"

"I'll let you know."

She gave me her phone number and address. She was living with her parents.

Then she paused at the door and turned enough to let me look at her lovely young body in profile. "If there's anything you want," she said softly, "be sure to let me know."

It was an ordinary enough line. But I had the feeling that it covered a lot of ground.

At 11:30 I picked up my car at the garage around the corner from my apartment.

The car is a Chevy convertible, an old one that dates from the pre-fin era. I left the top up. The air had an edge to it. I took the

East Side Drive downtown and pulled up across the street from Headquarters at noon.

They let me see Mark Donahue. He was wearing the same expensive suit but it didn't hang right now. It looked as though it had been slept in, which figured. He needed a shave and his eyes had red rims. I didn't ask him how he had slept. I could tell.

"Hello," he said.

"Getting along all right?"

"I suppose so." He swallowed. "They asked me questions most of the night. No rubber hose, though. That's something."

"Sure," I said. "Mind some more questions?"

"Go ahead."

"When did you start seeing Karen Price?"

"Four, five months ago."

"When did you stop?"

"About a month ago."

"Why?"

"Because I was practically married to Lynn."

"Who knew you were sleeping with Karen?"

"No one I know of."

"Anybody at the stag last night?"

"I don't think so."

More questions. When had she started phoning him? About two weeks ago, maybe a little longer than that. Was she in love with him? He hadn't thought so, no, and that was why the phone calls were such a shock to him at first. As far as he was concerned, it was just a mutual sex arrangement with no emotional involvement on either side. He took her to shows, bought her presents, gave her occasional small loans with the understanding that they weren't to be repaid. He wasn't exactly keeping her and she wasn't exactly going to bed in return for the money. It was just a convenient arrangement.

Everything, it seemed, was just a convenient arrangement. He and Karen Price had had a convenient shack-up. He and Lynn Farwell were planning a convenient marriage.

But someone had put a bullet in Karen's pretty chest. People don't do that because it's convenient. They usually have more emotional reasons.

More questions. Where did Karen live? He gave me an address in the Village, not too very far from his own apartment. Who were her friends? He knew one, her roommate, Ceil Gorski. Where did she work? He wasn't too clear.

"My lawyer's trying to get them to reduce the charge," he said. "So that I can get out on bail. You think he'll manage it?"

"He might."

"I hope so," he said. His face went serious, then brightened again. "This is a hell of a place to spend a wedding night." He smiled. "Funny—when I was trying to pick the right hotel, I never thought of a jail."

FOUR

It was only a few blocks from Mark Donahue's cell to the building where Karen Price had lived . . . a great deal further in terms of dollars and cents. She had an apartment in a redbrick five-story building on Sullivan Street, just below Bleecker.

The girl who opened the door was blond, like Lynn Farwell. But her dark roots showed and her eyebrows were dark brown. If her mouth and eyes relaxed she would have been pretty. They didn't.

"You just better not be another cop," she said.

"I'm afraid I am. But not city. Private."

The door started to close. I made like a brush salesman and tucked a foot in it. She glared at me.

"Private cops, I don't have to see," she said. "Get the hell out, will you?".

"I just want to talk to you."

"The feeling isn't mutual. Look—"

"It won't take long."

"You son of a bitch," she said. But she opened the door and let me inside. We walked through the kitchen to the living room. There was a couch there. She sat on it. I took a chair.

"Who are you anyway?" she said.

"My name's Ed London."

"Who you working for?"

"Mark Donahue."

"The one who killed her?"

"I don't think he did," I said. "What I'm trying to find out, Miss Gorski, is who did."

She got to her feet and started walking around the room. There was nothing deliberately sexy about her walk. She was hard, though. She lived in a cheap apartment on a bad block. She bleached her hair, and her hairdresser wasn't the only one who knew for sure. She could have—but didn't—come across as a slut.

There was something honest and forthright about her, if not necessarily wholesome. She was a big blonde with a hot body and a hard face. There are worse things than that.

"What do you want to know, London?"

"About Karen."

"What is there to know? You want a biography? She came from Indiana because she wanted to be a success. A singer, an actress, a model, something. She wasn't too clear on just what. She tried, she flopped. She woke up one day knowing she wasn't going to make it. It happens."

I didn't say anything.

"So she could go back to Indiana or she could stay in the city. Only she couldn't go back to Indiana. You give in to enough men, you drink enough drinks and do enough things, then you can't go back to Indiana. What's left?"

She lit a cigarette. "Karen could have been a whore. But she wasn't. She never put a price tag on it. She spread it around, sure. Look, she was in New York and she was used to a certain kind of life and a certain kind of people, and she had to manage that life and those people into enough money to stay alive on, and she had one commodity to trade. She had sex. But she wasn't a whore." She paused. "There's a difference."

"All right."

"Well, dammit, what else do you want to know?"

"Who was she sleeping with besides Donahue?"

"She didn't say and I didn't ask. And she never kept a diary."

"She ever have men up here?"

"No."

"She talk much about Donahue?"

"No." She leaned over, stubbed out a cigarette. Her breasts loomed before my face like fruit. But it wasn't purposeful sexiness. She didn't play that way.

"I've got to get out of here," she said. "I don't feel like talking anymore."

"If you could just—"

"I couldn't just." She looked away. "In fifteen minutes I have to be uptown on the West Side. A guy there wants to take some pictures of me naked. He pays for my time, Mr. London. I'm a working girl."

"Are you working tonight?"

"Huh?"

"I asked if—"

"I heard you. What's the pitch?"

"I'd like to take you out to dinner."

"Why?"

"I'd like to talk to you."

"I'm not going to tell you anything I don't feel like telling you, London."

"I know that, Miss Gorski."

"And a dinner doesn't buy my company in bed, either. In case that's the idea."

"It isn't. I'm not all that hard up, Miss Gorski."

She was suddenly smiling. The smile softened her face all over and cut her age a good three years. Before she had been attractive. Now she was genuinely pretty.

"You give as good as you take."

"I try to."

"Is eight o'clock too late? I just got done with lunch a little while ago."

"Eight's fine," I said. "I'll see you."

I left. I walked the half block to my car and sat behind the wheel for a few seconds and thought about the two girls I had met that day. Both blondes, one born that way, one self-made. One of them had poise, breeding, and money, good diction and flawless bearing—and she added up to a tramp. The other *was* a tramp, in an amateurish sort of a way, and she talked tough and dropped an occasional final consonant. Yet she was the one who managed to retain a certain degree of dignity. Of the two, Ceil Gorski was more the lady.

At 3:30 I was up in Westchester County. The sky was bluer, the air fresher, and the houses more costly. I pulled up in front of a $35,000 split-level, walked up a flagstone path, and leaned on a doorbell.

The little boy who answered it had red hair, freckles, and a chipped tooth. He was too cute to be snotty, but this didn't stop him.

He asked me who I was. I told him to get his father. He asked me why. I told him that if he didn't get his father I would twist his arm off. He wasn't sure whether or not to believe me, but I was obviously the first person who had ever talked to him this way. He took off in a hurry and a few seconds later Phil Abeles came to the door.

"Oh, London," he said. "Hello. Say, what did you tell the kid?"

"Nothing."

"Your face must have scared him." Abeles's eyes darted around. "You want to talk about what happened last night, I suppose."

"That's right."

"I'd just as soon talk somewhere else," he said. "Wait a minute, will you?"

I waited while he went to tell his wife that somebody from the office had driven up, that it was important, and that he'd be back in an hour. He came out and we went to my car.

"There's a quiet bar two blocks down and three over," he said, then added: "Let me check something. The way I've got it, you're a private detective working for Mark. Is that right?"

"Yes."

"Okay," he said. "I'd like to help the guy out. I don't know very much, but there are things I can talk about to you that I'd just as soon not tell the police. Nothing illegal. Just . . . Well, you can figure it out."

I could figure it out. That was the main reason why I had agreed to stay on the case for Donahue. People do not like to talk to the police if they can avoid it.

If Phil Abeles was going to talk at all about Karen Price, he would prefer me as a listening post to Lieutenant Jerry Gunther.

"Here's the place," he said. I pulled up next to the chosen bar, a log-cabin arrangement.

Abeles had J&B with water and I ordered a pony of Courvoisier.

"I told that homicide lieutenant I didn't know anything about the Price girl," he said. "That wasn't true."

"Go on."

He hesitated, but just a moment. "I didn't know she had anything going with Donahue," he said. "Nobody ever thought of Karen in one-man terms. She slept around."

"I gathered that."

"It's a funny thing," he said. "A girl, not exactly a whore but not convent-bred either, can tend to pass around in a certain group of men. Karen was like that. She went for ad men. I think at one time or another she was intimate with half of Madison Avenue."

Speaks well of the dead, I thought. "For anyone in particular?" I asked.

"It's hard to say. Probably for most of the fellows who were at the dinner last night. For Ray Powell—but that's nothing new; he's one of those bachelors who gets to everything in a skirt sooner or later. But for the married ones, too."

"For you?"

"That's a hell of a question."

"Forget it. You already answered it."

He grinned sourly. "Yes"—he lapsed into flippant Madison Avenue talk—"the Price was right." He sipped his drink, then continued. "Not recently, and not often. Two or three times over two months ago. You won't blackmail me now, will you?"

"I don't play that way." I thought a minute. "Would Karen Price have tried a little subtle blackmail?"

"I don't think so. She played pretty fair."

"Was she the type to fall in love with somebody like Donahue?"

Abeles scratched his head. "The story I heard," he said. "Something to the effect that she was calling him, threatening him, trying to head off his marriage."

I nodded. "That's why he hired me."

"It doesn't make much sense."

"No?"

"No. It doesn't fit in with what I know about Karen. She wasn't the torch-bearer type. And she was hardly making a steady thing with Mark, either. I may not have known he was sleeping with her, but I knew damn well that a lot of other guys had been making with her lately."

"Could she have been shaking him down?"

He shrugged. "I told you," he said. "It doesn't sound like her. But who knows? She might have gotten into financial trouble. It happens. Perhaps she'd try to milk somebody for a little money." He pursed his lips. "But why should she blackmail Mark, for heaven's sake? If she blackmailed a bachelor he could always tell her to go to hell. You'd think she would work that on a married man, not a bachelor."

"I know."

He started to laugh then. "But not me," he said. "Believe me, London. She didn't blackmail me and I didn't kill her."

I got a list from him of all the men at the dinner. In addition to Donahue and myself, there had been eight men present, all of them from Darcy & Bates. Four—Abeles, Jack Harris, Harold Merriman, and Joe Conn—were married. One—Ray Powell—was the bachelor and stud-about-town of the group, almost a compulsive Don Juan, according to Abeles. Another, Fred Klein, had a wife waiting out a residency requirement in Reno.

The remaining two wouldn't have much to do with girls like Karen Price. Lloyd Travers and Kenneth Bream were as queer as rectangular eggs.

I drove Abeles back to his house. Before I let him off he told me again not to waste time suspecting him.

"One thing you might remember," I said. "*Somebody* in that room shot Karen Price. Either Mark or one of the eight of you . . . I don't think it was Mark." I paused. "That means there's a murderer in your office, Abeles!"

FIVE

It was late enough in the day to call Lieutenant Gunther. I tried him at home first. His wife answered, told me he was at the station. I tried him there and caught him.

"Nice hours you work, Jerry."

"Well, I didn't have anything else on today. So I came on down. You know how it is . . . Say, I got news for you, Ed."

"About Donahue?"

"Yes. We let him go."

"He's clear?"

"No, not clear." Jerry grunted. "We could have held him but there was no point, Ed. He's not clear, not by a mile. But we ran a check on the Price kid and learned she's been sleeping with two parties—Democrats and Republicans. Practically everyone at the stag. So there's nothing that makes your boy look too much more suspicious than the others."

"I found out the same thing this afternoon."

"Ed, I wasn't too crazy about letting him get away. Donahue still looks like the killer from where I sit. He hired you because the girl was giving him trouble. She wasn't giving anybody else trouble. He looks like the closest thing to a suspect around."

"Then why release him?"

I could picture Jerry's shrug. "Well, there was pressure," he said. "The guy got himself an expensive lawyer and the lawyer was get-

ting ready to pull a couple of strings. That's not all, of course. Donahue isn't a criminal type, Ed. He's not going to run far. We let him
go, figuring we won't have much trouble picking him up again."

"Maybe you won't have to."

"You get anything yet, Ed?"

"Not much," I said. "Just enough to figure out that everything's
mixed up."

"I already knew that."

"Uh-huh. But the more I hunt around, the more loose ends I
find. I'm glad you boys let my client loose. I'm going to see if I can
get hold of him."

"Bye," Jerry said, clicking off.

I took time to get a pipe going, then dialed Mark Donahue's
number. The phone rang eight times before I gave up. I decided
he must be out on Long Island with Lynn Farwell. I was halfway
through the complicated process of prying a number out of the information operator when I decided not to bother. Donahue had my
number. He could reach me when he got the chance.

Then I closed my eyes, gritted my teeth, and tried to think
straight.

It wasn't easy. So far I had managed one little trick—I had suc-
ceeded in convincing myself that Donahue had not killed the girl.
But this wasn't much cause for celebration. When you're working
for someone, it's easy to get yourself to thinking that your client is
on the side of the angels.

First of all, the girl. Karen Price. According to all and sundry,
she was something of a tramp. According to her roommate she
didn't put a price tag on it—but she didn't keep it under lock and
key, either. She had wound up in bed with most of the heterosexual
ad men on Madison Avenue. Donahue, a member of this clan, had
been sleeping with her.

This didn't mean she was in love with him, or carrying a flaming
torch, or singing the blues, or issuing dire threats concerning his
upcoming marriage. According to everyone who knew Karen, there
was no reason for her to give a whoop in hell whether he got married,
turned queer, became an astronaut, or joined the Foreign Legion.

But Donahue said he had received threatening calls from her. That left two possibilities. One: Donahue was lying. Two: Donahue was telling the truth.

If he was lying, why in hell had he hired me as a bodyguard? And if he had some other reason to want the girl dead, he wouldn't need me along for fun and games. Hell, if he hadn't gone through the business of hiring me, no one could have tagged him as the prime suspect in the shooting. He would just be another person at the bachelor dinner, another former playmate of Karen's with no more motive to kill her than anyone else at the party.

I gave up the brainwork and concentrated on harmless if time-consuming games. I sat at my desk and drew up a list of the eight men who had been at the dinner. I listed the four married men, the Don Juan, the incipient divorcé and, just for the sake of completion, Lloyd and Kenneth. I worked on my silly little list for over an hour, creating mythical motives for each man.

It made an interesting mental exercise, although it didn't seem to be of much value.

SIX

The Alhambra is a Syrian restaurant on West 27th Street, an Arabian oasis in a desert of Greek nightclubs. Off the beaten track, it doesn't advertise, and the sign announcing its presence is almost invisible. You have to know the Alhambra is there in order to find it.

The owner and maitre d' is a little man whom the customers call Kamil. His name is Louis, his parents brought him to America before his eyes were open, and one of his brothers is a full professor at Columbia, but he likes to put on an act. When I brought Ceil Gorski into the place around 8:30, he smiled hugely at me and bowed halfway to the floor.

"Salaam alekhim," he said solemnly. "My pleasure, Mist' London."

"Alekhim salaam," I intoned, glancing over at Ceil while Louis showed us to a table.

Our waiter brought a bottle of very sweet white wine to go with the entrée.

"I was bitchy before. I'm sorry about it."

"Forget it."

"Ed—"

I looked at her. She was worth looking at in a pale green dress which she filled to perfection.

"You want to ask me some questions," she said, "don't you?"

"Well—"

"I don't mind, Ed."

I gave her a brief run-down on the way things seemed to shape up at that point.

"Let me try some names on you," I suggested. "Maybe you can tell me whether Karen mentioned them."

"You can try."

I ran through the eight jokers who had been at the stag. A few sounded vaguely familiar to her, but one of them, Ray Powell, turned out to be someone Ceil knew personally.

"A chaser," she said. "A very plush East Side apartment and an appetite for women that never lets up. He used to see Karen now and then, but there couldn't have been anything serious."

"You know him—very well?"

"Yes." She colored suddenly. She was not the sort you expected to blush. "If you mean intimately, no. He asked often enough. I wasn't interested." She lowered her eyes. "I don't sleep around that much," she said. "Karen—well, she came to New York with stars in her eyes, and when the stars dimmed and died, she went a little crazy, I suppose. I wasn't that ambitious and didn't fall as hard. I have some fairly far-out ways of earning a living, Ed, but most nights I sleep alone."

She was one hell of a girl. She was hard and soft, a cynic and a romantic at the same time. She hadn't gone to college, hadn't finished high school, but somewhere along the way she had acquired a veneer of sophistication that reflected more concrete knowledge than a diploma.

"Poor, Karen," she said. "Poor Karen."

I didn't say anything. She sat somberly for a moment, then tossed her head so that her bleached blond mane rippled like a wheat field in the wind. "I'm getting morbid as hell," she said. "You'd better take me home, Ed."

We climbed three flights of stairs. I stood next to her while she rummaged through her purse. She came up with a key and turned to face me before opening the door. "Ed," she said softly, "if I asked you, would you just come in for a few drinks? Could it be that much of an invitation and no more?"

"Yes."

"I hate to sound like—"

"I understand."

We went inside. She turned on lamps in the living room and we sat on the couch.

She started talking about the modeling session she'd gone through that afternoon. "The money was good," she said, "but I had to work for it. He took three or four rolls of film. Slightly advanced cheese-cake, Ed. Nudes, underwear stuff. He'll print the best pictures and they'll wind up for sale in the dirty little stores on 42nd Street."

"With the face retouched?"

She laughed. "He won't bother. Nobody's going to look at the face, Ed."

"I would."

"Would you?"

"Yes."

"And not the body?"

"That too."

She looked at me for a long moment. There was something electric in the air. I could feel the sweet animal heat of her. She was right next to me. I could reach out and touch her, could take her in my arms and press her close. The bedroom wasn't far away. And she would be good, very good.

Two drinks later, I got up and walked to the door. She followed me. I stopped at the doorway, started to say something, changed my mind. We said good night and I started down the stairs.

If she had been just any girl—actress, secretary, college girl, or waitress—then it would have ended differently. It would have ended in her bedroom, in warmth and hunger and fury. But she was not just any girl. She was a halfway tramp, a little tarnished, a little soiled, a little battered around the edges. And so I could not make that pass at her, could not maneuver from couch to bed.

I didn't want to go back to my apartment. It would be lonely there. I drove to a Third Avenue bar where they pour good drinks.

Somewhere between two and three I left the bar and looked around for the Chevy. By the time I found it I decided to leave it there and take a cab. I had had too little sleep the night before and too much to drink this night, and things were beginning to go a little out of focus. The way I felt, they looked better that way. But I didn't much feel like bouncing the car off a telephone pole or gunning down some equally stoned pedestrian. I flagged a cab and left the driving to him.

He had to tell me three times that we were in front of my building before it got through to me. I shook myself awake, paid him, and wended my way into the brownstone and up a flight of stairs.

Then I blinked a few times.

There was something on my doormat, something that hadn't been there when I left.

It was blond, well-bred, and glassy-eyed. It had an empty wine bottle in one hand and its mouth was smiling lustily. It got to its feet and swayed there, then pitched forward slightly. I caught it and it burrowed its head against my chest.

"You keep late hours," it said.

It was very soft and very warm. It rubbed its hips against me and purred like a kitten, I growled like a randy old tomcat.

"I've been waiting for you," it said. "I've been wanting to go to bed. Take me to bed, Ed London."

Its name, in case you haven't guessed, was Lynn Farwell.

We were a pair of iron filings and my bed was a magnet. I opened the door and we hurried inside. I closed the door and slid the bolt. We moved quickly through the living room and along a hall to the bedroom. Along the way we discarded clothing.

She left her skirt on my couch, her sweater on one of my leather chairs. Her bra and slip and shoes landed in various spots on the hall floor. In the bedroom she got rid of her stockings and garter belt and panties. She was naked and beautiful and hungry . . . and there was no time to waste on words.

Her body welcomed me. Her breasts, firm little cones of happiness, quivered against me. Her thighs enveloped me in the lust-heat of desire. Her face twisted in a blind agony of need.

We were both pretty well stoned. This didn't matter. We could never have done better sober. There was a beginning, bittersweet and almost painful. There was a middle, fast and furious, a scherzo movement in a symphony of fire. And there was an ending, gasping, spent, two bodies washed up on a lonely barren beach.

At the end she used words that girls are not supposed to learn in the schools she had attended. She screamed them out in a frenzy of completion, a song of obscenity offered as a coda.

And afterward, when the rhythm was gone and only the glow remained, she talked. "I needed that," she told me. "Needed it badly. But you could tell that, couldn't you?"

"Yes."

"You're good, Ed." She caressed me. "Very good."

"Sure. I win blue ribbons."

"Was I good?"

I told her she was fine.

"Mmmmm," she said.

SEVEN

I rolled out of bed just as the noon whistles started going off all over town. Lynn was gone. I listened to bells from a nearby church ring twelve times; then I showered, shaved, and swallowed aspirin. Lynn had left. Living proof of indiscretions makes bad company on the morning after.

I caught a cab, and the driver and I prowled Third Avenue for my car. It was still there. I drove it back to the garage and tucked it away. Then I called Donahue, but hung up before the phone had a chance to ring. Not that I expected to reach him anyway, since calling him on the phone didn't seem to produce much in the way of concrete results. But I didn't feel like talking to him just then.

A few hours ago I had been busy coupling with his bride-to-be. It seemed an unlikely prelude to a conversation.

Darcy & Bates wasn't really on Madison Avenue. It was around the corner on 48th Street, a suite of offices on the fourteenth floor of a twenty-two-story building. I got out of the elevator and stood before a reception desk.

"Phil Abeles," I said.

"May I ask your name?"

"Go right ahead." I smiled. She looked unhappily snowed. "Ed London," I finally said. She smiled gratefully and pressed one of twenty buttons and spoke softly into a tube.

"If you'll have a seat, Mr. London," she said.

I didn't have a seat. I stood instead and loaded up a pipe. I finished lighting it as Abeles emerged from an office and came over to meet me. He motioned for me to follow him. We went into his air-cooled office and he closed the door.

"What's up, Ed?"

"I'm not sure," I said. "I want some help." I drew on the pipe. "I'll need a private office for an hour or two," I told him. "And I want to see all of the men who were at Mark Donahue's bachelor dinner. One at a time."

"All of us?" He grinned. "Even Lloyd and Kenneth?"

"I suppose we can pass them for the time being. Just you and the other five then. Can you arrange it?"

He nodded with a fair amount of enthusiasm. "You can use this office," he said. "And everybody's around today, so you won't have any trouble on that score. Who do you want to see first?"

"I might as well start with you, Phil."

I talked with him for ten minutes. But I had already pumped him dry the day before. Still, he gave me a little information on some of the others I would be seeing. Before, I had tried to ask him about his own relationship with Karen Price. Although that tack had been fairly effective, it didn't look like the best way to come up with something concrete. Instead, I asked him about the other men. If I worked on all of them that way, I just might turn up an answer or two.

Abeles more or less crossed Fred Klein off the suspect list, if nothing else. Klein, whose wife was in Reno, had tentatively made the coulda-dunnit sheet on the chance that Karen was threatening to give his wife information that could boost her alimony, or something of the sort. Abeles knocked the theory to pieces with the information that Klein's wife had money of her own, that she wasn't looking for alimony, and that a pair of expensive lawyers had already worked out all the details of the divorce agreement.

I asked Phil Abeles which of the married men he knew definitely had contact at one time or another with Karen Price. This was the sort of information a man is supposed to keep to himself, but the mores of Madison Avenue tend to foster subtle backstabbing. Abeles told me he knew for certain that Karen had been intimate with Harold Merriman, and he was almost sure about Joe Conn as well.

After Abeles left, I knocked the dottle out of my pipe and filled it again. I lit it, and as I shook out the match, I looked up at Harold Merriman.

A pudgy man with a bald spot and bushy eyebrows, forty or forty-five, somewhat older than the rest of the crew. He sat down across the desk from me and narrowed his eyes. "Phil said you wanted to see me," he said. "What's the trouble?"

"Just routine." I smiled. "I need a little information. You knew Karen Price before the shooting, didn't you?"

"Well, I knew who she was."

Sure, I thought. But I let it pass and played him the way I had planned. I asked him who in the office had had anything to do with the dead girl. He hemmed and hawed a little, then told me that Phil Abeles had taken her out for dinner once or twice and that Jack Harris was supposed to have had her along on a business trip to Miami one weekend. Strictly in a secretarial capacity, no doubt.

"And you?"

"Oh, no," Merriman said. "I'd met her, of course, but that was as far as it went."

"Really?"

The hesitation was admission enough. "L-listen," he stammered, "all right, I . . . saw her a few times. It was nothing serious and it wasn't very recent. London—"

I waited.

"Keep it a secret, will you?" He forced a grin. "Write it off as a symptom of the foolish forties. She was available and I was ready to play around a little. I'd just as soon it didn't get out. Nobody around here knows, and I'd like to keep it that way." He hesitated again. "My wife knows. I was so damn ashamed of myself that I told her. But I wouldn't want the boys in the office to know."

I didn't tell him that they already knew, and that they had passed the information on to me.

Ray Powell came in grinning. He was a bachelor, and this made a difference. "Hello, London," he said. "I made it with the girl, if that's what you want to know."

"I heard rumors."

"I don't keep secrets," he said. He sprawled in the chair across from me and crossed one leg over the other. It was a relief to talk to someone other than a reticent, guilt-ridden adulterer.

He certainly looked like a Don Juan. He was twenty-eight, tall, dark, and handsome, with wavy black hair and piercing brown eyes. A little prettier and he might have passed for a gigolo. But there was a slight hardness about his features that prevented this.

"You're working for Mark," he said.

"That's right."

He sighed. "Well, I'd like to see him wind up innocent, but from where I sit, it's hard to see it that way. He's a funny guy, London. He wants to have his cake and eat it, too. He wanted a marriage and he wanted a playmate. With the girl he was marrying, you wouldn't think he'd worry about playing around. Ever meet Lynn?"

"I've met her."

"Then you know what I mean."

I nodded. "Was she one of your conquests?"

"Lynn?" He laughed easily. "Not that girl. She's the pure type, London. The one-man woman. Mark found himself a sweet girl there. Why he bothered with Karen is beyond me."

I switched the subject to the married men in the office. With Powell, I didn't try to find out which of them had been intimate with Karen Price, since it seemed fairly obvious they all had. Instead I tried to ascertain which of them could be in trouble as a result of an affair with the girl.

I learned a few things. Jack Harris was immune to blackmail— his wife knew he cheated on her regularly and had schooled herself to ignore such indiscretions just as long as he returned to her after each rough passage through the turbulent waters of adultery.

Harold Merriman was sufficiently well-off financially so that he could pay a blackmailer indefinitely rather than quiet her by murder; besides, Merriman had already told me that his wife knew, and I was more or less prepared to believe him.

Both Abeles and Joe Conn were possibilities. Conn looked best of all. He wasn't doing very well in advertising but he could hold his job indefinitely—he had married a girl whose family ran one of Darcy & Bates' major accounts. Conn had no money of his own, and no talent to hold a job if his wife wised up and left him.

Of course, there was always the question of how valid Ray Powell's impressions were. *Lynn? She's the pure type. The one-man woman.*

That didn't sound much like the drunken blonde who had turned up on my doormat the night before.

Jack Harris revealed nothing new, merely reinforced what I had managed to pick up elsewhere along the line. I talked to him for fifteen minutes or so. He left, and Joe Conn came into the room.

He wasn't happy. "They said you wanted to see me," he muttered. "We'll have to make it short, London. I've got a pile of work this afternoon and my nerves are jumping all over the place as it is."

The part about the nerves was something he didn't have to tell me. He didn't sit still, just paced back and forth like a lion in a cage before chow time.

I could play it slow and easy or fast and hard, looking to shock and jar. If he was the one who killed her, his nervousness now gave me an edge. I decided to press it.

I got up, walked over to Conn. A short stocky man, crew cut, no tie. "When did you start sleeping with Karen?" I snapped.

He spun around wide-eyed. "You're crazy!"

"Don't play games," I told him. "The whole office knows you were bedding her."

I watched him. His hands curled into fists at his sides. His eyes narrowed and his nostrils flared.

"What is this, London?"

"Your wife doesn't know about Karen, does she?"

"Damn you." He moved toward me. "How much, you bastard? A private detective." He snickered. "Sure you are. You're a damn blackmailer, London. How much?"

"Just how much did Karen ask for?" I said. "Enough to make you kill her?"

He answered with a left hook that managed to find the point of my chin and send me crashing back against the wall. There was a split second of blackness. Then he was coming at me again, fists ready, and I spun aside, ducked, and planted a fist of my own in his gut. He grunted and threw a right at me. I took it on the shoulder and tried his belly again. It was softer this time. He wheezed and folded up. I hit him in the face and just managed to pull the punch at the last minute. It didn't knock him out—only spilled him on the seat of his tweed pants.

"You've got a good punch, London."

"So do you," I said. My jaw still ached.

"You ever do any boxing?"

"No."

"I did," he said. "In the Navy. I still try to keep in shape. If I hadn't been so angry I'd have taken you."

"Maybe."

"But I got mad," he said. "Irish temper, I guess. Are you trying to shake me down?"

"No."

"You don't honestly think I killed Karen, do you?"

"Did you?"

"God, no."

I didn't say anything.

"You think I killed her," he said hollowly. "You must be insane. I'm no killer, London."

"Of course. You're a meek little man."

"You mean just now? I lost my temper."

"Sure."

"Oh, hell," he said. "I never killed her. You got me mad. I don't like shakedowns and I don't like being called a murderer. That's all, damn you."

I called Jerry Gunther from a pay phone in the lobby. "Two things," I told the lieutenant. "First, I think I've got a hotter prospect for you than Donahue. A man named Joe Conn, one of the boys at the stag. I tried shaking him up a little and he cracked wide open, tried to beat my brains in. He's got a good motive, too."

"Ed, listen—"

"That's the first thing," I said. "The other is that I've been trying to get in touch with my client for the past too-many hours and can't reach him. Did you have him picked up again?"

There was a long pause. All at once the air in the phone booth felt much too close. Something was wrong.

"I saw Donahue half an hour ago," Jerry said. "I'm afraid he killed that girl, Ed."

"He confessed?" I couldn't believe it.

"He confessed . . . in a way."

"I don't get it."

A short sigh. "It happened yesterday," Jerry said. "I can't give you the time until we get the medical examiner's report, but the guess is that it was just after we let him go. He sat down at his type-writer and dashed off a three-line confession. Then he stuck a gun in his mouth and made a mess. The lab boys are still there trying to scrape his brains off the ceiling. Ed?"

"What?"

"You didn't say anything . . . I didn't know if you were still on the line. Look, everybody guesses wrong some of the time."

"This was more than a guess. I was sure."

"Well, listen, I'm on my way to Donahue's place again. If you want to take a run over there you can have a look for yourself. I don't know what good it's going to do—"

"I'll meet you there," I said.

EIGHT

The lab crew left shortly after we arrived. "Just a formality for the inquest," Jerry Gunther said. "That's all."

"You're sure it's a suicide, then?"

"Stop dreaming, Ed. What else?"

What else? All that was left in the world of Mark Donahue was sprawled in a chair at a desk. There was a typewriter in front of him and a gun on the floor beside him. The gun was just where it would have dropped after a suicide shot of that nature. There were no little inconsistencies.

The suicide note in the typewriter was slightly incoherent. It read: *It has to end now. I can't help what I did but there is no way out anymore. God forgive me and God help me. I am sorry.*

"You can go if you want, Ed. I'll stick around until they send a truck for the body. But—"

"Run over the timetable, will you?"

"From when to when?"

"From when you released him to when he died."

Jerry shrugged. "Why? You can't read it any way but suicide, can you?"

"I don't know. Give me a run-down."

"Let's see," he said. "You called around five, right?"

"Around then. Five or five-thirty."

"We let him go around three. There's your timetable, Ed. We let him out around three, he came back here, thought about things for a while, then wrote that note and killed himself. That checks with the rough estimate we've got of the time of death. You narrow it down—you did call him after I spoke to you, didn't you?"

"Yes. No answer."

"He must have been dead by that time; probably killed himself within an hour after he got here."

"How did he seem when you released him?"

"Happy to be out, I thought at the time. But he didn't show much emotion one way or the other. You know how it is with a person who's getting ready to knock himself off. All the problems and emotions are kept bottled up inside."

I went over to a window and looked out at Horatio Street. It was the most obvious suicide in the world, but I couldn't swallow it. Call it a hunch, a stubborn refusal to accept the fact that my client had managed to fool me. Whatever it was, I didn't believe the suicide theory. It just didn't sit right.

"I don't like it," I said. "I don't think he killed himself."

"You're wrong, Ed."

"Am I?" I went to Donahue's liquor cabinet and filled two glasses with cognac.

"I know nothing ever looked more like suicide," I admitted. "But the motives are still as messy as ever. Look at what we got here. We have a man who hired me to protect him from his former mistress—and as soon as he did, he only managed to call attention to the fact that he was involved with her. He received threatening phone calls from her. She didn't want him married. But her best friend swears that the Price girl didn't give a damn about Donahue, that he was only another man in her collection."

"Look, Ed—"

"Let me finish. We can suppose for a minute that he was lying for reasons of his own that don't make much sense, that he had some crazy reason for calling me in on things before he knocked off the girl. Maybe he thought that would alibi him—"

"That's just what I was going to say," Jerry interjected.

"I thought of it. It doesn't make a hell of a lot of sense, but it's possible, I guess. Still, where in hell is his motive? Not blackmail. She wasn't the blackmailing type to begin with, as far as I can see. But there's more to it than that. Lynn Farwell wouldn't care who Mark slept with before they were married. Or after, for that matter. It wasn't a love match. She wanted a respectable husband and he wanted a rich wife, and they both figured to get what they wanted. Love wasn't part of it."

"Maybe he wasn't respectable," Jerry said. "Maybe Karen knew something he didn't want known. There's plenty of room here for a hidden motive, Ed."

"Maybe. Still, I wish you'd keep the case open, Jerry."

"You know I won't."

"You'll write it off as suicide and close the file?"

"But I have to. All the evidence points that way. Murder and then suicide, with Donahue tagged for killing the Price girl and then killing himself."

"I guess it makes your bookkeeping easier."

"You know better than that, Ed." He almost sounded hurt. "If I could see it any other way I'd keep on it. I can't. As far as we're concerned it's a closed book."

I walked over to the window again. "I'm going to stay with it," I said.

"Without a client?"

"Without a client."

A maid answered the phone in the Farwell home. I asked to speak to Lynn.

"Miss Farwell's not home," she said. "Who's calling, please?"

I gave her my name.

"Oh, yes, Mr. London. Miss Farwell left a message for you to call her at—" I took down a number with a Regency exchange, thanked her, and hung up.

I was tired, unhappy, and confused. I didn't want the role of bearer of evil tidings. I wished now that I had let Jerry tell her himself. I was in my apartment, it was a hot day for the time of year, and my air conditioner wasn't working right. I dialed the number the maid had given me. A girl answered, not Lynn. I asked to speak to Miss Farwell.

She came on the line almost immediately. "Ed?"

"Yes—I . . ."

"I wondered if you'd call. I hope I wasn't horrid last night. I was very drunk."

"You were all right."

"Just all right?" I didn't say anything. She giggled softly and whispered, "I had a good time, Ed. Thank you for a lovely evening."

"Lynn—"

"Is something the matter?"

I've never been good at breaking news. I took a deep breath and blurted out, "Mark is dead. I just came from his apartment. The police think he killed himself."

Silence.

"Can I meet you somewhere, Lynn? I'd like to talk to you."

More silence. Then, when she did speak, her voice was flat as week-old beer. "Are you at your apartment?"

"Yes."

"Stay there. I'll be right over. I'll take a cab."

The line went dead.

NINE

While I waited for Lynn I thought about Joe Conn. If one person murdered both Karen Price and Mark Donahue, Conn seemed the logical suspect. Karen was blackmailing him, I reasoned, holding him up for hush money that he had to pay if he wanted to keep wife and job. He found out Karen was going to be at the stag, jumping out of the cake, and he took a gun along and shot her.

Then Mark got arrested and Conn felt safe. Just when he was most pleased with himself, the police released Mark. Conn started to worry. If the case dragged out he was in trouble. Even if they didn't get to him, a lengthy investigation would turn up the fact that he had been sleeping with Karen. And he had to keep that fact hidden.

So he went to Donahue's apartment with another gun. He hit Mark over the head, propped him up in the chair, shot him through the mouth, and replaced his own prints with Mark's. Then he dashed off a quick suicide note and got out of there. The blow on the head wouldn't show, if that was how he did it. Not after the bullet did things to Mark's skull.

But then why in hell did Conn throw a fit at the ad agency when I tried to ruffle him? It didn't make sense. If he had killed Mark on Sunday afternoon, he would know that it would be only a matter of time until the body was found and the case closed. He wouldn't blow up if I called him a murderer, not when he had already taken so much trouble to cover his tracks.

Unless he was being subtle, anticipating my whole line of reasoning. And when you start taking a suspect's possible subtlety into consideration, you find yourself on a treadmill marked confusion. All at once the possibilities become endless.

I got off the treadmill, though. The doorbell rang and Lynn Farwell stepped into my apartment for the third time in two days. And it occurred to me, suddenly, just how different each of those three visits had been.

This one was slightly weird. She walked slowly to the same leather chair in which she had curled up Saturday morning. She did not wax kittenish this time.

"I don't feel a thing," she said.

"Shock."

"No," she admitted. "I don't even feel shock, Ed. I just don't feel a thing.

"I wasn't in love with him," she said. "You knew that, of course."

"I gathered as much."

"It wasn't a well-kept secret, was it? I told you that much before I told you my name, almost. Of course I was on the make for you at the time. That may have had something to do with it."

She looked at her drink but didn't touch it. Slowly, softly, she said, "After the first death there is no other."

There was a minute of silence. Just as I was about to prompt her into speaking, she repeated, "After the first death there is no other." She sighed. "When one death affects you completely, then the deaths that come after it don't have their full effect. Do you follow me?"

I nodded. "When did it happen?" I asked.

"Four years ago. I was in college then."

"A boy?"

"Yes."

She looked at her drink, then drained it.

"I was nineteen then. Pure and innocent. A popular girl who dated all the best boys and had a fine time. Then I met him. Ray Powell introduced us. You probably met Ray. He worked in the same office as Mark."

I nodded. That explained one contradiction—Ray's referring to Lynn as the pure type, the one-man woman. When he had known her, the shoe fit. Since then she had outgrown it.

"I started going out with John and all at once I was in love. I had never been in love before. I've never been in love since. It was something." For a shadow of an instant a smile crossed her face, then disappeared. "I can't honestly remember what it was like. Being in love, that is. I'm not the same person. That girl could love; I can't.

"He was going to pick me up and something went wrong with his car. The steering wheel or something like that. He was going around a turn and the wheels wouldn't straighten out and—

"I changed after that. At first I just hurt. All over. And then the callus formed, the emotional callus to keep me from going crazy, I suppose." She picked up a cigarette and puffed on it nervously, then stubbed it out. "You know what bothered me most? We never slept together. We were going to wait until we were married. See what a corny little girl I was?

"But I changed, Ed. I thought that at least I could have given him that much before he died. And I thought about that, and maybe brooded about it, and something happened inside me." She almost smiled. "I'm afraid I became a little bit of a tramp, Ed. Not just now and then, like last night. A tramp. I went to Ray Powell and lost my virginity, and then I made myself a one-woman welcoming committee for visiting Yale boys."

Her face filled up with memories. "I'm not that bad anymore. And I don't honestly feel John's death either, to be truthful. It happened a long time ago, and to a different girl."

"I don't think Mark Donahue killed himself," I said, "or the girl. I think he was framed and then murdered."

"It doesn't matter."

"Doesn't it?"

"No," she said, sadly, vacantly. "It should, I know. But it doesn't, Ed." She stood up. "Do you know why I really wanted to come here?"

"To talk."

"Yes. I've learned to pretend, you see. And I intend to pretend, too. I'll be the very shocked and saddened Miss Farwell now. That's the role I have to play." Another too-brief smile. "But I don't have to play that role with you, Ed. I wanted to say what I felt if only to one person. Or what I didn't feel." She rose to leave.

"And now I'll wear imitation widow's weeds for a while, and then I'll find some other bright young man to marry. Goodbye, Ed London."

I ALMOST FORGOT ABOUT THE DATE with Ceil. I'd made it the night before instead of the pass I would have preferred to make. When I got there, she said she was tired and hot and didn't feel like dressing.

"The Britannia is right down the block," she said. "And I can go there like this."

She was wearing slacks and a man's shirt. She didn't look mannish, though. That would have been slightly impossible.

We walked down the block to a hole in the wall with a sign that said, appropriately, FISH AND CHIPS. There were half a dozen small tables in a room decorated with travel posters of Trafalgar Square and Buckingham Palace and every major British tourist attraction with the possible exception of Diana Dors. We sat at a small table and ordered fish and chips and bottles of Guinness.

I said, "Donahue's dead."

"I know. I heard it on the radio."

"What did they say?"

"Suicide. He confessed to the murder and shot himself. Isn't that what happened?"

"I don't think so." I signaled the waiter for two more bottles of Guinness.

"It's possible that someone—probably Conn—killed Donahue," I added. "The door to his apartment was locked when the police got there, but it's one of those spring locks. The inside bolt wasn't turned. Conn could have gone there as soon as he learned Mark was released, then shot him and locked the door as he left."

"How could he know Mark was released?"

"A phone call to police Headquarters, or a call to Mark. That's no problem."

"How about the time? Maybe Conn has an alibi."

"I'm going to check that tomorrow," I said. "That's why I would have liked to see Jerry Gunther keep the file open on the case. Then he could have questioned Conn. The guy threw punches at me once already. I don't know if I can take him a second time."

She grinned. Then her face sobered. "Are you sure it was Conn? You said Abeles had the same motive."

"He's also got an alibi."

"A good one?"

"Damn good. *I'm* his alibi. I was with him in Scarsdale that afternoon, and I called Donahue's apartment as soon as I got back to town, and by that time Donahue was dead. Phil Abeles would have needed a jet plane to pull it off. Besides, I can't see him as the killer."

"And you can see Conn?"

"That's the trouble," I said. "I can't. Not really."

We drank up. I paid our check and we left. We walked a block to Washington Square and sat on a bench. I started to smoke my pipe when I heard a sharp intake of breath and turned to stare at Ceil.

"Oh," she said. "I just had a grisly idea."

"What?"

"It's silly. Like an Alfred Hitchcock television show. I thought maybe Karen really did make those phone calls to him, not because she was jealous but just to tease him, thinking what a gag it would be when she popped out of the cake at his bachelor dinner. And then the gag backfires and he shoots her because he's scared she wants to kill him." She laughed. "I've got a cute imagination," she said. "But I'm not much of a help, am I?"

I didn't answer her. My mind was off on a limb somewhere. I closed my eyes and saw the waiters wheeling the cake out toward the center of the room. Stripper music playing on a phonograph. A girl bursting from the cake, nude and lovely. A wide smile on her face—

"Ed, what's the matter?"

Most of the time problems are solved by simple trial and error, a lot of legwork that pays off finally. Other times all the legwork in the world falls flat, and it's like a jigsaw puzzle where you suddenly catch the necessary piece and all the others leap into place. This was one of those times.

"You're a genius!" I told Ceil.

"You don't mean it happened that way? I—"

"Oh, no. Of course not. Donahue didn't kill Karen—" I stood.

"Hey, where are you going?" Ceil asked.

"Gotta run," I said. "Can't even walk you home. Tomorrow," I said. "We'll have dinner, okay?"

I didn't hear her answer. I didn't wait for it. I raced across the park and jumped into the nearest cab.

I called Lynn Farwell from my apartment. She was back in her North Shore home, and life had returned to her voice. "I didn't expect to hear from you," she said. "I suppose you're interested in my body, Ed. It wouldn't be decent so soon after Mark's death, you know. But you may be able to persuade me—"

"Not your body," I said. "Your memory. Can you talk now? Without being overheard?"

She giggled lewdly. "If I couldn't, I wouldn't have said what I did. Go ahead, Mr. Detective."

I asked questions. She gave me answers. They were the ones I wanted to hear.

I strapped on a shoulder holster and jammed a gun into it.

TEN

The door to Powell's apartment was locked. I rang the bell once. No one answered. I waited a few minutes, then took out my penknife and went to work on the lock. Like the locks in all decent buildings in New York, this was one of the burglar-proof models. And, like just 99 percent of them, it wasn't burglar-proof. It took half a minute to open.

I turned the knob. Then I eased the gun from my shoulder holster and shoved the door open. I didn't need the gun just then. The room was empty.

But the apartment wasn't. I heard noises from another room, people-noises, sex-noises. A man's voice and a girl's voice. The man was saying he heard somebody in the living room. The girl was telling him he was crazy. He said he would check. Then there were footsteps, and he came through the doorway, and I pointed the gun at him.

I said, "Stay right there, Powell."

He looked a little ridiculous. He was wearing a bathrobe, his feet were bare, and it was fairly obvious that he had been interrupted somewhere in the middle of his favorite pastime. I kept the gun on him and watched his eyes. He was good—damned good. The eyes showed fear, outrage, surprise. Nothing else. Not the look of a man in a trap.

"If this is some kind of a joke—"

"It's no joke."

"Then what the hell is it?"

"The end of the line," I said. "You made a hell of a try. You almost got away with it."

"I don't know what you're driving at, London. But—"

"I think you do."

She picked that moment to wander into the room. She was a redhead with her hair messed. One of the buttons on her blouse was buttoned wrong. She walked into the room, wondering aloud what the interruption was about, and then she saw the gun and her mouth made a little O.

She said, "Maybe I should have stayed in the other room."

"Maybe you should go home," I snapped.

"Oh," she said. "Yes, that's a very good idea." She moved to her left and sort of backed around me, as if she wanted to keep as much distance as possible between her well-constructed body and the gun in my hand. "I think you're right," she said. "I think I should go home . . . And you don't have to worry about me."

"Good."

"I should tell you I have no memory at all," she said. "I never came here, never met you, never saw your face, and I cannot possibly remember what you look like. It is terrible, my memory."

"Good," I said.

"Living I like very much better than remembering. Goodbye, Mr. Nobody."

The door slammed, and Ray Powell and I were alone. He glared at me.

"What in hell do you want, exactly?"

"To talk to you."

"You need a gun for that?"

"Probably."

He grinned disarmingly. "Guns make me nervous."

"They never did before. You've got a knack for getting hold of unregistered guns, Powell. Is there another one in the bedroom?"

"I don't get it," he said. He scratched his head. "You must mean something, London. Spit it out."

"Don't play games."

"I—"

"Cut it," I said. "You killed Karen Price. You knew she was going to do the cake bit because you were the one who put the idea in Phil Abeles's head."

"Did he tell you that?"

"He's forgotten. But he'll remember with a little prompting. You set her up and then you killed her and tossed the gun on the floor. You figured the police would arrest Donahue, and you were right. But you didn't think they would let him go. When they did, you went to his place with another gun. He let you in. You shot him, made it look like suicide, and let the one death cover the other."

He shook his head in wonder. "You really believe this?"

"I know it."

"I suppose I had a motive," he said musingly. "What, pray tell, did I have against the girl? She was good in bed, you know. I make it a rule never to kill a good bed partner if I can help it." He grinned. "So why did I kill her?"

"You didn't have a thing against her," I said.

"My point exactly. I—"

"You killed her to frame Donahue," I added. "You got to Karen Price while the bachelor dinner was still in the planning stage. You hired her to make a series of calls to Donahue, jealousy calls threatening to kill him or otherwise foul up his wedding. It was going to be a big joke—she would scare him silly; and then for a capper she would pop out of the cake as naked as the truth and tell him she was just pulling his leg.

"But you topped the gag. She popped out of the cake covered with a smile and you put a bullet in her and left Donahue looking like the killer. Then, when you thought he was getting off the hook, you killed him. Not to cover the first murder—you felt safe enough on that score . . . because you really didn't have a reason to kill the girl herself. You killed Donahue because he was the one you wanted dead all along."

Powell was still grinning. Only not so self-assuredly now. In the beginning, he hadn't been aware of how much I knew. Now he was learning and it wasn't making him happy.

"I'll play your game," he said. "I killed Karen, even though I didn't have any reason. Now why did I kill Mark? Did I have a reason for that one?"

"Sure."

"What?"

"For the same reason you hired Karen to bother Donahue," I said. "Maybe a psychiatrist could explain it better. He'd call it transference."

"Go on."

"You wanted Mark Donahue dead because he was going to marry Lynn Farwell. And you don't want anybody to marry Lynn Farwell, Powell, you'd kill anybody who tried."

"Keep talking," he said.

"How am I doing so far?"

"Oh, you're brilliant, London. I suppose I'm in love with Lynn?"

"In a way."

"That's why I've never asked her to marry me. And why I bed down anything else that gets close enough to jump."

"That's right."

"You're out of your mind, London."

"No," I said. "But you are." I took a breath. "You've been in love with Lynn for a long time. Four years, anyway. It's no normal love, Powell, because you're not a normal person. Lynn's part of a fixation of yours. She's sweet and pure and unattainable in your mind. You don't want to possess her completely because that would destroy the illusion. Instead you compensate by proving your virility with any available girl. But you can't let Lynn marry someone else. That would take her away from you. You don't want to have her—except for an occasional evening, maybe—but you won't let anyone else have her."

He was tottering on the edge now . . . trying to take a step toward me and then backing off. I had to push him over that edge. If he cracked, then he would crack wide open. If he held himself together he might wriggle free. I knew damn well he was guilty, but there wasn't enough evidence to present to a jury. I had to make him crack.

"First I'm a double murderer," Powell said. "Now I'm a mental case. I don't deny that I like Lynn. She's a sweet, clean, decent girl. But that's as far as it goes."

"Is it?"

"Yes."

"Donahue's the second man who almost married her. The first one was four years ago. Remember John? You introduced the two of them. That was a mistake, wasn't it?"

"He wouldn't have been good for her. But it didn't matter. I suppose you know he died in a car accident."

"In a car, yes. Not an accident. You gimmicked the steering wheel. Then you let him kill himself. You got away clean with that one, Powell."

I hadn't cracked him yet. I was close, but he was still able to compose himself.

"It was an accident," he exclaimed. "Besides, it happened a long time ago. I'm surprised you even bother mentioning it."

I ignored his words. "The death shook Lynn up a lot," I said. "It must have been tough for you to preserve your image of her. The sweet and innocent thing turned into a round-heeled little nymph for a while."

"That's a damned lie."

"It is like hell. And about that time you managed to have your cake and eat it, too. You kept on thinking of her as the unattainable ideal. But that didn't stop you from taking her virginity, did it? You ruined her, Powell!"

He was getting closer to the edge. His face was white and his hands were hard little fists. The muscles in his neck were drum-tight.

"I never touched her!"

"Liar!" I was shouting now. "You ruined that girl, Powell!"

"Damn you, I never touched her! Nobody did, damn you! She's still a virgin! She's still a virgin!"

I took a breath. "The hell she is," I yelled. "I had her last night,

Powell. She came to my room all hot to trot and I bedded her until she couldn't see straight."

His eyes were wild.

"Did you hear me, Powell? I had *your girl* last night. I had Lynn, Powell!"

And that cracked him.

He charged me like a wild man, his whole body coordinated in the spring. I stepped back, swung aside. He tried to turn and come toward me but his momentum kept him from pulling it off. By the time he got back on the right track, my hand had gone up and come down. The barrel of the gun caught him just behind the left ear. He took two more little steps, carried along by the sheer force of his rush. Then he folded up and went out like an ebbing tide.

He wasn't out long. By the time Jerry Gunther got there, flanked by a pair of uniformed cops, Powell was babbling away a mile a minute, spending half the time confessing to the three murders and the other half telling anyone who would listen that Lynn Farwell was a saint.

They started to put handcuffs on him. Then they changed their minds and bundled him up in a straitjacket.

ELEVEN

"I guess I missed my calling," Ceil said. "I should have been a detective. I probably would have flopped there, too, but the end might have been different. We all know what girls become when they don't make it as actresses. What do lousy detectives turn to?"

"Cognac," I said. "Pass the bottle."

She passed and I poured. We were in her apartment on Sullivan Street. It was Tuesday night, Ray Powell had long since finished confessing, and Ceil Gorski had just proved to me that she could cook a good meal.

"You figured it out beautifully," she said. "But do I get an assist on the play?"

"Easily." I tucked tobacco into my pipe, lit up. "You managed to get my mind working. Powell was a genius at murder. A certifiable psychotic, but also a genius. He set things up beautifully. First of all, the frame couldn't have been neater. He very carefully set up Donahue with means, motive, and opportunity. Then he shot the girl and left Donahue on the hook."

I worked on the cognac. "The neat thing was this—if Donahue managed to have an alibi, if by some chance somebody was watching him when the shot was fired, Powell was still in the clear. He himself was one of the few men in the room with no conceivable motive for wanting Karen Price dead."

Ceil moved a little closer on the couch. I put an arm around her. "Then the way he got rid of Donahue was sheer perfection," I continued. "He made it look enough like suicide to close the case as far as the police were concerned. And Jerry Gunther isn't an easy man to bulldoze. He's thorough. But Powell made it look good."

"You didn't swallow it."

"That's because I play hunches. Even so, I was up a tree by then. Because the murder had a double edge to it. Even if he muffed it somehow, even if it didn't go over as suicide, Donahue would be dead and he would be in the clear. Because there was only one way to interpret it—Donahue had been killed by the man who killed Karen Price, obviously, and had been killed so that the original killing would go unsolved. That made me suspect Joe Conn and never let me guess at Powell, not even on speculation. Even with the second killing he hid the fact that Donahue and not Karen was the real target."

"And that's where I came in," she said happily.

"That's exactly where you came in," I agreed. "You and your active imagination. You thought how grim it would be if Karen had only been playing a joke with those phone calls. And that was the only explanation in the world for the calls. I had to believe Donahue was getting the calls, and that Karen was making them. A disguised voice might work once, but she'd called him a few times.

"That left two possibilities, really. She could be jealous—which seemed contrary to everything I had learned about her. Or it could be a gag. But if she was jealous, then why in hell would she take the job popping out of the cake? So it had to be a gag, and once it was a gag, I had to guess why someone would put her up to it. And from that point—"

"It was easy."

"Uh-huh. It was easy."

She snuggled closer. I liked her perfume. I liked the feel of her body beside me.

"It wasn't that easy," she said. "You know what? I think you're a hell of a good detective. And you know what else?"

"What?"

"I also think you're a rotten businessman."

I smiled. "Why?"

"Because you did all that work and didn't make a dime out of it. You got a retainer from Donahue, but that didn't even cover all the time you spent *before* Karen was killed, let alone the time since then. And you probably will never collect."

"I'm satisfied."

"Because justice has been done?"

"Partly. Also because I'll be rewarded."

She upped her eyebrows. "How? You won't make another nickel out of the case, will you?"

"No."

"Then—"

"I'll make something more important than money."

"What?"

She was soft and warm beside me. And it was our third evening together. Not even an amateur tramp could mind a pass on a third date.

"What are you going to make?" she asked, innocently.

I took her face between my hands and kissed her. She closed her eyes and purred like a happy cat.

"You," I said.

TWIN CALL GIRLS

ONE

Somewhere a phone was ringing. I reached out and touched something warm and soft. The something flowed into my arms like hot lava and purred *Oh, Ed* and drew itself against me from head to toe. Mouths kissed and hands fluttered urgently.

Somewhere a phone was ringing. The girl in my arms sighed lustily and made preliminary movements. I kissed the side of her face and her throat. A bedspring complained with a metallic whine. It was the world's best way to wake up except for that damned phone.

Somewhere a phone was ringing. The girl in my arms sighed a sigh pregnant with thoughts of what might have been. Her mouth stopped kissing, her hands stopped fluttering, and, reluctantly, she drew herself away.

"Ed, the phone is ringing," she said.

Lust coughed and died. I blinked cobwebs from disappointed eyes, swung my legs over the side of the bed, and picked up the damn phone. A female voice said, "No names. Please listen carefully—this is urgent. I need help. Are you listening to me?"

"Yes."

"I can't talk now, but I want you to call me this afternoon. At two. Have you got that?"

"At two this afternoon."

"From a pay phone. Not from your apartment. Call me at TRafalgar 3–0520. Do you have the number?"

"TRafalgar 3–0520," I said. "Whom do I ask for?"

"Don't worry," she said. "I'll answer."

The phone clicked. The girl in my bed wanted to know who had called. I told her I didn't know. She said well now, what the hell was this, anyway? That I didn't know either. I got out of bed and found a magazine and a pencil. On the magazine cover was a painting of a general. He had a high forehead. Across it I printed "TRafalgar 3–0520" and under that "2 P.M."

The girl in my bed yawned, a wide, open-mouthed yawn. No prelude to love-making. The damned phone had ended that. She got out of bed and started putting on clothes.

"It's morning, all right," she noted. "Make some coffee, Ed. I've got a head that's two sizes too big for me."

I made a pot of coffee which we drank in the living room. She asked about the phone call.

"Probably some crank," I said. "All cloak and dagger. That's one trouble with being a detective. You get a lot of idiot phone calls."

"And all at the wrong time, Ed. You're supposed to call her back. You going to?"

"Probably."

"And the number'll turn out to be the YWCA, or something. You lead a rough life."

I told her it had its moments.

At 2 P.M. I called TRafalgar 3–0520. It wasn't the YWCA. The same voice answered on the first ring, saying, "Ed London?"

"Yes. Who is this?"

A sigh of relief. "I'm in terrible trouble," she said. "Somebody is trying to kill me. I need your help. I'm scared."

I started to tell her to come to my place, but she cut me off. "I can't go there," she said.

"Why not?"

"It's not safe. Listen, I'll meet you in Central Park. Is that all right?"

"It's a pretty big place. Want to narrow it down a little?"

"There's an entrance to the park at 94th Street and Fifth Avenue. There are two paths. Take the one that bears uptown. A little ways up there's a pond, and the path divides to go around the pond. I'll be sitting on one of the benches on the uptown side of the pond."

"How do I recognize you?"

"I'm blond. Not too tall. Don't worry, just come. It never gets crowded there. I'll be alone. I'll . . . I'll recognize you, Mr. London."

"What time?"

"Four-thirty. Please be on time. I'm very scared."

She had picked a quiet part of the park. I walked in through the 94th Street entrance and passed a covey of maids pushing carriages. They milled around near the entrance and gossiped about their employers. I took the path that led uptown and walked toward the pond.

The pond came into view, flat, calm, and stagnant. Three beer cans and two ducks floated on the water. I thought of sitting ducks. I started walking around the uptown side of the pond and then I saw her, sitting alone on a bench and not looking at me. I wanted to call her name but she had never gotten around to telling me what it was.

"Hello there," I called.

No answer and no glance. I looked at my watch. It was 4:30, I was right on time, and she was the only person around. She was blond, young, and dressed nicely. I walked faster. She still did not look at me. I hurried along, worried now, and I reached her and looked at her and saw, finally, why she had not moved.

I was on time. But someone had gotten to her first, had found her before me.

Once she had been pretty, and once she had been frightened . . . and now she was dead.

TWO

I looked around. The park was as still as the girl. I went through the inane formality of holding her cool and limp wrist and feeling for a pulse. There was none. There is rarely a pulse in the wrist of a girl who has been shot through the middle of the forehead. She had been dead fifteen or twenty minutes.

If she had a purse, someone had snatched it. No identification. I did not know her name, who had scared her, who had followed her, who had killed her, or why. She had wanted help, my help, but I did not get to her in time.

I didn't want to leave her on the bench. There is something ineffably discordant about a lone corpse left to cool and stiffen on a park bench. But I turned and walked back around the edge of the pond and down the path. I stopped once to look back at her. She did not look dead from a distance. She looked like a young girl sitting quietly, waiting to meet a suitor.

I walked to Fifth Avenue, down to 86th Street, east toward home. There was a bar on Madison. I stopped there to use the phone booth. I dialed Centre Street Police Headquarters.

"There's a body in Central Park, a dead girl," I said, and quickly gave him the location. He kept trying to interrupt, to get my name, to find out more. But I had said everything I wanted to say.

The day had started off with an unreal quality to it. Private detectives do not get mysterious phone calls from anonymous people. They do not keep unexplained rendezvous with nameless voices in secluded parts of Central Park. It had all seemed a game staged by some more or less harmless lunatic, and I had gone through the paces like a dutiful clown.

The corpse changed all of that. The girl, so neatly shot, posed so unobtrusively on the park bench, was a jarring coda to the symphony of annoyance that began with a phone call's interruption of romance. I had made my call to the police without giving my name and, consequently, was not involved. I had gone through the motions and had stumbled on the death of a prospective client who had not lived long enough to pay me a retainer. I had gone to her aid without believing she really existed, and when I had found her she was dead, and I never had the chance to become involved.

But I still felt involved.

At 5:30 I was still nursing my drink. Time dragged. Outside, the street was still bright. Then a buzzer sounded: someone was downstairs in my vestibule. I got up slowly, drink in hand, and pressed the answering buzzer that would open the downstairs door. I waited and listened to footsteps on the staircase. The footsteps halted in front of my door. There was a knock.

I finished the cognac and went to the door. I turned the knob and flung open the door—to look into the face of the girl I had found dead in Central Park. I saw the blue eyes, the blond hair, the button nose. I saw everything but the little hole in the middle of the forehead.

"You're Ed London," she said.

"You're not you!" I exclaimed stupidly as she stepped inside my apartment.

"I don't understand."

I took a deep breath and stammered, "B-but I just saw you, in Central Park, where I was supposed to meet you. Only somebody else met you first and you were dead. Shot between the eyes."

It sounded idiotic now—her standing beside me, a living, breathing doll. But she made her way through the maze of my meaningless words and something soaked in. Her mouth fell open and she gasped like a fish on a line. Her eyes bugged. She said, "Oh no! Good God," and gave a shrill little scream and fell into my arms and cried her eyes out . . .

THREE

I held the girl until she got a half-nelson on herself, then eased her into one of the twin leather chairs that give my living room the air of a British men's club. She stayed in the chair and finished her crying while I poured cognac into a glass for her.

I made her drink the cognac.

After a long time she said, "I can't believe it, Mr. London. I can't believe Jackie's dead."

"Jackie?"

"Jacqueline Baron," she said. "She was my sister." She broke down again, suddenly regained her composure. "Not my twin sister. She was a year older. But we looked enough alike to pass for twins. My parents named her Jackie and me Jill. Jackie and Jill. Like the nursery rhyme. They thought it was cute."

"Who called me? You or Jackie?"

"She did."

"Because she was afraid?"

"Because we were both afraid," Jill said. She held the glass of cognac in her hand, stared at it a moment, then drained it. "This is very good," she said. "What is it?"

"Cognac."

"Oh. It tastes good, makes me feel warm. But I still feel cold inside. Somebody killed Jackie and now they're going to kill me. Oh, God, I'm scared."

She started to cry again.

After a while she calmed down again. I asked if she knew who had been trying to kill Jackie and her. She said she didn't know. I asked why anyone would want them dead. She didn't know that either.

"We'd better take this from the top," I said. "When did it all start?"

"Three days ago, I think."

"What happened?"

"There was a phone call. Jackie answered. We share an apartment—shared an apartment," she added morosely. "Jackie answered it. She listened for a minute, looked frightened, and slammed the phone down."

"Who was it?"

"She wouldn't say. Wouldn't tell me anything about it. Then, the next day, someone in a truck tried to run us both down. It was so frightening. We were crossing the street and a truck came speeding at us from out of nowhere. He missed us by inches. Luckily, we got across in time."

"Did you get a look at the truck?"

She shook her head. "No, I was too frightened. And I thought—then—it was just accidental. But Jackie was worried. I could tell something was wrong. When I prodded her, she told me about the phone call. Someone was going to kill us both."

"Did she say why?"

"She didn't know."

"No idea?"

"Nothing she told me about . . . But there's more. Yesterday, someone tried to kill me. Right on Park Avenue. A car whizzed by and somebody shot at me. Whoever it was missed. I was petrified."

"Why didn't you go to the police?"

"It's . . . We couldn't."

"And this morning Jackie called me. She wouldn't call the police either, but she called me. That doesn't make much sense."

She didn't answer.

"Look at me," I said. "This is no game. Somebody shot your sister. Killed her in cold blood. Right now the police are picking her body up from Central Park and trying to figure out who the hell she is. You can't afford to sit around deciding how much you can tell me and how much you can keep to yourself. You either open up or I'll pick up the phone and call the police and you can tell it to them. Which is probably a fairly good idea at this stage."

"No, don't."

"Then you'd better start talking."

"Yes," she said. "I guess you're right."

She started talking. Jill and Jacqueline Baron lived together in an expensive apartment on East 58th Street off Park. They were self-employed. They earned a good living.

They were call girls.

"We were going to be models," she said. "You know, everybody starts out to be a model. Only we never did make it."

"But we did all right," Jill said. Her eyes turned hard, bitter. "We had all the qualifications for our chosen work . . . I'm not bad to look at, am I?"

She was wearing a green sheath dress that hid her figure as effectively as Saran wrap. She had long legs, and they were crossed at the knee now so that I could see their shape, which was fine. Her breasts pushed out at me in a way that would keep her out of bounds for the fashion photographers but undeniably in bounds for any red-blooded man between the ages of eighteen and eighty. And she was beautiful to boot.

"Pretty," she said. She rolled the word on her tongue and her eyes clouded. "Our looks were our downfall. It's an easy life for a lazy girl, with looks and a figure, Ed. It doesn't take any talent at all. The men come and they tell their friends about you and pretty soon you have a date every night, and every date is at least a fifty-dollar bill and maybe a hundred, and no income tax out of that, either . . . Would you pay me fifty, Ed?"

She laughed softly. She was playing Little Miss Desirable now, running her tongue over her lower lip, pouting a little, arranging herself in the chair to make herself appear the personification of commercial lust. The act drained away her sorrow, and her fear. She got caught up in it and part of the reality of Jackie's death left her for the moment.

"It was handy," she said. "Jackie and I had good times together. We were closer than sisters, Ed. You . . . well, you say how much we looked alike. We've always been able to pass for twins. That was an asset in business, you know."

"Why?"

"Because we could cover each other's dates." She smiled, remembering. "If Jackie had two dates at the same time and I was free, I would take one of them and pretend I was Jackie. The tricks never knew the difference. They couldn't even tell us apart in bed."

"Handy."

"Uh-huh. Sometimes we would take a trick together. You know, a man would want to go to bed with both of us at once. A real sister act." She closed her blue eyes. "Men get their kicks in funny ways. Some need two girls in order to get their jollies. Men are all sick, Ed."

"You get a distorted picture."

"Do I?"

"Yes. You just meet the men who pay you. The straight ones, the sane ones, they're home with their wives in front of a television set with a can of beer close by. But you don't get to see that kind."

Her eyebrows went up a notch. "And you? Have you got a wife, Ed London?"

"I don't even have a television set. But let's forget my sex life for the time being.

"Let's take it from the top," I said. "You're both call girls and you live together. That is, lived together. Someone is trying to kill you and you don't know who or why. Any ideas at all?"

"None."

"Were you blackmailing anyone?"

"No."

"Was Jackie?"

"If she was, she didn't tell me about it."

"Okay. How about men? Any boyfriends?"

"The only men in my life are customers, Ed."

It was a sort of hopeless line of questioning. All she knew was that her sister had been shot and she was next in line.

"Why didn't you go to the police?" I asked Jill Baron.

"You should know that by now. Call girls don't look for help from the law. The police leave you alone if you live a quiet life and stay out of trouble, but if you draw them a map of who you are and where you live and how you earn your living, you might as well hang out a sign. The crooked cops come with their hands out and the honest ones haul you off to jail."

She worked on her coffee. "Jackie didn't even want to call in a private detective. She said you couldn't trust them. But your name had been mentioned somewhere, and I heard you were honest. So I insisted we call you."

"Well, now's a good time to go to the police, Jill. Whoever is after you is playing for keeps."

She shook her head. "But they'll just ask me questions," she said. "Questions, questions, questions, and I don't know any of the answers that count. So what good will it do me?"

Her voice broke off and her eyes dropped. I took one of her small hands in mine. Her flesh was cold.

"Ed, help me," she pleaded. "If you help me maybe we can find out what it's all about and then go to the police. It won't do any good to go to them now."

She had a point. She couldn't give the cops anything much to work on.

"Jill."

She looked at me.

"Think, now. Were you or Jackie ever arrested? I mean for any offense at all."

"Just a traffic ticket once. Nothing more."

"Did they fingerprint you?"

"No, I just got a ticket."

"Were either of you ever fingerprinted for anything? A government job? Anything?"

"I turned a trick with a UN diplomat once. But you don't get fingerprinted for that sort of thing. Why the questions?"

I filled a pipe and lit a match. Without prints, it was going to take them awhile to identify Jackie Baron's body. A corpse without identification is a tricky thing, and although police routine always comes up with an answer, it takes time. They run through Missing Persons files, they ship the prints to Washington, they play games with laundry marks . . .

So we had time to dig around a little.

"All right," I said. "We'll leave the police out of things, at least for the time being."

"And you'll help me, Ed?"

"I'll help you," I said.

FOUR

I put my gun in the shoulder rig where it belonged, went to the window, pulled back the shade, and peered across the street. A few old ladies were walking home. No one seemed to be lurking in the shadows.

"Did anyone follow you here?"

"No."

"Are you sure?"

"No."

I told her to wait there and left the apartment. I walked down-stairs, then left through the rear exit where the janitor drags the garbage. There is a low fence between the yard of my building and the yard of the building behind it that fronts on 84th Street. I pushed a garbage can against the fence, climbed onto the can, and dropped over the fence. I walked through that building, smiled at a curious seven-year-old boy, and came out on 84th.

The air was cooler now with the beginnings of a storm blowing up over the East River. The sky was a darker gray; in a few hours it would be completely black. I walked around the block to 83rd and headed toward my own building again, keeping my eyes open. All the parked cars were appropriately empty, all the doorways were now untenanted. If she had been followed, her shadow had melted. The coast seemed clear.

I went upstairs. She was standing by the fireplace looking at some of my books.

"Grab your purse," I said.

"Where we going?"

"Downtown. I'm hiding you."

We left the apartment. A cab drove up, and I gave the driver an address in the West Twenties. As he put the taxi in gear, Jill looked at me inquisitively.

"It's a friend's apartment," I said.

"Anyone I know?"

"Probably not. She's an actress, out of town with a road company. She won't be back for two months."

"And you have a key to her apartment?"

"Yes."

She smiled. "How cozy, Ed. Hiding one girl at a girlfriend's apartment. Won't she mind?"

"She won't be there to mind," I said.

She kept quiet the rest of the trip. Once or twice she dabbed at her eyes with a handkerchief. The cabby took Second Avenue downtown to 23rd Street, then cut west and doubled uptown a block to the address I had given him.

"Here?" Jill said, surprised.

"That's right."

"Your actress friend can't be making much money."

"It's a tough business."

"It must be. Maybe she should try my line, Ed. Or doesn't she have any aptitude in that direction?"

"Don't be bitchy."

She pouted. "Was I being bitchy?"

"Very."

"I'm sorry," she said. "I'll try to be good. It's just . . . I guess I'm cracking wise to get Jackie out of my mind, what happened to her, and, oh, it isn't really working, Ed."

Jill and I climbed an unlit and shaky staircase past the machine shop on the first floor and Madame Sindra's palmist studio on the second floor. She stood in front of Maddy's door while I found the right key and opened it. We went inside. She sat down on a couch while I turned on the lights.

"Well," she said. "Now what?"

I sat down next to her. "You'll be safe here," I said.

"I know."

"And you can stay here while I try to get a line on whoever is after you. But I've got to ask you a question I already asked you, Jill. And you have to answer it straight."

"Go on."

"Were you mixed up in anything besides hustling?"

"Isn't that enough?"

"I'm serious. Ever try blackmailing a customer? Or did you ever overhear anything you shouldn't have heard? Think about it. It's important."

Her face screwed up in concentration and then relaxed. She shook her head negatively.

"Nothing?"

"Nothing."

"And Jackie?"

"If she was, I never knew about it."

"Then it can only add up one way," I said. "Somebody had a reason to see Jackie dead. But you both looked alike and you both acted alike and he couldn't tell you apart. Maybe Jackie was working some sort of deal of her own. He couldn't be sure it was Jackie he was after, or that you weren't in on it with her. So he has to kill both sisters to make sure he gets the one he wants. Do you follow me?"

She nodded but looked perplexed. "Jackie wouldn't do anything like that," she said.

"Are you positive?"

"Well—"

I got to my feet. "I want you to stay here," I told her. "Don't leave the apartment, not for anything. Don't make any phone calls. As long as you're here, you'll be safe. Nobody followed us here and nobody's going to come here looking for you. Just stay put and wait for me."

"Where are you going?"

"To your apartment."

She stared at me. "Is that safe? The police—"

"I'm sure they haven't identified Jackie's body yet. It should take them two or three days unless they get lucky. And if I spot any cops, I'll come right back. If not, I'll have a look at your place and see if Jackie left anything around of interest."

"And suppose the . . . the killer is waiting there?"

"That's a chance I'll take. But I'm a big boy."

She looked me up and down, the kind of look I had given her earlier. "Yes," she said evenly. "You are."

"Give me your apartment key."

She went over to her purse and gave me a brown leather key-wallet. She started to hand it over; then she took it back and looked at it, frowning. "This is Jackie's," she said.

"What?"

"It happens all the time," she said. "We both have these things for our keys, same color, and we keep taking each other's—" She broke off and looked at me. Her eyes were bright, as though she were trying to put a smile on top of a scream. "I keep forgetting she's dead. I talk about her as if she's still here . . ." She collapsed in a chair and cried. Her shoulders heaved from her sobs.

I'm no good at that sort of scene. The reality of her sister's death was first hitting home, and for the next hour or so there wasn't anything I or anybody else could do for her.

I took her dead sister's keys and said, "Jill, I'll hurry back."

There were three other apartments on the second floor besides the one I sought, and someone was standing in the hallway in front of one of them. I didn't want an audience when I opened Jill's door—New Yorkers are tolerant people, but there is no point in straining this inherent tolerance. I walked up to the third floor and waited. Then I went back to the second floor, emptied my pipe in a hall ashtray, and stood in front of Jill Baron's door.

I took out the key to the apartment, listened at the door, heard nothing. On a hunch I dropped to one knee and squinted myopically through the keyhole. The apartment was dark inside.

I stood up again, stuck the key in the lock, and turned. I twisted the doorknob, pushed the door open, and stepped into a black room. I was groping around for the light switch when the Empire State Building fell on my head.

It was good but not good enough. He caught me on the side of the head just above the ear and I did a little two-step and wound up on my knees. He moved in the darkness, coming in to throw the finisher. My head was rocky and my legs wouldn't behave. I managed to swerve out of the way of the blow and got to my feet, but my rubbery legs didn't want to hold me. He came at me again, a blur in the darkness, and something hard shot past my head. I ducked and swung, aiming for where his gut should be.

My aim was good but there was nothing behind the punch—the shot on the head had drained my strength. He backed away from the blow and hit me in the chest. It wasn't a hard punch but it sent me reeling.

Somehow, I got to the light switch. I flicked it on and saw him, moving toward me and blinking at the sudden burst of light. A big man, a fast man. A chin like Gibraltar and a chest like a beer barrel. Hamhock hands, and a leather-covered sap in one of them. He swung the sap. I dodged, caught it on one shoulder. My arm went numb and my fingers tingled. I tried to make my hand fish the .38 out from under my jacket, but my arm was having none of it. It wouldn't behave.

He moved at me, grinning. I doubled up a left hand and pushed it at him. He batted it out of the way casually and kept coming. I lowered my fat head and charged him like a bull, and he picked up that sap and let me have it right between the horns.

This time it worked. I caught a knee in the face on the way down but I barely felt it at all. I just noticed it, thinking, *Ah, yes, I've been kneed in the face*, taking note of it but not caring a hell of a lot about it one way or the other. Then I blacked out . . .

FIVE

I wasn't out long. Five minutes, ten minutes. I opened both eyes and blinked in the darkness and tried to get up, which was a mistake. I fell down again. It was as though someone had cut the tendons in my arms and legs. They just wouldn't do my bidding.

This time I stayed down for a while. I took deep breaths the way they do in the movies, and I also took inventory. My head felt like a sandlot baseball after nine innings. My shoulder was aching and my arm was numb.

I got up and, this time, stayed erect. The room was dark—apparently my "friend" had shut off the lights before leaving—but I managed to find the light switch for the second time that night. This time, though, I was alone. I found a chair, collapsed into it, and smoked a cigarette.

There had been just the two of us, me and the man with the sap. But the room looked as if it had been the scene of a gang war. A bookcase stood empty on one wall, its contents heaped on the floor. Chair and sofa cushions were scattered around. My friend had been looking for something. Whether he had found it, I couldn't tell.

I got up a little shakily and checked out the rest of the apartment. There were two bedrooms branching off a hallway, one Jackie's, the other Jill's. Each came equipped with a huge bed, which more or less figured. Each had been searched, and was a mess. I gave the rubble a quick once-over, pawing through mounds of lacy underwear that would have given a fetishist a quick thrill. I didn't find anything very interesting. I didn't expect to.

It was beginning to look more and more like blackmail. My man was systematic, I reasoned. He had somehow trailed Jackie to the meeting place in the park, then got close enough to her to put a gun to her forehead and shoot. Then he had doubled back to the girls' apartment for a crack at Jill. Jill wasn't there, of course, so he'd jimmied the door and rifled the rooms for the pictures or tapes or whatever it was that she was holding on him.

He might have found them and he might not—I couldn't say. But it was an odds-on bet that, if he didn't find them, they weren't around. The place had been turned upside down.

It was too late to search the place. My friend had already taken care of that. But it made sense to straighten up a little. The way things stood, anybody who stumbled into the apartment for one reason or another was going to figure out that things were not according to Hoyle. A maid or a janitor might wander in and call the cops, and that would fix up their body-identification problem for them.

The longer it took the police, the more time I had to work. So I went through the apartment like somebody's maid, putting the books back in the bookcase, fluffing up cushions and placing them where they belonged, stuffing clothes into drawers and closets. I didn't go overboard. The place did not have to pass muster, just so long as it lost the aftermath-of-a-hurricane look.

There was a bottle of scotch in one of the closets. This slowed me down a little.

At which point the doorbell rang.

I sat down softly on an overstuffed chair and waited. Maybe they would go away. Maybe they would come back tomorrow. A feeble hope at best, but somehow I couldn't see myself going to the door, opening it, and saying hello to a couple of detectives from Homicide. They might get upset.

"Hey," someone yelled. "Hey, open up in there, willya?"

I got up reluctantly, walked to the door.

"Hey, Jackie," the voice yelled again. "Open up, Jackie. What the hell, open the door!"

This was no cop.

"Who's there?" I said.

"It's Joe Robling, dammit, and where the hell is Jackie?"

A customer. A drunk customer, from the sound of things. I dug my wallet out of a pocket, opened the door, flipped open the wallet, and shoved it in the man's face. He blinked and I pulled the wallet back and buried it once more in my pocket. I had given him a quick look at my driver's license but he didn't know the difference.

"Crawley, Vice Squad," I said. "Who the hell are you, chum?"

His eyes clouded, then turned crafty. He was sad because Jackie was not available and scared because I was there, holding him by the arm. "I—I made a mistake," he stammered. "I must have the wrong apartment."

"You know where you are?"

"Sure."

"This place is a cathouse, chum. You know that?"

He tried hard to look shocked. He didn't manage it at all. He looked lost and comical but I didn't laugh at him.

"Maybe I better be going," he said.

I gave him ten minutes to disappear completely, then turned off all the lights and left the Baron girls' apartment. The hallway was clear this time. I walked down carpeted stairs, through the vestibule, and out to the street. There was no one around. I walked two blocks without spotting a tail, stepped into a hotel lobby on Central Park South, and came out on Fifth Avenue without anyone behind me.

SIX

Jill Baron drew back when she saw me. "You look terrible," she said. "What happened?"

We sat on Maddy's couch and I told her. Outside, the night was soundless. We were in a business neighborhood and the businesses had all shuttered their doors long ago.

"Did he hurt you badly, Ed?" she asked.

"I'll live." I described him again, the hulking mass of him, the bulldog chin, the once-broken nose. "Try to get a picture of him, Jill. Think. Any bells ring?"

She screwed up her face and shook her head, "No bells, Ed. I'm sorry."

"Nothing?"

"I could probably think of a hundred men who fit that description. I might know the man if I saw him, but this way—" She spread her hands. "A better description might help. If you could tell me about his appendectomy scar—"

"I wouldn't be in a position to know about that."

"But I might," she said. Her face brightened. "You know, I would have given a thousand dollars for a look at Joe Robling's face. Was he very frightened?"

"A little."

"I ought to be angry at you," she said. "He was a good customer. Generally drunk, but a hundred-dollar trick who never got rough and never complained."

"He asked for Jackie."

"He always asked for Jackie," she said, a wry smile breaking through her generally somber mood. "But I took him a few times, now and then, if Jackie was busy. He never knew the difference. You don't think you scared him off for good, do you?"

"I wouldn't know."

She looked at me and pouted. "Oh, stop it," she said. "For heaven's sake, don't go moral on me, Ed. You know what I am and I know what I am, and if we can't relax and accept it, there's something wrong with us.

"You don't want to talk about my business," she said.

"No, I don't."

"What do you want to talk about?"

"Your sister."

"Oh." The somber mien returned.

"You didn't see that apartment after our unidentified friend got through with it. Either you or Jackie had something he wanted badly. If it wasn't you—"

"It wasn't, Ed."

"—then it must have been Jackie. She had something or knew something and it got dangerous for her. And now it's dangerous for you, too."

She frowned. "I don't know, Ed. Suppose it was just some . . . well, some nut. You meet them in my business. I know you don't want to talk about the world's oldest profession, but that much is true. The oddballs you meet!"

She closed her eyes, reminiscing. "Why couldn't it be like that? What if one of them, some man who was a customer, what if he got it into his head to kill us? A Jack-the-Ripper type."

"It doesn't add."

"Why not?"

"Look, a psycho might have his own reasons for wanting to kill a couple of hookers, I'll grant you that. But a psycho wouldn't play it so cool. He might come after you with a knife, might bust down your door and try to beat your brains in or shoot you or whatever. But I doubt if he would carefully trail Jackie to Central Park and put a neat little bullet in her forehead and then methodically search the apartment.

"He might go on a destructive rampage, just trying to rip up everything he could get his hands on. But that isn't what our boy did. He gave the place a thorough search and let it go at that. He's got a reason, Jill." I stopped for breath. "It looks like blackmail to me."

"But Jackie—"

"Tell me about her, Jill."

"She—" She stopped there, and then grimaced. She took a deep breath, and tried again. "She liked good clothes, fancy restaurants, expensive furniture. She hated nightclubs but sometimes she had to go to them on dates. She liked the Museum of Modern Art and modern jazz—"

"Men?"

"She didn't have a sweet man. Neither of us did. I think she was seeing someone, not business, but I don't remember his name. I'm not sure if she ever told me his name."

"Did you ever meet him?"

"I don't think so. Is he important?"

"I don't know yet. Keep talking. Was Jackie having money troubles?"

She stood up, walked across the room. Her dress was snug on her professional body. She lit a fresh cigarette, stood at the window, blew out smoke. "I know what you're thinking," she said, "but you're wrong. She couldn't be a blackmailer, she couldn't. She was my sister. We had differences, but she was still my sister, and I can't believe that of her—"

"Tell me about those differences, Jill."

"What's there to tell? The usual minor spats over nothing."

"How about money?"

"No problem at all. We kept separate bank accounts. No community property. What was mine was mine and what was Jackie's was Jackie's. I don't know what she had in the bank. I've got ten or fifteen thousand saved, and she certainly earned as much as I did, except . . ."

"Except what?"

"I don't know. Something was bothering her. She had a weakness for horses, phoned in bets every morning from our apartment. Possibly she was a heavy player."

"And got in deep?"

"Maybe. She didn't talk about it, but I think she owed a little money here and there. She dressed well, I told you that, and of course we both had charge accounts and credit cards and all that. She may have run up some fairly heavy tabs around town, and owed her bookmaker."

She paused, then said, "This is guesswork, Ed. A guess I don't particularly like to make. My sister was no more of a saint than I am, but I hate to think . . ."

Her voice trailed off. She leaned over and ground out her cigarette in one of Maddy's ashtrays. "I would have loaned her the money. I would have been glad to."

"Did she ever ask?"

"No. Never." She narrowed her eyes, remembering. "But there was something. She mentioned how nice it would be if a pile of money fell into her lap. We always talked like that; it was nothing special. But if I had only thought to offer her money, if I had only asked her—"

"Don't blame yourself, Jill."

"Why shouldn't I?" Her voice nearly broke, but she controlled it.

I stood up, took her arm. "Jackie was riding for a fall," I told her. "If you had bailed her out this time, she would have gotten in over her head some other time. Blackmail's an easy out in your line of work. You must have thought of it yourself once or twice."

"Not seriously."

"But for all you knew Jackie did think of it—seriously. She might have tried to squeeze somebody before. But this time she picked on the wrong man and he squeezed back. There was nothing you could do about it, Jill."

She drew close to me and her perfume was heady. I felt the warmth of her before her body actually touched mine. Her head was tilted and her eyes were misty and half-closed. "You're good for me," she sighed. I was holding her arm, and she drew even closer to me.

"I'm cold and I'm scared and I'm shaky, but I'm no frail petunia, am I, Ed? But right now I wish I was. I wish I could make you believe I *need* to be treated like a frail petunia."

I made some sort of motion toward her, and inexplicably she now backed away from me. "You know what's worst, Ed? I feel guilty."

"Guilty? What for?"

"Jackie's dead, but I'm alive, and I'm glad I'm alive. I'm glad it was Jackie instead of me. That thought's been in my mind ever since you told me she was dead. I've been trying to make it go away, but I can't. Isn't that terrible, Ed?"

"No, it isn't," I told her. "That's the most normal reaction in the world."

"My God, are you good for me. I'm cold and I'm scared and I'm a no-good prostitute. And poor Jackie's on some cold slab someplace; and I'm—I'm—I know, I'm cold. She's cold but she doesn't know it, she—Ed, for the love of God, make me warm."

I looked at her, and I told myself she was just another hooker. There were thousands of them, and none of them were worth it. That's what I told myself. But I went over anyway and put my arms around her, and she was trembling.

"I'm a stranger here," she whispered, with a pathetic attempt at coquettishness. Her voice trembled like her body, but she persevered. "A stranger who doesn't know her way around. Show me where my bed is, Ed."

I showed her . . .

It was very dark in the bedroom, with the barest bit of light coming in through the window from a streetlamp down the block. I got out of my clothes in the darkness and found her in the bed. Her body was naked and waiting.

Her mouth was a warm well. Her arms went around me, drew me close. Her body moved beneath mine, twisting and writhing in a horizontal dance as old as time. My hands went all over her and all of her was smooth and soft and fine.

"Oh, hurry, hurry—"

I had stray thoughts. I thought how disloyal it was to Madeline Parson to embrace another girl in her bed, and I thought, too, that this display of affection was Jill's own way of paying me a retainer instead of cash. Unhappy thoughts, those.

But she was good, very good, and the thoughts went away. One thought came back at the end, one that was almost funny. That morning her sister Jackie had interrupted something along these lines, and now sister Jill was making up for it. It was ironic.

Then that thought, too, vanished. The scene dropped off and the world went away, and there were only the two of us alone in some special bracket of space and time. We visited a special place devoid of call girls and criminals and sudden death. We went there together.

A pleasant trip. Afterward, sleep came quickly.

SEVEN

In the morning, no telephone intruded. The smell of coffee woke me. I yawned, rolled over, and buried my face in the pillow. The room was heavy with the air of spent passion. I yawned again, opened my eyes, and saw her come in with a steaming cup in her hand.

"I made coffee," she said.

I didn't say anything. She was wearing some sort of silky black thing and the sight of her brought memories in a flood.

"But it's too hot," she said.

"What is?"

"The coffee, silly." She turned and stared. "What did you think I meant?"

"Forget what I thought. What about the coffee?"

"It's too hot." She set it down on the bedside table. "While it cools—"

While it cooled, we warmed. She slipped the nightgown off and came back to bed. She said *Mmmmm, what a way to wake up* and then she did not say anything for a very long time. The phone stayed respectfully silent.

Later she curled up beside me while I drank the coffee. She made good java. She would murmur something from time to time, and from time to time I would run a hand over her. I touched the arch of her hip, the strawberry birthmark on the side of her thigh. A large measure of reality faded away. Intimacy does that. It pushes away unpleasant things, things like Jill's profession and Jackie's death and the big-chinned murderer-at-large.

But these things came back, slowly. I finished the coffee and got out of bed. Jill asked me where I was going.

"To get a paper," I said. "I want to find out what the police know about your sister. Wait here."

It was somewhere after nine. The sky was overcast and the air thick with overdue rain. People hurried by in blankets of sweat. Later, with any luck, the sky would open up and the rains would come. I walked down Eighth Avenue to 23rd Street and picked up the four morning papers. I carried them back to the loft.

I found Jill Baron as nude as I'd left her. She wanted to know if there was anything in the papers.

"I haven't looked yet," I told her. I gave her the *News* and *Mirror*, kept the *Times* and the *Tribune* for myself. We sat side by side on Maddy's couch and went through the papers looking for a report of Jackie's murder.

The *Times* didn't print the story, but the other three papers did. It wasn't an important one. There was no obvious sex angle and the body had not been identified, at least not by the time they made up the papers.

The journalistic tone varied from paper to paper but the message was the same in each story. Acting on an anonymous phone tip, police had found the body of a girl in her middle twenties on a bench in Central Park. She had been shot once at close range in the forehead and had died instantly. Her body had not yet been identified, and no clues as to the probable identity of her killer had been announced.

"Then they don't know anything," Jill said.

"The papers don't. Or didn't, when they went to press. That was awhile ago. The police may know a lot more."

I reached for the phone. "I'm calling them," I said.

"To tell them—"

"No. To ask them."

I asked the desk man at Centre Street for Jerry Gunther in Homicide.

"Ed London, Jerry. How's it going?"

"Well enough. What's up?"

"I just read something about a dead girl in the park. The one who was shot in the head. Know who she was?"

"Are you mixed up in this one, Ed?"

I laughed that off. "I don't think so. I have a Missing Person to look for and she comes close to the description in the *Tribune*. Have you got a make on this girl yet?"

"Nothing. We're working on it. Think it's your pigeon?"

"I hope not. Mine is a blonde, not too tall, pretty face—"

"So's this one."

"—brown eyes, slender build—"

"This one is blue-eyed and stacked. You sure about the eyes?"

"Positive," I said. "I guess it's not my girl. I didn't think so but I wanted to check it out. I've got a hunch the girl I'm after skipped to Florida."

We said pleasant things to each other and he hung up.

"No identification," I told Jill. "They don't even sound close. We've got time."

"Well, where do we go from here?"

"Good question." I dug out a pipe and tobacco, filled the pipe, and lit it. "Jackie was blackmailing someone—either the guy who sapped me or whoever hired him. She could have been blackmailing him with something she knew or with something she had. The ape-man turned your apartment inside out, so it must have been something she had. You follow?"

"Uh-huh."

"Which leaves two possibilities," I continued. "Possibility one is that the goods were stowed in your apartment, in which case the killer has them by now. The other possibility is that Jackie parked the stuff elsewhere." I drew on the pipe. "Did she have any friends who might be holding it?"

"I don't think so."

"Any hiding place that might appeal? Think."

She thought and her eyes narrowed. She said, "Oh!"

"What?"

"She has a—a safe-deposit box. The Jefferson Savings Bank on Fifth Avenue. She took the box about a year ago because she wanted a safe place for her insurance policy. We both took out policies a long time ago payable to each other, and she kept hers in the box. I don't know what else she kept there."

"It wasn't a joint box? You don't have access to it?"

"No." She smiled. "I told you we kept money matters separate. I think there were a lot of things Jackie didn't tell me. I didn't have a key. But she had the box. I know she still has it, because they bill every year and she got a bill not too long ago."

"Did she go to the box often?"

"I don't know. I never asked her about it." She took out a cigarette and I gave her a light. "That would be the obvious place, wouldn't it? If she had something to hide—"

"Of course," I said.

She took a deep breath. "But it doesn't do us any good. Now that Jackie's dead, we can't get to the box. Unless, if we could tell them she was dead—"

"You'd still need a court order."

"Then we're stuck."

I stood up, walked over to the window. "They don't know Jackie is dead—"

"So?"

"Do you know how she signs her name?"

"Yes, but—"

"Could you fake her signature? After all, you have her keys. One of them may be the key for the safety-deposit box."

She hurried into the bedroom, came out again with her purse in tow. It was a large black bag. She dipped into it and came out with Jackie's key-wallet. She sat down on the couch and inspected the keys one by one.

"Let's see—this is to the apartment, and this is the outer door and . . . Does this look right?"

It was a large brass key with a number on it. "That's the key," I said. "And that would be the box number. Two-zero-four-three. Now we need something with her signature on it."

"I can forge her signature," Jill said, "and she can—I'm sorry."

"What?"

"I was going to say, she can forge mine. Wrong tense." Again she repressed tears, sighed, and continued. "We used to practice copying each other's signatures when we were kids. It's been a long time, but I think I can come fairly close. Not exact, though. Do you think I can get away with it?"

I nodded. I did think so. The signature they require with each visit to a safe-deposit vault is more a matter of form than anything else. Not many people sign their name identically every time.

"There are little things," I said. "You won't know your way around. Won't know which is your box or where you're supposed to take it. Jackie might even have known the guards well enough to have exchanged a few words."

"I think I can manage it."

"Are you sure?"

She looked at me bravely. "Do we have a choice, Ed?"

We went inside together. It wasn't immediately apparent where they kept the safe-deposit vault, but it would have been somewhat out of character if we had wandered around asking directions. Then I saw a sign at the head of a staircase and nudged Jill. We walked down the stairs together, broke an electric eye beam, went up to a long desk. A little old man looked up at us over the desk and smiled at Jill.

"Miss, uh—"

"Baron. Jacqueline Baron."

"Yes," he said. She told him the number of the box. He got a card from a drawer, wrote the time and date on it, and gave it to her. I held my breath while Jill signed her sister's name. He glanced at the signature, set the card aside, walked around the desk, and unlocked a swinging iron gate. Jill turned, smiled sweetly, and entered the restricted area.

I watched her go into the vault room and hand her keys to the guard. He fitted his key into the double lock, then used her key. He withdrew the box and pointed toward a row of cubbyholes. She went into one of them and closed the door.

THE DOOR OF THE CUBBYHOLE OPENED. Jill came out with her purse over her arm and the metal box in one hand. The guard hurried back with her and locked the box away, going through the two-key ritual a second time. He led her to the gate, unlocked it, stood aside to let her pass. She winked quickly at me and I took her arm. We climbed the stairs, broke the electric eye beam once more.

On the street she said, "I have to believe it now. Jackie was a blackmailer!"

"What did you find?"

"I'll show you. But not here. Can we go someplace?"

We walked over to Sixth Avenue and up a few blocks. There was a small, run-down tavern at the corner, with one man behind the bar and two drunks in front of it. Otherwise the place was empty. We took a booth in the back and sat together, facing the door.

I pointed to her purse. "Well, what did you find?"

She reached into the purse and pulled out a long white envelope, a short fat manila envelope, and a thick roll of bills. The bills were secured by a doubled-up rubber band. I riffled them. There were thirty or forty, most of them hundreds with a sprinkling of fifties.

"Three or four thousand here," I said.

"Three thousand. I counted." I reached for the white envelope. "That's the insurance."

I opened it. The policy had been written by the Ohio Mutual Insurance Company. It had been drawn about a year and a half ago and the face amount was $50,000.

"You come into a lot of money," I said.

"If I live to collect it."

I opened the manila envelope. There were a dozen pictures inside, black and white glossies. The precise scenes varied in form but the game was the same in each. There were two persons in each photograph, a man and a woman. Both were nude and busy; and this photographic record of their activities would have sold well in the back room of a 42nd Street pornography shop. The prints were good and clear, the composition fine.

The girl was Jackie, and a look at her showed that the resemblance between the Baron sisters was just as striking when the girls were unclad. She was a dead ringer for her sister. A very dead ringer, now.

And the man was no stranger, either. When I had seen him he had clothes on, which constituted an improvement. He wasn't beautiful. When I had seen him, for that matter, he had a sap in his hand and had been swinging it at my skull.

"The man," I said, feeling my scalp. "I recognize him."

"So do I," Jill murmured.

EIGHT

I picked up my glass and drank the brandy. They do not stock fine cognac in the Sixth Avenue joints. But it went down anyway and the warmth spread.

"His name is Ralph," Jill said. "That's all I know."

"A customer of Jackie's?"

"Not a customer." She lowered her eyes. "I think I told you she was seeing somebody. I couldn't remember his name then. Seeing his picture, I remembered. His name is Ralph. I saw him with her . . . oh, maybe three times altogether. I never talked with him but I saw him. He came over to take her out. Where they went, I never knew."

"When was this?"

"The first time was maybe two months ago, and then again two or three weeks after that."

"Did she talk about him?"

"Not much. Jackie wasn't that much of a talker."

"What did she say?"

"That she had started seeing him. That he wasn't a customer but a friend. The first time I got a little bitchy, I think. I don't remember it very well. I was slightly stoned and I'm not too good at remembering things that happen when I drink."

"Give it a try. It's important."

"I asked her if she was taking a pimp," Jill said suddenly. "I remember now. And Jackie . . . slapped me. Not hard, but slapped me."

"Did she say anything?"

"She said she was thinking about marrying him, but I don't believe she really meant it."

"Was this the first time you met him?"

"Yes."

"Did she ever say anything about it again?"

"No. Maybe she felt I disapproved of the whole thing, I don't know. I met him one more time, but we just said hello and passed like ships at night. She never mentioned him again, or marriage." She paused. "He was the man in the apartment?"

I nodded.

"I don't understand," she said. "She might blackmail a customer. But her boyfriend—"

I thought about that and it started to make more sense than she thought it did. Jackie met Ralph, then either fell in love with him or pictured him as a good prospect for marriage and a way out of her debt-ridden state and call girl routine. She was in hock up to her eyeballs and she needed an out in the worst way—this made more sense than the love bit, which sounded out of character. So she played him hard, and she gave away something she usually sold at a good price.

And then some roof fell in on her. Maybe he had a wife somewhere. Maybe he wasn't interested in marrying her. One way or another, she turned out to be the sucker and she had the money worries without any help from Ralph in the offing. So she decided to make him pay through the nose for the free samples. She set up a date, rigged a camera or hired a cameraman, and took a flock of pictures. Then she used them to put the squeeze on Ralph.

That was a mistake. It changed everything, turned the whole world upside down. Ralph paid her off—this was what the three grand in the safe-deposit box represented. But he didn't pay her enough and she kept squeezing, and he was willing to take only so much. He shot her, turned her apartment upside down looking for the pictures, and would kill Jill if he got a chance, since she was the only possible link to him and Jackie.

I knew the killer now. I had his picture and his first name. The rest would take some finding, but the police were the ones who could pull it off.

"I have to make a phone call, Ed," Jill said. "My answering service. And I want to use the little girl's room." She started to leave, then called back. "Ed, I could use a drink now. Will you order me a highball?"

She scooped up her purse and left the table. I sat there with an insurance policy, a roll of bills, and a stack of dirty pictures. I looked at the pics again—solely for investigational purposes, of course—and put them in their envelope and tucked the envelope into my jacket pocket. I put the policy in its envelope and pocketed the roll of bills. Then I went to the bar and got myself a fresh brandy and a rye and ginger ale for Jill.

When she came back to the table, she sipped her drink and smiled at me. We talked some more until we finished our drinks. Then we rose to leave. I gave her the insurance policy and the money. She didn't ask for the pictures.

"What are you going to do now?"

"Call the police."

"Why?"

"Why not? They can run down Ralph a lot faster than we can. And the sooner we level with them, the easier it will go. Do you know how many laws we've broken in the past twenty hours?"

"I'm used to breaking laws," she said.

So was I, but I never felt too secure about it.

"Ed, wouldn't it be better if we could give them Ralph's full name? Wouldn't that make it simpler all around?"

"Sure it would."

"Jackie had a little black book," she said. "It's one of the tools of the trade, along with a bottle of Enovid and a strong stomach. I know where she kept hers."

"Where?"

"In the apartment, and in a place where Ralph probably couldn't find it."

"Would his name be in it?"

"Of course. And if I could go there—"

"We could go to the police first," I said. "Then we could hunt down the little black book."

Jill made a face. "Let's do this my way," she said. "Please, Ed? Please?"

The cab stopped outside her building. Her key opened the outer door. Then she turned toward me and said, "Wait here for me, Ed. I'll be down in a minute."

"I'll come up with you."

"No. Wait here. If the police are there, Ed, it's sensible for me to come walking in; it's my home. But if you're with me and they find out you're a private detective, they'll start asking a lot of questions we can't answer."

She had a point, but I said, "What about our friend Ralph?"

"He's already been here and searched the place," she said. "Why would he come back?"

I shrugged. "All right."

Her feet led her hurriedly up the flight of carpeted stairs. I stayed in the hallway at the foot of the stairs, poised to ward off imaginary intruders. No intruders appeared. I reached for a pipe and listened as her key entered the lock upstairs and the door opened. I hauled out a pouch of tobacco and her door swung shut. I opened the pouch and started to fill the pipe and Jill screamed, "Ed . . ."

The scream was shrill and brittle. I dropped the pipe and the tobacco and dug my .38 out of the shoulder rig, simultaneously charging up the staircase. I was halfway up when a gun went off. The apartment had thick walls and a heavy door but that shot echoed loud and long through the building, and another scream followed its shattering concussion.

Her door was locked. I put the mouth of the .38 to the lock and shot it to hell and gone, gave the door a kick, and watched it fly open.

Jill was standing in the center of the room. She had a little gun in her little hand. Her dress was torn, her hair messed up. She was through screaming and she stood staring downward with wild and stricken eyes.

He was on the floor. Ralph, the mystery man, he of the bulldog jaw and the descending blackjack. He was on his back with his legs tangled awkwardly under him and his hands clutching out at nothing and a fountain of blood still gushing from the raw red wound in his throat.

She turned, saw me. I went to her and the gun spilled from her fingers and clattered on the floor. She put her head against my chest and wailed. I held her and her wailing stopped. After a while, she pushed me away, sucking in gulps of air. She looked ready to keel over. I led her to a chair and she sagged into it.

She said, "I should have . . . I should have let you . . . come with me. I didn't think—"

"He was waiting for you."

She managed to nod. "I came in. I closed the door . . . turned around and . . . he was pointing a gun at me. I tried to grab it and he grabbed at me and he tore my dress and—"

"Take it easy."

"I can't take it easy. I killed him. Good God, I killed him!"

I calmed her down. A cigarette helped. She smoked it greedily. Then I asked her how it had happened.

"I fought with him, I didn't even fully realize what was happening. I just knew he was trying to shoot me, and I screamed. I must have deflected the gun . . . It went off and—"

Ralph lay dead, a bullet wound in his throat. I looked at Jill. The intruder had torn her dress and her bra in the struggle. Her body was visible to the beltline. She pulled the dress together in unnecessary modesty.

"It's over now," I said. I crossed the room and picked up the phone.

NINE

"I thought you were a friend of mine," Jerry sneered.

"I am."

"You should have called me when you found the girl in the park. You should have called me when the sister showed up at your apartment. You should have called me when you ran up against Traynor the first time. You should have—"

The dead man was Ralph Traynor. It said so in Jackie's address book and on a batch of cards and papers in his wallet. He lived somewhere in Brooklyn.

"You should know better, Ed."

I gave Jerry my side of it. I told him that my first aim was to keep the girl free and clear and save her from publicity and the killer. "You would have spotlighted her," I said.

"I would have stuck her in a cell."

"And we never would have gotten anywhere. You know that and I know it, dammit. My way worked."

"It did?"

"Yes, Jerry. You have the killer. He's dead, but he would have been just as dead in a year after a trial and a batch of appeals. The state comes out a few dollars ahead and the case is closed out that much faster." I took a breath, smiled. "I know I played it cute. Maybe I was wrong. My reasons seemed good at the time."

He sighed, then punched me in the arm to show that we were still friends. I took Jill by the arm and went down the stairs behind Gunther. A police car was parked in front alongside a fire hydrant. Jerry's uniformed driver was at the wheel.

Jerry got in next to the driver and Jill and I sat in the back. The driver didn't use the siren. We drove moderately across town, then went down to Centre Street on the East Side Drive.

It took time for them to get our statements. I gave them mine as quickly as possible in a little room with Gunther and a police stenographer. I took it from the top, starting with the first phone call the day before and concluding with the arrival of the law. I left out little things like the interlude with Jill at Maddy Parson's apartment. Certain facts don't belong in a police report.

Jill took a little longer with her statement. The stenographer typed them both up and we signed them.

"You can both go now," Jerry said. "We'll be getting a report from ballistics and a run-down on Traynor pretty soon. So far everything checks out."

Jill nodded. She got to her feet and turned to me. "Are you coming, Ed?"

"I'll stick around for the ballistics report," I said. "But how about dinner?"

"Wonderful," Jill said.

Jill said goodbye to Jerry, and we watched her go. Afterward we sat for a few minutes without saying anything. Then Jerry commented on Jill's looks. He poked me in the ribs. "Hearty appetite, tonight." He smiled. Then, serious again, he said, "Ed, you certainly fall into some bizarre cases."

"I guess so."

"But it all works out. Ballistics should confirm what we've already pretty well established. Jacqueline Baron was shot with a slug out of a .25 caliber automatic, probably foreign-made. The gun that finished Traynor was an Astra Firecat. It fits."

"A little gun."

"Uh-huh. Easy to hide in a pocket. No bulge under the jacket, like the cannon you're wearing." He tapped me over the heart. "No gun for deer hunting, but good enough at close range. And he got close enough to the Baron girl to leave powder burns on her forehead."

"I know," I said. "I saw them." I lit my pipe. "A peculiar gun for a man like Traynor to use. A little gun would get lost in those big mitts of his."

Jerry grinned. "Sure. Chances are he'd have bought himself a Magnum, if he had the choice to make. But when it comes to picking up an unregistered gun, you take what you can get. We had a little old lady who shot her husband with a Super Blackhawk. The recoil on that thing must have knocked her into the next room. And then a hulk like Traynor uses a little job like the Astra. Those foreign guns—the thing is you can get 'em sent to you through the mail, Ed." He frowned. "Traynor's gun did a job though. Killed the Baron girl, then killed him."

He had things to do. I went outside and walked around the corner to a lunch counter.

When I finished, I went back to Headquarters. The ballistics report had confirmed what everyone already took for granted. The same gun had killed both Jackie Baron and Ralph Traynor.

Gunther passed me in the hallway. He said, "Go home now, Ed. We have everything we need. We'll want you and Jill Baron for the inquest in a day or two. Let her know, will you?"

TEN

Something stank.

I spent a long time sitting at my window watching the rain come down on 83rd Street.

The packet of pornographic pictures was still in my jacket pocket. Gunther had not wanted them. They were evidence, but with Traynor dead there would be no trial, just the formality of an inquest to tie up what loose ends remained so the file could be marked closed.

I took out the manila envelope and opened it. I spilled the black-and-white glossies into my lap. Then, one by one, I examined them again.

An odd sensation. Pornographic photos, sure to arouse the libido of any vicariously oriented lecher. But this was a special case: both subjects engaged in such lively activity were lively no more. The nubile blonde was dead, and the massive man was dead, and neither would again have the chance to play bedroom games.

I looked at the pictures again. Three of them had similar scratches, little seemingly meaningless spots . . .

At a quarter after four I called Centre Street and got through to Jerry Gunther. "I was wondering about Traynor," I said. "Get anything more on him?"

"A little. Listen, it's over, Ed. And you're out of it anyway. What's your interest?"

"I've got to type up a report for my client."

He didn't argue. They had found a little more about Traynor, not a hell of a lot but enough. He was in good shape financially, though not rich. He had been seeing a lot of Jackie Baron, and his wife knew he was playing around—but not with whom. She had been thinking of divorcing him, had even gone to a lawyer to ask what a divorce would entail. She wanted to get rid of him, but she also wanted to gouge him for every nickel she could get.

"That made him a good blackmail prospect," Jerry Gunther said. "With those pictures in her lap, Mrs. Traynor wouldn't have to take a plane to Reno. She could get a New York divorce and a nice piece of alimony. But Traynor wasn't rich enough to pay forever. He forked over money once or twice, which accounts for the dough you found in Jackie's safe-deposit box. Then she squeezed too hard and he decided to kill her instead."

"Did you check his bank account for large withdrawals?"

"Ed," he said exasperatedly, "we're not working on this case. We're closing it. Something eating you?"

"No. Just routine, Jerry."

I thanked him. He said what the hell, call him anytime, he was just a public servant.

I took him up on it twenty minutes later, after two cups of coffee and a lot more thought. I got him on the phone and heard him growl something to somebody else; then he asked me what the hell I wanted now.

"A favor."

"Shoot."

"Has Jackie Baron's body been released yet?"

"No."

"It's still at the morgue?"

"Yes. The sister hasn't claimed it yet, probably won't until tomorrow, I guess. Why?"

"Call the morgue for me. Tell them I have permission to look at the body."

He didn't say anything at first. Then he spoke softly. "Ed, you're onto something."

"Partly."

"You think there's something funny?"

"There could be. Make the call for me, will you?"

The little man at the morgue had thick glasses and no jaw. He was not a lovely man and he had an ugly job.

"Here we are," he said finally. "Miss Jacqueline Baron. We didn't know who she was, you know, until a few hours ago. That's dreadful, isn't it?"

"What is?"

"To be dead and unknown. I'd hate that. People should have serial numbers." He clucked his tongue. "Do you want to see the girl?"

"Yes."

He nodded, drew the sheet down as far as her neck. They had performed an autopsy. It wasn't pretty.

"All the way," I said.

He took the sheet off and we stood viewing the body like a pair of necrophiliacs in paradise. I tried not to look at the chinless man's eyes. His job might have unwritten compensations for him, and I did not want to think about them.

I looked at the body, at the legs. Smooth white skin everywhere. No scars, no blemishes. Nothing but clear flesh frozen in the gray permanence of death.

I turned away. The little man covered her with the sheet and joined me. We walked to the exit. He asked me if I had known the girl. I said I had seen her once, not mentioning that she had been dead at the time. He did not say anything more.

At 7 P.M. I parked in front of the building on 58th Street. I went up the stairs for Jill Baron. She was ready, and she looked better than ever. "You're on time," she said. "Let's go, I'm starving."

We drove to a steakhouse on Third Avenue.

Afterward I said something about a club downtown where they played good jazz. She took my arm, stepped up close, and let me smell her perfume. "We don't have to go anywhere," she said.

"I thought you'd want to celebrate your deliverance from terror."

"I do." Her voice turned husky. "But we can celebrate at my place, can't we?"

I smiled. Who was I to argue with a woman?

We drove back to her apartment.

She poured drinks and we sat on the couch and imbibed them. Traces of chalk marks remained on the carpet, and a throw rug did not quite hide the stain of Traynor's blood.

"I won't be living here much longer," she said. "I may even leave New York. One thing is sure . . . I'm getting out of this business, Ed."

I didn't say anything.

"I can't say I hated every minute of it because I didn't. It was easy and profitable. But it does things to a girl, makes her start hating herself. Jackie wasn't a blackmailer, not at heart. The work changed her. It must have. I don't want to turn into something that would fill me with self-loathing. It's important to like yourself, Ed."

We finished our drinks. On cue we turned to each other. Her face was flushed from the drink and her lips tasted of it. She snuggled up against me and whispered sweet somethings.

The bedroom was neat and clean, the bed turned down. She moved to turn off the light. I told her to leave it on.

"You want to see me naked, Ed?" A narcissistic smile showed I had scored one hundred percent with an apt remark.

"Yes, from head to toe."

"I'm glad," she murmured. "I like that."

We kissed. She undressed slowly, sensuously. We stretched out on the bed. She lay back, her eyes closed, her arms at her sides. A nude goddess, waiting.

I touched her cheek, her shoulder. My hand moved over silken flesh. My finger touched the strawberry birthmark on the side of her thigh and she quivered beneath my touch.

The birthmark. The one that had been scratched from the negatives of the pornographic photographs. *The one that was nowhere to be seen on the body in the morgue!*

Her eyes opened and she looked at me. There was the shadow of a question on her face but she kept it back, waiting. I took my hands away from her body.

"It was a nice try, *Jackie,*" I said. "It almost worked."

Her mouth made an O and her eyes bugged. She was already out of her clothes. Now she jumped out of her skin.

ELEVEN

She wasn't talking. She lay naked on the bed with beads of sweat already starting to emerge upon her forehead. Her eyes were trying to say that she didn't know what I was talking about. Their message didn't convince me.

"I've been calling you Jill," I said. "But you're not Jill. Jill's in the morgue. She's there because you put a gun to her forehead and killed her!

"You're not Jill. You're Jackie. And some of the things you told me about Jackie were true. Jackie had money worries. Jackie was a gambler and Jackie owed a lot of tabs around town. Jill had money in the bank but Jackie didn't. Jackie owed money."

I stopped for a breath. "So Jackie killed Jill," I said. "You needed money, fast. A long time ago you and Jill took out policies naming each other as beneficiaries. If Jill was eliminated, then you got the money you needed in a hurry. So you thought it all out and decided to kill your sister."

"You're insane—"

"No. You figured it all out and somewhere along the line you saw a way to do it better. It was one thing to kill Jill—then you got the money and paid your debts. But it was even neater to kill her and assume your sister's identity. Then your debts would be written off completely. You could start fresh with no one mad at you. You could be Jill."

I looked at her coldly. "Probably Jill was a nicer girl, anyhow."

The room was quiet. I looked at her naked body and looked quickly away. Flesh in and of itself is no stimulant. She kindled no desire, not after I'd proved to myself that she had killed her own sister, and Ralph Traynor.

"There was more to it than that," I went on. "You might have had a lot of trouble figuring out a good way to kill Jill. But it became infinitely easier when you made it look as though Jackie had been murdered. Jill didn't have any reason to work a blackmail dodge. Jill had money in the bank. But you had plenty of reason to be a black-mailer, and if you made your sister look like a blackmailer nobody would look your way if she got herself murdered. They would just look for the person she had been blackmailing.

"You probably started to play a little blackmail at the beginning. Figured on squeezing some money out of Ralph Traynor. Hell, you're not the sentimental type. You wouldn't have put Traynor on the free list because you liked his looks. You started seeing him because you thought you could blackmail him. You had a set of blackmail pics taken and were ready to start showing them to him; but then you realized he couldn't come up with the big money you needed."

Jackie had a pack of cigarettes on the night table. I took one and lit it. "That was one thing I wondered about," I continued. "Traynor made a good living but he wasn't rich. I could see him coming up with three thousand dollars in a pinch, but I couldn't see how you figured on getting any more than that from him. But you never blackmailed him at all. You had the pictures taken, and when you saw the prints and thought about the money you needed, you got the idea of killing Jill.

"And you went right ahead with it after you put a pile of money and the pictures in your safe-deposit box. That set the stage. Jill never suspected a thing. Maybe she noticed you were a little nervous. Probably not. You're a good actress, Jackie."

She looked at me. Her face showed no expression whatsoever, as though she was waiting patiently for me to finish spouting my nonsense and to return to reality.

"A damned good actress. Maybe you have to be a good actress to be a good whore. Anyway, yesterday morning you got away from Jill and called me. You were all mystery on the phone. You were willing to risk my writing the whole thing off as a gag because you wanted things to work out just right. And you wanted to make sure you had me playing ball with you. If I didn't call you back, you'd just postpone the murder a day or two and phone some other private eye.

"But I cooperated. You were there when I called you back and you arranged a meeting with me at four-thirty. Then, about an hour ahead of time, you took Jill for a walk in the park. She thought the two of you were just going out for some fresh air. You went to the spot where you were supposed to meet me, took the automatic from your purse, and blew your sister's brains out."

For the first time, she shuddered. It was a momentary reaction, a quivering of the upper lip, a brief outbreak of gooseflesh over her naked body. It passed quickly.

"You stuck the gun back in your purse and left the park, Jackie. Maybe you hung around long enough to make sure I discovered the body. Maybe not. Either way, you had plenty of time to double back to my apartment and wander in like a little lost lamb. You staged that part beautifully. You hadn't told me anything about sisters over the phone and as far as I knew there was only one of you, and that one was dead on a park bench. You came into my arms with a whole load of shock value working for you, and then you let yourself fall apart in tears when I told you your sister was dead. You played the scared act to the hilt and made it look as though you were in a hell of a lot of danger."

She sat speechless—mouth agape, looking ludicrous in her nudity.

"And that worked, too. If the nonexistent blackmail victim had only been after your sister, I would have taken the whole thing straight to the police and they would have picked it to pieces. But the killer was supposed to be after you, too—and I had to catch him and keep you in the clear at the same time. I stowed you at Maddy's, and you got busy setting up a frame for Traynor.

"You were cute about it," I went on. "You never did get around to blackmailing Traynor, so he still thought he was your loving boyfriend. As soon as I left Maddy's you got on the phone and called him, told him to get over to your apartment. Or maybe he was there all along—it's the same either way. You told him some pest was on his way over and that he should knock the pest out and leave him there.

"Traynor didn't know anything about murder. All he knew was that he was crazy about you, the poor fool. So he waited in the dark until I came in, and he slugged me. Then he turned your apartment upside down to make it look as though it had been searched. I don't know what you told him to get him to go along with that. It must have been good."

She laughed. "Ralph would do anything for me," she said. "He didn't need a reason."

"Sure. Anyway, he knocked me out and gave me a good look at him in the process. I believed your story right off the bat, but this made it perfect. The whole blackmail pattern was fixed now. I had to believe in Traynor because he damn well existed and I had an aching head to prove it. I went back to Maddy's with my head in a sling and you let me coax a little more information out of you.

About Jackie being in debt, and about Jackie having a boyfriend—all of that. If you gave me all of it at once I would have tried to pick holes in it, but you were too smart for that. You made me pry it out of you and I swallowed it whole."

"You said I was a good actress, Ed."

She was smiling now. I had her pegged and she knew it, but she could still manage a smile. God knows how.

"I didn't get a chance to look for holes in your story, not that night," I said. "You kept me busy in bed. More acting, Jackie."

"That wasn't *all* acting."

I ignored the line. "A repeat performance in the morning," I said. "And then the safe-deposit box—hell, that was something. You let me talk you into impersonating Jackie, and what it amounted to is that you impersonated yourself. No wonder you didn't have any trouble with the signature. It was your own signature.

"You did a good job there, you know. You had to look uncertain enough to make me think you were Jill and confident enough not to make the guard suspicious. You got the money and the pictures from the box and you were home free, or close to it."

She moved a little on the bed, a coldly calculated but subtle and seductive maneuver that made her breasts jut out. She wanted to make me conscious of her body, but didn't want to act whorish about it.

She could have saved herself the trouble. Her body was now about as exciting to me as Jill's, stretched out on a slab in the morgue. She stretched like a cat and ran her tongue over her lower lip and not a single spark flew.

"We went to the bar and looked at the pictures, Jackie," I continued. "Then you got up to make a phone call. You didn't call your answering service. You called Traynor, told him to get to your apartment right away. I don't know what reason you gave him, but you pulled the strings and he performed on schedule. You worked a stall act at the bar to give him time to get there, dawdled in the john, all of that. Then we got to your apartment to look for Jackie's address book. You made me wait downstairs. What would have happened if I went up with you?"

"I knew you wouldn't, Ed."

"The hell you did. You hoped I wouldn't but you had it all figured out if I did. I was lucky I stayed downstairs."

Her eyes went innocently wide.

"Because you would have killed me. You would have used your
gun on me and then you would have used my gun on Traynor to
make it look as though we shot each other. That would have been
a little tricky to pull off but you would have done it if necessary.
Then with both of us dead you could try your story on the police.

"It might have worked too. But it wasn't as sure a thing as it
could have been, and that was why you wanted me to stay downstairs to back you up. However, you would have made your play
either way."

"Oh, no, Ed. That's not true!" She put her heart into it. "I never
could have killed you, Ed."

"No?"

"Ed, I—"

I told her to save it. "You went upstairs and let yourself in," I
continued. "Traynor came over to kiss you and you screamed your
head off. His face must have been something to see just then. You
had him running around in circles anyway, and a good loud scream
must have rattled the hell out of him. But he didn't have much time
to worry about it. You took out the gun and shot him. Then you
gave out with another scream.

"This afternoon I thought about that part of it. The door was
locked when I got upstairs. I had to shoot it off. Why would you
lock the door when you were ducking into the apartment for a minute? When would you get a chance to close the door with Traynor
waiting to kill you?

"You did it to stall. It gave you a few extra seconds to tear your
dress and build the scene. By the time I shot my way through the
door you were into your act, and from then on everything was set
up. It couldn't miss, could it?"

She didn't answer.

"The gun checked out, the same weapon used for both killings.
I backed your story every step of the way. You ran one hell of a

lot of risks but things broke right for you each time. And by the time you left Headquarters you were clear. There would be a coroner's inquest, maybe a few more questions that you could answer with your eyes closed. Then Jill's body would be buried with your name on the headstone. You'd be Jill, with no debts and whatever money she had had, plus fifty thousand dollars worth of insurance money."

She didn't answer. Her hands moved down over her own naked flesh in a calculated movement that was supposed to look unconscious and automatic. I remembered making love to her, the flavor of her embrace, the touch of her body.

"You almost made it," I said.

"What—tipped you off, Ed? The birthmark?"

"Partly. That clinched it, of course. As soon as I got the idea that it was you in the photographs, I knew you had lied to me. And that was the trouble with the whole gambit, Jackie. It was all built on a pyramid of lies. As soon as one of them broke down, the whole thing collapsed. All the little inconsistencies that I had glossed over came back in spades. Every loophole showed up bright and clear."

"Then I should have gotten those pictures back. I could have said I wanted to burn them—"

"I would have figured it anyway."

"How?"

I thought for a second. "It was too pat," I said. "You timed everything so perfectly, Jackie. So damned perfectly. Traynor was always at the right place just at the right time. Somebody had to be calling his signals.

"And another thing—the powder burns on Jill's forehead. That was too neat and cute. If she knew Traynor was after her, she wouldn't have let him get that close. She would have run or tried to fight or something. The death scene looked as though it had been the handiwork of someone she knew, someone she wasn't afraid of." I frowned. "Someone like her sister."

"I . . . I wanted to make it fast."

"Uh-huh. You should have walked away and fired three or four shots into her. It would have looked better that way."

"I wanted Jill to die quickly. I didn't want it to hurt her."

"Sure. You're an angel of mercy and an angel of death all rolled into one. *There was a little whore and she had a little bore right in the middle of her forehead.* You should have stuck to the other nursery rhyme."

"What rhyme?"

"The one about Jackie and Jill going over the hill," I said. "Get dressed."

"You're turning me in?"

"What do you think?"

But she wasn't through yet. Her lush body flexed and her lips curled in a sensual smile. "Look at me," she said.

I looked.

"I'm well off now financially, Ed. I'm not good at arithmetic but I'm sure you can figure it out. I'll bet it's a lot of money, right?"

"It's a lot of money."

"And there would be more than money, Ed." Her hands touched her breasts. "I have a good clientele."

I stood up. She swung her legs over the side of the bed, got to her feet, and came toward me. "Get dressed," I sneered. "I can't stand the sight of you."

She blinked. Maybe no one had ever told her that before. She stood still. I pushed her aside, walked past her, and picked up the phone. I started dialing. I was making more work for Jerry Gunther, but I had a hunch he wouldn't mind.

PERMISSIONS

B. L. Lawrence, pseud. "One Night of Death." *Guilty*, November 1958.

B. L. Lawrence, pseud. "Sweet Little Racket." *Trapped*, April 1959.

Sheldon Lord, pseud. "Bargain in Blood." *Off Beat*, February 1959.

Sheldon Lord, pseud. "Just Window Shopping." *Man's Magazine*, December 1962; reprinted in *Guy*, October 1968.*

"The Bad Night." *Guilty*, November 1958.

"The Badger Game." *Trapped*, February 1960.

"Bride of Violence." *Two-Fisted*, December 1959.

"The Burning Fury." *Off Beat*, February 1959.

"The Dope." *Guilty*, July 1958.

"A Fire at Night." *Manhunt*, June 1958.

"Frozen Stiff." *Manhunt*, June 1962.

---

* This story was discovered by Lynn Munroe in *Guy*, October 1968; somewhat later Mr. Munroe located an earlier appearance in *Man's Magazine*, December 1962. The author recalls writing "Just Window Shopping" for Pontiac Publications circa 1958, but it has not been located in any of their magazines.

"Hate Goes Courting." *Web*, June 1958.

"I Don't Fool Around." *Trapped*, February 1961.

"Lie Back and Enjoy It." *Trapped*, October 1958.

"Look Death in the Eye." *Web*, April 1959.

"Make a Prison." *Science Fiction Stories*, January 1959.*

"Man with a Passion." *Sure Fire*, July 1958.

"Murder Is My Business." *Off Beat*, September 1958.

"The Naked and the Deadly." *Man's Magazine*, October 1962; reprinted in *Guy*, December 1963.

"Package Deal." *Ed McBain's Mystery Book*, Issue 3, 1961.

"Professional Killer." *Trapped*, April 1959.

"Pseudo Identity." *Alfred Hitchcock's Mystery Magazine*, November 1966.

"Ride a White Horse." *Manhunt*, December 1958.

"A Shroud for the Damned." *Keyhole*, April 1962.

"Stag Party Girl." *Man's Magazine*, February 1963; reprinted in *Guy*, February 1965.

"Twin Call Girls." *Man's Magazine*, August 1963; reprinted in *Guy*, August 1965.

"The Way to Power." *Trapped*, June 1958.

"You Can't Lose." *Manhunt*, February 1958.

---

* "Make a Prison" is here published as "Nor Iron Bars a Cage."